IN THE DEPTHS OF A MAN'S MIND

DAVID McCANN

First published 2025
© David McCann, 2024
Imprint: DMc publishing
dmmccann.com

Paperback ISBN 978-1-7637164-0-7
e-Book ISBN 978-1-7637164-1-4

The content of this book is protected by copyright law. No part may be reproduced and reused for any commercial purpose without explicit written permission from the author.

Editor: Tyrone Couch, Tyrone Couch Editing Services, ty@tced.au, ABN 99269754429

Book cover design and typesetting by Alicia Grady, Struck by Violet. www.struckbyviolet.com
Elements of this cover have been generated with the assistance of AI.

A catalogue record for this book is available from the National Library of Australia

The past is your lesson.
The present is your gift.
The future is your motivation.

~ Zig Ziglar

Time has no master
but time itself

Neleuwen

N E S W
Norto
Finnaclands
Cantabria
Hamidara
Lunan Ranges
Chain of Hill
Gyrockgenri
(Hotlands)
Yillion Pass
Neleuwan
Middle Stream
Tonecius Ocean
Grey Ocean
Sonder
Hills
Pillion

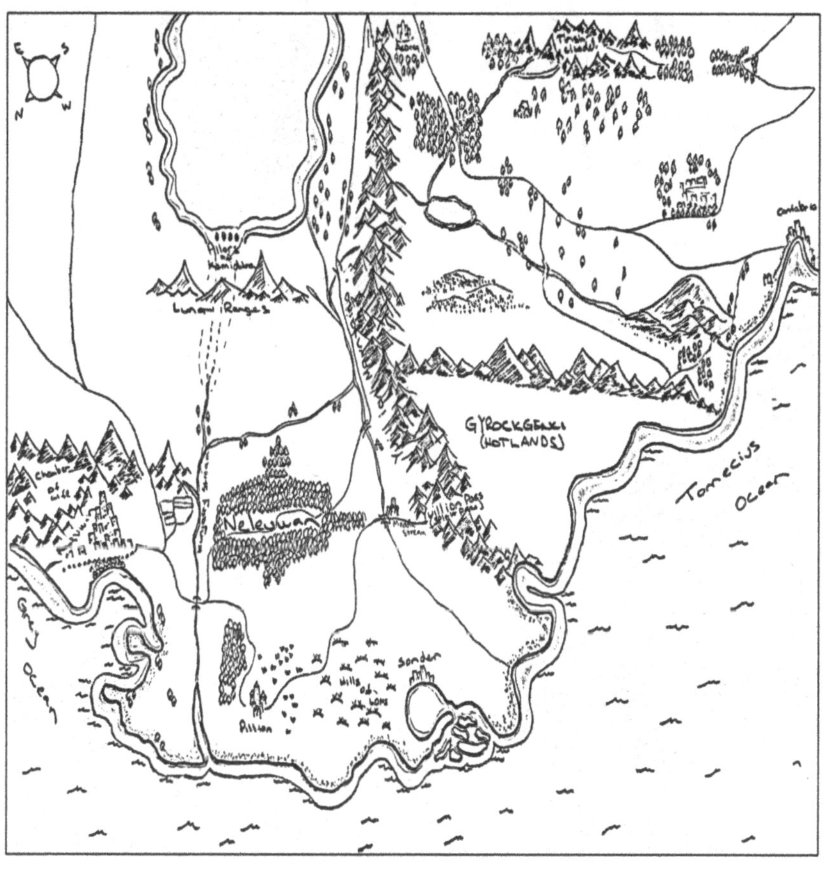

CHAPTER ONE

TEACHER

In the dark recesses of Castle Neleuwan, a wizened man descended the cold narrow steps towards an old meat cellar. Revered as an advisor of kings and queens, his words had shaped nations and history alike. Today, he had a different purpose. The echo of his shoes hitting the stone beneath his feet grew less noticeable as the loud roar from beyond the door became more prominent the closer he moved towards it. Uncertain of what he would find beyond it, he proceeded with haste—not with fear, but excitement.

Reaching the door at the base of the stairs, he held for a moment as if considering something, then suddenly pushed through. In the same instant, the noise that had been heard all the way from the top of the stairwell fell to silence. For a fleeting moment, all eyes turned towards the figure that had entered the room. A sudden cheer went up, and the room's occupants moved to their proper places.

The boys' excitement had turned to reverence at the arrival of their new teacher: an imposing figure in brown robes with a grey beard cascading down the front, stopping just short of the simple runic pattern just above the belt wrapped at his waist. The figure strode across the room and took his place at the front of the boys, now seated around the small, dark chamber. The meat cellar, having been converted to a classroom of sorts, smelled of damp and dirt, doing nothing to give away its true purpose.

As a teacher, the man had great influence over the minds of the young men who'd settled into their places beneath his heavy eyebrows. Only now would they come to understand his true intentions.

"Good morning, squires," came a deep, resonant voice from within the hood. It was tinged with great wisdom and knowledge, and a sense of optimism for what was to come.

Of course, the boys had been told about their teacher, and each had been excited in their own way to meet this robed figure. His voice felt familiar and comforting to them, as if he'd known them all for years, and a good friend was returning into their presence. Before he went on, he turned around to gesture to the only other man in the room, signalling that he could return to his duties. The man nodded and exited, leaving the robed man to his work.

The boys had been waiting for this lesson for some time, and their banter about what to expect had stirred them into a frenzy. Whoever this robed figure was, their expectations of him were exceptionally high.

The figure turned back to face his students once more, making sure his face could not be seen. The mood in the room grew to one of even greater anticipation, as each boy had formed an image in his mind of what this figure might look like, and were eager to compare their vision to the reality. For many years, this figure had fostered intrigue, rumours, and misgivings with his historic words, stories, and tales ... but ultimately, he was a man like any other. Teaching the squires firsthand was one of his greatest joys, and he continued to make sure he visited the new boys each year—sometimes for one lesson, sometimes for many more.

On this occasion, he had yet to make up his mind which it would be.

He let the anticipation build for a little longer than the boys had expected, standing in front of them without saying a word, waiting for the uncomfortable silence to fester. Finally, now that he had their undivided attention, he slowly drew back his hood. Whenever he did this, he always made certain that he drew it back to reveal a sunny countenance and a positive smile. His smile was bright and friendly, with eyes that showed his caring and wisdom.

The boys released a collective breath, his disposition putting them at ease.

"A question for you, boys … or could it be a riddle?" The man grinned, looking around the room and making eye contact with each boy. "If you wanted to influence our world from somewhere beyond it, how would you go about it?"

The room was silent for a long time before a young boy raised his hand.

"Sir?"

"Yes, Montague!" he said, pointing at the boy.

The boy was surprised the man knew his name, to the point that it threw him off his answer. He had to physically shake his head to get his thoughts back in order.

"Well, I'd probably come in a dream or premonition," he said, apparently trying to convince himself of his own answer.

The robed man nodded in appreciation.

"You are close, Montague, though that is not quite the answer I was looking for."

Located in the lower parts of the palace, the makeshift classroom was not well lit, even with candles. As such, the meek voice that came from a dark corner at the far reaches of the room came as quite a surprise to all but the man himself.

"Prophecy!" the voice squeaked.

"Correct, Forgrand."

A smile was all the robed figure could see, but it practically lit up the darkened corner. He could only smile in return.

"Prophecy, gentlemen! For over four millennia, we have had reported incidences of prophecy—some which have come to pass, and others that have not. Take, for example, the prophecy known as The Contingent. This prophecy alone predicted the downfall of the Igerian State." The figure began to walk the front of the room as he spoke. "Naturally, every philosopher and mage at the time was cautious of prophecy … and when Igerian politicians decided to send the Carsian government a demand for the surrender of their city, who would've thought they were even capable of responding in such a way that, by the next day, the State of Igeria would be razed to the ground? The connection was not understood at the time, but when you relate the incident back to the prophecy, the answer presents itself. Listen carefully.

"'The wolf strikes, but the beast turns on its master to burn its own heart. Fire rains, earth moves, and time is lost to the wolf.' Now, who can tell me how we might interpret this prophecy?"

"Sir?" said a young man, slowly raising his hand.

Notably smaller than the others, the boy wore the attire of a squire, though it seemed to swim on him. The depth of his voice, however, belied his impish figure. His face was covered in smudges of dirt, and he'd taken off his shoes. He was most unusual for a squire, and quite out of place among the other boys. He sat removed from most of the others, save for a boy the man recognised as Marcus, several years Higant's senior. The two boys served as squires under Baron Vandeguild, the king's second cousin, and appeared quite close.

"Higant. What say you?" said the man, intrigued that the youngest of the students had put himself forward.

The moment the boy started to answer, ever so slightly, his eyes flared a light blue. Were it anyone else, they might not have noticed … but it did not escape his teacher's attention.

"Firstly, sir," Higant began, "the words of The Contingent alone weren't much to go on. I can't imagine them being enough to connect this prophecy to the Igerian State, nor the relevant time period."

He paused for several moments more, pulling together his thoughts.

Finally, Higant asked, "Did the prophecy have markers?"

The question came as a surprise to the robed figure—and by the look on Higant's face, they'd come as something of a surprise to him, too. In contrast, the rest of the boys turned to look at the boy with annoyance. Unaware of the significance of what he'd said, the room was quickly filled with well-targeted jibes.

"Boys, that's enough," said the robed man, a hard edge to his voice. The room fell silent. "Higant. I'm not sure of your heritage ... but you're quite right. Markers are important, especially in prophecy. I will let you all in on a little secret, unknown even to most scholars. When a prophecy is scribed, there is always a marker placed somewhere on the parchment. For centuries, the purpose of these markers eluded all who looked upon them, and the events foretold by prophecy were often only connected to them after they'd occurred ... that is, until about a year ago, when a very wise woman cracked the code."

One of the boys scoffed. "A woman, sir? What do *they* know about prophecy? She must've had help from a wizard," he said, his chest puffing up in front of his friends. Several of the other boys echoed his sentiment.

The man's voice was calm, composed, and strong.

"Gentlemen, it's past time you let go of your beliefs about what the world should expect of women. Some of the most revered, strong, and wise people in all the world are women, and I for one am very glad that's true. I hope you will all consider your words around the fairer sex, and make sure you show them the respect they deserve."

The one who'd spoken looked down at his shoes, his chest deflating.

"Sorry, sir," several of the boys said in unison.

"Now, as I was saying," said their teacher, his eyebrows rising as if to make the point. "One day, a woman appeared before the priests and mages of Acoreq, the centre of all prophecy in the world, asking their leave to access the recorded prophecies and aid in the search for the meaning of the mysterious marks. Just as you boys reacted to her gender, so too did they, being all male at the time. A moot was held, and it took ten full days and nights for the Council to come to a consensus. Had they not voted in her favour, we may never have understood the markers, and history may have taken on a very different shape. In the end, it was a boy no older than yourselves that won over the Council ... but that is a story for another time. Let me tell you why prophecies have markers, and how they were unlocked."

By now, most of the boys were transfixed. The man smiled.

"This young lady spent many months searching the prophecies for the key to the markers. She was passionate about her work, so much so that all else became superfluous to her. Her family, her friends ... even the mages of the Acoreq thought she was a ghost for many months, only seeing her late in the hours of the evening and up before the calls of the roosters in the early dawn.

"In the eight months that passed after she'd been given access to the prophecies, she toiled through thousands of documents—some easily read, others no more than scribbles on loose parchment. She'd said little in that time, and written less ... until late one spring evening when, on her way to her bed, she'd had a revelation. Deciding that she needed an immediate answer to a question that had been burning in her mind, she navigated her way to the chambers of The Luminary, the head of the Council of Acoreq. She needed an answer only he could provide."

"What was the question?" came a unified voice from the room, holding onto every word.

No matter how many times the man had told this story, the reaction was always the same. His smile broadened.

"The question, gentlemen—"

There was a loud bang against the oak door, causing the room to collectively jump.

The robed figure moved towards the door and opened it to reveal a young messenger, wearing robes similar to his own. The messenger bowed his head in reverence and reached into the sleeve of his robe, withdrawing a roll of parchment. The parchment bore the seal of Acoreq.

The messenger stood upright, holding out the parchment. A silence had fallen across the room, the boys eager to see what the messenger had brought.

"Time turns for no man but the one true prophet," said the messenger, kneeling as he handed the parchment over.

The more perceptive of the boys' jaws dropped. With that, their teacher's identity had become clear to them. The robed figure before them was none other than Master Vandrune, the true prophet. The boys had been told they'd be taught by a mage today, and that the lesson was not one to be missed ... but they never would've imagined that the mage would be the true prophet himself.

"Time has no master but time itself," responded Vandrune.

The messenger rose, bowed his head, and headed back the way he'd come. Master Vandrune looked down at the seal on the paper, then turned back to the boys, a smirk slowly coming to his face.

"You may close your mouths, boys, before you catch something."

The boys, realising they must have looked ridiculous, did so.

"Are you truly a real prophet, sir?" asked Marcus, who'd been looking back and forth between him and Higant excitedly.

"I am simply what I am, boys—nothing more and nothing less," he said in a forthright manner, placing the parchment inside his robes. "Now, where were we?"

Looking around at the boys, searching their faces for an answer, Vandrune realised they were in shock, and one would not be forthcoming.

"Ah, yes. The question the young lady had posed to the head mage at Acoreq."

The young men quickly remembered their curiosity, which only seemed to have deepened with the knowledge of who he was.

"She asked of The Luminary, 'Do prophecies ever overlap?'"

And so, Vandrune continued his tale.

The Luminary was a little stunned by this question. No one, let alone a young woman with no formal training in prophecy, had ever thought to ask it.

"As head of the Council of Acoreq, it is my duty to protect prophecy from those who would take it and abuse it for their own benefit," he said eventually. "When you first arrived, I took you for someone who was after nothing more than a way to better your position in this world, and take all for granted. Had it not been for the boy who convinced me otherwise, I would've turned you away quick as a spell, and sent you far away from here."

The Luminary paused for a moment, regarding her with renewed warmth.

"However, I have watched you these last many months, and have found your commitment to your cause of choice quite compelling."

The young lady appeared somewhat perplexed by the phrase 'cause of choice', but said nothing.

"In fact, for you to come before me now with a question that others have not asked, or even formed, is a truth revealed in your purpose. Nearly a hundred and fifty years ago, I received my first prophecy. Only now do the words I wrote that day finally fall into place, their meaning presenting itself as clearly as a sunrise lights my face. Whether you are a prophet, mage, or otherwise, I am glad I find myself here at this moment in time. I hope I do not disappoint in my answer."

She nodded eagerly. "Thank you, Luminary. I would hear it."

"I have one last question for you before I answer. Come," he said, ushering her into his private study.

It was a large, round room with two fireplaces, each bringing warmth and light to the dark recesses. A number of tables dotted the room, scattered with all manner of books and experiments.

"Please, have a seat. Would you like some tea?"

The woman nodded, sitting in the comfort of an old leather-bound chair draped with an animal skin to keep the warmth. She watched as the older man moved about making tea for her to drink, his robes and smooth movements belied his age and physic.

The Luminary returned with hot tea, handed her a cup, and sat opposite her in a larger chair, facing her. He took a sip of his tea, and as he swallowed his mouthful, his voice took on a different tone. It was comforting, yet deadly—purposeful, yet cautious.

"Why do you seek the truth?"

Unsettled, the young lady began to answer, her eyes not leaving the floor.

"I seek to understand prophecy better. If I can figure out what the markers mean, then maybe I can help to prevent disaster."

"A good answer ... but I believe there's more to it than that," he said, his eyes as kind as they were intense. They seemed to see right through her.

Slowly, she began to recall the memory.

"I was working late one night with my husband at our bookbinding shop. We'd just closed up for the night and started to clean, the same as we did every night ... until suddenly, I felt a cold chill come over me. My husband tells me I fell to the floor on the spot, and felt deathly cold to the touch. Not showing any signs of life, my husband thought me dead, and within the hour, he'd carried me back to our bed in preparation for my last rites. He left to find a priest ... and that's when I woke up."

She looked up at The Luminary, and he motioned for her to continue.

"I was disoriented, covered in sweat, my head throbbing. I tried to get up, but I had very little feeling in my body. Slowly, painfully, the feeling started to return, and when I was able to move again, I stumbled over to a small table in the room and sat down. My eyes glazed over, and my hand started to write on its own. It was the most unusual sensation. It felt like someone had taken control of my hands, and I was watching from afar."

"A prophecy," said The Luminary.

Strangely, he didn't seem surprised.

She nodded hesitantly. "My husband returned to the house with the priest right in the middle of it, and they were shocked to see me not only upright, but writing strange words and not responding to them. When I came back to myself, I had written two full parchments of writing in a language I'd never seen before ... and yet I knew both what it said, and how to speak the language. I was lucky to have such an understanding husband, and a priest who didn't think me a spirit returned from the dead.

"What I *didn't* understand were the strange symbols I'd drawn at the bottom of the page. In the days to come, my husband and I searched through all of our books, but couldn't find anything that even remotely resembled them. It was then that we wondered if the mages of Acoreq would be able to help. And so, we set out for the closest mage we knew of: Aukestra of Meddle Stream. When we explained to her what had occurred, she offered to guide me here, and my husband returned home to run our business until my return.

"It took a number of weeks to make my way here, and in that time, I tried many times to reread the words on the page ... yet I had lost the words and the translation from my mind, as if it were all a bad memory. The only thing I knew was that they were *important*. So to answer your question ... I seek the truth so that I might regain the words, and remember what I must do. No more, no less."

The head mage had a strange look on his face.

"What is your name?" he asked pointedly.

"Catherine de Halt," she said, visibly nervous.

"Yes ... that is the name you gave when you first came here. But I want to know your *real* name," he said, his tone both firm and commanding.

How could he have known? No one, not even her husband, knew her true name.

"Sara," she said, tears coming unbidden to her eyes. "Though it has been many years since I called myself that name, let alone others. I apologise for concealing it."

As rivulets flowed down her cheeks, the mage stood and walked over to comfort her. Lost in her thoughts, her body shook in his arms at the exposure of the lie.

Slowly, she composed herself, and then pulled away from the mage. He met her eyes, and she was again struck by their kindness and curiosity.

"You, who seeks the truth, whose own facade yet hindered you from finding it," he said gently. "Now that it has melted away, I can finally answer your question."

She pulled the cup of tea to her lips and drank deeply.

"Prophecy, as you well know, is difficult to predict. Some are easy to decipher, whilst others are more challenging and are left unsolved. This issue has persisted for several generations, and in an effort to resolve it, many have tried to reveal the secret of the markers. All have failed. Until now, I had lost all hope of finding a solution. You see ... my prophecy was about you, Sara."

Her eyebrows furrowed. "About me?"

"Yes. My first prophecy came to me in the same manner as yours, and its words escaped me in much the same way. Since then, I have trained myself to manage these telling's, and to bring meaning to the confusion. When the words returned to me, they told of a young woman who would come to challenge the status quo—to find meaning in the dark, and to lead us into the light. However, the prophecy also came with a warning; that if we *do* follow the light, the darkness will bring forth many who will try to gain power from those who are powerless. Whatever your prophecy contains, I cannot imagine it is unrelated.

"So you see, your arrival here is cause for both concern and delight." The Luminary smiled. "Still, quite frankly, I am glad you still haven't found a way to understand the markers. If you had, then great change would be upon us, and I don't know that we are ready."

It was at that moment that it all fell into place.

She had to tell him. No longer living with the burden of a lie, she could not return to living with another so quickly.

"There's more," Sara said slowly and deliberately.

The Luminary leaned forward, without breaking eye contact. "Surely you don't mean ..."

Tears came to her eyes once more. The room seemed to take on a gloom, even with the warmth of the fires.

Composing herself, she wiped her cheeks with a hand.

"I know how to read them."

The Luminary was truly stunned. Perhaps for the first time in his life, he struggled to find the words, or get his thoughts in order.

"The greatest minds in all of Neleuwan have been working on this for over a century. You've only been here for a matter of months," he said in disbelief. "When did you find out? And how?"

"The pieces have been there for some time, but they only came together moments ago. When I travelled here from Meddle Stream, I didn't have much to keep me away from the elements, so I slept under the sky. It's beautiful out there at night ... you can see so many lights in the vast darkness of the sky. One night, I realised that part of the sky looked very familiar, almost like it had been burned into the back of my mind. But something about it wasn't quite right. I didn't think much of it at first ... but night after night, I looked up at the stars, and was struck by the same feeling. I've been called out there every night since—and tonight, it was different. The feeling was gone, and the stars were a perfect match for the image in my head. It was like a door had been unlocked to my mind, and the words of the prophecy came forth, as if I had written them mere moments before.

"Once you realise what the markings are, it's really quite simple: the markers are star charts."

"Star charts?" A look of disbelief came across The Luminary's face. He stood and started pacing the room. Halfway across, he stopped and turned to look back at Sara. "That can't be right. We've looked to the star charts before, and nothing we've seen has ever aligned."

"That's just it. The alignment is only correct at the time of the prophecy. The stars can change from day to day, and year to year ... but if you can predict what the stars are doing, and where they will be in the sky, you can derive a date for when that prophecy should occur. My prophecy told me of this day—told me the story of my journey here, and of piecing this together."

She looked away.

"There is ... still more. However, I cannot speak it. Time will tell if it is truly as the prophecy predicts, but I will say this. My work here is done, Luminary. I have committed all of this to parchment, and with your approval, I will present it to the Council tomorrow."

The Luminary sat silently, a smile and a look of sheer wonder upon his face.

"Too many years have passed with us believing that the solution to the markers was in the prophecies. At no point had we considered that it was the other way around—that the solution to the prophecies was in the markers. Thank you, Sara. Your contribution to the Council of Acoreq and the lands of Neleuwan will surely become legend. You are now a part of the mage alumni, and will forever be welcome here."

"So, there you have it, Higant," said Vandrune happily. "In the days of The Contingent, we had no such way of knowing when the prophecies would occur. Often, we didn't even know to which events they pertained. We had nothing to rely on but our wits. It was only after the fact that someone was able to identify that this particular prophecy related to Carsian and the Igerian State. Thankfully, we now know we can look to the stars for answers."

All the boys had leant in to hear the tale, and now that it was at an end, they relaxed and returned to their places.

"That was fascinating, sir!" one of the young men pronounced, and the others chattered in agreement. "Amazing!"

Higant, who had fallen silent, finally looked up.

"I think I know how they figured it out ... The Contingent, I mean. But there's something I don't understand."

"Oh? Go on," Master Vandrune encouraged.

"The Igerian tabard features a crest, on which a wolf plays a large part. The prophecy talks of a beast turning on its master, and some hundred years before The Contingent, the Carsians were annexed by the Igerian State. That part makes sense. But what is the reference to fire from the sky?"

Master Vandrune had his eyes fixed firmly upon the young lad. The boy continued to surprise the prophet. At his age, most of these lugs could barely string a sentence together, let alone make sense of prophecy law.

"In the region that was Igeria, there was once a mountain by the name of Centorn," said Vandrune. "What the Carsians knew, but the Igerian State did not, was that Centorn was an active volcano. The Carsians had been mining near the base of the mountain for years, and had long since discovered this. And so, when the Igerian State sent them the demand for surrender, they responded by inciting the volcano to erupt, sending molten lava flying across Igeria. By the next day, there was nothing left but charred remains."

The boys, amazed by this detail, started talking amongst themselves.

"Well, gentlemen, that should be all for today. I shall see you again soon. Thank you for such a rousing spectacle of smarts, wit, and good humour. About your business, then. It comes on noon, and I believe the lords will want their squires back."

As the last of the boys left the room, Vandrune made note of the young man named Higant. He would keep an eye on this young man. He was sure to be something interesting.

Once the room was empty, Vandrune walked to the door and closed it, placing a sealing spell on the door so he would not be disturbed.

It was time to find out what was so urgent.

CHAPTER TWO

Parchment

Vandrune reached into his sleeve and retrieved the missive. The seal of Acoreq was intricate in its design, and he knew it was more than just intricate—it was also a magic ward, and one that only the person it was keyed to would be able to break. With a broad smile, he reflected on the many times he'd tested his students of magic to try to unbind a seal that was not meant for them. It was effectively impossible, but he hoped to one day find someone who was able to achieve it.

Vandrune understood magic in a way most could not fathom. His understanding of prophecy and the unorthodox teachings he received when learning the arcane arts gave him a unique perspective on things. This seal was more than just a seal to him: it was poetry, just as much as it was a powerful magic.

Closing his eyes and concentrating, he sent his mind to the seal. Subtly, he felt for the string with his mind's eye. Finding it, he uttered a command.

"Time turns for me."

At the command, the seal began to glow, as if the wax were growing hot from the inside. Glowing brighter and brighter, small cracks started to appear in the seal, and as they reached its edges, the pieces of it separated and fell to the floor. The parchment, unaffected by the glow or the way the seal had reacted, was now free to be unfurled.

Vandrune opened his eyes and unfolded the parchment. It had to be important for The Luminary to send it directly to him, and to use the words from yesteryear as security.

It still made Vandrune uncomfortable when people found out his heritage of prophecy, though it was always wonderful to see young men's eyes brighten upon finding out.

As the last fold opened, a look of confusion came across his face. The parchment was blank. Certain that The Luminary would not have sent him an empty page, a look of concern appeared upon his brow. If something was hidden there, and even he couldn't immediately see the trick to it, whatever the parchment conveyed must be of grave importance.

Vandrune started to pace the room, hand scratching at his chin. He turned the parchment over and over to see if he'd missed anything, whether on the back of it or where the seal had resided before opening. He even reached down to the floor, looking for anything that might have fallen when the seal was released. Ultimately, he concluded that nothing had been missed ... so then what was needed to reveal what was surely written?

He rolled the parchment back up and slid it back into his sleeve pocket. Looking around the room, he once again reflected on the group of young men, focusing on the spot where Higant had sat. He had truly been a rare surprise.

And that flare of his eyes ... he would have to enquire after him.

Leaving the room, he closed the wooden door and latched it, heading up the now-quiet stairwell once again. As he reached the landing and entered the hall, his mind continued to ponder the problem before him. Why so many layers of security? Was the seal meant to feed the parchment, rather than fall from it?

Lost in thought, Vandrune kept mumbling to himself out loud. Those he walked past must have thought him strange, several of them giving him a wide berth.

Had he followed the opening spell correctly? Could he have used the wrong command? No ... he dismissed both answers immediately. The parchment had survived. Intended recipient or no, if the seal had not been broken correctly, the page would have turned to ash in his hand. It had to be something else.

The Kings of Neleuwan had ever welcomed Vandrune's counsel, and so he was a regular visitor to the capital. The quarters he'd been assigned were located in the main castle, and his presence there never came as a surprise to its inhabitants. As he advanced past the guards and into the portico leading into the main castle, he turned left down the hall and headed back towards his quarters, continuing to examine the problem all the while. His footfalls were those of a well-trodden path, one he had made many times over the years. Despite being lost in thought, he never slowed or quickened his pace, his stride as constant and consistent as it had ever been.

Towards the end of the hall was a courtyard, and as Vandrune headed out into it, he came to a stop. It was widely known that the fountains of the palace depicted significant moments in history, and this fountain in particular was one of exquisite beauty. He always slowed to look upon it whenever he walked through the passage. It depicted a strong, robust warrior standing beneath a dragon's glare. The dragon had its maw open wide with fire bellowing forth, leaning down, about to strike the warrior. Its razor-sharp claws were almost twice the size of the armoured combatant.

In contrast, the warrior was not preparing to defend themselves at all, but standing before the dragon with his head bowed, calm and solemn, a solitary figure of strength. The warrior's weapons were left sheathed at his side, a battle axe still in its cradle. Hanging from the warrior's arms were four glowing golden bands, two on each side, attached by way of a chain that draped from the upper arms down to the wrists.

It was evident to Vandrune that this statue was not just created by hand, but by a master mage who understood art as a form of magic. Metalworkers and artisans were capable of creating extraordinary masterpieces, but magic was able to bring life to the features and details of such works in a way that no other craft could. It made him proud to be called a mage whenever he saw craftsmanship like this statue.

Looking down at the feet of the warrior, he saw the relief of a blade carved in front of him, as though the soldier had set his arms down. It was a detail he'd noticed before, and one he'd felt was rather strange. With all the detail they'd put into the statue, why settle for a recess here, rather than an actual blade?

Then, a new detail caught his eye: a symbol or a rune, etched into the recess of the blade. It seemed strange he had not noticed the symbol before, even though he'd admired the statue many times. Was it a recent addition? If so, who had put it there, and why? On closer inspection, at the very least, he determined that it posed no threat to the castle ... and with the missive from The Luminary currently front of mind, it would have to wait.

Before turning to head off, he once again took in the magnificence of the fountain and the statue. He couldn't help but wonder at the story behind the figures before him. He was familiar with the events depicted by most of the other fountains, but this one escaped him.

As he stared at it, it was as if time slowed, and time was moving at one-tenth its usual speed. He became lost in its details. The dragon. The warrior.

When he came out of his reverie, it felt like he'd been standing there for a long time.

"Better keep moving," he mumbled, looking around as if expecting to find someone. He turned onto the soft, cool grasses that surrounded the fountain and proceeded towards the far corner of the courtyard.

As he moved off the grass, he entered through a large archway and advanced along the palatial corridor towards the east wing of the palace, lined with statues of marble and gold. His soft shoes made little to no noise as he moved down the corridor towards the Dome of Lillifor, another magnificence of the castle that had him in a state of perpetual awe. The dome, covering a junction of a number of central corridors of the castle, had been inlaid with coloured glass, and was open to light from above. When lit by the rays of the sun, this glass gave the floor below a complete outline of the kingdom and its surrounding lands. It was a marvel that had captured the people's imaginations for many years. That the builders of ages past had been able to map out such advanced geographical calculations was nothing short of a marvel of ingenuity.

Vandrune took his time to savour the dome, but unlike he had with the fountain, he did not lose his sense of time. It was time to shift his focus back to the problem at hand. He moved on down the corridor on the left, between the golden statues of the old kings and queens and onward towards the east wing. Turning the last corner into the east wing, he stopped in front of the third door on the right.

Vandrune withdrew the key the steward had given him from his robe. The stewards looked after him well, and served him with great reverence whenever he was present. During his visits, Vandrune worked very hard to demystify the rumours and stories that surrounded him, and responded to the caretakers' kindness with just as much respect and consideration. It had served both parties well, their mutual respect fostering many friendships over the years.

As he entered his quarters, he found them exactly as they always were. It was a quaint little room with a four-poster bed on the wall to his right, and a small desk to his left. In the middle of the room stood a small boy wearing a leather tunic, the royal crest pressed into its centre. His leather-strapped boots came up to his mid-calf, and at his waist sat a small leather pouch and an ornate dagger.

Curiously, his tan-coloured pants seemed a little darker down the left leg today.

"Who might you be, young squire?" Vandrune asked with a smile.

"I am Syng, Master Vandrune," the boy answered, hands behind his back and head up straight. "My lord welcomes you once again to the palace of Neleuwan, and hopes you are comfortable while you are here. He wishes to dine with you this evening. Until then, I am at your beck and call, sir."

"You may tell King Frederick I am honoured by his request," said Vandrune, nodding his head in subtle acknowledgement.

"I will pass on your acceptance, sir. Is there anything else you require?"

"No, thank you, Syng. It is wonderful to make your acquaintance. May your day be full of joy for this meeting, for I know mine will be."

At this, Syng smiled broadly, and just about bounced out of the door.

Shaking his head and smiling, Vandrune headed towards the window. The view from his room was nothing short of spectacular. Opening the window, he looked out upon the lush green plains that surrounded the city, and out towards the rolling hills of the south fields. The castle sat on an outcropping from the flat plain above the lower levels of the mountainside, stretching out across it. His quarters looked over the beauty of the land, and it was a wonderful thing.

Vandrune moved back towards his desk and took off his robe. He'd been travelling for a number of days, and the attire below his robes was much less formal than most would believe. Mostly, he wore simple travelling clothes as he moved through the lands.

Before setting his robe aside, he withdrew The Luminary's missive from its sleeve pocket, then pulled the stool out from underneath his desk and sat down. He unravelled the parchment again to reveal that still, nothing was written there.

A frown pressed down above his eyes. Still, the mystery persisted. He closed his eyes and put his mind to work. What was he missing?

Ten minutes passed with Vandrune suspended in what looked like a trance before his eyes opened suddenly. Once more, the noises from the city below floated in through his window, and it was a comfort to him—a sign that life around him was going on as it should.

"Could it be so simple?" said Vandrune, scolding himself for not seeing it before.

He reached for his robes to gather the object within that might hold the answer.

Inside the hidden pouch, he found the smooth item he had been looking for. He wrapped his fingers around it and pulled it free. Placing it in front of him, he looked down upon the small black stone. The oval was nothing short of perfect, free from all flaws and imperfections. Its surface was so smooth that a drop of water would not roll off in a single direction, but disperse every which way around it.

Picking it up once more, he placed the midnight-black stone upon the parchment.

"Day to night, night to day," he muttered.

As if the stone understood its purpose, it instantly started to drain of its colour, coalescing into a puddle on the parchment and then moving across it with a mind of its own. As it travelled, it found the grooves of a channel and started to disperse.

At first, no pattern was discernible ... but then letters, then words, began to form. It was at this point that Vandrune understood. Midnight stones, an ancient encryption tool, were incredibly rare, and only a handful of mages possessed them. He'd had one for many years, but had never had cause to use it. That The Luminary had sent this message to Vandrune directly and used a midnight stone to conceal it meant whatever it contained was important indeed.

When the stone's colour had drained away in its entirety, Vandrune pulled it from the parchment, and upon lifting it, he found it to be translucent, nearly transparent. He put it aside on the desk and turned his attention to the words on the parchment.

Immediately, he understood why The Luminary had been so careful.

CHAPTER THREE

PROPHECY

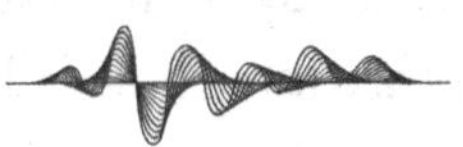

As the evening sun set over the castle, a lone figure sat upon the king's throne, lost in his thoughts as the group in front of him moved slowly towards his judgment. Sitting there on his dais, he wondered how it had come to this. It was not that long ago he'd been a young boy, carelessly running around the halls of this very castle.

Now, he sat here as king.

Frederick had been ordained several summers before, not long after the death of his father, the seventeenth King of Neleuwan. Even now, it was a strange thought that he should've become king at such an early age, and had such high expectations thrust upon him.

The death of his father had been sudden. Frederick had felt great loss and grief at the passing of the man he'd loved wholeheartedly. To this day, he still wished that he might speak with him once more.

Since his father's death, with the quickness of his ascension to the throne, he'd had no time to truly find peace in what his life had become. The pace at which he'd moved from son to king, and the fact that he hadn't been able to grieve in the way he'd wanted, made finding it all the more difficult.

His father's loss had not been the first he'd had to deal with in his young life. Frederick's mother had died when he was much younger, so to find himself elevated to king with no other family to shelter or nurture him through that difficult time had left a feeling of emptiness in his heart. Frederick had always wanted siblings, but he'd been an only child, and his parents had loved him with such passion that losing them was like losing a limb, and they were equally difficult to replace.

Taking up a mantle as heavy as the leadership of a people whilst dealing with personal loss had been a challenge. In his mind, it was no time for a celebration of a new king—it was a time to mourn the passing of a great man, king, and father. Instead, he'd had to grieve in his own time, and present a stoic front for the people. It was nothing one could conceivably prepare for.

The people of Neleuwan were a proud and gracious people. They enjoyed their lives, finding pleasure in the small, intimate times with their families and the fun and laughter of festivals and celebrations. Many of them were wondrous creators, some of them responsible for the multiple fountains and stained-glass pavilions of the castle, as well as artworks that were on display across the country. Neleuwan also had a large contingent of merchants, whose reputation for being some of the best cooks in the land was well established. Their stews, banquets, spices, and combinations of savoury desserts had earned them great renown all across the world.

After the loss of the king, Fredericks's advisors, had explained he would need to be there for the people so they would continue to feel stability and the guiding hand of leadership. Thankfully, Frederick had always been well-liked by the people, so it was not hard for them to see him as king. They'd regarded him as a nice enough young man, and though he'd never had to lead, he'd always been of help to those of the kingdom who had less than most.

In the seven summers that had passed since the death of his father, King Frederick had proved himself to his people time and again. His ability to achieve that which no one before him had, and in such a short rule, still baffled many of his advisors and peers. Frederick believed that while the old ways were to be revered and learned from, they were not to be followed blindly in all respects, but learned from, and adapted where necessary. This behaviour had presented a challenge to his advisors, who had long relied upon tradition. The new ideas that Frederick proposed were in complete contrast to the old ways, and he often led the way without consultation or discussion.

The people, however, had prospered since his time on the throne, and loved and revered him for it, as much as they had his father. Without a doubt, Frederick was gifted. He innately understood those whom others had avoided, dismissed, and regarded as less than. He saw them as people to be understood, helped, and allied with—and ally with them he did.

His ability to bring people together was exemplified when he turned his skills towards bringing peace to the barbarian clans that roamed across the Lunar Ranges north of Neleuwan, near to the Qhillip Falls. A nomadic people, the barbarian clans had fought for hundreds of years over who amongst them should be king—and as an outsider, he'd managed to find a peace that had been lost to them for over three hundred years.

In that time, the clans had fought amongst themselves, plotting and warring upon the rise of any man who might try to be king. The hate that each clan held for the next was imbued in their culture, carried forward by generations of bloodshed and endless war. It seemed the cycle would never end ... yet Frederick, even before his rise to king, had possessed a keen interest in the barbarians. He'd been schooled by scholars from all over the world, and above all, he'd been tutored by Vandrune. His father had wanted his son to understand the importance of the world outside of Neleuwan, and there was no better instructor in this than the prophet Vandrune. He'd been a good friend to the former king, and considered his request to help educate his son an honour.

Their discussions about philosophy, culture, and politics went long into the night. Of course, Vandrune's knowledge of these subjects was part of the reason Frederick's father had asked him ... but more than anything, he'd needed Frederick to understand prophecy.

Vandrune too knew this to be of the utmost importance, but he also understood that a king must grow to become more than those who came before, without losing the support and reverence of the people. He knew that Frederick must become a knowledgeable king, not just a man to rule, and he could not teach him prophecy without imparting the other elements taught to a mage.

With that in mind, Vandrune had gone well beyond his intended scope, teaching the young king-to-be about the world beyond the borders of Neleuwan—not just its physical borders, but its ideological ones, too. To be king, one must understand all of the pieces on the board, and play at a level far above those who might rise to challenge him.

Frederick had been a good student, consuming all that he could. Was it any wonder that Vandrune, at the time of Frederick's father's death, returned to the kingdom to advise and guide him? Not only did Vandrune become akin to the father figure that Frederick had lost, and a confidant for his grief, he also became a good friend.

It was during this time that Frederick had devised his strategy for managing the barbarian clans. Vandrune had talked with him many times about the clans, and even before his father died, he'd come up with many possible solutions ... but he was not king yet.

It wasn't long after he became king that he'd put his plan into motion.

His idea that the barbarians were a people destined not to be ruled, and must govern themselves without a hierarchy seemed contradictory, and his advisors said just that.

But to a barbarian, the idea was revolutionary.

Frederick organised individual meetings with each of the clan's chieftains and went travelling from clan to clan, discussing his idea with them, and the vision he had for helping them to become a unified land. When the head of each clan met Frederick, they'd thought it a wild idea for him to meet with them, considering they'd wanted his father's head on a platter. His brazenness, combined with his intimate knowledge of their people, made them warm to the young lad instantly.

It turned out that the clans were tired of fighting. They needed to move away from war and into a place that allowed them to live in peace and prosperity. Frederick had made a few assumptions when formulating his ideas about how to proceed, and this one had been at the heart of it. It wasn't that much of a stretch: even for a warlike people, war can be very taxing, especially when the warring had been going on for centuries. Perhaps, then, if they had been born into war, they might find an alternative that didn't result in the deaths of their loved ones appealing.

Some, of course, had been a little sceptical about a boy trying to bring peace, but once they had listened to his proposal and heard all he had to say about unity, they started to voice their own opinions and ideas. At Frederick's request, the chieftains came together, and each of them was given a voice. There, they started to express their views and grievances, and thus began the process of healing a people.

By the end of these meetings, totalling one hundred and thirteen over many moons, the clans finally agreed that their search for a king was what drove them to battle, and that clanship with a council of peers would allow for collaboration and discussion in place of war. As the first point of order, they settled upon a common name for the land they had collectively roamed.

When the moon was full and Lunarflowers bloomed across the valley, as the moon set slowly across the sky, it dove down behind the range at the end of the river systems, which gave a peaceful glow to the lands of the barbarian nation. At the point where the moon descended, the river system opened up into a large natural cave, and at its entrance lay the Pillars of Kamiditra. These pillars were known to all the clans as the Setilim of Peace, and were revered alongside the moon and its presence in the sky. Thus were their lands renamed the Lunar Ranges after their beloved moon and the peace that came with the night.

To convene a council was a task that came with risk, and not all of the barbarians were in favour of the decision. The most significant of these dissenters were the Avarie, a legendary group of female warriors with abilities not fully understood. Feeling that the council was a departure from the glory days of old, they'd taken the opportunity to attack during the very first council session, expecting that the nineteen clans, only so recently allied, would start fighting amongst themselves. At the same time, they'd set out to assassinate King Frederick, the man who'd been the driving force behind the change.

They certainly had not imagined that the clans' warriors would band together so readily and effectively to fight a common foe, nor that they would protect the king of the lands they'd fought hard to conquer.

It was a true testament to the hard work that Frederick and his advisors had put in. He'd managed to expand the clans' narrow thinking that they had no purpose but war, encouraging them to see their commonalities rather than their differences: their love of the moon, their common use of the underground waters they held sacred, and their love for their people were all the same. Once they'd realised this, it was only a matter of time before the council was formed ... and with the clans presenting a unified front, the Avarie suffered a bitter defeat, and were quickly disbanded.

When Frederick had returned from his time on the Ranges to govern his own lands, the kingdom had prospered in his absence, in no small part due to his efforts to increase trade between nations and the inclusion of the clans. Taxes had decreased due to the good fortune he'd established in the east, in the shape of sapphires and gold. The kingdom's population had grown considerably, so much so that the theologians named this decade the Decade of Prosperity.

Instead of feeling pride at this accomplishment, the title of king made the hairs on Frederick's neck stand up every time he heard it. Often, he felt himself an imposter, and being praised for his successes only added to his uncertainty. He wasn't blind to the good he'd done in the last seven years, but nor was he blind to all the ways it could fall apart at any moment.

True, the vocal majority supported his rule, but not everyone in the kingdom was happy about a boy ruling a kingdom designed for a man. Plotting and conniving had been at the very heart of many of its previous kings' reigns, and he'd be a fool to think his own was any different. His only defence against such machinations was his natural desire to follow a different path than his predecessors—one of truth and justice, and of upholding right and wrong.

But the definition for right and wrong was far from universal, and it was days like today he felt the most unnerved.

Frederick watched the party slowly making their way towards him, their fates in his hands. The hall around him was cavernous and ornate, with columns of pillars lining either side. Tapestries hung on the walls, and fires roared in deep culverts off to the corners of the hall. These culverts were designed in such a way that their heat would travel the length and breadth of the hall, heating it and the rooms above evenly. Frederick marvelled every time he thought of it, and the many other advancements his people had made in this last century.

His colours hung from the ceiling in long, straight stripes of material dyed a shade of deep grape with gilded trim, upon which his family crest was emblazoned: an eagle with a sceptre in its talons. The majesty of the hall was imposing, even to Frederick himself. He felt a chill in the air about him on this day—a day he had to pass judgment on one of his own.

Slowly, three men and one small boy approached the dais. Recessed behind it was a second, smaller throne fit for a queen, but being as young as he was, he had not yet found a suitable lady to fill this position.

The eyes of the men were downcast, but the child among them looked about himself with complete wonder, taking in every moment and splendour before him. It hadn't registered to him at first, but now that it had, it was very unusual. The men to be judged this day were soldiers in his army, charged with insubordination.

Why, then, was there a child among them?

When the four reached the bottom of the platform that led up to the king, they bowed and knelt, the child following the adults' lead.

In his official tone, Frederick spoke, his voice projecting to all corners of the hall.

"All here have borne witness to the infamy of the supplicants before me." He hated using the word 'supplicant', but where the law was concerned, his hands were tied. "Lift your eyes to me, so I can see that you know my words."

The four of them did so, each of the men's faces bearing grim resignation.

"I want you men … and you, boy … to know this before I say anything further. In my position, I have many official duties to perform, and of all of them, this is the one I enjoy the least."

The stern look on his face faded to one of uncertainty as his eyes were drawn to the child. It was as if he were being pulled in by them—compelled to focus on the boy.

Several others in the hall who were awaiting their own audience with the king looked at each other strangely, trying to follow the king's eyes, wondering what it was that held his stare. The men standing next to the child did the same, looking back and forth between the king and the space next to them. The child, caught up in the moment, smiled back at them, his teeth showing through.

For a long moment, Frederick's eyes fixed on the boy. He did not blink, nor move—he simply stared. Suddenly, all those present watched as the king's face turned to a look of surprise. The guards, who had been anxiously watching the scene unfold, saw this and started moving defensively towards the dais.

To Frederick's eyes, in place of the child, there now stood an old man with a long, white beard, brown robes cinched by a green belt, and a gnarled wooden staff in his old, wrinkled hand.

The boy was an illusion. Paired with the old man's staff and attire, Frederick could only imagine the man before him had revealed himself for what he truly was: a mage, and a powerful one at that.

"How is it you appear where a boy once stood?" said Frederick.

The congregation in the hall looked at each other, troubled by the king's words.

"Funny," said the mage. "The same could be said to you, my liege."

Frederick rose from his seat.

"Who are you, and why have you come?"

The old man bowed his head in supplication. "I've come to request an audience with you, Your Majesty."

With surprising speed, the mage snapped back upright and raised a hand, and a sudden shimmering of white light descended upon the room.

Frederick stared in amazement. The hall stood deathly still. Not a sound could be heard, or a breath of wind could be felt. All Frederick could hear was his heart in his ears, pounding rapidly. He looked around to find that all who'd been active before now stood like statues, as unmoving as the hall's many pillars.

Frederick's gaze came back to land on the mage, who was now standing with his arms at his side, clearly enjoying Frederick's reaction.

"What is this sorcery?" he bellowed.

The king's voice was tinged with anger … but the mage didn't miss the fear in it, either.

Smiling, he said, "As I said, milord, I humbly request your attention for a short while. For matters as sensitive as these, it's imperative that the words do not reach the wrong ears."

"Then speak," Frederick demanded. "What is it you have to say?"

"I will be brief, my liege, as I do not have much time," the mage said coolly. "I am a wanderer of sorts ,who it seems fate has dealt a cruel hand. You see, I have the ability to see things that most take for granted. I come before you today, for my foresight has seen something of significance for you and your family."

"I must intercede here, mage, for I have no family," Frederick stated matter-of-factually.

"Not *yet*."

The gravity of these words was not lost on the king.

"Go on."

As if obliging, the mage's eyes rolled back into his head, and the hall around him suddenly became cold, turning the world before Frederick dark and lonely.

Words, sounding distant and surreal, came forth from the mage's mouth.

"Two boys, one lost and one found, hold truth. Seek that which is lost. Keep that which is found. Both will reveal their core. When the rune flares and the spirit calls, send them home."

The mage's eyes returned to their normal colour, and he slumped forward. The hall became warmer as the fires regained their intensity and warmth. Frederick descended the dais to the mage to offer his aid, but before he reached the man, a hand shot out from under his robes, palm facing out. Frederick stopped instantly.

"Come no closer. I am fine," he said, shallow breaths returning to his body.

It occurred to Frederick that if the mage were a threat, he would've struck already, and wouldn't have made himself vulnerable. Frederick sat slowly upon one of the steps up to the dais, suddenly fatigued. The mage—and apparent prophet—rose slowly and stood once more. As he came to his full height and regained his composure, he straightened out his robes and gestured to the supplicants.

"What are their crimes?"

Frederick looked over the men and sighed.

"'Failure to comply with a direct order in the king's army' ... which is an officious way of saying they enjoyed a bit of mead while in uniform. They weren't even on duty. The advisors expect me to set an example, but frankly, I don't see the problem."

The mage chuckled. "Thank you for your honesty, sire. Your vision is a thing to be commended, in more ways than one. It seems you noticed something was amiss well in advance of the moment I intended to reveal myself."

Frederick frowned. "You mean to say I saw through the disguise of a prophet? I may be a king, but I'm only a man. How could that be?"

A knowing smile appeared upon the mage's face.

"Far be it from me to say, milord ... but time reveals all, to be sure."

The mage's hands lifted to join in front of himself. He muttered a few small words, and the room light up brighter than the sun, blinding Frederick. The king shielded his eyes from the light until darkness slowly descended, and the room regained its usual illumination. Frederick pulled his arms away and opened his eyes slightly to test if it was safe to do so, and found that as soon as the mage had cast the spell, time had returned to its normal speed.

The many eyes that had stood still and statuesque moments before now looked towards the king in complete shock. To them, the king had risen from his throne and come to sit on the lower steps of the dais instantaneously. The three soldiers to be judged jumped back in surprise at the proximity of the king, now only feet away from them. In their minds, and the minds of all present, the king had moved far too quickly for any man.

It was only now that Frederick realised that the robed man—be he mage or prophet, friend or foe—had vanished without a trace.

The Home Guard, the king's personal guard, appeared like mist from out of the shadows, and again people were frightened by the sudden apparition. Once materialised, they moved at pace towards the king.

Frederick, realising how this must look, stood and moved back up the stairs onto the top of dais and towards his throne. There, he turned and spoke in a resonating voice, full of purpose and strength.

"All in the presence of this court!"

The soldiers at the bottom of the steps straightened and resumed their place, looks of sudden fear descending once again upon their faces. The Home Guard paused in their advance towards the king, and the people within the hall, transfixed by what had occurred, listened intently to what was coming.

"These men here," Frederick said, pointing to the three soldiers, "are nothing more than men of the crown. As such, they are bound to serve the kingdom. It is therefore decreed that they will serve out the next year in the outer borders. Once that term has ended, they may once again join the king's army to perform their duty, as previously ordained. This is my judgement. Let no man speak otherwise."

His advisors started to talk amongst themselves. Once again, the king had gone off script, though there was the sense that this was something his advisors were getting used to. As the tension of the previous few minutes passed, the hall started to return to normal.

The people of the court returned to their allotted space, waiting for their turn to discuss their items of business. The Home Guard that had materialised out of thin air had vanished. No one really saw them leave: they simply were no longer there.

To the king's right stood his advisors, the most senior of which was Chancellor Portlief. The chancellor was an older man with a greying, neatly trimmed beard and long grey hair tied back into a ponytail. He wore a tight-fitting shirt that revealed a sturdy build beneath a leather tunic, upon which his coat of orange and lilac stood in contrast to his black pants and boots. To most ladies' eyes, he was a handsome gentleman. To Frederick, he looked like a man who was uncertain why he had acquitted soldiers from the penalty of discharge and banishment from the kingdom. Frederick and his advisors had discussed the terms, and he had acted entirely out of alignment.

Portlief was a wise advisor, having spent many years with the former king, and the last seven with Frederick. He had experience well beyond Frederick's years, and Frederick had relied upon his counsel on many occasions. He understood the fluctuating nature of the world, and so was quick to understand, rather than to judge. Being of a similar mind, Frederick appreciated this about him ... but that wasn't to say they never clashed.

Frederick sat and indicated for Portlief to come forward. Portlief walked forward and leant down to consult with Frederick.

"My lord," he stated formally, his lips somewhat pursed.

"I need your ear, your knowledge, and to get the hell out of this session," he said, his ears turning red with irritation.

The change in Frederick's mood was surprising to Portlief. He had never seen him so worked up, and for no reason he could discern.

"As you require, my lord," he stated, standing up and bowing.

"All of you, hear this," Portlief stated in a booming voice. "Today's session is at an end. The remaining business of the day will be brought before the guilds of business, and decided upon there. So sayeth the king, and in the king's court, his word is law."

Looks of disgust came from the people who'd waited to present their case before the king. It was not terribly unusual for the guilds to take up such issues when business of state and kingdom needed to be dealt with, but they had already endured a lengthy wait, and would likely have to do so again.

The Home Guard appeared once more, encouraging the people of the court out of the hall and closing the doors behind them. Once the room was empty, Frederick rose and headed to the back of the dais, where his office of business and law was located. He entered the room, his advisors in tow, and removed his ceremonial garb, throwing it across the armchair in the corner. Underneath his robes, he wore a simple pair of tan pants and a loose-fitting white shirt.

"Those damnable robes are far too thick for this weather," he said, advancing towards his chair.

At all times, the king had two guards posted to protect him. These men were sworn to secrecy and loyalty above all and beyond … and it was precisely for instances of 'the beyond' that Frederick needed these men. Frederick had learnt to fight from a young age, honing his skills as his father had wanted, and he fancied himself a capable defender. As such, it had bothered Frederick at first to have two shadows whenever he walked a few yards from his office to relieve himself … but since the Avarie's attempt on his life, he'd decided their presence wasn't so bad after all. Not always convenient or comforting, but useful nonetheless.

Frederick had taken his time getting to know and understand his many and varied guards, and though he dared not voice a preference, his favourite among them were those present today, William and Katarg. The two had been with him from the start, and having spent many an hour with them at his side, he considered them to be good friends.

Shortly after the king entered the room, his advisors had descended upon the doorway.

"Gentlemen," he indicated to William and Katarg." A moment, if you please."

Immediately, the guards turned from their charge and advanced towards the door to prevent the advisors from entering the room.

"Portlief. Enter," said Katarg.

William and Katarg allowed him, and only him, to pass, then shut the doors and barred them. A smile spread across Frederick's face. He felt nothing but pride for his guards, who'd understood him well enough to know what he'd wanted with just a few words.

"Portlief, what did you see in the hall just now?"

The king's tone was unassuming but inquisitive, the irritation slowly leaving him.

"Your Majesty—"

Frederick raised a hand to cut him off.

"We are old friends, Portlief. I've asked you a thousand times. Please, call me Frederick."

"Yes, sir. Ah ... Frederick, sir. You ... were about to hold court for the three supplicants, whereby you stated your business and then ... stopped, in favour of staring at the space next to the men. That's when it happened, milord. Within a split second, you moved from your chair to the bottom step. I'm afraid I cannot explain that, sir. Can you?"

"Did you not see the young boy?" asked Frederick, scrutinising his advisor's answer.

A look of concern came over Portlief's face.

"What boy, sire?"

Frederick sighed. "Thank you, Portlief. I suspected my experience may have differed from your own, and indeed from all others present."

He then explained what had happened in the hall.

"That almost sounds like a prophecy, Your—Frederick."

Frederick nodded. "I thought the same. Thankfully, Vandrune is in the capital, instructing the squires on the very subject. Please, let him know I require his counsel."

Portlief nodded, visibly concerned for the king. As he moved towards the door, still watching Frederick, he bade the king's two most loyal shadows keep an eye on him.

"Never take them off him, sir," said William in a deep, resonating voice.

"Thank you all," said Frederick. "I need some time to think on this mage's words. Please make sure I am not disturbed."

Finally, Portlief pulled open the door and advanced towards the other advisors, who looked lost and dismayed at having been locked out. Frederick could see the concern on their faces as the door glided shut, but was in no mood to placate them.

Inside his chamber, Frederick went over the apparent prophecy over and over again, trying to make sense of it. One thing kept standing out above all else:

"Two boys, one lost and one found."

Who was that mage? Was he truly a prophet? Had he been one of the boys the old man had referenced, and if so, what was this 'core' he'd mentioned?

Whatever the answers, Frederick couldn't help but feel that troubled times lay ahead for the kingdom of Neleuwan.

SQUIRES

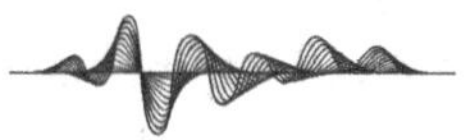

Sunlight crested the rampart's crenulations as the boys moved from the makeshift lesson room up through the castle proper, each of them heading off to follow up with their masters and complete their allotted duties. As they made their way, they couldn't stop talking about the lesson. Their teacher was a prophet, and none other than Master Vandrune himself. They couldn't help but relive the moment again and again.

Of the group, none were more excited than the pair from House Vandeguild.

"It was all I could do not to stare," said Higant.

"Who would've thought—our teacher, a true prophet! No one will believe this. I can't wait to tell the others," Marcus said excitedly.

The boys proceeded on through the halls towards the ante-chamber of the great hall and out into the palace grounds. The sun was high in the sky, and the brightness of its rays caused the boys to shade their eyes. After a few moments, they turned from the front of the hall and headed down the passage to the right along a connecting pavilion to the Hall of Lords, and onto the chamber of Lord Baron Vandeguild.

They entered the baron's office and found him writing at his desk, upon which sat large piles of parchment, doubtless filled with menial tasks that the boys would have to take care of. Baron Vandeguild was a podgy man with a round face, his fat filling in any wrinkles he might've earned had he been slimmer in stature, making him look far younger than he was. Despite his penchant for indulgence, he was a kindly soul, and worked hard for the good of the kingdom.

"Boys! It is good to see you," the baron said with a knowing smile. "Finished your lesson for the day, have you? I trust it was to your liking?"

"To put it lightly, sir," said Marcus, beaming.

"Given the build-up, we'd expected a mage, but a prophet? I'd never thought to meet one, much less learn from one!" said Higant.

"Good, good. Before you take your rest for the day, I've one last task for each of you. Higant, take this message to Sabr, the Captain of the Guard. A scout must depart at once for the southern border. It is a matter of great importance that this gets to the outer barracks."

"Yes, sir!" he said, taking the rolled-up scroll and heading out of the office, winking at Marcus as he passed.

After Higant left, the baron was suddenly coy. Marcus stood where he was for a few silent moments before the baron raised his head again and indicated for him to approach.

As he drew close to the baron, he caught wind of an unfamiliar scent. It was faint, but unmistakable in its sweetness.

"Marcus, my boy," the baron said sheepishly. "I need to ask a favour, as it were. As my eldest squire, I need your maturity in the task at hand. It is a matter that requires ... discretion."

Judging by his behaviour, Marcus suspected he knew where this was going.

In addition to a good meal, the baron had another vice: women.

"What is it you need, sir?" Marcus squinted, trying to seem unassuming.

Baron Vandeguild looked around surreptitiously, as if trying to make sure no one would hear his next words. Being the only two in the room, the exercise felt a little futile.

His words were almost a whisper.

"What do you know of the whorehouses down in the poor quarter?"

Astoundingly, being not much older than fourteen summers, the whorehouses were not a place Marcus frequented all that often.

"A little, sir," was all he could say.

"I am ... in need of company tonight, and it would look a little out of order if someone of my stature were to be seen in that area of the poor quarter at night ... or at any other time, for that matter. I was wondering if you could help me organise some kind of ... rendezvous?"

Marcus thought it would be out of order for a young boy to be seen around those parts as well, but he kept that to himself. He couldn't help but think it strange that the second cousin to the king would be asking after a prostitute when, despite not being the most appealing man to look at, he could (and often did) secure a lady of the court just as easily.

"I'll see what I can do for you, sir," he said, turning and heading for the door.

Before he was able to reach it, Baron Vandeguild said, "Ah, Marcus ... this is our little secret—just between you and me, yes?"

"My word is my bond, milord," Marcus said formally, suppressing a sigh.

"My villa, an hour after sunset. Understood?"

The boy nodded quickly, and then was gone.

Waiting until he was sure Marcus had left, the baron rose from his chair and walked over to the door to his office, shutting it and turning the lock. He leant against the door and faced the back wall of his office, upon which hung a tapestry of extreme beauty and magnificence. It celebrated the visage of the palace and the lands around.

"Privacy at last," the baron said shyly.

"One rendezvous to conceal another, is it? Quick thinking, milord. I wasn't sure the boy would go along with it ... but he is a squire, after all. They never think for themselves."

Out from behind the tapestry stepped an alluring woman, wholly undressed, with flowing brown hair, lips of red, and cheeks of a similar shade. Her supple skin shimmered with sweat, and was tanned to perfection.

The baron looked at her with hungry eyes. Licking his lips, he walked slowly towards her.

"You are a vision of beauty, my dear," he said, unbuttoning his shirt.

"Only to you, milord, am I bound to be beautiful," she said with lust in her eyes.

The woman stood completely still, her hands behind her back, waiting for the baron to reach his objective. The baron was halfway across the room and still advancing, shirt off and his pants around his ankles, causing him to shuffle.

"You do make me giggle, milord," she said with mock laughter.

"Come closer, my love, and let me show you how a real man makes a lady giggle."

She took a step closer to him, teasing him to move closer to her.

"I see you have a present for me," she said seductively, eyes low.

The baron shuffled a little further towards the voluptuous woman, only three feet from each other now. The heat in the room was oppressive and made her sweat even more, causing her naked body to glisten. Beads of sweat ran down between her supple breasts on their way to the flesh below. The baron reached for her and felt soft, supple skin beneath his fingertips, then enveloped her in his arms and his bare chest.

Kissing her soft pink lips, he pressed hard against her curvaceous body, feeling its warmth. She kissed him in kind and ran her hands up into his hair, then down his less-than-muscular back. She pulled away a little, then moved his hand to her breast. He squeezed it firmly, and her eyes closed with pleasure.

Finally able to free his ankles from his pants, the baron picked the woman up and carried her as best as he could through a hidden door behind the tapestry. Inside stood a four-poster bed with sheets that shone in the candlelight, and advancing awkwardly towards it, he fell forward onto the soft mattress, trying not to crush his lady as he fell. Her head landed upon feather-filled pillows, and was quickly forced to the left as he kissed her neck. Her eyes took in the rest of the room, which amounted to a decanter and a pair of wine glasses on the bedside table and pink-hued lanterns on each of the four walls, the candles within casting romantic lighting throughout the chamber.

The baron moved her up the bed and placed her softly in front of him, where she sat up and then pulled him up with her so they were eye to eye. She once again moved his hand to her breast and he responded by slowly, softly caressing the soft pink skin and nipple. She leaned back on the bed and he moved his hands across all her body, slowly caressing her breast, her thighs, her legs, her belly, and finally, her love. The softness and the wetness of it made him lust for her all the more.

He slipped his fingers in and out, listening as he slowly but surely brought her to the climax of ecstasy. Soon enough, she moaned and withered, and the baron was quite pleased with himself. Once recovered, she then manoeuvred the baron onto the bed next to her and rolled over on top of him. She held his hands above his head and moved her body in ways the baron had not even thought possible, sliding upon his manhood and starting to excite him.

The room echoed with their heavy breathing and moans. Just as they were reaching the height of their passion, the women subtly moved her body down so her breast was in his face. With that, her hands were free, and she slowly reached under the pillow on the bed. Now that the baron was almost at the critical part of his lovemaking, the woman pulled him upwards into a full sit, where she straddled his waist with his manhood deep inside her. His eyes meeting hers, he was almost there, almost there—and then suddenly, he stiffened. His eyes rolled up into his head, and he collapsed into the headboard.

With the deed done, the woman rose up off him and slid off the side of the bed. The baron did not move. She looked at him and giggled to herself.

Of course he was still: the blade in his back had made sure of that.

Before she dressed, she washed herself at the basin to rid herself of the big oaf's stench. She dressed in her lady's attire, a formal gown made of jade and mauve, colours which were striking in any man's eyes ... to say nothing of the plunging neckline and the split up the side. It made the men go wild, and had been her favourite for a long while.

"Well, my lord, thank you for your kindness ... and now you must play your part by vacating an office that was never fit for a pig such as yourself, and delivering the Blade as the scrolls ordained," she said with a smile.

She drew aside the tapestry, exiting the hidden chamber and stopping at the baron's desk. There, she reached down and picked up a piece of parchment, rolled it up, and tucked it between her breasts and out of sight. Finally, she opened the door and exited, pulling it closed behind her before making her way out of the palace.

As if she'd made this trip many times, she navigated the roads down to the poor quarter to a tavern called The Whistling Sailor, a seedy establishment at the best of times. Today, it was empty save for the barkeep and his waiter. He noted her as she entered, then continued on with his duties. She crossed the common room and proceeded up the stairs at the far end, leading to the rooms overhead.

At the end of the hall, she pushed her way through a door and out onto a balcony. Looking to her right, there was a ladder that led up onto the roof, which she quickly ascended and then moved stealthily to the east side of the roof. From her vantage point, she could see the vastness of the ocean and the harbour below, stopping for the briefest of moments to appreciate it before moving to a corner of the roof that overhung another balcony. Once there, she grappled the ledge, swung down in a feat of athleticism, and leveraged herself onto the balcony, pausing again to make sure her dress had made the journey unharmed. No longer exposed, she casually advanced through a nearby window into a small room.

The room was adorned with red wallpaper and a four-poster bed that almost consumed the room, covered in silk bedsheets and soft feather pillows. The floor was lined with aged wood that had been laid when this building, one of the oldest in the area, had been constructed.

Without missing a beat, she slipped out of her dress, pulling the parchment from her cleavage and placing it onto her bedside table. Completely exhausted, she fell backwards onto her soft sheets.

A knock sounded at the door, startling her.

Without bothering to dress herself, she walked to the end of the room and opened the small door, which looked out into a narrow hallway and set of stairs at the other end.

In the doorway stood a young man of light-coloured hair, no older than fourteen, maybe fifteen summers. Stout-looking for his age, he was a handsome lad, if a little dishevelled-looking. Above his black undershirt and brown slacks was a green cotton tunic emblazoned with a familiar coat of arms. She'd seen this young boy through the tapestry in the baron's office naught but an hour earlier.

Out of all the prostitutes he could've found, he'd stumbled across her.

"Good afternoon, my lady," said Marcus with formality and pride, hands behind his back, though slightly startled by the bare skin of the woman before him.

She was proud of her naked form, and in it, her confidence didn't wane one bit.

"And to you too, young sire," she said with mock formality. "What brings you to my door on such a lovely day?"

"I was sent by my lord to find a suitable lady for his company this evening," he said, trying his best to maintain eye contact.

"A lady, is it? Well, I do believe I've gone up in the world," she said, a smile appearing upon her face. "And whom will I have the honour of sharing some time with this evening?"

"I'm afraid I cannot discuss that with you at this time," he said, looking over his shoulder for eavesdroppers, then turning back to her, making sure his eyes started high.

"I'm not sure I'm the lady you're looking for," she said, slowly closing the door.

"Please," said the boy, jamming his foot between the door and the doorframe. "I was told you were ... exceptionally good at your profession, ma'am, and my lord would be most pleased if you would attend."

"So, my reputation precedes me, does it?" she said, slowly taking in the stature of this young boy—no, young man. "How can you be sure I'm as good at my, as you call it, *profession* as they say?"

"I asked more than your fair share of people, milady, and they all said the same: if they felt the need for ... true pleasure ... you were the lady to call upon."

"Well, with that sort of endorsement, I'm not surprised you turned up at my doorstep." Her lips curled into a grin. "I wonder ... would you know true pleasure if you encountered it, young man?"

The lad's face was flushed a deep shade of red.

"Ah … well, that's—no, ma'am … I've had neither the chance nor the pleasure," he said, looking down at his shoes.

"Well then," she said, reaching for him and drawing him into her room, "I believe it's about time you did."

She placed the young man down on her bed, then made her way back to the door.

"My name is Crimson," she announced, closing the door slowly and turning back to face him. "What might yours be?"

"M—Marcus, ma'am!"

She walked towards the bed and smiled.

CHAPTER FIVE

Murder

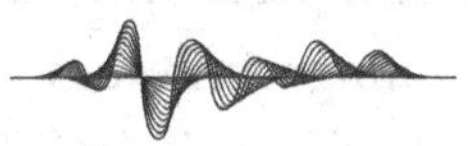

It was well past dark by the time Marcus walked out of the tavern. A cool wind had rolled in from the grey ocean, and with it had come fog and rain. He pulled his tunic closer about himself and strode off towards the palace and his quarters.

His mind was awash with feelings, mostly of the sort he'd never felt before. It had been his first time with a woman, and for it to have been with one so experienced had only heightened his emotions.

He walked slowly up towards the castle with a light smirk on his face, trying to keep and then recall the wonders of the experience he'd just had. The woman named Crimson had shown him things he could not yet comprehend, yet he felt certain that in years to come, he would be grateful to this woman for showing him what it was to love.

His spirits soared as he made his way through the poorer quarter of the city towards the rich and palatial houses surrounding the palace.

While lost in thoughts of his last couple of hours, he suddenly thought of the baron, and realised he'd completely forgotten about the rendezvous he'd been asked to organise. The whole reason he'd been out there was to secure a lady of the night for the baron's pleasure, not his own. He would surely get in some measure of trouble for leaving the baron lonely, but considering the secretive—and, frankly, tawdry—nature of the request, he supposed there was only so much his lord would do to punish him.

Nevertheless, his strong sense of duty confounded him. Marcus started to run towards the palace, his pace quickening with every stride. His mind was spinning with excuses, searching for one that could explain both his lack of completion of the task and the reason he'd been missing until long after dark had fallen.

He entered the castle through the east gate, hurrying past familiar guards and then running all the way to the baron's office. As he rounded the corner into the hall in which it lay, he saw there was still light emanating from inside. Could he still be working? He dared to hope that the baron had forgotten as well, though the more likely scenario was that he'd returned from his empty villa and waited here to scold him upon his return.

Bracing himself, Marcus reached for the door and turned the latch, only to find the door was locked.

He knocked on the door a few times, each time getting louder. It was not out of the question that the baron may have drank himself into a stupor while working long hours at his desk. Only a few moons ago, Marcus and Higant had returned here to report the completion of their tasks and found him in just such a state, slumped over his desk next to an empty bottle of absinth, drooling on some important paper he'd been writing. Even together, it had taken the two of them some time to get him to bed for the night, and Marcus was not excited about the prospect of having to attempt it alone.

When it became apparent that his lord was not coming to the door, it was time for a different approach. Marcus had learnt to adapt to these sorts of situations, and had acquired many tools and skills along the way. He reached inside his tunic and removed two small metal pins. If someone discovered them, they would think them no more than bent metal nails ... but to Marcus, they were every bit as good as lockpicks.

Just as he was about to get to work on the lock, he remembered that the lock had seized up recently, and the baron had had him oil it only a few days ago. A well-oiled lock would be nearly impossible to pick, even with the proper tools.

Marcus rose to his feet and considered his options.

He turned his attention to the hinges upon which the door sat. Looking at the old door and its warped, wonky hinges, he wondered if the pins might be able to be removed, thus allowing the door to be lifted off them and into the office.

He placed the tip of one of his metal nails under that of the lowest of the three hinge pins and pushed down with his palm. The pin didn't budge. Undeterred, Marcus reached around his waist and pulled his dagger free from its hiding place at the back of his belt. With the butt of the handle, he struck the metal pin, which seemed only send reverberating shockwaves through the door, not to mention his arms. The second strike made more of a hollow sound, still sending shockwaves up his forearms. It was the final strike that did the trick. The hit made a crunching sound, then a click, and he knew then he'd succeeded. Sure enough, the pin cleared the top of the bracket and fell to the floor.

Moving onto the last two pins, Marcus repeated the process, and as the final pin popped free from its holder, the door swung inward and fell off its hinges, the lock breaking free as the full weight of the door landed heavily on the ground.

"That noise would've woken the dead ... or a drunk baron," he chuckled to himself, putting away his dagger and pins.

Impressed with himself for figuring out the puzzle of the door, he stepped through the opening he'd created and stood just inside the doorway, waiting for his eyes to adjust to the comparatively bright room.

The first thing he noted was not with his eyes, but his nose—a scent that seemed somehow familiar. He made his way into the room and towards the baron's desk, still stacked high with all manner of parchments, on the other side of which he expected to find the baron's sleeping face.

However, as he reached the desk and peered over the piles, he saw that the desk was empty. Strange. The baron was many things, but he wasn't negligent enough to let the lamps burn in a room full of parchment with no one around.

On further inspection of the desk, Marcus noticed a blank piece of parchment and the baron's quill resting on the desk, not in its holder. Again, this struck Marcus as odd, as the baron had always been particular about those sorts of things.

Marcus walked around to the back of the desk and placed the quill back into its holder next to the inkwell. There, he caught another whiff of that scent. It was deeply familiar, but still he could not place it. Using it as a guide, he paced about the office, trying to find the source of the aroma, as well as any reason the baron would've left his lanterns burning, his desk out of order, and no indication as to why.

As he looked around, another strange thing caught his eye: the baron's pants, crumpled up on the floor. He was amazed he hadn't noticed them earlier. Picking them up, a frown descended on his brow.

"Of all things, why are there pants in the middle of the floor?" he asked of the room. Of course, the room did not reply, but he'd felt it strange enough to warrant the remark.

He placed them on the back of the chair that sat opposite the baron's desk. Again, that scent greeted his senses. The next thing he noticed, near the foot of the desk, was the baron's shirt. Indeed, it seemed to Marcus that the baron had undressed. Blushing as he remembered his own rendezvous, Marcus wondered if perhaps his lord had grown impatient while waiting for his return and found his own lady to entertain, right here in the study.

Still, that didn't explain why he'd left the place in such a state.

After several more minutes of searching without finding any new information or answers, Marcus resigned himself to the enigma and prepared to leave, but not before taking care of that which his master had failed to. He walked over to the desk and extinguished the lantern, then walked the perimeter of the room, doing the same for each of the wall lanterns.

Bizarrely, as the light from the last lantern dimmed, the room was plunged into darkness … and yet at the same time, a sliver of light remained.

At first, Marcus thought it was one of the lanterns he'd already turned off finishing its wick, but as he turned around to investigate, he noticed the light was coming from beyond the ornate tapestry on the wall behind the baron's desk.

Stranger still, the light that remained was pink.

He moved slowly towards the tapestry, feeling around in the near-darkness to find its edges. When he drew it back, he found that the strangely hued light had been emanating from out of a hidden doorway.

The baron had a hidden chamber in his office, and Marcus had had no idea.

"Lord Baron?" he whispered, leaning in quietly and peering into the doorway.

He could not have prepared himself for what he saw. Sitting up on the bed, slumped to the side, was Baron Vandeguild, naked and still.

Marcus quickly pulled his head away from the entrance, hoping the baron had not seen him. Hearing no movement, he risked looking again, and after watching him for a second or two, it was evident something was wrong.

He walked slowly up to the four-poster bed, praying the baron was simply drunk and passed out, but instinctively, he knew better. Then there was that damnable scent, growing stronger and more intense with every step he took towards the baron.

When Marcus made it to the bed, he reached out to touch the baron, and his eyes turned to saucers. The baron was cold—ice cold. He pulled his hand away quickly and moved to see the baron's eyes, lifeless and still. The blood drained from Marcus's face and he instantly took a few steps back, his eyes still locked on the baron as he backed towards the doorway. When he reached it, he turned and ran out from the tapestry, pale and stricken by what he'd seen.

Marcus burst out of the office door and into the night, yelling at the top of his lungs, tears streaming down his face.

"Home Guard! Home Guard!"

He frantically looked up and down the corridor, waiting for the guard to appear ... yet no one came. He didn't know what to do.

"Home Guard, please! There's been a murder!"

And still, no one appeared. In a way, it made sense—after all, their sole charge was to guard the king. Still, surely someone should've heard his cries and come running? Furiously searching his mind for someone he could call upon, as if out of nowhere, a name planted itself in his mind.

Vandrune.

Marcus was off running at pace, sweat running down his face and mixing with his tears for the departed baron. He headed for the east wing of the palace and the visitors' quarters, where the assigned rooms of visiting dignitaries were common knowledge to the squires in case they needed to deliver messages.

As Marcus sprinted through Dome of Lillifor, he didn't even register the deep red colour pouring in through the dome above and illuminating the floor below. Unbeknownst to him, a blood moon hung in the sky above, but surging through the hall in his haste, the irony was lost on him.

Marcus turned down the third corridor and ran, passing statues and fountains and all manner of doors. He turned right and found the third door on the right, and when he reached the door, he noticed another squire standing at the entrance, sound asleep, leaning against the doorframe on a chair. Marcus was running so fast he slid on the floor and crashed into Syng, who was swearing at the sudden intrusion into his dreams, trying to disentangle himself from Marcus all the while.

Finally, the two squires removed themselves from each other. Syng looked at Marcus hard and said, "What are you doing running around this late at night, Marcus?"

"I *must* see Vandrune," said Marcus, frantic. "It is vitally important."

"Vandrune has asked not to be woken until dawn. If you'd like to come back, I'll—"

Marcus pinned him to the wall, knocking the breath out of him.

"I need to see him *now*, Syng. If you get in my way, you'll regret it." His voice was filled with panic. He hadn't meant to be so aggressive, but this was more than urgent.

Marcus let Syng go, and the young squire straightened himself out. In a split second, he'd pulled his dagger and spun Marcus around with amazing speed, pinning him against the wall in kind, blade at his throat.

His quick movements had caught Marcus by surprise, but once the shock of it faded, the severity returned to his eyes. All he wanted was to see Vandrune, and for good reason.

The two squires looked each other hard in the eyes.

"Don't *ever* touch me again," said Syng.

Before Marcus could respond, they both realised they were being watched. Marcus' eyes moved to see who was watching them, and Syng turned to see Vandrune's silhouette in the doorway of his room.

"What's all this noise, gentlemen?" said Vandrune in a calm, resonating voice.

Syng made no move to release his grip, nor his blade. "Sir. This young ruffian says he needs to talk to you. Per your request, I—"

"I appreciate your enthusiasm, but I didn't mean *under any circumstances,* lad. Plainly, his business is important."

"It is, Master Vandrune," said Marcus, straining not to move into the blade.

"Lower you blade, Squire Syng. I will take charge from here."

Vandrune reached for the dagger and Syng acquiesced, allowing Marcus to move into the room. Syng followed closely behind.

"Master Vandrune," said Marcus, his voice strained. "My Lord Baron Vandeguild is dead, sir. I found him in a hidden room behind his office. I called for the Home Guard, but none came. I didn't know what to do, sir. You were the only one I could think of."

Syng's eyes became wide with shock. A baron? Dead in the palace?

Vandrune swiftly pulled on his robes and boots.

"Lead the way."

As they left the guest's quarters, Vandrune pulled from his robes a small blue stone. He placed it in his hand and muttered some words into it, which sounded to the squires more like musical notes. The stone glowed blue and suddenly, before him as they walked, the disembodied head of the king appeared in the same blue light. Both Marcus and Syng jumped back with surprise.

"Vandrune. How may I be of service at this time of night?" said Frederick, looking a little perturbed by the interruption to whatever he'd been doing.

"My lord," he said with sincerity in his voice, "I require your immediate presence at your cousin Baron Vandeguild's office."

"I'm on my way."

The blue light dimmed, and Vandrune placed the blue stone

back inside his robes. They continued moving back through the castle the way that Marcus had come, and soon came upon the corridor in which it lay. Vandrune stopped the boys at the far end, and from there, they could see the king had just appeared at the other side, flanked by William and Katarg.

"Hold position, my lord. I believe the Home Guard may be necessary."

Understanding immediately, Frederick held his hands at his side and closed his eyes, and without warning, the king spoke.

"Ku-Da-Ru."

Out of nowhere, figures started appearing in the corridor, as if materialising from nothing. It took a mere second for the corridor to fill with the Home Guard, leaving the two squires amazed at the ten soldiers who'd appeared out of thin air between them and the king.

The commander of the Home Guard moved towards the king to understand the need, and the king directed to speak with Vandrune. As the man moved back towards Vandrune, Marcus realised that something was not quite right with him, like something from his countenance was … missing. He didn't have time to think it through, however, as his attention was drawn back to Vandrune.

"Good evening, sir," said the commander, his voice strange and yet familiar, almost wavering. "How may we serve?"

"This young man here," said Vandrune, indicating to Marcus, "has reported that Lord Baron Vandeguild is dead. I ask for a sweep of the room and its contents. Please, report to me before the king, as he does not yet know."

"I understand, sir."

The man bowed his head and turned to the other Home Guard, and just as suddenly as they'd appeared, they were gone. Marcus blinked twice to make sure his eyes had not been playing tricks on him, but indeed, the corridor was once again empty.

A minute passed, and everyone in the corridor stood silently, waiting. In far less time than they'd expected, the captain reappeared again suddenly, making Marcus and Syng jump a second time.

"The room is secure, sir. No sign of any other presence. The Lord Baron is dead," he said formally.

"What are the circumstances?" Vandrune questioned.

"A six-inch blade was driven into the baron's back," he said, as if giving a written report. "The weapon remains."

"Thank you, Commander. Please maintain a guard upon this corridor."

"Yes, sir."

Contrary to his words, the commander disappeared from sight ... though Marcus felt he and his guards were still here in some form or another.

Vandrune turned to the squires and indicated for them to wait where they were, then walked to the other end of the corridor to meet the king. The boys couldn't hear what was being said, but watching Frederick's face turn from red to pale, they might've guessed.

William and Katarg, who had receded into the shadows whilst the Home Guard had completed their task, now moved back into the light after the revelation that the baron was dead—partly to support the king in this time of grief, but mostly to stay close and protect him from any threats.

Marcus turned to Syng, tears running down his cheeks. Filled with adrenaline and terror, he hadn't yet had a moment to mourn the loss of his lord.

"I'm sorry for the way I acted back there," he said, true sorrow sounding in his voice.

Syng met him in kind. "I too feel shame for my actions."

He held out a hand, and Marcus grasped it.

They both turned to see Vandrune and the king move towards the office door. To their surprise, Vandrune indicated for them to come inside. Syng moved easily towards the door, though Marcus was a little more reluctant. Inside, the lanterns were once again alight, but the room was more stifling than it had been before. Marcus caught that sweet scent once again, and still he couldn't place it. Frederick and Vandrune moved towards the tapestry, which had been pulled back to reveal the doorway. They entered and disappeared into the room. Marcus knew what was in there, and so he decided to wait in the office proper, staying as close to the door as possible.

Frederick came from the room first, tears falling from his cheeks. Vandrune, it seemed, was using magic to determine the circumstances of the murder.

He too returned a little while later with a look of concern on his face.

Frederick moved towards him, and they talked in hushed tones. Finally, Vandrune looked towards Marcus.

Slowly, both the king and Vandrune walked over to Marcus.

"Marcus," said the king, his voice solemn and deliberate. "I am sorry you had to find my cousin like this. It must've been a terrible shock, and I'm sorry to ask you to relive the memory ... but I need you to tell me when it was you last saw the baron. Any details—anything that might help us find who's responsible."

Marcus recounted his meeting with the baron after Vandrune's class, of Higant's task and his own, though hesitating to voice the baron's request for a prostitute. Sensing this, Vandrune placed a reassuring hand on his shoulder, helping him to stay the course and tell the truth of the matter. In the end, he omitted his interlude with Crimson, but otherwise recounted the story as he knew it.

And then, at the thought of her, it all fell into place.

"Of course," he said aloud.

Everybody in the room turned to look at him.

"What is it, Marcus?" Frederick asked.

"Well sir, when I first discovered the hidden room, I smelled a familiar perfume or scent. Until now, I could not recall where I had smelled it, nor why it was familiar. I can scarcely believe it, but ..."

Only then did Marcus realise he had no choice but to tell the story in its entirety, including his dalliance with Crimson. He felt sick to his stomach.

"Instead of a lady for the lord's pleasure, I think I found his killer. The prostitute I chanced upon in my search wore that very perfume, I am certain of it. I know, because s—she seduced me," he blurted out.

Marcus blushed with embarrassment as he recounted the whole story in what may have been unnecessary detail. Once again, Vandrune placed a hand on his shoulder, and he hung his head.

"I feel sick to my stomach for such treachery," said Marcus. "She must have known who I was."

Vandrune raised an eyebrow. "How could she have known?"

"The first time I caught wind of the scent was while Lord Vandeguild was still alive, before he sent me on my task. She must have been waiting for him in the back room. I went straight from here to the poor quarter, and it took some time for me to find the most ... experienced lady for my lord—more than enough time for her to have done the deed and return to her quarters. It had to be her."

Frederick turned to Vandrune. "How long has he been dead?"

"Long enough for young Marcus' story to fit, I fear."

"Do you recall where she resides?" Frederick asked of Marcus.

"I do, sire. The Whistling Sailor."

At the thought of returning there, Marcus felt a fire building in his stomach: it was revenge, and a sudden urge to seek it.

Vandrune sat down at the baron's desk.

"While I have faith in your account, we still need evidence that she was the one," he said, looking for any sign the baron might've left behind.

At that, Marcus felt the heat in his belly subside. He knew she had done it—he knew that he'd smelt the perfume for what it was, but how could he prove it?

Vandrune looked down at the blank parchment on the desk in front of him. They had not been visible before, but sitting in the baron's chair, he was able to see indentations upon the paper—some form of writing. It seemed the baron had been shrewd in his business with the supposed lady.

Vandrune removed a thin piece of something that looked like charcoal from his pocket, then started to rub it across the paper on the desk in front of him.

He lifted his head and looked up at the king.

"I have an idea."

CONFESSIONS

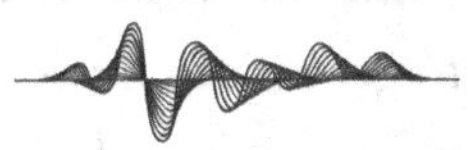

It was well after midnight by the time Marcus returned to the squires' sleeping quarters. He did not want to wake Higant or any other of the boys stationed in the room, so he crept in and hopped on his bunk fully clothed.

His mind was racing with the evening's events, not least of all the death of the baron, a man who had taken him in and treated him like a son. He'd been caring in his own way, looking out for the boys as much as he'd been gruff with them. Above all, he had loved them, and Marcus would miss him dearly.

Exhausted, it did not take long for him to start to doze off. His thoughts drifted about, remembering times he'd shared with the baron. He started to yawn and close his eyes, and the closer he came to sleep, the more his thoughts moved to his experience with a woman. As giddy as he'd felt before learning the truth, it now only turned his stomach to think on it.

The woman who'd seduced him had done so mere hours after killing his lord, in full knowledge of who he was.

She was wickedness incarnate, and he would have his revenge.

Finally, Marcus fell asleep, though it was fitful at best. His dreams were filled with visions of the baron dead on his bed, causing him to wake suddenly in a sweat, only to then drift back off to sleep with visions of Crimson.

When morning came, he woke with a start. Someone was shaking him and trying to get him to move. Marcus opened his eyes slowly and saw Higant, still in his bed clothes.

"Get up, you lazy son of a horse," Higant hissed at Marcus.

Startled, Marcus started waving his hands around. "Get off me!"

Higant jumped back to avoid the swinging arms.

"We're late! The baron's going to kill us!" said Higant, rushing over to wash his face in the basin by the door.

Marcus's face sank. He leant back against the wall that his bunk was pushed up against.

"I don't think the baron will mind," he said quietly.

"Are you out of your mind? Have you already forgotten last week, when we were late to meet his sister's future husband? If we're late *again,* he'll flog us himself!"

Higant was starting to undress and pull on the brown pants customary to the squirehood. He was just about to tuck in his shirt when he noticed that Marcus hadn't moved an inch. He hadn't really paid that much attention to him while waking him up, but seeing his face now, he stopped in his tracks.

"What's wrong, Marcus? Come to think of it ... where were you last night?"

Marcus had been dreading this moment since the night before.

"There's something I need to tell you," said Marcus, his eyes starting to glaze over. He indicated for Higant to sit next to him, and he obliged.

"I was late last night for many reasons," he said, tears now flowing down his cheeks.

Higant placed a hand on his friend's shoulder.

"It's alright, Marcus. Whatever it is, you can tell me."

Marcus was amazed at the calmness of his friend's words. He lifted his head.

"The baron is dead."

Higant's face paled. He'd expected something serious, but not this. He tried to say something, but the words would not come.

Slowly, he managed to form the word, "How?"

Marcus recounted his story in its entirety, without holding back on any detail. Higant listened intently to every word. Neither of them had realised it, but the rest of the squires had woken up to the conversation, and had gathered around for Marcus's story.

They sat there for more than an hour as Marcus spoke, and once it was done, the boys could do naught but stare.

"Gentlemen."

The boys were shocked by the sudden intrusion into their private moment. They turned to the doorway to see Portlief sitting on the floor.

"How long have you been there?" asked Marcus, wiping his face.

"Long enough, young squire," he said, standing and walking into the quarters. He walked over to where Higant sat, crouching down so he was face to face with him.

"Higant, isn't it?" he said with a soft, caring voice.

"Yes ... sir."

"I am Portlief, the king's first advisor. His Majesty has asked if you would accompany me to his offices."

Sensing the shift in tone, the rest of the squires gradually began to disperse, returning to getting ready for the day.

"I've seen you around the castle, sir," said Higant, standing up from the bed they'd been sitting on with shaky legs. "I must ask ... why me? And what of Marcus?"

Portlief turned to Marcus. Little did Higant know, his friend had met with the advisor shortly before returning the night before.

"It is time," said Portlief.

Marcus nodded, then looked over at Higant.

"Go with Portlief, my friend. I have a task to complete. I cannot speak it, but I will see you soon."

He reached out his hand and grasped his friend's wrist. Confused and reeling, Higant did the same, and struggled to let go. Marcus was as much a big brother to him as he was his only real friend— someone who protected him and looked out for him. Right now, he needed him more than ever.

"Please don't go," Higant whispered. "Not now."

"The king needs us, Higant. You and me both," said Marcus, standing. "Portlief will keep you safe from harm. Hold yourself high, and be strong. I'll be back shortly."

With that, Marcus walked to the door, splashed his face with water from the basin, and left the room without looking back.

Higant looked at the empty doorway, feeling lost and alone. Portlief looked down at the young man.

"It is as Marcus says. I will keep you safe, young Higant. I have sworn it to the king."

Higant looked up at Portlief and saw the compassion in his eyes.

Taking a deep breath, he stepped off the bed, tucked his shirt the rest of the way in, put on his boots, and proceeded to get his coat from the hooks behind his bunk.

"If I am to see the king, I must look my best," he said, trying to compose himself.

A look of pride came over Portlief's face. Much like his friend, the young lad was made of stronger stuff than most boys his age. Though he grieved for them, he knew they would be alright. They proceeded out the door and headed up the stairs to halls above.

A short while later, after a quiet walk, they passed into the antechamber outside the great hall in which the king conducted his business. The hall was empty today, which Higant thought unusual. They proceeded down the length of the hall and walked up the stairs of the dais.

Lost in his thoughts, Higant had simply trailed along behind Portlief, and it was not until they stopped that he realised they'd come all the way up to the dais. Seeing the throne sitting empty atop it, he stopped and looked at where he found himself in complete awe. He'd never been this close to the throne, and never expected to be. No one but the king and his closest advisors were allowed to walk upon the dais, yet here he was, looking out at the hall, sharing in their view. He felt both privileged and very much out of place.

After composing himself, they walked to the back of the dais and through the long sheafs of material that hung from the roof behind the throne. On the other side, Higant found they were heading towards two large golden doors. Outside of these doors stood two guards, and as they approached, they both inclined their heads towards Portlief.

Bowing his head, Portlief said, "Good morning, William, Katarg. May I introduce Higant, squire to Baron Vandeguild."

The two guards, understanding immediately, both knelt to the ground, weapons still at the ready.

"You have our greatest sympathy for your loss, young squire," they said, eyes fixed upon him.

"Thank you," said Higant, tears starting to fall once again.

They stood, looked at Portlief, and said, "The king is waiting for you, First Advisor. Vandrune is with him."

At that, Portlief smiled. He hoped the king had told the mage of the recent prophecy, though it was possible he may have kept it to himself, considering the circumstances.

The guards knocked on the door and opened it. Portlief lead the way, with Higant in tow. The office was, to Higant's eyes, the most amazing place he had ever seen. It was a cavernous room with a large desk and chair towards the back. In the middle of the room sat a lounge and three armchairs around a small table, upon which many different pieces of parchment were spread.

The room was decorated in gold and velvet trim, the house colours of the king. The lilac and gold blended together to give the room a glow like no other. Beyond the desk, a large windowed door lay off to the right, with a balcony beyond.

Higant's new teacher, the prophet Vandrune, stood vigil by the door. For a moment, the three men in the room looked warmly at the young boy, allowing him a moment to take in his surroundings.

Finally, Portlief said, "King Frederick, I present to you Squire Higant of House Vandeguild."

Higant recognised the face of the king instantly. He looked him in the eyes and bowed deeply. The king, who'd had countless people present to him, had never seen one bow so low. He smiled at the boy and walked towards him.

"Please rise, young squire. You have fairly won my heart with your stature alone."

Higant was not sure how to react, but he slowly lifted his head and straightened his back, feeling pride swell in his chest.

"Please, call me Higant, sire."

"Well, in that case, call me Frederick," the king said, still smiling at the sheer charm of the boy. Again, Higant was lost for a response, so he simply smiled back at the king.

Frederick indicated for to the boy to sit on the lounge, and he proceeded to do the same. Portlief also took his place at one of the chairs surrounding the table.

"Milord—Frederick, sire—young Marcus has proceeded with his task," said Portlief.

At that, Higant's ears pricked up.

"Excellent," said Frederick, looking over towards Vandrune by the door.

Nodding, Vandrune locked the door, then to Higant's surprise, he took a couple of steps backwards from the door and started making swirling hand gestures. His hands moved in a fluid motion until a blue glow started to appear in the air before him, growing brighter by the moment. As the glow intensified, the light drifted forward into the door and started to coat it until the whole door, and several inches beyond it, were entirely covered by it. Once the entire door was glowing, he moved towards the glass door onto the balcony and repeated the same, for this and all other openings to the world beyond.

Once finished, he said, "The room is sealed, Frederick."

"Thank you, old friend."

Vandrune returned to his seat, and Portlief took the floor.

"Before we begin," Portlief said, looking pointedly at Frederick, "have you told Master Vandrune of your recent visitation?"

Frederick smiled. "Such little faith, my friend! I informed him last night, after we'd seen to the baron."

"What do you think, Master Vandrune?" said Portlief.

Vandrune's brow furrowed.

"It seems to me our king has had a visit from Kyruarth."

"Kyruarth, sir? Who might that be?"

"He is a long-lived mage whose continued existence is known only to a few people of power," said Vandrune. "Acoreq was founded around him over three hundred years ago. I have seen him in prophecy, but have never met him. My master, The Luminary, spent nearly fifty years with him at the temple ... but today, Kyruarth is a nomad, a man with a purpose understood by none other than himself. He's been known to appear whenever trouble is brewing. As for this prophecy ... it's hard to know what to make of it. The kind of prophecy he bears is hard to predict due to its lack of a marker."

Higant, who hadn't intended to speak until spoken to, let his curiosity get the better of him.

"Master Vandrune ... I'm sorry to interrupt, but aren't all prophecies supposed to have markers?"

"That's correct," said Vandrune, still amazed at the boy's understanding. "Though it was not always this way. The prophecy we have today universally comes to us via writing, and always bears a marker. Kyruarth, however, hails from a time long past, when prophecy came to us verbally. Seeing as verbal prophecy is not written down, it lacked the markers we now know to be reflections of the stars."

His mind hard at work, Higant pulled his legs underneath himself upon the couch to make himself more comfortable.

"If verbal prophecy had no markers, then in theory, it should've been just as difficult to interpret as written prophecy was before the markers were understood. However, history shows that many age-old disasters were prevented with the help of prophecy. In contrast, prophecy doesn't appear to have played much of a part in recent history, and efforts to decipher it haven't been met with much success. Could it be that verbal prophecy actually did have markers of its own, or some other way of interpreting when the events would unfold?"

Vandrune smiled broadly at the boy's intellect and curiosity, apparently deep enough for him to forget his considerable anxiety about the company he kept.

"A very good question, young man, and not at all unrelated to the matter at hand. However, it is an explanation I believe would be better left to another."

Vandrune rose from his seat, pulling the blue stone he'd used to call the king the night before from his robes. He held it in his palm and called forth the name of the person he wished to speak to.

"Luminary."

The rock glowed a light blue, and right in front of him appeared the head of an old man who looked older than his years. The wizened man had flowing white hair, and a sparse beard to match. His face was deeply wrinkled, and though he wore glasses, his eyes were full of life, piercing in their intensity.

"It is good to speak with you again, old friend," said The Luminary, his voice raspy.

"And you, my master," said Vandrune.

"What need have you?" the old man asked.

"For one, it appears the king has had a visit from Kyruarth."

At this, the older mage frowned a little. His interest piqued, he appeared to lean in and listened more intently.

"Beyond that, a young pupil of mine has a question for you. In the days of verbal prophecy, how did we predict the moment that prophecies would come to fruition?"

Higant's face was flushed. His present company was intimidating enough; he certainly hadn't expected his question to be elevated to the head of the Council of Acoreq.

The old mage, still frowning, nodded his head. A slight grin crept across his face.

"Vandrune, my friend, place the stone in the middle of the table so I may see the others and our young charge."

Vandrune did as he was instructed, while Frederick wondered how the head mage had known the layout of his office.

"Now, Vandrune. Please retrieve the parchment I sent you. We will have need of it in a moment."

Vandrune had completely forgotten about his master's missive. The events of the evening just past had pushed it from his mind.

"I trust you've been able to reveal what was written by now?"

Vandrune nodded in agreement and pulled the parchment forth in preparation.

"Good." The Luminary's head turned to face Higant. "Young man. What is your name?"

"My name is Higant, sir," he said, feeling a little silly speaking to a floating head.

"So it is. My name is Matthew but people call me The Luminary and it is a pleasure to meet you. And it was you who asked this question?"

Higant nodded.

"You are a smart young man. We must keep an eye on you," the old man said with a smile and a hearty laugh. "Indeed, before the markers' purpose was revealed, many prophecies went unsolved as to when and where they would occur ... and for the most part, the same can be said of the time before there were markers at all. Most of the prophecies of old, verbal as they were, were never written down, for the simple reason that the majority of people were illiterate. For the few prophets who were able to have their prophecies inscribed, the timeframe between their prophecy and finding someone who could write it down was usually quite a time, so the words became lost and distorted. To make matters worse, at the time, there was no Acoreq. Prophecies were scattered upon the open world, were difficult to validate, and rarely found their way into the hands of those who may have been able to act upon them.

"Then, about three hundred years ago, an individual of keen intellect was found to possess a remarkable skill. Not only could he understand prophecy instinctually, he could predict when it would occur just by hearing it one time. Wanting to make use of this gift, he travelled the world in search of prophecy ... and by the time he was finished, the land was at peace, relations between nations were amicable, each race had enough space to live peacefully, and the world was a happier place. A reclusive man who valued his privacy and freedom, he insisted that his contributions be kept secret, and thus was his name obscured from local history.

"Despite this, it was decided at a meeting between nations that a place should be established for the interpretation and storage of prophecies, to be centred around this unique man who was able to interpret them. Due to his kind-hearted nature, the man was unable to refuse ... and so Acoreq was born. That man's name was Kyruarth.

"For the first hundred and fifty years, many prophets came to Acoreq to deliver their prophecies. Some of them even stayed, trying to better understand what the prophecy they told meant and predicted, but most eventually went on and tried to live a normal life. In all that time, the one man who was able to translate and officiate the prophecies remained. He slept little, ate even less, and worked from morning till late into the night.

"A member of the council myself at the time, one night I found him atop one of Acoreq's towers, looking up at the full moon. In the fifty years I'd been there, it was the one time I'd seen him do anything other than work. As I walked towards him, he turned and looked me in the eye. He said a young lady by the name of Sara would one day come to me, and she will change what we know. It was time for him to leave, and to find his purpose once more.

"I was distraught. The one person who could foretell when a prophecy was meant to occur was leaving ... but I had sympathy for my friend. His eyes were no longer bright and alive—they were lost, and changed. He needed to find himself again, and be a part of the world. As torn as my heart was between letting him go and persuading him to stay in Acoreq, I ultimately knew he had to leave, and I did not fight the inevitable.

"What I had not known then, as I do today, was that the nature of prophecy had changed. No longer would they be received by word of mouth, but inscribed by hand in alignment with the stars. Even now, it is not understood why this change occurred, but occur it did. We happened upon the change sometime later, when disparate prophecies from distant lands made their way to Acoreq on parchment, all of them containing the star-like symbols. Stranger still, the prophets themselves had been the ones to inscribe the prophecy, one of whom was blind and many others illiterate. At first, we were uncertain what to make of it. Not only had the method of prophecy changed across the board, they now included markers, and neither physical nor intellectual capacity had any impact on the prophets' ability to deliver the prophecy.

"Then, not long after my friend left Acoreq for whatever life lay beyond it, I was alone in my study examining a recent prophecy with the newly discovered markers when suddenly, I had a prophecy of my own. It happened so unexpectedly that when I came to, I found myself lying on the floor hours later, cold and in pain from the position I'd been in. It wasn't until I stood back up that I saw the prophecy upon the desk. It told of the arrival of the woman named Sara, speaking of a key phrase that I would speak, thus unlocking her true identity and thereby revealing the truth of the markers.

"It would be many years before that prophecy came to fruition. We waited a century and a half to see her come, and to learn the truth of the markers. In fact, it was only a year ago that she finally arrived. As Kyruarth and my own prophecy had foretold, it was through her that we came to understand the markers, and reclaimed the ability to determine when they are set to occur."

Higant turned to Vandrune. "The same story you told us in your lesson."

Vandrune looked down at the young squire and smiled. "Yes, it is."

Having been listening intently, lost in his thoughts, Higant's expression had appeared clouded and uncertain. Suddenly, just as they had in the old meat cellar, his eyes flashed that same shade of blue, sharpening with unmistakable clarity.

He started to speak in a soft and deliberate tone.

"Luminary, Vandrune ... you mentioned there are two kinds of prophecy: verbal, and written. What if there's a third?"

Both mages turned to Higant, perplexed.

"What gives you that impression?" said Vandrune.

Higant slowly stood up from his chair and started to walk along the length of the rug beneath the chairs. When he got to the end of the rug, he turned and looked at the men watching him, focusing upon The Luminary with piercing eyes.

"You said that your prophecy about Sara contained a key phrase. Is that correct?"

The Luminary frowned. "Yes, that is what I said, Higant."

"You also said that the purpose of the key phrase was to have Sara show her true self, which would ultimately lead to making sense of the markers, yes?"

The whole room had gone quiet, everyone's eyes fixed on Higant, trying to understand what he was getting to.

The Luminary again replied, "Yes."

Higant did not move a muscle—he just stared intently at The Luminary.

"Taking Vandrune's account into consideration, I believe your prophecy was not only a key, but a lock—and the same can be said for Sara's. I think your prophecies were twinned."

This caught everyone by surprise.

"Twinned?" The Luminary echoed, truly curious as to the mind of this young man.

Vandrune as well had lifted his hand to stroke his beard and ponder the boy's words.

"What about my retelling of the story leads you to believe that?" he asked.

Higant smiled.

"You see, the stars align in the sky the same way for what seems like many years. The world turns, and every night, they are locked in their dance with the sky above. To us, it seems that the stars are moving ... but in truth, it is we who move, not the stars."

He paused, as if for dramatic effect.

"If we look at the sequence of events, it would seem that The

Luminary's key phrase was the words, 'Why do you seek the truth?' ... and shortly before that, Sara—or, in that moment, Catherine de Halt—had rather poignantly spoken the words, 'Do prophecies ever overlap?'"

The room lapsed into another contemplative silence.

It was Frederick who broke it.

"I still don't think we follow you, Higant. Please, continue, and we may yet find the truth you seek."

Higant began to pace back and forth along the edge of the rug, explaining as if he were some learned teacher explaining how the sun stays in the sky.

"King Frederick, the key phrase that The Luminary used as part of his prophecy was not only to unlock Sara's name, even though it did help her to reveal her true self. Its true purpose was to unlock the prophecy that she had made as Catherine de Halt. Her prophecy simply suggested that she would travel to Acoreq and reveal the secret of the markers—nowhere within it was it stated what that secret was. It wasn't until she made her journey and The Luminary spoke his phrase that it became clear to her. Likewise, The Luminary's prophecy stated that a woman named Sara would appear and reveal the truth of the markers ... and it wasn't until Catherine de Halt asked *her* question that he was able to ask his, thus prompting her to become Sara and discover the truth for herself.

"So you see, both of their prophecies relate to the same event, and set them on the proper path to meeting one another. It was only once they came together that either of them had meaning, or were able to come about. Thus are the prophecies twinned."

Having given voice to all that had been in his mind, Higant sat down in the same chair as before, suddenly feeling very tired.

It had been a very long day, and it was starting to weigh upon him.

Vandrune, who had not moved save to stroke his beard, turned to The Luminary.

"He's right."

The Luminary looked up at Vandrune. "He is. To think that all this time, a third form of prophecy has been upon us ... and that this young man would be the one to reveal it. Vandrune. The parchment, if you please."

Nodding, the prophet spread the missive on the table before them for all to see.

"I sent this to Vandrune two days ago with an Acoreq seal," said The Luminary. "In it, I asked him not to reveal its contents until I advised it was time. It seems that time is upon us."

Vandrune began to read aloud.

TWINNED AT BIRTH, KI AND AWE,
THE CASCADE WILL RISE AND TAKE ONE OR ALL.
PRAYER UPON RUNE WILL MAP THE WAY,
THE LOCK AND KEY WILL HAVE THEIR DAY.
SET THE COURSE OF THE ONE TO SEEK THE TWO,
REVEAL A PLACE WHERE THE END IS DOOM.
IN THE DEPTHS OF A MAN'S MIND,
A MYSTERY LOCKED IN TIME.

As Vandrune finished reading the parchment, he looked back to the head mage, whose eyes were fixed upon Frederick.

"King Frederick ... this prophecy speaks of many things, some of which I believe I understand, and many more I do not. However, there is one piece that is clearer to me now more than ever."

The head turned to look at Higant, who had fallen asleep on the chair, his head fallen to the side.

"'The one' is here. As to who the two might be, I am sure we will find out in time. In the meantime, look out for this young squire.

He is wise, and talks like a scholar, yet there is likely more to him than meets the eye. If asked to recount his theory, it would not surprise me if he found himself lost for words."

He turned his attention to Vandrune. "You have my permission to address the king with all that you know, my young friend. It is time he knew."

Vandrune bowed. "I will do as you ask, master."

The Luminary's visage turned towards the sleeping squire.

"You are a rare gem, Higant. I hope we will meet again someday."

After that, the blue head of The Luminary disappeared, and Vandrune's blue stone stopped glowing. The mage picked it up and placed it back in his pocket, folding the parchment and sitting back in the chair opposite Higant.

He looked to the king.

"There is much I have to say, Frederick. You must listen carefully, and without interruption, for I can only say what I have to say once."

"I understand."

Suddenly, there was a knock at the door.

CHAPTER SEVEN

MARCUS

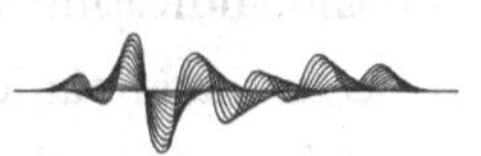

Another knock came from the door, louder and more urgent this time. Frederick rose to his feet, on alert. He advanced towards the door and realised that William, his personal guard, was knocking and yelling. It seemed the seal that had been placed on the doors also limited sound.

"Vandrune, the seal!"

After a moments hesitation, Vandrune proceeded to the door, and with a simple hand gesture, he removed the seal.

The door burst open and William, who'd been trying to get inside, fell through the door. Picking himself up from the floor, William rushed the rest of the way in. Katarg, as well as a gentleman no more than three feet tall, trailed in behind him.

"Sire. We have news of Marcus," said William, his breath ragged and puffed. "I only hope it is not as bad as it sounds."

At the sound of Marcus's name, Higant woke with a jolt.

Katarg stepped forward with the short gentleman in tow.

"Milord, this is Fanton. He is an informant we've used in the past, and is as reliable as they come. He has told us some very worrying information."

Katarg indicated for Fanton to come forward, and he did so without fanfare, stopping in front of the king without so much as a bow or salute.

"Speak man," said Frederick, in no mood for formalities.

"My friends here," he said, indicating to the two guards, "asked me to tail the young squire as he accompanied the soldiers in search of a lady of the night. I followed him from the east gate down into the city and towards the poor quarter. I was his shadow. He didn't even know I was there. He moved with purpose and determination ... but I was surprised to see he didn't have any soldiers with him.

"He walked into a tavern near the harbour called The Whistling Sailor, which is really a front for a seedy brothel by the name of The Lovely One. I waited by the entrance for about an hour, but the boy did not appear again. William and Katarg had said he was only supposed to be in there for a short time, so I went around the back of the building to look for a less obvious way in. As I came 'round the corner and headed down the lane that runs behind the brothel, I saw the young man bound and gagged, being dragged onto a cart by a person in grey robes and a hood. Slung over his shoulder was a very curious weapon. A sciver, sire."

Frederick plainly did not understand the significance of the word, but at its mention, Vandrune had turned a pale shade of green.

"Vandrune? What is it?" the king asked uncertainly.

"It relates to the matter The Luminary had asked me to talk to you about ... though it seems we have more pressing matters at hand. There is another prophecy at work here, and the sighting of a sciver in that context is quite unnerving."

Frederick turned to the small man who had stopped to watch the king.

"Continue, please," he said with urgency.

"Well, once they'd loaded the boy onto the cart, the person in the grey robes drove out of the city and off to the southwest. I returned to the brothel to see if the lady whom the boy was meant to meet was there, and was able to climb in through her window. Inside, I found a pool of blood on the floor, and this."

Fanton pulled a piece of parchment from his robes and handed it to Frederick. To his alarm, it was a letter granting admittance to the palace for an audience with the king, signed by his cousin Baron Vandeguild and affixed with the royal seal. Now he understood what the woman's business with his cousin had been ... but why kill him? And why go to all that trouble to obtain the letter, only to leave it behind? What purpose would that serve but to arouse suspicion?

Either way, it was confirmation that this woman named Crimson had murdered his kin.

He turned to the diminutive man.

"Thank you for your service, Fanton. My men here will attend to you for your trouble and pay you for your time."

"If it's all the same sire, rather than gold, I would dearly love a place to call my own," said Fanton. "There is a small farm on the outskirts of the city, in an isolated place overlooking the Grey Ocean and the forest to the west. I visited it as a child, and I would love to be able to retire there someday, should it ever become vacant."

"I will certainly consider your request, Fanton. Thank you once again."

At this, Fanton turned and strode back to the door and out of the room, saying thanks to William and Katarg.

When he left the room, Commander Kai appeared, which startled both William and Katarg. He spoke to them both and handed them something. William took the item and turned, walking towards the king.

"Sire, Commander Kai advises this is the blade they found in the baron."

"Bring it here," said the king.

William walked back to the king and held out the blade, but before Frederick could reach out for it, Vandrune stayed his hand.

"You mustn't touch it," the mage said in a forceful voice.

He noted that while William was wearing gloves, the king's hands were unprotected. Vandrune pulled a cloth from his robes, indicating for William to place the blade inside of it. Vandrune observed the intricate patterns upon the handle of this otherwise simple looking blade, he then wrapped it up in a bundle and secreted it away.

"Vandrune, what is it?" Frederick asked, a look of concern upon his face. "Is it one of those 'scivers'? What is its significance?"

"For better or worse, this blade is not a sciver. Far from what might be considered a conventional weapon, a sciver is a blade infused with the power of the mages of old. They can kill with nothing more than a word from its holder. If there is one in Neleuwan, it is a bad omen ... and yet, the blade that Commander Kai brought us here tonight may be of even greater concern. I have my suspicions, but I would verify them before I speak them. Until then, I will keep this blade, and seek out the truth of its origin."

"A weapon that can kill with but a word," said Frederick. "I've never heard of such a foul thing."

"Indeed. But there is more," said Vandrune. He turned to the others. "A moment, please."

Vandrune strode over to a corner of the room, indicating for Frederick to follow. There they stood, speaking in hushed tones for a number of minutes, the contents of their conversation unclear to the rest of the room. Higant was beside himself with worry, but he dared not interrupt.

Eventually, they turned and strode back to the group, and Frederick came to a stop before William and Katarg.

"Gentlemen, have an advance scouting party set out at once. We'll meet them on the road. We're going after Marcus ourselves."

Both men strode from the room without hesitation.

Vandrune addressed the rest of the room.

"I'm afraid our young squire Marcus is indeed in great peril. We must seek him out, no matter the cost." He focused on Higant. "Worry not, my boy. We'll see him home."

Higant stood up tall, tears rolling down his cheeks.

In a louder voice than expected, he said, "Master Vandrune, Your Highness, I wish to join you."

Frederick crouched down to Higant's height and looked him in the eyes, where tears continued to fall.

"Higant, you are a young and wise squire who has been dealt a blow these last days. On top of all that has happened, a dear friend of yours has now been taken. To join us, you would have to be a squire, and due to my cousin's death, both you and Marcus have lost that title."

Before he could protest, the king continued.

"You have done the realm a great service on this day. And so, to allow you to regain your position and aid in the search, I will have both you and Marcus transfer into my service. Henceforth, the two of you are squires to the king."

Higant, transfixed by the depth of the king's eyes, let the gravity of what the king had said wash over him. It was a noble gesture, and one that quickly dried his eyes.

He'd said nothing before dozing off, and wasn't quite sure what he'd done to serve the realm ... but nonetheless, his chest swelled with pride.

"I am honoured, sire," he said. "Forgive me, milord, but when do we leave?"

Frederick smiled.

"At once."

CHAPTER EIGHT

PATH OF DARK

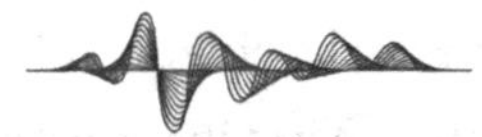

As soon as the horses were prepared, twelve people rode out after Marcus, including Vandrune, Higant, the King, his two favoured guards, and several of his ethereal Home Guard.

Half an hour into their journey, they crossed paths with the advance scouting party the king had ordered, returning after having picked up Marcus's trail from the poor quarter. The scouts reported having caught up to his captors three miles out of the city, catching sight of a wagon manned by a grey-hooded rider and a solitary figure at its side, sitting atop a steed of great magnificence.

However, they had been unable to retrieve the boy.

"The pace they were making was extremely fast, sire—unnaturally so," said the lead rider. "Every time our party got close to the wagon, it would accelerate away at a speed far beyond that of our horses."

"Understood," said the king. "It is well that we brought the Home Guard. They will help us to see that which is beyond our sight."

The scouts passed them by to return to the capital, and after another gauntlet of hard riding, the party slowed the horses for a brief rest. They had just passed the bridge over Kunjarry Stream on the outskirts of the city's farming fields, and were heading along the east road for Pillton. They had enough supplies for three days, and would resupply in Pillton if they didn't catch up to their quarry beforehand.

Their plan was simple: a smaller part of the party would get ahead of the cart and block the road from the front, then the remaining party would split into three more groups, two of them flanking whilst the king and his guard brought up the rear. Once the cart was surrounded, they would have Marcus back, and have their answers as to who was attempting to steal a citizen of Neleuwan.

Looking at the Home Guard in formation around them, Higant recalled the strangeness of his encounter with them in the baron's corridor. Sidled up next to the king, he couldn't help but ask.

"I don't mean to be rude, sire … but what *are* the Home Guard?"

King Frederick smiled.

"I cannot blame you for your curiosity. The Home Guard, otherwise known as the Ku-Da-Ru, are elite guards loyal only to the Neleuwan king. They possess abilities beyond that of a simple human, and power beyond that which even I don't fully understand. To hear my father tell it, the Ku-Da-Ru were created by a mage of great knowledge and power."

Higant was taken aback. "*Created,* milord? Are they not men and women?"

"They are … and yet they are not," the king said grimly. "All I was told is that they were given a choice, and this is what they chose. We refer to them as the Home Guard in an effort to demystify them, though I understand they may be unnerving. Rest assured, however, they are at my command. None save for the mage who created them may direct them unless given my explicit permission … and command aside, I like to believe they made their decision out of loyalty to the kingdom."

So said the king, and yet he himself didn't appear wholly convinced.

Eventually, after some more hard riding, the advance party fell back to inform the others that the cart had been sighted.

The men who were due to block the road veered off the main road and headed parallel at a faster pace. It was well known that the road ahead curved as it headed towards Pillton, so they decided to cut a shorter path along the scout tracks to get ahead of the cart. The trails were no stranger to palace traffic, and were quick and easy to traverse, making them perfect for this type of ambush.

The sun was setting in the west, and it cast long shadows of the men as they rode on into dusk, the sky lit up with dark streaks of oranges and purples. The mood of the king's group was solemn, though their pace was brisk and controlled. For most of the journey, Higant had been lost in thoughts of his friend. He only hoped that Marcus was unharmed.

Having traversed the long bend, the carriage was now heading in a straighter line towards Pillton. The group that had ridden ahead were almost certainly in place, ready to block the road. With that, the king and his entourage bore down upon the carriage and its passengers ... and just as the wagon crested the hill, stopping just short of the ambush, it came to a sudden stop.

A dark figure climbed out of the driver's seat and proceeded around behind the wagon. A short time passed, then the figure returned with a smaller figure at its side. It was hard to make out exactly who it was in the fading light, but the king, Vandrune, and the guards assumed it had to be Marcus. There was no urgency in their movements, and if they'd spotted their pursuers, they certainly weren't letting on.

The two figures headed further down the road, closer towards the advance group that was in hiding just ahead, waiting to ambush them. Frederick had brought his party to a halt, keeping as out of sight as was possible in this light.

Why would they do this? It didn't make sense. Frederick looked to Vandrune, who also was at a loss. Higant just sat atop his horse, watching, wondering, hoping his friend would be alright.

Frederick indicated for the party to move further up the road, as no further movement had been detected from the figures since they'd disappeared over the crest of the hill. Even as they drew nearer to the wagon, they saw no further activity. The group was no more than a couple hundred feet from the wagon when Frederick stopped, dismounted his horse, and indicated for the Home Guard to come forward. The lead guard materialised out of thin air right in front of Higant, who had been riding next to the king and dismounted at the same time.

"Scout ahead, Jamir. Find out the purpose of this sudden stop."

The man nodded, then quite literally disappeared into the surrounding forest, like vapour in the night.

The rest of the party moved off the road and into the forest's edge so as not to be seen. The light of day was long gone, but the moon had risen high and was full in the eastern sky. As they entered the trees, leading their horses behind them, Vandrune felt something was amiss. Searching for the cause of the odd feeling, he worked slowly through his senses. First, his smell ... nothing unusual. The taste of the air, nothing again. He did not feel any strangeness upon his skin, either. He closed his eyes and listened, and it was then he realised the cause of his concern. The forest they had entered was quiet. Not a squeak was to be heard—no crickets, no birds, no nocturnal creatures of any type. It was deathly silent.

"What does it mean?" Vandrune whispered to himself, a look of concern still etched on his face.

Jamir returned a short time later.

"The wagon is empty. The boy is gone."

The king mounted his horse, nudging it forward and out of the forest's edge. The rest of the party did the same, following him onto the road.

They headed towards the wagon at speed. Within minutes, they reached the wagon and dismounted to investigate.

"Nothing out of the ordinary," Frederick said, exasperated.

Inside the wagon was a soft mattress and a handful of blankets, but nothing of note.

"Why stop here and leave the wagon behind?" said Frederick. "Is it not strange to leave a good, solid horse and wagon in the middle of the road in the dark and then disappear?"

As they were about to mount back up and ride on to see if the advance group had any more information about this strange turn of events, they felt a sudden thud under their feet, which was followed closely by a thunderous boom. The sound was so loud that it forced them to place their hands over their ears, rising in intensity to the point of almost being deafening.

They looked around to find its source and saw a black light rimmed with a white glow flaring out from the depths of the thick forest to the left of the road. Before their eyes, the light flared brighter than day, and they were impacted by a force that sent all of them to the ground. Some of the party were even thrown clear of the road and into the surrounding shrubs.

Vandrune felt like he had been struck by lightning. He tried to get up, but was shaky at best. The Home Guard materialised out of the dark and helped King Frederick to stand, and in moments, they had done the same for the rest of the party. William and Katarg, who'd been standing in front of Frederick when the blast came, had been among those thrown into the bushes, both of them staggering out of the bushes with their armour askew. As soon as their bodies would allow them, they returned to their post with Frederick and straightened their gear.

"Seek the source!" Frederick called to the Home Guard. Again, they moved like smoke on the breeze—here one minute and gone the next.

The king turned to assist anyone he could back onto the few horses that had not been harmed by the blast, and they took off like men possessed, all fearing for what the noise and the black light could mean for Marcus.

Frederick's mind raced as his horse took a left and dove into the brush off the road and back into the tree line. He cared for all of his citizens, but his concern for the well-being of this young boy Marcus surprised even him. He was not sure why Marcus had struck such a chord with him, but he felt a powerful compulsion to save the boy. Perhaps it was Higant and his love for his friend that pulled at his heartstrings.

As the horses came out of the forest's edge and into the forest proper, instead of a thicket of aged trees looming overhead, the scene before them opened up to the sky. At their feet, a low-hanging mist rose up to their knees. Frederick slowed the horses and dismounted, taking in the devastation. In a wide circle around them, the trees that had once stood tall were charred and burned, and the silence around was deafening. Vandrune again felt that same uneasy feeling as before.

"Ku-Da-Ru!" Frederick called.

A solitary figure emerged from the mist ahead.

"This way, sire," the Ku-Da-Ru officer said in a deep voice. "The Commander requests your presence."

Frederick followed after the officer, and the world closed in around them as they proceeded forward. An eerie feeling lay about the land, heightening Frederick's senses as he moved through.

Frederick had known this land very well as a child. He'd hunted and fought pretend battles here whenever he'd had the chance to sneak out of the palace and get away from his minders. Now, it was a foreign world, one of darkness and pain—a world that, unfortunately for Frederick, seemed to be becoming all too common.

"He is just ahead, sire," said the officer, and in the next instant, he vanished.

It still amazed Frederick the way they were able to conceal themselves right in front of his eyes.

Ahead, Frederick found the Commander, just as the officer had said. The man stood on top of a small pile of disturbed earth, arms folded.

"Commander Kai, report."

"Sire. I've not seen one firsthand, but our creator imparted us with the knowledge of many potential threats to aid us in our defence of the realm. This," he said, gesturing to the ground beneath his feet, "is a truant mound."

"Truant mound?" said Frederick, confused. "What is a truant mound? Or a truant, for that matter?"

"Of course, sire. A truant is, in essence, a mage ... but unlike mages, who use the energy within themselves, truants have no inner source of power. They can only pull from the earth around them. When they do so, it scars the earth, as you can see around you. For centuries, this practice threatened the very life of the planet, which eventually culminated in the Lolariane War some three hundred years ago. Mounds such as these were trademarks of the time, and are evidence of an especially foul use of the practice: the expenditure of an innocent party's life energy in order to harness the power within their soul. The mound remains where the soul meets its end, and lies at the centre of the destruction. It is a forbidden practice in the teachings of mages, and to my knowledge, this is the first mound that has been identified since the war."

"Well, this one has come to life in a way I don't wish to experience again," said Frederick, still rubbing his arms after the explosion. "Why have none been seen for such a long time? And why resurface tonight?"

"As for the former, milord, the end result of the Lolariane War was—or was thought to be—the extinction of the truants, though tonight's events seem to suggest otherwise. For the latter, I'm afraid I cannot say," said the commander. "What I can say is that the life used in this ritual was not that of the boy we seek."

At this comment, Frederick lifted his eyes from the mound.

"How can you tell?"

"When a person's soul is expended, it leaves a scent upon the wind. If it had been a male, it would've been akin to cut grass. A female, however, produces—"

"A floral scent," Frederick stated, catching it from the air.

Commander Kai nodded. "You have a good nose, sire."

"What now, Commander? Where did they go, and how do we find out where they went? I don't see any tracks leading away from this area."

"In that, I believe Prophet Vandrune might be of assistance," said Commander Kai, looking past the king and motioning towards where the rest of the party was waiting.

"Come forward, Vandrune! I need your assistance!" Frederick shouted.

Hearing the voice of the king, the whole party started moving towards it.

Navigating the mass of fallen trees along the way, the mist grew thicker about them, and their visibility declined. Vandrune was the first to emerge from the mist, exiting at what appeared to be the other side of the explosion site, where the ring of collapsed trees ended. At no time did he see the king. Shortly after, the rest of the party came through the mist and emerged next to Vandrune.

"What is this?" said Higant, looking up at the sight of a frowning Vandrune and no king. "I could've sworn His Majesty's voice had come from this direction."

Once again, the king called out to them to move forward to his position, but this time, the voice echoed from back the way they'd came. Again, they attempted to advance towards the king's position, but were unsuccessful.

However, it was not a wasted effort. Vandrune noticed they did not end up in the same position from which they'd started, and could only imagine that another crossing would more than likely land them somewhere else, and ultimately in the same predicament.

"Gentlemen," Vandrune proclaimed, "if you don't mind, I think I've had about enough of this."

He strode several feet ahead of the party, and a small, iridescent blue glow started emanating in front of him. From where the men behind him stood, it looked like a halo of blue light had outlined the prophet.

A gentle murmuring sound caught the ears of the men. Its intensity waxed and waned as though it were a heart beating, becoming rhythmic as they listened further. The horses, which had been on edge since entering this part of the forest, started to ease, their folded ears lifting to a more sedate position. The men, too, seemed comforted by the light and the low beating hum of the chant, almost transfixed by it. They looked on in wonder as the prophet stood before the soothing blue light ... and then without warning, the light flashed brightly, and was gone.

Vandrune turned to motion the party forward.

"Shall we?"

The mesmerised men were quite startled by Vandrune's gruff voice.

"Of course, Master Vandrune," they all said in unison.

They moved forward towards the king, who was calling on them again. This time, there was no mystery—they found the king standing exactly where they'd expected to after hearing his voice, standing next to Commander Kai atop a small mound in the middle of the clearing.

"There was a blue glow, then a flash," said the king. "What happened?"

"It seems there is magic about, Frederick. Just a little trick to pierce the veil," Vandrune said with a smile. "The mist was preventing us from reaching you ... though how and why, I am yet to understand."

"Curious," said Frederick. "How were Commander Kai and I able to make our way here?"

"Perhaps they intended to separate us? Either way, all appears to be in order. A mystery for another time, sire."

Looking about the clearing, Vandrune's eyes fixed upon the mound. His eyes went wide, and he quickly inclined his head, searching the air for a scent.

"A woman," the prophet said solemnly. "The poor thing. Such a senseless waste of life."

"Indeed, Master Vandrune," resounded Commander Kai's voice.

Vandrune walked around the mound, testing not only the air, but the dirt as he went. His hands hovered above the ground, palms down, chanting words under his breath once again. Every so often, he would pause and close his eyes for up to a few minutes, then open them again and continue his testing. Frederick supposed that he too was trying to make sense of how something that had not been seen in over three centuries had appeared in the middle of a sundered forest.

Up until now, Higant, Marcus's friend and now squire of the king, had simply watched in wonder and awe, underlined by a sense of urgency and fear. Finally, there was the faintest of blue flashes, and he mustered up the courage to say something.

It was as much the way he said it as it was the words he spoke that made Vandrune immediately stop what he was doing and look intently at the boy.

"What level is the truant mound?"

CHAPTER NINE

Secret Revealed

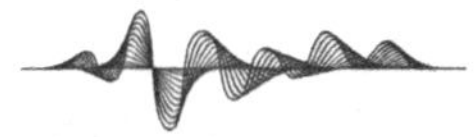

Marcus was sore, tired, and fed up with his situation. His task was supposed to have been a simple one—go with the soldiers and arrest the lady who killed the baron. What he hadn't anticipated was the snivelling little twerp had grabbed him and dragged him to the Whistling Sailor, where *she* had been waiting for him. In hindsight, it was madness to have expected any less.

There she'd stood in black leathers, revealing all of her shapely figure. At her waist had been a wicked blade, of a make that Marcus had never seen before. A coat had hung from her shoulders, its hood obscuring her slicked-back hair and eyes, though not enough to prevent Marcus from feeling them boring into him.

"Hello, my pet. Back for more, are we?"

The plan had been foiled from the outset. His only hope left had been a bluff.

"You are to come with me to the castle, my lady," he'd said, trying not to let his disdain show through. "I've been sent with a request from the king himself. You are under suspicion for the murder of Lord Baron Vandeguild, and must be brought in for questioning"

"Really," she'd said, a sly smile emerging from beneath her hood. "And how do you propose to take me there?"

"There is a carriage and an armed escort waiting for you just up the road. You are to be taken to him immediately." Fanton shook his head in amusement.

With the speed of a blink, she'd drawn the blade at her hip and held it at Marcus's throat, making that the second time he'd had a weapon at his neck in the last day.

That time, however, it was not held by a fellow squire. He'd been sure he was about to die—and yet all he'd been able to think about was the pain Higant would feel for his loss.

Instead of having his throat cut as he'd expected, however, he'd been struck hard in the head, and had quickly hit the floor. Several minutes had passed before he'd regained a sense of his surroundings. The leather-clad woman, who'd given him so much pleasure only a few hours earlier and then caused him so much pain, had come to stand over his crumpled form, hood drawn back, showing her face in all the light.

What he'd seen there had made his knees go weak.

Her face had been pale, save for the twin markings above her eyes, crossing her forehead like butterfly wings split by a wicked blade that dove to the tip of her nose. Below her eyes and across her cheeks had been symmetrical blood-red marks, each of which had borne the appearance of having been scratched into the skin. Her eyes, too, had been as red as blood.

"Who are *you* to arrest *me,* you waste of a seed?" she'd spat.

Still dazed and unsure of what to do, Marcus had remained still on the floor. The leather-clad woman had then walked to the other side of the room, turning to indicate to the little man who'd grabbed him to gather him from the floor.

It was then Marcus had noticed how the colour of her eyes had changed to a dark shade of blue. Even in his half-aware state, it had occurred to him that the changes seemed to be linked to her mood. Right before striking him, they'd flared a deep shade of red, and had then seem to ease a little after taking her rage out on him. Still, he couldn't be sure. So much was happening, he was having trouble taking it all in. The only reason he'd even known he'd been hit was because of the searing pain in his head, and that he'd ended up on the floor.

"On the contrary, Marcus, it is you who will be coming with me."

Crimson's voice had carried a sinister tone that had sent a chill down his spine.

"Fanton? Tie him up, gag him, and throw him in the wagon."

"Of course, milady."

Since then, it had been a long ride from the city out into the surrounding farms. All the bumping about in the back of the wagon had done nothing for Marcus's position, and the rock that had made its way onto the wagon floor and underneath him was not doing him any favours, either. Every bump exaggerated the pain he already felt.

How is it I have ended up here? he thought. *I've let down Higant, the baron, and now the king himself. Twice now, I've been sent to do a job, and twice I have failed in my duties. What have I done to deserve—*

His thoughts were interrupted by the sudden stop of the wagon.

He heard the vicious voice of the small man, starkly contrasted by Crimson's seductive whisper. His stomach churned every time he remembered the passion they'd shared.

The back flap of the wagon came loose with a loud bang, and the small man's head appeared in the opening. Fanton grabbed his bound arms and pulled him off the wagon's tailgate, sending pain radiating through Marcus's head once again as it hit the ground.

"They are not far behind, my lady," Fanton said whilst dragging Marcus after him.

Marcus was sore from head to toe. He'd lost most of the feeling in his hands and legs, and his head was killing him. Blood had started to trickle down into his eye, blurring his vision.

They dragged him ahead of the wagon, down the crest of the hill, and then turned left off the path.

"Where is she?" Crimson hissed at Fanton.

"I am here, my lady of the night," came a sultry voice from roadside.

Instantly, Crimson's voice shifted from angry to affectionate.

"We are pursued, my love. We must hurry into the woods to avoid detection."

"Your will is my command," the young lady purred.

In both of their voices, Marcus heard love in its truest form. It was the sort of passion that could stem the tide of time, slowing it down until every creature of the earth stood still. Unfortunately for Marcus, it did little to ease his pain. Fanton was certainly not gentle with his handling of him. He had at least untied the bonds on Marcus's feet, which had allowed him to walk, but the blade sticking an inch into his back made it feel like a cold comfort.

After a time of running into the depths of the forest, Crimson slowed to a halt.

"This will be far enough. Fanton, hold on to him so he won't get away."

"Yes, my lady."

While Fanton tightened his grip on Marcus's restraints, Crimson turned to her female companion, her eyes turning a light shade of magenta.

"My love," she spoke softly," I love you with all my heart and soul."

She pulled the girl close, and as their bodies touched, the young woman moaned at her lady's touch. Their lips met, and Crimson's eyes danced in all the colours of the rainbow.

Fanton, who'd been standing behind Marcus, dragged him alongside as he moved behind the enraptured lady, reaching out one hand to touch the small of her back and another clamping tight to Marcus' shoulder. As he made contact, he felt a tingle trickling in at first, then it came like a torrent, flowing in and out of his body.

The girl was moaning in near ecstasy with whatever was occurring. Suddenly, the eyes of the two women met and the girl's body jerked, her head snapping back at a macabre angle. The lady started to float slightly off the ground, and a shockwave was sent slamming into the earth, coalescing and moving outward away from them.

Strangely, at that moment, Marcus felt peace. No pain, no hurt, no joy, no sorrow, no love, no night, no day … just peace.

The ground hit hard as he collapsed, and the wind was knocked from him. Gasping for air, he tried desperately to remain conscious. Though focusing intently on pulling air into his lungs, his eyes were drawn to his right, and were then blinded by a bright light that felt like it was piercing deep into his eyes, like it was drilling into the back of his skull. The light was so bright, he lost all sense of his surroundings, or of anything other than the intensity of the searing light shining upon the inside of his brain. His whole body felt numb and yet in extreme pain, all at the same time.

After who knows how long, the light began to dim, and his sight, pierced by the light as it had been, slowly returned to darkness.

It took him a while to get the courage to open them again.

At the exact moment he'd thought the world around him had finally settled, another bright light, somehow even closer and more intense, tore through him. It felt like his insides were being ripped out, and the shockwave that followed slammed into him with unbelievable force.

The last thing he remembered was a feeling of weightlessness, as if he were flying through the sky ... and then the sudden stop, right before blackness took him.

CHAPTER TEN

TRUANT MOUND

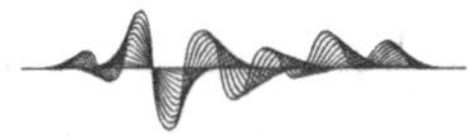

"What a peculiar question," said Vandrune.

"It is important to determine the height of the truant mound, is it not?" Higant asked, looking quizzically at the dirt mound as though he'd asked the obvious question.

"Firstly, Squire Higant, the level of the truant mound is two-and-a-half hands high," said Vandrune, eyeing him closely. "Secondly, could you tell me the significance of that?"

Vandrune was always asking questions of his students in class, but there was much more to this question than a simple pop quiz. Evidently, Higant was privy to things he should've had no way of knowing ... but strangely, it only seemed to surface on occasion.

And so, the master was testing the depths of his pupil's locked knowledge.

One of the reasons was that he wanted to know what Higant knew, for it may hold some clue as to why Marcus was taken ... but more importantly, it could help him to understand what exactly this reserve of hidden knowledge was, and what it was doing locked away in this young man's mind.

In his musings, Vandrune had even wondered if it was conceivable that the young man had been responsible for his friend's disappearance in one way or another.

In matters as complicated as this, nothing could be ruled out.

The only way to know the boundaries was to probe when opportunity knocked.

Higant, who had pondered the question for a good while, finally spoke.

"When a truant mound is discovered—which is unusual in the current time, as it has been over three hundred years since one was last reported—the height of the mound becomes significant for multiple reasons. This is especially true when the surrounding area is devastated so thoroughly."

He paused and looked around at all three, who had stopped everything to look at him—some in surprise, and others in awe of how a boy so young could talk with such authority on any subject, let alone this one.

He continued on.

"There are three primary issues that arise when a truant uses such power, which are referred to as the Truant Triad. The first is that most people who arrive after a truant event such as this overlook the mound, putting the explosion down to some other cause. If they weren't looking for it, the mound would be of no significance to them anyway.

"The second is a little more complicated. For some time after the event, the mound is covered in mist, making it hard to see ... but obscuring visibility isn't the mist's only effect. When a truant uses their power, they traumatise the earth. When the earth is traumatised on this scale, the earth defends itself."

Again, he stopped for a moment, giving his audience a moment to catch up.

Vandrune took advantage of the pause.

"Higant, what do you mean, 'the earth defends itself?' And what does that have to do with the mound or the mist?"

Higant looked at Vandrune with surprise. "You experienced it yourself, Vandrune—we all did! When we tried to make it to the king, who'd arrived there before the protection could form, the mist moved us through and away from the area. Even though we could hear the king from the epicentre, we could not reach him. In the past, this protection has been perceived as a spell cast by the truant ... but the truth is that the earth is simply defending itself after the assault."

Higant had the attention of everyone around him, each of them hanging onto his every word.

"It's worth noting that a truant's power is derived in part from moving natural earthly energies into themselves, where they are able to magnify it. By pulling the energy from the earth, they are essentially raping it of its ability to sustain itself. This leaves a scar on the earth at the point of ignition—in other words, the truant mound ... though the wound is often much greater than the mound alone. And to answer your question, Vandrune, the level of the mound indicates how much power was used in the spell that was cast. The greater the power, the higher the mound."

It was all Vandrune could do to nod slowly, dumbfounded.

Higant seemed about to leave his explanation there, but Frederick wasn't satisfied.

"You said the mist was the second of three. What is the third issue of the Triad?"

Higant thought about how to explain the third thing, and did so with cold precision.

"The third issue is the reason we had the explosion. A low truant mound, less than a hand's height, indicates that the power drawn for the spell was minimal. At most, it causes a thud—a concussion to the air, like the one that threw us all back on the road."

Higant paused again for effect. Even the Ku-Da-Ru, who were able to appear and disappear at will, had materialised to pay close attention to his words.

He was plainly enjoying this.

"But the explosion that came afterward was something else entirely. You see, you only get an explosion like *that* when a person's soul energy is consumed. If that alone weren't frightful enough ... such a transference of power is only possible when the victim truly loves the truant. In other words, a mound of this level indicates that someone has been murdered at the hands of someone they love."

Frederick exchanged a knowing look with Commander Kai, and then caught Vandrune's eyes. To his surprise, tears trailed down the sympathetic old mage's cheeks. It seemed this detail had been something that even he hadn't known.

Again, this begged the question ... where was Higant's knowledge coming from?

Something in Higant was beginning to falter. He still had more to say, but he was visibly exhausted, and his cocky demeanour was starting to crack. When next he spoke, his voice was more sorrowful—more like himself.

"Mounds of this size are often the result of a truant travelling over a great distance." Tears welled in his eyes. "They ... they knew we were following them. They must have used Marcus's soul to escape."

Vandrune's head cocked to the side. This suggestion of Higant's conflicted with the explanation that he himself had just given. Surely he didn't think Marcus loved his kidnapper? Then again, given what had happened between them, it wasn't impossible.

Higant fell to his knees, and Frederick stepped in to support him.

"It wasn't him, Higant. I am certain that Marcus yet lives."

The squire's eyes were red with tears.

"How can you be sure?"

Frederick relayed what Commander Kai had explained about the scent of a soul.

Vandrune kneeled down and patted Higant's shoulder, deciding to keep his observations to himself for now.

"You've done well, my boy. Take a moment to rest."

Nodding quietly, Higant lowered himself to the ground, overcome by fatigue.

After a moment, Vandrune stood and turned to the king.

"Frederick, by all accounts, your kingdom may be the first in hundreds of years to be threatened by the truants. If you have one, then you may have more," he stated directly, and didn't stop there. "However, that is not my biggest concern."

Frederick's face settled into a deep-set frown and a look of concern beyond his years.

"I'm loath to ask, but what *is* your biggest concern, if not that? What could be worse than this mess?"

Vandrune looked to where he had left Higant, and was not surprised to find the boy sound asleep on the ground, curled up into a ball.

"It is amazing to me that we stand here with a boy, no older than eleven summers, reciting knowledge thought lost to history."

The mage allowed himself a brief smile, but his expression quickly turned grave.

"While young Higant here explained facets of the truants' power that even I did not know, one thing that is well known in the annals of history is this: at the apex of the Lolariane War, when the truants had their backs to the wall, they attempted to ignite an event known as a Truant Cascade. It was a complex rite of resonance between most of the remaining truants ... and the full extent of what they might've accomplished with it is unknown, for the Cascade failed, and they destroyed themselves in the process.

"My lord ... my friend. From the evidence we've seen here tonight, it would seem the truants have returned. How and why, I do not know, but I foresee a difficult road ahead," said Vandrune, his head dropping as he spoke his last words.

The gravity of the situation was slowly dawning on Frederick. He moved away from the group of men, lost in his thoughts as the Ku-Da-Ru set up a permitter around the group.

"Seek that which is lost ... keep that which is found," he muttered to himself.

Frederick slowly turned his eyes to rest upon Higant, who was beginning to stir. Could this boy be part of the mage's prophecy? Was Marcus that which was lost? It was all too coincidental to be a coincidence, but so much had happened in the last day, he was not sure what to make of it all.

His voice came shaky and uncertain.

"Vandrune? Your ear for a moment."

Vandrune walked towards Frederick, and they slowly moved away from the group. The group watched as the two men spoke in dull whispers of things they could only guess at. Higant, risen from his brief slumber, could only hope they were not entertaining the thought of leaving Marcus to the ravages of the truants.

As Vandrune and Frederick returned to the group, they headed to Commander Kai, and the king dismissed them. Without a word, the Ku-Da-Ru withdrew and vanished, no doubt keeping guard from a distance.

Frederick turned to Higant, beckoning him over.

"Higant ... can you recall what you were saying to us before your nap?" asked Frederick.

Higant looked at both men and frowned, trying to remember the last thing they'd spoken about.

"I recall we found the king," Higant said slowly. "Then I felt tired and laid down."

Vandrune nodded silently.

"My boy," he said, "the king and I have spoken, and we believe it is time to change tack. Frederick is king, and as such, he has responsibilities that come along with his stature. The group will head back to Neleuwan."

As he spoke, the king was busy mounting his horse, and beginning to lead the party back towards the road.

Higant shook his head. "Frederick said Marcus was alive. Why would we not keep searching for him?"

Despite his protests, Vandrune ushered Higant to his horse and helped him upon it, leading it and his own horse after the king. Higant was starting to get angry. Was he the only one who cared what happened to Marcus?

When they arrived at the road, they found the king waiting for them to catch up. Frederick gathered the party, then moved his horse to face Higant's.

"Time to make a choice, my squire. Stay with me, or go with Vandrune?"

"Milord?" Higant was unsure of the request.

"Vandrune and I have spoken, and we feel it's best if he pursues Marcus alone, while I stay here to continue the work of a king. However, it is my belief that when a man comes to a crossroads, whether by coincidence or by duty, he should be the one to decide which path he takes. This, I know all too well." The king smiled. "So I ask again. With me, continuing in your duty as a squire in defence of our lands? Or with Vandrune, in the pursuit of your friend Marcus?"

At the sound of his friend's name, his choice was made. His emotions rose to the surface, and the tears came easily. It was only then that his voice truly found its power.

"Marcus, sire."

"With Vandrune it is," Frederick said with a knowing grin. "It is good to know my faith in you is not unfounded. Congratulations. You have passed your first test as my squire, and performed admirably."

Higant beamed through his tears.

"I won't let you down, my lord."

King Frederick gave the boy a reassuring nod.

"Vandrune?" he said, turning towards him. "Look after my squire, will you? I do hope he will be well educated when he returns."

Vandrune laughed. "At this rate, he'll be the one educating me."

The mage reached for Frederick's arm, and they grasped each other's forearms in a friendly goodbye.

"Well, hop down, then," said Vandrune, who'd set about untethering their packs from their horses.

Higant was unsure why they were leaving their horses behind, but didn't question it. With that, they strode off down the road, away from the carnage of the forest where the truant mound lay and further along the road to Pillton.

Frederick watched as the mage and the boy walked on down the road, hoping they would return safely with Marcus and any news they could gather. It was a risk to let go of 'that which is found' as the prophecy had foretold—at least, in his interpretation—but Frederick knew better than to perceive the prophecy's words at face value. It was unlikely they were as simple as finding something, or someone like Higant, and then keeping them under lock and key.

He felt that in time, it would all be for the best, and had no doubt that Vandrune was right—there was something of great significance locked away in Higant's mind.

Though neither of them knew what it was, nor how to unlock it, he was hopeful their journey would bring them closer to the answer.

CHAPTER ELEVEN

STRANGER

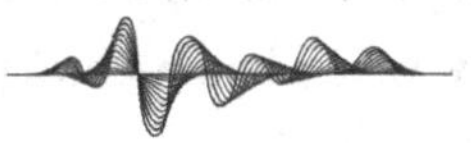

Marcus opened his eyes slowly and tried to lift himself up, the blood rushing back to his head, making him feel dizzy and nauseous. His eyes hurt when he finally opened them, as if hot needles had been pushed into his brain. Moving was not much better. His arms and legs all hurt to move. The rough and bumpy wagon ride to get to the forest and the rope that had cut into his wrists along the way were just the tip of the iceberg.

His heart felt like it was trying to pull away from his chest at the pace it was pumping. His breathing was rapid, and pain coursed through his fingers, sending tingling sensations up his arms. The sound of thunder rolled across the sky, and sweat came seeping into his mouth and eyes, salty and sharp. Confusion rained down upon his senses as he tried to orient himself in his surroundings.

Lost in a darkened world with no escape, panic started to overcome him. Darkness was all that came to him—nothing but darkness.

After what felt like an eternity, glimpses of light began to mix in with the dark, swirling across the inside of his eyelids. No matter how he tried, they would not open. Pain swelled in his mind once more ... until with sudden, unexpected relief, he finally passed out.

When he woke again, his body ached as though it had been set aflame. His mouth was dry, and it felt like a thousand needles were being pressed into his cheeks. Any small movement bore more pain down upon his skin, and yet as each movement caused discomfort, it went away just as quickly. Like a bad memory, the pain would return, and he would find himself again in darkness, his unconsciousness fraught with fitful dreams.

Hours passed before he stirred again.

This time, it was different. He felt peace. No pain ... just peace.

Still, he remembered. He kept his eyes closed and was reluctant to move a muscle, in case the pain returned.

A subtle light fell across his face, and he felt the warmth of it. Slowly, he opened his eyes, anticipating the pain and the fear ... and yet, there was none. The discomfort he'd thought would come, did not.

He slowly scanned his eyes around the room he found himself in. Moving his head slowly, still not fully convinced that the pain would not return, he found that the room was not as small as he'd thought, and was actually quite large and pleasant.

He lay on a sizeable bed protected by mosquito netting, with the sweet warmth of the breeze upon his face and skin. As he took in his surroundings, he noticed that he was naked, with nothing but a sheet across his lower half and otherwise exposed upon the soft covers of the bed.

He tentatively moved his fingers, and again found no pain. He slowly worked his way up his limbs, and eventually found that all the pain had gone. Sitting up to test the dizziness, none came ... but as he moved himself to the edge of the bed, he realised that he was out of breath.

Even without pain, that such little exertion would drain him of energy and render him breathless was a little disconcerting. As he sat there, hoping for his breath to settle, he noticed there were windows surrounding the bed. He turned to look around and found that the windows were all open, thus allowing the outdoor elements into the bright room.

Marcus's physical ability was still being tested, but his senses were starting to return. He could smell many different scents coming in from outside the windows, but one scent was stronger than all the rest: the smell of wet salt. It was one he had never smelt so strongly before, and one that would change everything.

Marcus stood up slowly to test his legs and found that they were solid, but still not as strong as they'd been. He quickly became aware that his stomach was grumbling. He needed something to give him energy.

He attempted to move towards the door and closer to the smells coming from outside, but fell into the doorframe, the sheet wrapped around his waist. The sky outside of the room was a blue as deep as the most beautiful woman's eyes, and the clouds he noticed were white like sheep in its vast fields. The warmth he felt as he stood in the sunlight made his body feel as if its strength was rebuilding, growing, filling up like a long-empty cup replenished with the finest mead. He closed his eyes and drank in every drop.

As he felt the warmth grow within him, he opened his eyes again, feeling something nagging at the back of his mind. Not sure what it could be, he turned back into the room.

He noticed that against the far wall opposite the door was a chair, his squire's clothes sitting cleaned and dried upon it. The clothes had been patched in places where it seemed he had sustained some injuries in whatever that was that had happened to him. He slowly made his way towards the chair, which was still not an easy feat.

Halfway there, he looked around to see the rest of the room, noticing the other furniture. There was a dresser set back against the rear wall on the opposite side of the bed to the chair, and atop it was a tray of food, complete with cheeses, dry biscuits, bread, and honey wine, all there waiting to be consumed.

Forgetting all about his clothes, he worked his way towards the food, holding the sheet around his waist and trying his hardest not to trip over it. Bumping into a few things along the way, he almost collapsed into the dresser. It rocked perilously as he rested all of his weight upon it, nearly spilling the mead. Steadying himself, he ate with gusto, consuming the spread within minutes and leaving nothing but a few crumbs, washing it all down with mead.

Having used the last of his energy to eat, and the food not yet metabolised, Marcus sank down to the floor, more exhausted than he'd ever been. Eventually, he would make his way back to the clothes on the chair, but he needed to give himself time to recoup. Resigning himself to his position on the floor, he rested his back against the dresser and looked over at the bed he'd woken up on.

The thing that had been nagging at him suddenly hit him like a ton of bricks.

"How ... did I get here?"

Still, Marcus couldn't shake the feeling there was more he was missing. He searched his mind for it, but it eluded him. His stomach starting to settle, he moved towards his clothes, stumbling in his haste to get dressed and find answers.

Picking himself up from the floor for a third time, he rested his head against a second doorway near the chair, the sheet from the bed still firmly grasped in his hand. As he lifted his head from the doorframe, the curtain blew open, and Marcus's thinking was stopped in its his tracks.

Now he knew what that smell was.

It was the smell of the ocean.

The building stood at the top of a cliff, looking straight out over the ocean. It was a view he had never seen, and thought he never would. The smell, the sound of the waves, the movement of the ocean, the ships sailing in and out of the harbour, all floating up to him from the small fishing village below …

In that moment, a word came to him.

"Home," he whispered aloud.

It was the thing he had been seeking all his life—his most personal dream, one of freedom, to be and to do whatever he desired. Just like that, it had suddenly materialised in front of him.

But just as quickly as the feeling of hope and freedom and life had been thrust into his mind, the door slammed shut just as fast. He had no idea where he was, or why he was there … but wherever it was, it was Crimson who had brought him there.

He turned around in a flash, looking through the room for any trace of her or Fanton.

He'd recovered a little of his strength after eating, but he still stumbled in his efforts to find some sign of them. After flailing his way through every inch of the place, he'd had to conclude that nowhere in the room or the surrounding gardens and cliffs were his captors to be seen. That didn't rule out the possibility that they would return, of course. But if they'd wanted to keep him there, then why were his hands not tied? Why had he been lying on a soft bed with food nearby, and all his wounds tended to?

Marcus made his way back to the chair and quickly dressed himself, throwing the sheet back on the bed. Motivated to find more food before leaving if he could, he headed for the nearest internal door. As he stepped through the door into a small adjoining room, a deep voice resonated from a chair in a dimly lit corner.

"Good morning," it said, rising from the chair.

Marcus froze in mid stride.

"Who are you?"

"The man who saved your life, young squire," said a gruff, weathered voice.

"I wasn't aware I was in danger," Marcus lied, grasping for any advantage.

"Well, if that be the case, it appears I've stumbled upon a fool," the voice said with a slight chuckle.

Despite his situation, Marcus was taken aback.

"How dare you insult me without knowing who I am?"

"I don't much care who you are, young squire. All I care about is that you live."

The man moved into the light, revealing the most hairy, weather-beaten, kindly old man he had ever seen.

"You look like you've lived a thousand lifetimes," Marcus said before he could stop himself.

The man chuckled again. "Well, after your ordeal, you're a picture of beauty yourself."

"I—I'm sorry. Forgive my rudeness ... I'm just a little confused as to what happened last night."

Running his hands through his hair, Marcus felt a little wobbly. Sensing that he wasn't in any danger, he collapsed into a nearby chair.

"Last night? I do believe you mean two moons ago."

The elderly man strode across the room to another tray of food, which he picked up and placed in front of Marcus.

"Two moons?" Marcus put his head between his hands.

"Aye, boy. 'Tis a minor miracle you woke at all."

"What happened?"

"Well now ... let me start at the beginning. There I was, out at sea, enjoying the relaxing nature of the lady of the ocean. My boat and I travel to many places, but that afternoon I was only a mile offshore, enjoying the day's take on my way back to the harbour. Clouds had been brewing over the land all day, see, and a storm looked to be on the way.

"With my eyes on the horizon, I noticed lightning firing off from those storm clouds ... but it shot out at an odd angle, and it didn't have the feel of something natural. At first, I thought it might be mage magic, but mages are strange creatures—keep their magic hidden, if they can. Nothing subtle about this.

"At first, I let it go, making landfall and working my way back up the cliff. Let me tell you, it's a steep climb, and it takes an old man like me a while to reach the top. But reach it I did, and then settled in on the deck, keeping an eye on the clouds for any more strange lights. The strikes continued, and strangely enough, they seemed to be concentrated in a particular area, not far from the edge of the forest on these very cliffs.

"Being a nosey kind of fellow, I decided to investigate. Not sure what it was, but something in me was telling me I was needed. When I finally made it to the area, it turned out the strikes were landing in a ridge, surrounded on all sides by high stone faces. I hid in a couple of bushes right by the edge and looked down into it, and there I saw a rock formation, like a bowl near the centre of it. I crept a little closer, and what I saw was something that hasn't been seen in three hundred years: a truant calling."

Curious as he was, Marcus was getting a little restless, unsure how any of this related to his arrival here or being unconscious for a number of days. Still, he figured he owed it to the man to let him continue his story.

"What's a truant calling?" he asked.

"It's a group of truants acting as an anchor, focusing on a single point for the purpose of pulling another truant through to that location once they enter the breach. In other words, they were intentionally bringing someone to them."

Again, Marcus wasn't really sure what any of these things were, but was done asking questions for now.

The old man continued.

"Every time the lightning flared and hit the ground, the energy would bring through someone new. It seemed a large number of people had already come through the breach, likely on the lightning I'd seen earlier. Each one that arrived joined the others, all of them forming a circle around the bowl and chanting.

"Eventually, the chanting got louder, and there were three more lightning strikes, far more powerful than the last—one, then another two in quick succession. As it happened, the first of these did not strike the middle of the bowl, but just off to the right of me, about thirty yards or so. When the light settled, I ran over to see what had happened ... and that's when the next two strikes hit, right on target. Shockwave knocked me clear off my feet, it did," he said, rubbing his behind. "Anyway, once I got back up and reached the site of the first strike ... well, there you were, lying bruised and bloodied. Seemed strange that no one from the bowl came looking for you, but I suppose they were tending to the others. Either way, it didn't seem proper to leave you in the care of folks who'd put you in such a state ... so I picked you up in a hurry and brought you back here."

Pip turned around from the window he'd been staring out of and looked over at Marcus, a bright smile on his face. "Wasn't easy, mind you. You're quite heavy when you're not awake," he said, chuckling to himself.

Marcus was stunned. He owed the old man a lot more than he'd realised.

"Thank you, sir. I owe you my life."

"Please. Call me Pip."

"Thank you ... Pip. My name is Marcus."

Pip smiled.

"Marcus, eh? I must say, Marcus, you were pretty banged up when you arrived. I treated your immediate wounds, but being as bad as some of them were, I was going to need help. I was just about to head down to the village to seek aid from the town healer ... and then there was a knock at my door."

CHAPTER TWELVE

BEGINNING

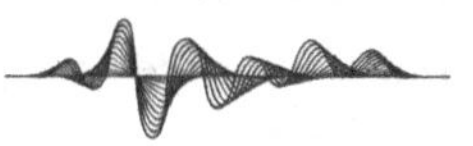

It had been two days since Higant and Vandrune had left the king and his guards to make their way along the road to Pillton, then out into the world beyond. They'd picked up fresh horses in Pillton, along with supplies and a change of clothes into something more suitable for a long trip. Then, they had ridden hard, stopping only to sleep and eat.

Not many words were spoken between them while they travelled, and they were making a good pace ... but Higant had no idea where they could possibly be headed at such a clip. Marcus had disappeared into thin air. There was no trail for them to follow. He trusted Vandrune, but the longer they travelled without a clear destination, the more anxious he became.

On the third day, as the sun started to set across the mountains, Vandrune decided they should walk for a while, letting the horses rest after riding so hard. The horses seemed pleased with the change of pace, taking a moment to eat some of the grasses that grew at the sides of the roads whenever the chance presented itself.

Another reason Vandrune had suggested the break was because he thought it might help to get the two of them talking … and indeed, they'd only been walking for a little while before Higant finally spoke up.

"Master Vandrune … we've been riding hard for two days now, and we've barely had a moment's rest. I've no issue with that if it gets us to Marcus sooner … but where are we even going? How do you know which direction to head?"

Seeing Higant's pained expression, with a soft, simple look, he said, "A fair question, my boy. To be perfectly honest, I simply thought if we continued in the direction their carriage had been heading, it might help us to define our direction. Alas, given that they travelled through a truant calling, they could be just about anywhere."

Looking around, Vandrune took in the surrounding landscape, then returned his attention to the track they found themselves upon. Eyes forward, he didn't even notice that Higant had stopped dead in the middle of the road, looking at him with complete surprise.

The boy didn't know what he'd expected him to say, but it certainly hadn't been that. His look of surprise quickly turned to one of anger, burst free of its chains.

"When you and King Frederick spoke before offering me my choice, I thought you knew what you were doing," said Higant, his face turning red and his voice hitting a high pitch. "You made it sound like you had a plan—a direction to take. My friend is lost, and you mean to tell me that even Vandrune, a true prophet, has no idea where he is?"

His voice had built into a yell, now coming straight from his lungs.

Despite the narrowed eyes burning holes into Vandrune's back, the mage continued strolling up the track for a time before coming to a stop, standing silently next to his horse, his face obscured by his cloak's hood.

To Higant, it felt like an eternity before Vandrune slowly turned to face him, even though it had only been a few moments. When he did, his expression was totally unreadable. Instead of offering Higant any semblance of an explanation, he turned and headed off the track with his horse in tow, moving towards a thicket of trees not far from the road and disappearing into the brush.

Higant hadn't imagined he could get any angrier than he already was, but his rage flared even hotter. Why was Vandrune ignoring him? Was he not owed an explanation?

Higant stormed through the brush after him, dragging his horse with him in an effort to follow Vandrune and give him a piece of his mind. The horse struggled to pull free, but Higant had no mind for the poor animal, holding its reins in a death grip.

Coming through the brush, he found it opened up to a vaulted tree ceiling. After navigating the relatively dense bushes, he hadn't been expecting it to lead to such a wonderful, cosy space, and the peace of it took the wind out of his sails.

He found Vandrune standing close to the trunk of the tree that was the centre of this magnificent space, already busy staking his horse and unpacking his gear. Seeing him acting so casually fired his anger right back up again. Just when it looked like he was about to explode, he heard something that shifted his focus away from Vandrune. He started to look around for the source of his distraction, but couldn't tell where it had come from. He looked all around the space, to the edges and back the way they'd come, but failed to find the source of the noise.

By the time he'd finished looking for it, he realised his anger had abated. Shifting his focus had made him much calmer, but his frustrations were far from resolved. Now thinking a little more clearly and feeling the weariness of the road, he decided to start setting up his bed for the night.

Higant lay out his bedroll on the opposite side of the clearing to Vandrune's. As things stood, he just didn't want to be near him. After that, he focused on his horse. He apologised to the beast for being so gruff, taking off his saddle and bridle and brushing off the soil and dirt that had kicked up while they'd been riding. Tying him loosely to a tree branch near his bedroll so he could eat some of the nearby grass, Higant then took his own fill and drank some of the water from his skin.

The light had gone out a long while before the two had finished sorting their horses and gear, but soon enough, they had a fire started and had settled around it for warmth.

Higant, whose anger had cooled earlier, had had time for it to bubble up once again. It seemed the more Vandrune ignored him, the more frustrated he became.

But before he could say anything, Vandrune spoke, with all his years of wisdom reflected behind his eyes.

"Master Higant ... as a keeper of knowledge, it is my duty in this world to provide counsel, offer insight, and be a protector of those within my reach. You are one such person," he said, voice measured and calm. "However, you are also one of the greatest threats to the others I would protect."

Higant's anger finally exploded.

"A threat? I am barely eleven summers old. How can I be a threat? To you, and to everyone else, I am but a child, am I not?" He had stood up without even realising it, his hands fisted at his side. "I have done *everything* I have ever been asked, and my reward for that has been losing both my lord and my friend, through no fault of my own. On top of all that, you lead me into the woods on some wild goose chase, and then claim I am a threat? I am no threat—I am a victim!"

Even with all of Higant's anger directed at him, Vandrune stood as a calm statue in the middle of a squall, continuing without missing a beat.

"You are a victim, true ... but there is no denying you are also a threat," he said with a calm, soft voice to counter his. "You have knowledge ... knowledge of what has occurred."

Vandrune pulled his hands behind his back and took on the air of a teacher about to impart an important life lesson.

"A truant mound has not been seen in three hundred years, and yet you were able to identify one before even prophets and kings. Furthermore, you understood the significance of its height—again relaying information that has been thought irrelevant for centuries as though it were common knowledge. While extremely unlikely, it's not impossible that you might've obtained this knowledge after undertaking extensive research on the history of truants ... but that would not explain how you knew about the mist and the Truant Triad, information to which even I was not privy. It also would not explain why you were able to clarify how the nature of prophecy has changed, revealing the existence of a third form of prophecy as easily as if you had been schooled in prophetic lore for thousands of years. Even the most seasoned of scholars could only dream of making such a discovery, and you spoke of it as though it were trivial. These are all things you have done in a handful of days."

Vandrune paused to see what reaction he would get from the boy.

"I don't remember any of that, Vandrune," he said, a look of complete distress upon his face. "I ... I remember saying *something*, and asking a few questions, but for the life of me, I can't recall what they were. I didn't think what I said was that important."

Higant started to relax his fists, his breathing slowing as the fire in his belly went out once more.

Vandrune's expression was one of great sympathy.

"It's because of this that I actually have some idea of the path we must tread, and not for the reasons you believe."

"But you said—"

"It is less about where we must go, young squire, and more about what we must do," he said gently. "When I spoke with King Frederick, we both agreed that there is much more to his cousin's murder, to Marcus's kidnapping, and to you than there might seem. It is time we understood the greater threat. In doing that, I am all but certain we will find Marcus."

Higant's facade of anger now lost, his pain came to the surface, sending tears running down his cheeks.

"He's my only friend. The only person who has ever really cared for me. More than that, he is my brother. Maybe not by blood, but he's always been there for me. It's time I was there for him."

Vandrune moved forward to comfort him, Higant leaned into the old mage, sobbing into his robes.

"I'm sorry, Vandrune. I'm just scared for him. I don't know what to do."

After allowing himself to be with his feelings for a time, Higant pulled away from Vandrune and looked up into his calm, inquisitive eyes.

"I still don't understand. How is this knowledge a threat?"

"The question is not how, but why," Vandrune offered. "You see, for you to possess the knowledge that you do, there are only a number of possibilities. My first thought was that you'd been exposed to matters of prophecy at a young age, imparting you with knowledge to be tapped into later in life … however, I soon dismissed this theory, as the level of detail and your understanding of it all is far too advanced."

The mage hesitated before continuing.

"Before I tell you this next theory, understand that I have already rejected it, and I will tell you why in a moment. After the truant mound, I considered that you may have been an unwitting truant spy, planted in a position that allowed you access to the king. First, you were squire to the king's cousin, and now to the king himself … paired with the information you had, it was not a difficult conclusion to draw. Ultimately, I dismissed it because your knowledge extends far beyond the subject of truants, and a spy would not have drawn attention to themselves by volunteering that information."

Higant, now that he was calmer and no longer angry with Vandrune, simply listened intently, following the mage's logic in hopes of understanding his situation.

"And what is your current theory?" he asked.

"What we know is that you're able to access the knowledge when the need arises, though you are unable to recall it afterward," said Vandrune. "This suggests two things: one, that the knowledge is being blocked by something; and two, that pieces of it are allowed to slip through that blockage when the need is great, if only for them to be forgotten and return there afterwards. There's also the fact that, so far, those pieces have only made it through the blockage at times you've had some sort of personal connection or need for them. Thus, there is a certain logic to whatever force is regulating your access to the sealed knowledge.

"As for the reason the knowledge is there in the first place … I'm afraid your guess is as good as mine. Beyond this extraordinary ability—and a sharp wit of your own, of course—you are simply a young squire who goes about his day, unaware of the knowledge and skills he possesses."

By the time he was done, they had both come to sit down next to the fire.

"I still don't get it, Vandrune," said Higant, his head low. "How is the knowledge dangerous, especially if I can't access it without some sort of trigger? Even when I do manage it, I can't remember it."

"Exactly!" Vandrune proclaimed, as if the boy had hit upon the very issue. "You said it yourself. All that has happened to you has been through no fault of your own. If my suspicions are correct ... someone is manipulating the events around you, doing things that—as you say—trigger you to access this sealed knowledge. Perhaps they intend to have you reveal to them what lies hidden in your mind."

Higant frowned in thought.

Slowly, he said, "So you're saying they killed the baron and took Marcus just to trigger me? To access the knowledge that supposedly exists in my mind?"

"An unpleasant thought, to be sure, but one I fear may be quite close to the truth. There is also the possibility that it isn't the information itself they seek, but the act of unlocking that which is locked, and thereby releasing whatever seal has been placed upon you. Either way, whatever this entity hopes to accomplish with you is one of the reasons I am forced to consider the risk you might pose."

"What is the other?" Higant asked hesitantly.

"Do you recall how angry you were when you entered this grove earlier?" said Vandrune. "And how every time it nearly overwhelmed you, there was something there to distract you?"

Higant blushed at the thought of his misplaced fury.

"I remember," he said sheepishly.

"I confess, it was I who created that sound, laced as it was with an energy that helps to calm anger," said Vandrune. "See, emotions can be very powerful things ... particularly in those who possess great power. We still don't understand the nature of whatever it is that lies inside your mind, but it's entirely possible that a strong emotion like anger could cause you to release something even more devastating than knowledge. Forgive me, but I wasn't ready to test that particular theory, so I had to help you calm down."

Higant had some ideas about how the mage might've avoided angering him to begin with, but decided to keep them to himself.

"Of course, at present, we have no way of confirming any of this," Vandrune continued. "Thus did the king and I think it best to keep you far afield from those who might harm you. We will keep Marcus in focus at all times, but he is not our direct point of travel. We must first seek out those who might shed light on the situation."

"Does that mean we're going to Acoreq? To The Luminary?" Higant asked, a little excited at the prospect despite the circumstances.

"At first, I had thought that was where we needed to go ... but I now believe we need to consider the bigger picture as it relates to the prophecy revealed in King Frederick's office. 'In the depths of a man's mind; a mystery locked in time' ... I believe this relates to you, young Higant. How and why, I do not know, but it can be no coincidence."

"If not there, then where?" said Higant, struggling to come to grips with all of this.

Vandrune smiled.

"There's only one man I can think to ask. It is time we met Kyruarth."

CHAPTER THIRTEEN

SEEK

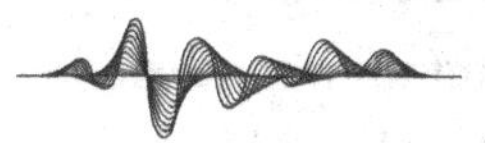

After leaving the safety of the grove, Vandrune and Higant rode in the direction of the Yuill Ion Pass, a barren path over the mountain that connected the continents of Neleuwan and Gyrockgenci. Vandrune explained to Higant that while the continents had collided long ago, the Yuill Ion Pass and the harsh mountain over which it crossed remained the only passage over land, separating the lush green earth of Neleuwan and the dry stony deserts of Gyrockgenci. The reason for their destination was that, according to The Luminary, it was Kyruarth's last known location.

Moving towards the slopes leading up to the pass, the grass thinned out and the trees gradually became smaller until nothing but the odd shrub remained. With every step they took up the mountain, the heat grew more and more oppressive. For most mountains, the higher you climbed, the lower the temperature fell ... but this was the complete opposite. As they ascended, waves of heat from the dry lands of Gyrockgenci flowed over the top of the mountain and down towards their advance, the arid air making sweat bead upon their brows.

It was no secret that many a traveller had found themselves out of water and died of dehydration while navigating the pass and the deserts beyond. So many people had set out from the nearby villages on the Neleuwan side and never returned that the locals had come to refer to it as Spirit Pass, as it seemed to be as much a passage to the spirit world as a path to the neighbouring continent.

As sharp as their minds were, there were moments when Higant and Vandrune—a child and an old man in body—felt that they too might succumb to the mountain pass, but their ample preparation and determination to press on saw them through the worst of it.

It took them the better part of a day, but finally, they saw the crest of the mountain pass. By now, their lips were cracked and dry, and dust had caked itself across their faces, having mingled with the sweat that had been pouring off them all day.

At the moment they crested the top of the pass, a breeze cooler and more refreshing than any they'd thought possible hit them in the face. It came as such a surprise after the harrowing ascent that they instantly came out of their stupor, and couldn't help but let out a laugh.

They decided to stop there for a moment and give water to the horses, who were also visibly thrilled by the sudden change in temperature. Looking out over the new land, blanketed a pale yellow that contrasted with the vibrant green at their backs, it seemed the sky over Gyrockgenci shimmered and merged with the land at the horizon.

The breeze, it seemed, would only be a temporary relief from the stifling and sweltering climb, for the shimmering could only be an intense heat radiating from the ground.

Regardless of what lay ahead, they did not pass up the opportunity to feel the cool, fresh air upon their faces. Higant closed his eyes and let the breeze wash over his face and body, imagining it like a waterfall washing away the sweat and heat.

Since their discussion in the grove, the two of them had shared a singular focus: find Kyruarth. Vandrune had been impressed with Higant's resolve. Once the boy got his mind focused upon a goal, he was like an arrow to its target. That sort of drive was something quite formidable, particularly given that he possessed it this early in his years. It did come with some concern, however—was this behaviour truly a part of his personality, or had it come from whatever was locked away in his mind?

Vandrune had been watching Higant from time to time to judge if anything had changed in the boy, but so far, it seemed the only thing that had changed about him was his need to get to Kyruarth. Whenever he questioned the lad about this shift, he always stated the same thing: "I need to find Marcus." It made Vandrune feel great affection for the young squire. Even with all of the uncertainty surrounding him, he was more worried about his friend than anything else.

All too soon, their reprieve was over, and it was time for them to continue on.

"Careful of the shale as we head down the other side of this pass," said Vandrune. "It's hot and dry, and will cut the horses' legs if not carefully trodden."

A number of hours passed, and already, the cool breeze was like a distant memory. They'd had to dismount from their horses early into the descent, as their hooves had started to slide on the loose rocks and they were concerned the horses might fall, taking them down with them.

Higant had become fond of his horse on the ride.

"I'm trying to think of a name for him," he announced.

Vandrune, on the other hand, was apprehensive.

"I don't recommend it," he said. "I don't mean to be cold, but if they injure themselves, they won't last long out here. Best not to get attached."

Higant was undeterred.

"If you won't name her, I will," he said, nodding to Vandrune's horse before returning his attention to his own. "But not before we come up with one for you, eh? How do you feel about Dusty?"

The horse looked at him, but otherwise gave no indication it was listening.

"Alright then, what about Fuzzy?"

Again, the horse just plodded along behind him.

Off in the distance, far to the north, they could see a storm brewing. The lightning and rolls of thunder were faint, but visible and audible nonetheless.

"What about Thunder?"

At this, the horse's ears pricked up, and it lifted its head free of the reins that Higant was holding.

"Looks like we have a winner," Higant smiled, patting Thunder's head while he gathered the reins. "I declare that my horse shall now be known as Thunder!"

Vandrune chuckled at the wonderful name Higant had given his horse, silently hoping that nothing happened to it and brought the boy more sadness.

"If your horse is Thunder, than what about mine?"

"Well, your horse is female, and all the girls I know love flowers. What about Flower?"

Vandrune relayed the name to his horse. No reaction.

"Sorry, Higant. It appears we have a hard no on that name."

"Hard no, eh? Then what about Blossom?" Higant thought, trying to think of something similar, but more specific to her.

"Well, Blossom? What do you think?" said Vandrune, looking back at his horse.

To his surprise, the horse was almost smiling back at him, ears pricked up and tail swinging as if she were a girl skipping down the road.

"You've done it again, my boy!"

The pair laughed along the path with their horses, now christened Thunder and Blossom.

Time passed, and the light had faded into twilight. They were close to the base of the pass in the hotlands of Gyrockgenci, and desperately needed to rest.

"Will we make camp soon, Vandrune?" said Higant, taking a drink from his waterskin.

"Once we're on level ground, we'll find shelter and rest. After we've regained our energy—if such a thing is possible in this land—we'll travel through the night. It'll be cooler that way, and we'll cover much more ground. Not to mention, it will be much more pleasant for Blossom and Thunder."

"How will we find our way in the dark?"

"We'll navigate our way by the stars," said Vandrune. "The direction we're heading will be in the same general direction we've been travelling all along: due south, straight through the heart of Gyrockgenci."

Exhausted as he was, Higant was concerned they wouldn't make it, but he didn't voice that to anyone—not even Thunder.

Not long after the horses had received their names, Vandrune had taken the lead, as he was able to see and understand the path better than Higant. He'd travelled the land for many years, and though Gyrockgenci was new to him, he knew exactly the pitfalls to look for in such terrain. Higant was still young, and had not ventured far from the confines of the castle, much less Neleuwan.

It took a few hours, but by the time they'd finally made it down the slopes to the land below, it was well past dark. The air was slightly cooler, and a breeze had picked up, giving them some relief from the heat. Even with the breeze, the temperature was not much better—it just felt good to have something blowing through their hair to cool the sweat.

Vandrune spotted a rocky overhang not that far from where they'd come level with the hot sands, designating it as their camp for the night. The moon was high and full, casting an eerily bright glow across the land. With that in mind, they decided not to light a fire, lest they draw unwanted attention, and it was too hot already.

They ate dried meats and fruit that Vandrune still had in his saddlebag from the resupply all the way back at Pillton. It seemed so long ago that they'd been there, but in truth, only a number of days had passed. The pace they'd moved at since their destination had been decided was impressive, but it came at the cost of tiredness and fatigue, both of which were now catching up. The horses were showing it too, especially after a day of walking up and down the mountain. Higant found a place to stake them for the night, giving them what he could in the way of chaff and water, then leaving them to sleep and recover as much as they could. It was not long after that both Higant and Vandrune lay out their bedrolls and fell to sleep.

After a few hours of sleep, Vandrune woke with purpose just after the zenith of the moon. It was time to narrow the search.

Without rising from his bedroll, Vandrune crossed his legs and closed his eyes. He focused slowly on his breathing to bring himself to a calm state, which didn't take long, then started to recite the chant in his mind's eye. Slowly and surely, he felt the words take shape, and the vision he held in his mind started to become clear.

Finally, he found what he was looking for.

A figure, standing alone in a sea of darkness, looking back towards him. It stood quiet, solemn, still. It wore a cloak with a hood, and from within the hood glowed piercing green eyes. Intense as they were, there was nothing to fear from them.

The eyes portrayed safety. Sanctuary. Home.

"I have come, master of my master," said Vandrune. "I seek that which does not wish to be found."

In this place, his voice felt ethereal—light and lost, as if a slight breeze would blow it away. In contrast, the voice that returned was not wistful like Vandrune's, but clear, strong, and powerful.

"Truants have come, and the Cascade is upon us," it echoed. "It is time. Come to me."

Focused as Vandrune was upon, his chanting, the figure, and its words, an image appeared in his mind. There was no colour, and the picture was indistinct, like a negative of a drawing scrawled in the dirt.

Suddenly, Vandrune's eyes opened. He looked over at Higant who, like him, was now sitting cross-legged, watching him from his own bedroll.

"How long have you been awake?" said Vandrune, wiping a cold sweat from his brow.

"Since I heard your words in my mind," said Higant.

If this surprised Vandrune, he didn't let it show. He turned away from Higant and reached for his waterskin, taking a long drink. The work of a wizard was draining and dehydrating, especially when communing with others.

Vandrune reached into his pocket and pulled forth a bound book of numerous pages. From within the binder, he removed a writing implement and started to recreate the image he'd seen, no doubt the place they needed to travel to.

As he finished the drawing, clearly some sort of topographical map, he did not recognise the location.

"Vandrune, what are you drawing?"

With a quick glance at the boy, Vandrune placed a finger between the pages and closed the book upon it, then moved to sit beside him.

"Something I saw whilst Reaching."

"Reaching?"

"It is a general term for extending your will to find and speak with other users of magic," said Vandrune. "A difficult task, but one made easier when you know the markers of the one you seek, and vice versa."

"Who were you seeking?" Higant asked.

"If you were able to hear my words in your mind, I suspect you already know," said Vandrune, his eyes mischievous.

"Kyruarth!" said Higant, beaming.

"Indeed," Vandrune confirmed. "It seems he gave me a location for our meeting, though I can't say I know the place it refers to."

Vandrune went to open the book, but Higant caught his hand before he had a chance. He looked up into Vandrune's eyes, and there, the mage saw a familiar flare of blue.

"We must travel to the Pinnacle of Osciros," said Higant. "To a west-facing cliff overlooking the Tonnecius Ocean."

Vandrune was astonished.

"H—how can you be certain?"

Higant smiled.

"Like I said ... I heard your words in my mind."

CHAPTER FOURTEEN

The Fountain of the Dragon

King Frederick, having just finished attending to the business of those who'd needed an audience for the day, was returning to his private rooms behind the dais with a satisfied smile. The variety of ideas, problems, gifts, and countless other matters brought before him by his citizens and outlanders alike never ceased to interest him. He truly enjoyed meeting the people and aiding them where he could. Most of his advisors grumped at him when he spent too much time answering one 'supplicant' or addressing their issues, as he often got to talking to them, wanting to know what they did, where they were from, and so much more. It slowed down the proceedings, but it was an enjoyable experience for Frederick, and one he felt was necessary in order to properly attend to his people's needs.

Entering his office, he went to sit in one of the chairs surrounding the small table. He slumped down in it, tired after a particularly long day of audiences. Looking out at the table, he remembered the night that Vandrune, Higant, Portlief, and his private guards had listened to The Luminary and the details of the prophecy. It seemed like a lifetime ago that Higant had surprised them all with his knowledge on the intricacies of prophecy, and they'd set out looking for Marcus. In truth, it had only been a few days, and already, life in the castle had all but returned to normal.

Once word of his cousin Baron Vandeguild's untimely demise got out, the people had held a lovely ceremony for him, celebrating his life in earnest. Though he'd been a man renowned for enjoying his drink and the pleasures of the flesh, he was equally well known for his generosity and cheerful disposition. Many people turned out to his celebration to remember the wonderful person he was, and none were more grateful to him than Frederick himself. As his junior, Frederick had spoken with him regularly about the world around him and the inner workings of politics as he was preparing to rule, and not once had the baron expressed any disdain about his younger relative rising to a higher station. The king was grateful for his cousin's unselfish insights, and would miss him dearly.

Thinking back on that day, he wondered what had become of Vandrune and Higant. He hadn't heard anything since they'd parted ways, and that in itself was not out of character for Vandrune, but under the circumstances, it seemed strange not to have heard anything.

He rose from his chair, leaving behind the ceremonial robes that were part of the pomp and ceremony of the receptions and then headed out the door, moving off down the hall to take a stroll through the castle. He was so accustomed to William and Katarg being around that he hadn't even noticed they'd fallen into step a few feet behind him. The giveaway had been the subtle sound of their weapons bumping against their waist as they walked.

Both soldiers were seasoned battle agents, each with personalities soft and tender enough that to see them leap to the defence of the king and utterly destroy all those who might pose a threat to him was a sight to behold.

Of course, to date, they'd never really had to … but it was precisely because of that tenderness and love for their king that they were always on alert, and continued to further their training at every opportunity.

By now, they had made their way down the formal stairs and towards the guest wing in which Vandrune resided. The main hall was on the other side of the castle, so walking there meant taking a number of paths and turns, but the journey was made pleasant by the ability to look upon the amazing ceilings, glasswork, and fountains that the castle had accumulated over many generations.

Whenever Frederick made his way through the castle, he always stopped to look up at the glass ceiling of the Dome of Lillifor, projecting the map of the whole of Neleuwan upon the ground below. The fact that its architects had managed to position the glass in such a way that it captured the light from the sun and reflected the image of the land so accurately was truly amazing to Frederick, and whenever he came upon it, he wished he had more chances to do so.

Slowly, he moved on from the dome, the sun having started to descend and the map moving beyond the reach of the display as the light diminished. Thankfully, the wonders of the castle were far from over.

He soon came upon the one fountain that had fascinated him all his life: the Fountain of The Dragon. In the oldest texts he'd studied on the area, and in conversation with scholars of history, they'd all referred to this fountain as one that had been built at the same time as the castle … and yet, something about it felt *older,* different to the others somehow. It wouldn't have surprised him if the castle had been built for the fountain, rather than the other way around.

Today, more than ever before, it captured his attention.

Frederick asked William and Katarg to keep watch. He wanted a moment alone with the fountain. Not one to disobey an order, however odd it might be, they stood guard at each of the entrances to the courtyard.

Frederick walked slowly over to the bench that sat opposite the fountain. He sat down and closed his eyes, listening to the running of the water. It was so tranquil and calming that soon, all the tension and frustration and tiredness left his body, and what was left was a quiet centre.

He sat there for a long while, just enjoying the solitude.

The sound of the running water was so relaxing and peaceful that he felt totally at ease, surrendering his awareness of his surroundings. He felt like he was floating, as if being swept away on its gentle flow to a more serene place.

In his meditation, the water took him on a journey through the fountain and around the back, through an opening and inside the fountain itself. It was as if he *was* the water, swirling through the intricate pipes that worked to bring it back to the top and let it flow outward again so it could start its journey over. It was exhilarating … and almost too real.

Frederick travelled through the system of pipes a number of times, and each time it felt *nearly* the same … but there was something about that slight difference that nagged at him, like it was calling for his attention. As he continued to repeat his journey, he swore he could hear a voice off in the distance, though he couldn't quite make it out what it was saying.

Every time he went through the pipes, he would hear a little more of the voice, clearer and getting closer. It felt like he'd gone through the pipes hundreds of times, yet he still felt calm, and in no way in danger. He just needed to focus on the voice.

Finally, he started to make out words—faintly at first, but he simply continued on his journey until he could hear them all with absolute clarity.

His eyes opened, and he felt the world around him close back in. He could see the Fountain of The Dragon again, and the words were etched into his brain. Somehow, he knew exactly what they were for and why they were important, as if their meaning had been sent along with them from the beyond. Carried along with the words had been a series of images, telling the story of a time long past.

He stood slowly and walked towards to the fountain. He'd looked upon it so many times in his life, but only now was he really seeing it for the first time. The dragon loomed over the man with his weapons at his side, as if resigned to be burned by the fire bellowing from the dragon's mouth ... but even before his meditation, Frederick had felt that the man exuded too much strength and composure for that. It was clearer to him now than ever that the dragon was in fact protecting the man, and the man was bowing his head to the dragon in reverence. It was not hostility between them, but trust, and mutual respect.

And then, there was the rune at the foot of the man, now glowing just below the surface of the water. He'd never noticed it before, but now it glowed an iridescent blue, like it had been sent from the spirit world itself.

"Home Guard," Frederick called instinctively.

The words had barely passed his lips before Commander Kai appeared out of the mist.

"At your command," said the man, devoid of emotion.

"Commander ... look into the fountain before me and tell me what you see."

The commander followed the king's eyes and froze.

"I see ... home," he said, almost talking to himself. "It is my home, sire."

It was as he'd suspected.

"Commander Kai, I know this might be a difficult question to answer, and I thank you for your honesty in advance. Could you explain what you mean by home?"

The commander pursed his lips.

"I believe you are aware we were once given a choice, my lord. The choice I made was to remain with my family, no matter the cost."

The king did not waver. "Your family, Commander. How long ago did they move on to the spirit world?"

The commander's eyes were fixed upon the rune.

"Eighty-nine years, seventeen days, and three months ago, sire."

"Commander, how many others in the Ku-Da-Ru are like you?" King Frederick asked.

"All of them, milord. We chose to serve this kingdom, to make sure that it does not fall. In doing so, we had a good many years of watching over our loved ones ... and continue to stand vigil even after they move beyond."

At that, an almost imperceptible emotion came through on Commander Kai's face.

"Commander," King Frederick said calmly, "would you bring your men and women before me, here and now? All of them, please. As they leave, please have them appear to the regular soldiers, and ask them to take up posts where they would normally hold station until further notice."

"We will return within the hour," the commander stated.

While the king waited for his return, he moved towards the opening where he'd left William and Katarg.

"I need you both to do something for me," he said. "Head out of this hall and stand guard at the entrance to the building. After that, I need you to bar the door, and let no one in or out. I know this goes against everything I've ever asked of you both, but it is imperative that no one come near here in the coming hours."

In unison, both William and Katarg said, "What about you, sire?"

"I will be here. This is my request, and it is on my authority. Do not worry—I will have the entirety of the Ku-Da-Ru guard with me."

They nodded their agreement, if somewhat reluctantly, and headed for the door.

Frederick took a deep breath and exhaled. This was not at all how he'd expected this day would end, but if things were truly as they seemed, there was nothing for it.

The king sat back down on the bench and waited for Commander Kai to return. It seemed it had taken a while for him to gather all his men, but return they all did, and the large hall was soon accommodating the full company, a hundred-plus strong.

Frederick stood up on the bench and addressed the group.

"I asked Commander Kai to look upon the rune etched into this fountain, and he called it 'home,'" said the king. "Am I right to assume you would all say the same?"

A ripple of acknowledgment went through the group. Frederick braced himself.

"Tonight, I received a message, which I now know came from the spirit world. The rune at the foot of the soldier is forged of ancient magic, known only to those long gone from this land. It glows before us now to tell us that change is upon our world."

He paused for a moment.

"This rune is your home ... and I have been tasked with getting you home."

Frederick could feel the change in the room. For a group thought to be incapable of expressing emotion, there was a clear message of hope written upon their faces.

"I want to say thank you," he said finally. "You chose to stay when death was upon you, and have served far beyond that which was expected. Now is the time to become that which you were always destined to be—to rest, and to return to your loved ones. *When the rune flares and the spirit calls, send them home.*"

As he finished reciting the words given to him by the old mage all those days ago, the rune flared, and its iridescent blue shone so brightly that the light was blinding. The Ku-Da-Ru moved slowly towards it, losing their shape and being consumed by the light. Shielding his eyes from the intense light, though Frederick could not see, he knew all too well that they were returning home.

Finally, the light dimmed to a point that he could take away his arm, and he found just one person remaining in the courtyard. It was Commander Kai—no longer a commander, but simply Kai, the rail-thin boy he'd been before making his choice. He smiled broadly up at Frederick and reached out to take his hand, guiding him down from the bench.

"Thank you, Frederick," said Kai. "You have fulfilled the prophecy, and reunited us with our loved ones. Our time is over now ... but yours has only just begun. I've been sent back with a message: it is time for you to do something greater than yourself."

Though a little nervous, Frederick stood firm.

"What must I do?"

"Upon this fountain lie many unique items. Some of them are known to the world, and are already upon it. Others are yet to find their right time. In response to the trouble upon your lands, the Bands of Awe have awakened, and are now free of the stone. When the eyes flare, the Bands will unlock the knowledge in the barred mind. You know of what I speak ... though this is not their only purpose. In the Chamber of Life, the Bands of Awe must be given to the one who is twin to the prophecy foretold. Only then can he find the way forward."

Frederick clasped Kai's hand, his eyes expressing true love for the man and his men.

"Thank you for this. Please thank those who helped us to make sense of this, too."

Kai grasped Frederick's forearm with an echo of the strength he once held.

"You've been the best of us, Frederick. You showed it with the way you treated each and every one of us, despite our condition.

Know that this message was sent so that you, and those you charge with finding the twin cores, can have a fighting chance."

Releasing the king's arm, Kai turned to step into the water, but before he climbed in, he looked back to his king once more.

"Thank you again, Frederick. Know too that we are at peace. As a result, however, your kingdom lies unprotected ... but fret not, for your realm will soon have guardians again."

Having spoken his piece, the blue light flared a final time, and Kai was gone.

The hall dimmed, and the fountain's water continued to bubble and flow. As the light of the rune went out, Frederick noticed something in the water he hadn't noticed before.

He reached into the fountain and pulled out two sets of gold-coloured bands, each connected by an ornate chain, apparently having fallen from the arms of the praying soldier.

Frederick held them up to what remained of the light.

"The Bands of Awe," he marvelled. "An appropriate name for such an artefact."

He dropped the bands into his coat pocket, then strode for the door with purpose. Commander Kai's warning had not been lost on him.

Your kingdom lies unprotected.

CHAPTER FIFTEEN

PIP

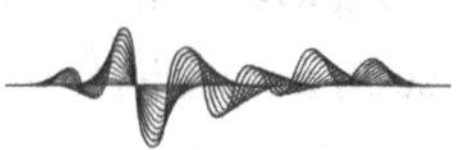

Kyruarth had ridden hard from Neleuwan through the hot-lands to get to the Pinnacle of Osciros, the highest point of the cliffs overlooking the town of Cantaloria and the Tonnecius Ocean. There, at its apex, was where his friend Pip made his home. It had been many months since he'd first visited the Cantalorian cliffs, but he was in great need of seeing the ocean and bathing in its blue waters again.

The tale of how the two had met several months ago was strange, to say the least.

After leaving Acoreq, Kyruarth had spent many years wandering across the land, seeing the countryside and living a new life free from the pressures of Acoreq and prophecy. He had spent the hundred and fifty years since he departed from Acoreq seeing all the sights that his solitude there had deprived him. For every one of those years, his soul was being uplifted from his travels through the world around him, and the peace within it. Before the day he met Pip, he hadn't had any further prophetic events.

When he first came across the small fishing town of Cantaloria, he'd stopped to take advantage of the beautiful shoreline and clear blue ocean. He'd quickly shed his footwear and placed his feet in those cool, refreshing waters.

Feeling almost like a normal citizen, he'd closed his eyes, felt the cool water on his feet, and lost himself in the sounds of the world around him. It had been such a wonderful experience …

… until his eyes burst open, and he was violently thrown back, hitting his head hard.

Dazed, lying flat on his back, Kyruarth looked up to see the cliffs above him. Standing far above him on the apex of the cliff was a person—a young man, standing on the cliffs looking out to sea, a glow emanating from his body.

The glow enveloped him, pulsing with an iridescent blue. It reminded Kyruarth of the bioluminescent plankton that came to life when waves crashed to the shore, something he'd once seen when visiting the Lunar Ranges. The young man looked down to Kyruarth where he lay and spoke to him, his voice as clear as if he'd stood mere feet from him.

"You must seek what can't be found, high above or underground. Between two times, the cores combine; reveal the place now lost to time."

The voice then drifted away, like a breeze had lifted the words from the boy's lips and blown them out to sea. Kyruarth felt his whole body relax … and then he lost consciousness.

It was late into the night when he awoke, but he was no longer on the beach. He opened his eyes to find himself in a bed, looking up at a roof.

He sat up slowly and looked about the room, wondering where he was and what had happened after his vision on the shoreline.

He worked his way to the edge of the bed and rested his feet on the ground, and as if on cue, an older man's voice came from across the room, heading his way.

"You might want to take it easy," he said. "Hit your head pretty hard, you did."

As the man made it to the bedside, he placed upon the bed some fresh clothes, then proceeded to open the curtains and let in some morning light. There was food on a small table at the end of the bed, and a couple of chairs set in a nook on the far wall.

"The name's Pip. Found you out cold on the beach down by the shore," he explained as he was fussing with the curtains. "Saw you as I came into the harbour to moor my boat. I'm a bit nosey, I'll admit, but I hadn't seen you move in a good while, and I couldn't imagine you'd be catching sunrays that late in the day. Thought I'd investigate, and good thing I did! You had plenty of blood caked on your head where the rock had got you, but after a good clean, I patched you up nice and proper. Looks like a good night's rest has done you good, too."

When no response was forthcoming, Pip turned around and saw that the stranger had his eyes fixed upon him.

"What's your name then, stranger?" he said, going back to his fussing, not particularly concerned by the stare.

Kyruarth had seen many things on his travels, and had learned better than to trust that a situation was exactly as it appeared. For all he knew, it was this man who'd injured him in the first place. Still, he was not about to let his past experiences make him discourteous to a man who had, by all appearances, shown him much goodwill.

"I am Kyruarth," he said, kindness slowly coming into his voice. "Thank you for tending to me while I was unconscious."

"Well, as my mum used to say, 'Kindly deeds to those around, will soon return to flower your ground.'"

Pip recited the words in a way that suggested he'd said them a thousand times before.

Kyruarth smiled. He liked the man's whimsical attitude to life and people. Sensing he was a gentle soul, he determined he should be befriended as such.

Settling in, Kyruarth stood and turned his attention to the food, reaching for some of the smaller items on the plate. After eating a few morsels, he took a long drink of water from the jar on the table. It had been a long while since he'd eaten, and this small amount of food felt like a banquet.

After his mind and body were refreshed, he returned to Pip's side.

"I can't thank you enough for the kindness you've shown me," he said. "How might I repay you?"

"No need for that, my friend. It's just nice to talk with another old soul such as yourself," Pip offered with a smile. "If you really must repay me, why not sit outside with me and enjoy the lovely breeze we have today?"

Kyruarth took him up on his offer, and ended up staying a few days, getting to know Pip quite well in that time. Of course, Kyruarth was a wanderer these days, and it wasn't long before he had to go and find his next adventure. At least, that's what he told Pip, for he didn't want to worry the man. In all truth, the vision he'd had by the shore was the first prophetic event he'd had in many, many years, and he wasn't sure how to proceed.

The vision felt personal somehow, not quite the same as his previous prophetic events ... and yet he knew that the boy and his words were meaningful nonetheless.

As he was leaving, Pip stopped him and handed him a bag. He looked inside and saw it contained a number of items, from food to waterskins and fresh clothes, none of which Kyruarth had asked for.

"This isn't necessary, Pip. I've already taken your lodgings and food for a number of days. You cared for me when I was vulnerable, and I'm truly grateful, but this is too much," said Kyruarth, trying to hand Pip back the bag.

"Nonsense. It's been wonderful to have another person to spend time and enjoy my home with. It's been many years since my wife passed, and I've not had much company since. You're the first who's been willing to hear an old man's stories and spend time appreciating the world around us for a good while. Think of it as a gift to make sure you're safe on your way, and can make it back here again someday."

Pip's words and smile were as impossible to refuse as the bag, and so Kyruarth graciously slung it over his shoulder.

"If the need take you," Pip continued, "you'll always be welcome here, no matter the day or hour. I'll always have a room for you."

Kyruarth welled with a great affection for the man, and reached out to hug him.

"You truly are a one of a kind, Pip," he said, pulling away and heading for the door.

Having returned to Cantaloria at last, Kyruarth slowed and dismounted his horse. Pip didn't have a stable, and considering he lived at the top of a cliff, that only seemed appropriate. Kyruarth walked into the small town and lodged his horse at the town stable, then headed towards the steep stair that led up the cliff to Pip's house. The weather had started to come in—possibly a follow-up to the storm that had been through earlier that afternoon. Kyruarth had seen it in the distance, and it had been quite the light show.

He slowly made his way up the steep stair that clung precariously to the side of the cliff, taking the occasional moment to drink in the spectacular view of the Tonnecius Ocean and the glistening waters that had started to settle after the storm. The last of the light was fading below the thinning clouds, reflecting off the waves as they crashed upon the shore.

As he often was, Kyruarth was astounded by the beauty of the world they lived in. His journeys had taken him all across the land, and he'd found that all of it was precious and hopeful, full of life of all shapes and sizes.

Of course, since the prophetic vision he'd had with the boy on this very cliff, he'd had several more of them, and their dark tidings had made him fear for the land. He only hoped that his visit to the king of Neleuwan would bear fruit, and that the young monarch would figure out what he needed to do.

King Frederick aside, Kyruarth himself was still not quite sure of his own role in the vision he'd had about the glowing boy. He hadn't been able to determine a time for the occurrence of the prophetic event, which was both unusual and unsettling.

He pushed it from his mind and continued up the stairs. As the stair ascended and got closer to the summit, the path moved further inland, away from the cliff's edge. It finally came out upon a small road that ran across the top of the cliff and away to the east. Pip's house was just up ahead, and down a small lane that moved back towards the edge of the cliff. Looking over the town and the beach below on a clear day, one could see a long way out over the ocean from Pip's abode.

The view aside, it would be wonderful to see his friend again. He had so enjoyed his last visit, and how they'd connected over their talks, their stories, and their love of the land. Coming to Pip's would afford him exactly the rest he needed, and his friend, he was sure, had many more stories to share.

As Pip's abode came into view, Kyruarth saw the light coming from the window at the front of the small house where the kitchen resided.

With a smile, he headed up onto the small porch and knocked.

CHAPTER SIXTEEN

HEALING

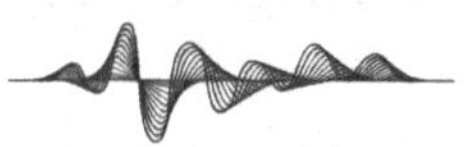

The door pulled open, and there standing in front of Kyruarth was Pip, looking a little dishevelled. A look of surprise came across Pip's face.

"Hello, my friend," said Kyruarth. "Sorry to call upon you so late in the day. I hope I'm still welcome in your home?"

The surprise faded from Pip's face, and was replaced by alarm.

"Kyruarth, thank the gods you're here. Come with me. I need your help."

In moments, Pip was rushing towards the back of the house. It was not quite how Kyruarth had anticipated the conversation playing out, but he did as his friend had asked. Entering the kitchen and dropping the bag Pip had given him all those months ago upon the table, he moved passed it and through a door at the back of the room. Turning right down the hall, he followed Pip left and into 'the back room', as his former host had called it.

Entering the room, he stopped short. There on the bed was a young man, heavily lacerated and unconscious. Even more unsettling than the boy's wounds was his face.

It was the boy Kyruarth had seen atop the cliff in his vision.

Pip, who'd already made it to the bedside, looked beside him, expecting Kyruarth to have followed. Confused, he turned to find him still standing in the doorway, staring.

"Kyruarth, are you coming?" Pip asked, ushering him towards the bed.

"Y—yes, of course," Kyruarth said, shaking himself from his thoughts. "What happened here, Pip?"

"There was a truant calling not far from here," he said. "The boy appeared where the lightning hit the ground."

For the second time in as many moments, Kyruarth stopped dead in his tracks.

"Did you say a truant calling?"

"Yes, near the old ruins, over the rise of the next hill. The ruin had been undisturbed for decades, but earlier tonight, there were a number of people in a circle using the chant of calling," said Pip, having relaxed significantly in the presence of his friend. "Lightning struck the circle many times, but one of the strikes went astray. Where it landed, I found him in its place. He was somehow thrown clear of the calling, and the force of the strike had sent him through the brush, causing a number of injuries. I was just about to head to the town to get the healer when you arrived."

Kyruarth knew that Pip had been around a while, but few men were around long enough to know what a truant calling was, and the intricacy of his knowledge of the subject suggested he'd known more than he'd let on when he was last here. For now though, the focus had to be on the health of this mysterious boy.

"Tell me what you know of his injuries," said Kyruarth, removing his travelling coat and throwing it across the chair.

"A bump to the head, and a number of deep cuts across his face and legs. There's also a contusion on his back that's starting to show dark blood under the skin, and his breathing is rapid and shallow."

Kyruarth listened intently, though it was difficult to fully push Pip's earlier comments out of his mind.

"Roll him over and let me see his back," he said. "We need to get him out of these clothes so we can assess him properly."

As they manoeuvred the boy onto his back and removed his shirt, Kyruarth could see the extent of the contusion and the flush of blood. He also found an unseen lower rib fracture, which might explain the shallow breathing, introducing the concern that his lungs may be filling with blood. Once they had his pants removed, maintaining his dignity with a sheet, they saw that he did indeed have a number of cuts. The worst of the deep cuts were on his face, along with the one accompanying the contusion on the back of his head and a cut deep on his right arm, stoppered by whatever dirt the boy had rolled in when he'd hit the ground.

Pip set up some water and cloths by the bed while Kyruarth knelt on the bed next to the boy, placing one hand on top of his head and the other over his heart. He closed his eyes and found the centre of his mind, then projected his energy outward through the boy, back and forth from one hand to the other. This allowed him to map the nerves and the electrical impulses throughout the boy's muscles and inner body. In his mind's eye, he now had a good picture of the landscape of the boy's internals, and could see the injuries with great detail.

He started at the top of the boy's head and focused on the contusion, working it with his energy, sending it across the vessels to help promote healing. This type of work took a lot of energy, even though Kyruarth was well seasoned in the ways of the mage. Nonetheless, he was an expert, and knew how to conserve, recoup, convey, and supplant the energy between the boy and himself.

Once the contusion had been repaired using his energy and the triggers of the boy's own bodily systems, Kyruarth then moved to the chest. He would normally have gone to sort out the broken rib and his breathing first, but after assessing the boy in depth, he'd found that the breathing was sustaining the young boy well enough to keep him alive, while the head injury had been fast developing into a greater concern. It was something he'd seen time and time again in healers who were only able to look from the outside—they only got half the picture, and by necessity, some of what they did was guesswork. With his way, he was able to see all the facets of an injury, and had greater insight into what was the most immediate threat.

In a way, it was an approach he took into all aspects of his life. To those without full visibility or understanding of his actions, they often appeared irrational, strange, and at times totally backwards. Of course, that was never the case. They were always measured, well thought out, and considerate of the circumstances.

Once he moved to the chest, he went to work helping to repair the rib and rectify the blush of blood at his back. After that was resolved, he moved to the facial lacerations, repeating the same process of imbuing them with his energy and stimulating the boy's natural defences. With satisfaction, he recognised that in time, there would be no scarring at all.

Finally, he sent his energy all throughout the young man's body, giving his entire system a kick to help him sleep and maintain his healing into the night. Kyruarth then receded from him, slowly cutting his connection and removing his hands.

He knelt back on his haunches and took a deep breath, trying to clear his mind and bring his focus back to the world around him.

As he opened his eyes, he noticed that dawn was fast approaching. Out over the ocean, the sun was starting to reflect off the waves below. He smiled broadly. This was the view he'd come to see. Slowly, he moved back off the bed and walked to the chair where he'd thrown his coat and then flopped down onto it, exhausted from the effort of the healing, but happy to have found the boy from his vision.

Pip came to sit in the opposite armchair. He had placed some food and tea on the table whilst Kyruarth had been working, knowing that Kyruarth would need replenishing when he was done.

"Did you repair all his ailments?" Pip asked, his concern for the boy evident.

"He's repaired on the inside. It's up to him when he decides to wake," said Kyruarth, leaning forward and taking some of the morsels and the cup of tea.

As he ate and drank, he felt his energy returning faster than expected.

"What tea is this?" he asked of Pip. "Its restorative properties are spectacular."

"Mage's Tea," Pip said with a smirk on his face.

If Kyruarth's interest hadn't been piqued before, it certainly was now. Only mages were taught the secrets of the tea, and Pip was no mage.

"Alright then, my friend. Out with it. How is it you know what a truant calling looks like, and are able to prepare Mage's Tea?"

Having come to trust the man, Kyruarth was not concerned about the answer to his questions—he was just extremely curious as to how this seemingly average older man, a fisherman in a small town, knew so much about mage's secrets and long-lost history.

"Do you want the short answer, or shall I tell you a story?" Pip said playfully.

"It'll take some time for my energy to return, so I do believe a story is in order," said Kyruarth, settling back into his chair.

"Well then, where to begin! If you hadn't guessed, I wasn't always a fisherman," Pip said mischievously. "I was raised in a place called Kelenex, in the Guardian Valley. It was a wide, grassy, and forested place, but the temperature did not rise above freezing most of the time. It rarely snowed, but it was always cold from the air blowing down off the peaks of the nearby Wyvern Mountains. I lived there with my mother and father till I came of age. Wouldn't have been any older than this lad here," he said, pointing to the boy on the bed.

"My parents believed it was never too early to learn, and that learning ought to be broader than the basics. There's more to life than staying alive, they'd say. They taught me the history of the lands of Kelenex, but they also taught me history as they knew it from the stories of old—stories from well before their time. I was like a sponge, too. I locked it all away in my mind, hoping that one day it would be useful.

"Of course, history was not the only thing they taught me. They also taught me how to look after myself, how to survive, and how to provide for myself and my future family. Those were some of the happiest days of my life. Loved my parents with all my heart, I did," Pip said, looking off into the distance across the ocean beyond his open door. "When I did come of age, I ventured out into the world and, with my parents' blessing, went to find my place in it. I tried many different things: soldiering, crafting, serving, helping ... but none of it really felt right. All good learning, of course, but not the right fit for me.

"So one night, after working all day in the field on a ranch I'd been a farmhand for, I ventured back into the town and headed to the local establishment for some dinner and refreshments. I moved around a lot, see, and I didn't have many friends as a result. I'd usually eat alone, then return to my lodgings, and that was it. That would go on for a while before I realised it was time to move on ... and on that evening, in that tavern, I was deciding where I should go next, ready to leave that very night."

"The place was called The Hugarband, and the barman, Tybith, got me situated in one of the tables at the back. The cook delivered one of his best meals and a pint of mead. It was a wonderful meal.

Helped me think of where to go to next, as it happens. In hindsight, I can't even remember where that was," he said, smiling wistfully.

"It didn't take long for the place to fill up, as most farmers and farmhands returned to The Hugarband for their end-of-day meal. Started to get quite loud in the room, and I was about ready to move on anyway. A number of meads later, I started to pull on my coat and headed for the door, ready to leave town for the last time. Only made it a single step before I saw a beautiful young lady making her way through the mass of people towards me. She was so beautiful, I stopped and caught my breath. While I was standing there entranced, she happened to trip over someone's boots, knocking me back onto my chair and falling back with me.

"The minute our eyes met, I knew I couldn't leave until I'd found out her name. Didn't realise at the time that my world was about to change. It was like someone had turned down the volume of everyone else around us, and we were the only ones in the room," said Pip, looking his companion in the eye. "Do you know what I mean, Kyruarth?"

Kyruarth gave a slight smile, nodding in recognition.

"In that moment, I remembered a story my parents had told me when I was young. I'd asked them what it was like when love hit your heart, and they'd said, 'The world slows down, your heart picks up its beatin', and you see into your true love's soul.'" A smile came across his face. "That's exactly what I felt. She was a star in the deep dark night, and she lit up my life from that moment on. We spent many hours talking and getting to know each other that night. Turned out she was a drifter too, going from place to place and helping people with their troubles.

"So, I became her support. I became her guard. I became her everything. All my life, I'd been searching for the one thing that would fulfill my life ... and there it was, right in front of me. It wasn't a job, or a purpose, or even a service to others. It was the love of my life."

Kyruarth, while moved by his friend's tale, found there was still a piece missing—something that just wasn't adding up.

"Not to whisk you away from her embrace, my friend ... but are you saying you learned about truant callings from your parents' stories?"

"No," Pip affirmed. "They taught me many things, but they never spoke of the truants. I may be old, and they were even older, but that's the stuff of history."

Taking this to mean Pip's story was not quite over, he gestured for him to continue.

"Ally was her name. The most beautiful name ever to touch these lips," said Pip. "She was my ray of sunshine. I was utterly smitten, and it wasn't until a number of weeks went by and we'd travelled all over that I acknowledged something wasn't right. She could do the most amazing things, well beyond my comprehension ... and whenever I asked her about them, she wouldn't give me the truth. Not all of it, anyway. When you love someone as I loved her, you can just tell. But one day, that all changed.

"We were riding to the next place along a back road to somewhere—the name escapes me, and is really unimportant. We came across a wagon that had lost its load and rolled down an embankment. There was a family on the road waving us down to stop and help lift the wagon, which had pinned their mother in the collision. There were a number of them, but not all of them had come out unscathed, and there weren't enough hands to lift the wagon. Of course, we stopped and ran down to the wagon to help.

"So, we coordinated the people who were uninjured and lifted the corners of the wagon she was caught under. The wagon had fallen at an awkward angle, and some of the load was still in place, so it was heavy to lift, but we got her out nonetheless. Still, she was in bad shape. We didn't think she was going to make it. And that's when she did it," said Pip. "Once the mother was free, Ally did something that even to this day mesmerises me, even just to remember. She laid her hands on the mother's head and her other hand on the lady's heart, just like you did tonight ... but unlike you, she started to glow a shimmering blue, not unlike the plankton in the waves at certain times of the year."

That was exactly how he'd conceptualised the glow he'd seen from the boy lying on the bed behind him.

That was not a coincidence, but a sign.

"Please, go on," Kyruarth indicated with a hand.

"When she lit up like that, everyone around her stepped back. The glow that surrounded her slowly enveloped the injured woman and we stood, watching it ebb and flow in intensity around them both. A matter of minutes passed before the glow disappeared, and Ally opened her eyes. She looked down at the woman, and they both stood up as if nothing had happened. Every last one of the injuries the woman had sustained was gone. She was whole again, and free to move about as she'd always done.

"The people who'd surrounded the scene were amazed at what had happened. Ally then tended to the injuries of the others in a similar way, but no blue glow was seen after that first time. They all thanked Ally for everything she'd done, and we went on our way. It wasn't until we stopped for the day by a Walloway pine and set up camp that we finally discussed the events of the day.

"Figuring it was time she explained herself, she told me she was a mage, but unlike any other. She was descended from a line of mages known as the Guardian Accord. Of course, I had no idea what that was, but I drank in every word. She explained that her bloodline had a task it must fulfil in the future, and so it must endure—must pass on its knowledge so that when the time comes, its descendants will be ready to do what they must. If the line was lost or broken, the future would be in jeopardy.

"In that moment, I selfishly thought of what that might mean for us ... or for me, really. I asked her, 'Am I worthy of your love? To be part of your future? Or does your duty to your bloodline preclude me from loving you the way that I do?' She just smiled and said she had been travelling for many years, searching for something ... and hadn't known what it was until she fell into my arms that night. I was her centre, her beating heart ... her love. She chose me to be the one for her, if I would have her. It was everything I had felt for her."

A tear started to fall down Pip's cheek as he leaned forward to pick up his tea. He took a sip and Kyruarth slowly leant back in his chair, regarding Pip gently.

"I loved her more than all the fish in the sea. I do so miss her," Pip said, his eyes shedding more tears. He looked at Kyruarth and smiled. "Memories of an old man."

"Memories of the one you loved," Kyruarth said quite tenderly.

Pip nodded shakily.

"And so, we married ... found our place here on the cliffs over-looking the ocean. It was a view that helped to lift our hearts no matter what was going on." Taking a long, slow breath, he smiled. "You asked how I knew about the truant calling. Ally told me more than enough about things from before—things intended for the inheritor of the Guardian Accord's will. She told me many things I'd had no idea had occurred in history, or the telling of which had been misconstrued over time. She also told me of the powers of the Mage's Tea, includ-ing how to make it, what goes in it, and how to get the ingredients right. As you can see, I eventually perfected it, and now I can make it in my sleep. And ... as I'm sure you've gathered, I lost Ally a number of years ago now."

Kyruarth carefully placed his tea on the table, trying to work out how to proceed respectfully.

"Do you mind if I ask a personal question?"

"Of course," said Pip in that fatherly tone Kyruarth had become familiar with.

"Did you have any children?"

"A little girl," he said, smiling at the memory. "She was as beautiful as her mother, and twice as bright … having picked up a thing or two from me, of course. She was … lost. She was no older than five summers when Ally passed, and she took it very hard. I tried my best to be the mother *and* the father, but she had a connection with her mother that I just couldn't recreate. I think some of that had to do with the Guardian Accord."

"Lost, Pip?" said Kyruarth.

Pip sighed. "We were down in the town, getting some food for our dinner that night. Somehow, we got separated in the bustle of all the people, and I lost sight of her. I searched through the town and the surrounding lands, and as night fell with no sign of her, I was heartbroken. The next morning, the townsfolk came together to search, and search we did—but for days, weeks, years, I could find no trace of her. No footprints, no sightings … nothing.

"I searched until my bones grew old, and I could search no more. One day, I simply had to accept that no matter what I did, I … I would never see her again. She was lost to me, and I didn't know how to find her. My little girl, and the only connection left that I had to Ally … lost."

Tears formed in his already red eyes.

Kyruarth's heart ached for the man.

"I'm deeply sorry for your loss, Pip."

"It's been many a year since I last dredged up those memories, and still they continue to sting. I only hope she's still out there somewhere, and that wherever she is, she's happy," said Pip, sorrow in his voice.

After a moment more, Pip shook his head gently, then wiped his eyes.

"Thank you for listening to my ramblings, my friend. It truly is great to see you again. It occurs to me now that I still haven't asked why you've returned."

Kyruarth smiled. "Truth be told, I was on my way here to spend some time with my friend, and regale him with tales of my latest adventures. Unfortunately, it would seem that the fates have brought me back here for a different purpose. You see that boy there is the same one I saw in my vision the last time I was here ... and the fact that he arrived shortly before I did, tells me that what I saw that night is upon us.

"There's also the matter of the story you just told. I've heard about the Guardian Accord in passing, but never truly believed it was real. If I'm correct, then this young man is part of that accord, whether he's aware of it or not."

Without a word, Pip stood up, walked out the door, and out into the hall, heading into the first bedroom. Moments later, he returned with a small pebble affixed to a strap of leather like a necklace, no bigger than his fingernail. Eyes fixed upon the keepsake, he sat back down.

"My wife wore this around her neck for as long as I knew her," he said, then looked over at the boy. "It glowed a faint blue whenever she wore it, but it stopped glowing the day she died. It's been grey ever since."

Kyruarth's eyes lit up.

"You think if this young man possesses the power of the Guardian Accord, the stone may come to life, as it once did for Ally."

Pip nodded, and the two of them moved quickly to the bedside. He lowered the necklace onto the boy's chest, and as soon as it hit his skin, the little pebble started to glow an iridescent blue.

As confused as he was astounded, Pip looked up at Kyruarth.

"It seems he is indeed of the Accord ... but he's not my son. So whose son is he?"

THE LADIES TRUANT

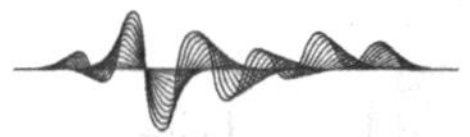

Crimson's body surged with ecstasy, a pleasure unlike any other. It was always a rush travelling this way. The use of another's essence made the already satisfying intake of great power from the earth feel like heaven when ignited. Fanton's journey, however, had not been quite as pleasurable, least of all in his landing, having hit the ground hard. As Crimson appeared in the ritual circle, he was still being gathered from the ground by the truant callers. In a flash of lightning, she arrived on steady feet in the open air, inhaling the scent of the ions expelled by the strike. The ion aroma mixed with the power she'd expended made her feel alive in a way that few things could.

Savouring the taste in the air, she opened her eyes slowly to find the Ladies Truant gathering around her.

"Lady Shen. Are preparations in order?" said Crimson, her tone indicating she expected nothing less than a yes.

Lady Shen bowed her head down and to the side.

"They are, my lady Crimson."

"Lady Hytern."

A woman towards the back of the group moved forward through the robed figures.

"Yes, my lady," she said, making the same bowing gesture.

"Where are our pursuers?"

"It's been a number of hours since you travelled, Lady Crimson. The king's retinue is heading back to the castle, while the mage and the squire continued on to Pillton in search of the boy. They appear to be preparing for a journey."

"Thank you, Lady Hytern," said Crimson, placing a hand on her cheek.

Standing tall, she addressed the gathering of robed women.

"Ladies Truant, tonight we advance the prophecy, power, and future we have all sought for. The taking of this boy is the key to breaking the seal that will bring forth our cascade across time."

At the mention of the boy, there was a change in the atmosphere.

Crimson turned her head from left to right, looking for Marcus. Unable to see him, she started to pace around the Ladies Truant, searching for where he'd landed.

She turned to Lady Autarious, who'd been near to where she'd landed not moments before, and thrust her face an inch away from hers.

"Where is he?!"

Lady Autarious's face blanched.

"He … did not come through with you, my lady. We assumed he'd been recovered."

Crimson's face went red. Her eyes changed colour to a hot, fiery orange, giving her a wicked, angry look. Her blade came up in her hand faster than the lightning had struck the ground and cut Lady Autarious across the throat, dropping her like a stone, her blood splashing across the earth.

Without missing a beat, she turned to Fanton, who was still trying to right himself. Crimson picked him clear off the ground and held him just inches from her face.

"You were supposed to hold on to him. You were supposed to keep him close. What happened?" The words dripped from her mouth like poison from a venomous snake.

"I had him, I—I swear!" Fanton stammered, feet dangling off the ground. "As we were transitioning, it was like we were struck by some force, knocking him off course."

Crimson dropped him and he hit the ground hard, but managed to roll, lessening the impact.

"Search the area. If he came through with us, then he must have arrived on one of the strikes. I want this whole ruin and surrounds covered before first light!"

The robed ladies quickly dispersed, looking in and around the bowl and the surrounding cliffs for any sign of Marcus.

Hours passed before Lady Forstant returned to the calling site, explaining that she'd found a strike mark on a nearby cliff and several patches of blood nearby, but there was no trail leading away from the area, and no sign of him anywhere near it.

Lady Shen appeared shortly after Forstant's return.

"My lady, the sun will soon crest the horizon. We must make haste and return to the Citadel to prepare for the next stage. The boy, if he truly made it through, has eluded us for the time being, but it is of little consequence. You have put the Blade in play, the Higant boy is on the move, and preparations for the Cascade are almost complete. All that remains is to locate the Chamber."

With a curt nod of assent, Crimson turned and headed to the east in the direction of the Citadel, towards the horses waiting above. The rest of the group fell into line.

Lady Shen was right, but nonetheless, Crimson was frustrated by the loss of Marcus. He was to be the bait that would draw in

Kyruarth and Higant, and ensure that the seal would be broken. She'd planned to kill him in Higant's presence, sending the boy into a fit of rage powerful enough to release that which was sealed away. At that moment, she would release the Cascade, sending all of his power and rage through the channels of time.

Thus, would the door be opened for the truants to reshape the world in their way ... and to bring back all that had been lost.

Even without Marcus, however, Higant and Kyruarth were all but sure to arrive to try to stop her. It may be enough to simply bluff that she'd killed Marcus, and it was entirely possible that he *had* died in the failed transition.

And then, Crimson had an epiphany.

She stopped her ascent up the sides of the bowl and turned to the group, who'd stopped as well at this sudden change in momentum.

"I know his frequency. He resonated when we made love." A sinister look came over her face. "We must hurry to the Citadel to perform the resonance rite. It seems we haven't lost our advantage after all."

The rest of the group hurried past her, heading to their horses and mounting before galloping away. Crimson, the last to remain, looked back down into the bowl, her eyes turning a bright ruby red.

"I will find you, my pet."

The wind picked up her coat as she turned, revealing her naked body in all its beauty. She mounted her horse and rode off at pace towards the eastern mountains and the Citadel within.

CHAPTER EIGHTEEN

COMING OF AGE

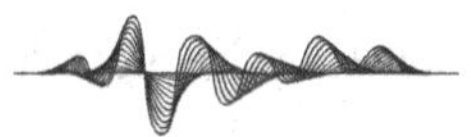

Before long, the Ladies Truant arrived back at the Citadel. The entry was hidden in a culvert within a ravine, carved into the side of a mountain deep in the mountain ranges of Thrish. They entered the large archway and ventured into a vast open chamber, large enough to hold an army ten thousand strong. Once inside, Crimson quickly dismissed the others and then walked to the far end of the chamber, where a smaller entrance leading to an upward slope would take her to the living chambers.

The Thrish Citadel had been carved out of the rock by masons of old, thousands of years before Crimson's time. It was from a past long forgotten, its original purpose lost to time. It could well have been an ancient temple, with its unusual symbology and carved statues appearing more frequently the further it delved into the mountain range. It was not the only one of its kind: there were many of them scattered about the land, and many of them had been repurposed as homes for the truants. Crimson's kind had lived in isolation for millennia, their birthright and practices considered taboo by all. Not for the first time in history, their flame was thought to have been extinguished ... but her parents, along with hundreds of others, had lived in secret, keeping the traditions of truants alive and hidden until they were thought forgotten to the annals of history.

On the contrary, they'd been working tirelessly to make sure their culture survived—and that those who'd persecuted them and denied their very existence were repaid in kind.

Crimson entered her chamber and removed her coat, revealing her slim, muscular, and tanned body. She walked to the water channel that flowed throughout the chamber, scooped some up, and let it splash upon her face, sending droplets running down her supple skin and across her body, proceeding to wash herself of all the dirt and grime of her travel.

Crimson had lived in the Citadel with the truants her entire life. Her parents had been influential truants who'd led the efforts to preserve their people, and she'd been destined to do the same. Only a few times over the years were the reclusive truants, having learned to be suspicious and wary of anyone, discovered for what they were.

Usually, those who learned their secret earned themselves a swift and sharp blade, ensuring that it died with them ... but in the case of Crimson's parents, their oppressors had got the better of them.

That morning, a scout had returned to the Citadel from their patrol of the mountain pass to report a wagon they'd spotted broken down on the side of the road, a number of travellers taking shelter within. It was the middle of winter, and a snowstorm was on the way. Doubtless, if no one went to assist them, they would all perish.

Advising caution, most of the senior truants voted in favour of abandoning the hapless travellers to their fate ... but Crimson's parents had always had kind hearts, and set out together to offer them aid, taking a wagon of their own and posing as fellow travellers on the road.

As the couple approached the wagon, they found men and women huddled together in the back of the wagon, shivering from the cold. They gave them some warm drinks to fight off the chill, and used supplies they'd brought with them to help fix the wagon and get them back on the road.

Just as they'd had the wagon back on the road and were about to depart, out of nowhere, the surrounding trees lit up like the night, and two of the men from the wagon jumped off, standing as mages do when about to send energy into battle. The wagon came to be surrounded by a number more mages, their power gathered in their hands and at the ready.

Crimson's parents didn't understand—they hadn't used any of their powers while fixing the wagon, and had only sought to help those in need. Had the Citadel been compromised somehow? What could these mages want with them?

A single mage moved off the snowy slope towards them.

"Who are you, and what are you doing on a mountain in the dead of winter?" he said, stopping a number of feet away.

"We live in an isolated cabin not far from here," said Crimson's father. "We're low on rations, and are heading over the pass to resupply."

"With a snowstorm blowing in?" the mage said, taking an offensive stance. "If you truly lived up here, you'd know better. And besides, there are no cabins within a hundred miles of this place."

"Couldn't we say the same to you? We can show you to it if you like," said Crimson's mother, tinging her words with frequency energy, trying to influence his thoughts.

The mage looked at her strangely, apparently detecting something, though not quite sure what it was.

He shook his head, then narrowed his eyes.

"It seems the prophecy was true. Men—"

Crimson's father was the first to react. He moved so fast that the mage had no time to think before the blade hit him, dead in the centre of the chest. The second mage from the cart was about to send his power forth when the blade sliced his neck, severing an artery and painting the pristine white snow red. Now in full response, the surrounding mages all released their energy at Crimson's father, but he was moving too fast for any of them to land a hit. Still, he couldn't keep up the pace forever, and they were closing in on him with every release.

In the chaos of his onslaught, no one was paying any attention to Crimson's mother, which would prove to be a grave mistake. She'd started to chant in various resonances, releasing energy with every change in pitch. She was a well-trained senior truant, and had many years of experience—enough to know that up against this many mages, this would be her last stand.

Even in the thick of battle, she and her husband had managed to exchange a knowing glance. They could not allow themselves to fall here and let a single one of these mages live to lead others to their location, or to their beloved daughter.

Her resonance building, she fed it around all of the mages while her husband kept them distracted, creating a resonance bubble. Once connected and closed, she would trigger the explosion.

It didn't take long for her to complete the enclosure. Now, no one could run—not even her. Her husband, who'd already killed five of the mages, was starting to slow. The energy he'd drawn and consumed to move as deftly as he had had taken its toll, and the mage's barrages were starting to find their target.

Before detonating the energy within the resonance bubble, Crimson's mother sent a message to her daughter's frequency on the winds of resonance.

"Your father and I love you very much," she whispered. *"Live a full life, and never let anyone tell you you're not worthy of one."*

The Citadel below shook with the explosion of power. The

drawing of energy gathered from the soil beneath the snow left scars in the mountain that would never heal—a testament to the loss and love they felt in their final moments.

It took a number of hours before the rest of the truants at the Citadel were able to determine what had happened. Forced to inform Crimson that she was now an orphan, being only seven summers old, the senior truants tried to comfort her by telling her it had been an accident … but having heard her mother's message, and after hearing the whispers around the Citadel, she knew it had been no accident.

One day, she would seek revenge upon the mages, and the one who'd sent them.

Crimson spent years travelling the land, honing her skills and power to be ready for the day she met the one responsible for her parents' death, interrogating and cutting down every mage in her path. Eventually, she extracted a name from the last gasp of a mage: Kyruarth, the old prophet, who had prophesised of her parents at the pass long ago. The mages had been led there by his word to end the truant threat.

He was the enemy, and he would be made to pay tenfold.

Thus, she worked tirelessly to bring about the Ladies Truant, a group of elite female truants who had lost their loved ones to the mages. Utterly devoted to her cause, they would aid her in completing not only her revenge, but a total reset.

And in so doing, they would bring their families back to life.

Once clean, Crimson moved to the shelves and retrieved her favourite red dress. This was no ordinary dress. Wicked leather straps ran across the back, connecting to a revealing square-cut leather bodice in the front. The silken elements of the dress ran down to her mid-thigh and flared outward, revealing much of her shapely legs.

Her hands reached down to attach a scabbard to her waist, holding host to the wicked blade. As she placed it upon her hip, she felt a sense of power within herself surge.

It would not be long now. She would have her revenge upon the one who took her parents from her, and upon the world that had turned the truants to dust all those years ago.

The time of truants would rise again.

RETAINED

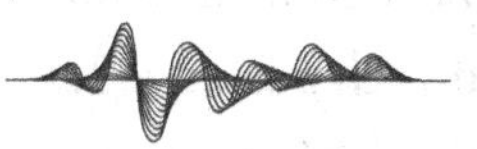

After Vandrune had received the location from Kyruarth, he and Higant had travelled long into the night and through to the early morning. Higant, having heard everything in his mind's eye, did not question the direction they were heading, and it seemed like he could even lead the way if it came to it. It was strange—word for word and image for image, Vandrune and Higant both recalled the same event, as though Higant had been present in that liminal space between the prophets when they'd communicated.

The only difference was that Higant had been able to identify the location, where Vandrune had not.

Concerned, Vandrune had questioned Higant extensively about what he'd seen, heard, and above all recalled after the event was done. Unlike his earlier brushes with the sealed knowledge, Higant had not fallen asleep afterward, and was able to recall it in detail almost a full day later.

Though Vandrune had decided not to trouble Higant with it, the way that things were unfolding was playing upon his mind. He was concerned about what might happen if Higant continued to pry at the seal that kept that mysterious knowledge in the depths of his mind at bay—what that might result in, or what unknown powers might be unleashed. He also feared that his own power may be influencing the boy. Was it possible that his communication ritual had affected Higant somehow? But how could a chant he'd performed thousands of times before have had such a strange result, connecting the boy to both the sender and recipient in such an intimate way?

This was becoming even more of a mystery than it had already seemed.

Shortly before day was about to break, Vandrune located a cave near the base of the cliffs they were travelling alongside of in the heat-filled valley, figuring it would be a good place to sleep and shelter Thunder and Blossom through the temperature of the day.

As they readied their camp, Vandrune ran through the same questions he'd asked Higant several times since learning the boy heard the details of his communication, and he gave the same answers once more.

"Why do you keep asking me these questions?" Higant asked, stopping partway through unrolling his bedroll.

"This is the first time you've recalled the details of a knowledge event many hours afterward," said Vandrune. "I was testing to see if you would forget, and if so, how long it would take. What do you suppose was different this time?"

Higant frowned.

"Could it have been your chanting? Perhaps the rhythm and the words somehow helped to contain the detail?" he suggested. "Or maybe I wasn't actually accessing the knowledge? After all, it was more like I came along for the ride than remembered something."

Musing over his words, Vandrune began to setting up a small fire to cook what sparse rations they had.

"I considered that the chanting may have had an impact ... but no matter how I try to explain it, that chant shouldn't have reached anyone other than the intended recipient. The latter is an interesting theory, but I can't imagine the event is unrelated to the power within you."

Now puzzling over the problem himself, Higant started towards the horses to give them water, brush their coats, and talk to them.

"Could it have been the heat? Maybe heat is a factor in remembering?" Higant asked while brushing Blossom, who was enjoying every minute of the attention. Thunder, on the other hand, was not impressed. He seemed to think that he should've been first, and was stamping his hooves to show his displeasure.

"I don't think so," said Vandrune. "We'd been in the heat for no longer than a day at that stage, and if anything, the heat would've lessened your ability to recall, not enhanced it."

Vandrune spoke his thoughts aloud, trying to make sure his thinking was sound. After a short pause, he nodded, shrugged, and went about the cooking.

Higant finished brushing Blossom and gave her a scratch under the chin, which she returned in kind with a gentle nudge him. Thunder appeared even more displeased by this, stamping a little harder to drive the point home.

Turning his attention to Thunder, Higant walked towards the beautiful beast and gave a mock bow, imitating one he might've given to a royal figure like Frederick.

"Apologies, Your Majesty, for taking so long to attend to your needs," he said theatrically. "May I brush your coat and scratch your chin?"

To Higant and Vandrune's awe, Thunder extended his right forelimb out in front of him, bent the other, and then dropped his head low.

Unmistakably, Thunder was bowing before him.

"I—I was just kidding around," Higant said to Thunder, looking back and forth between him and Vandrune. "Vandrune, why is he bowing?"

Thunder stayed there for a long moment before returning to his natural stance.

Vandrune, who'd just started to boil some of the remaining water from his skin, stood up and walked over to Higant to join him in appraising Thunder. The horse simply stood there, looking intently at Higant.

"Have you ever seen a horse do that before?" Higant asked.

"I've seen animals do a lot of strange things in my time," said Vandrune, "but that was more than strange. That was *regal*."

Vandrune just stared at Thunder, waiting for him to do something else.

Unsure how to proceed, Higant walked to Thunder's side and went to brush him ... but just as the brush was about to make contact, Thunder moved away from it and turned to face Higant. Higant tried again, and again Thunder moved away from the brush.

"What in the world is going on?"

Vandrune stroked his beard with consternation.

"I'm not sure either, Higant ... but could I ask you to bow to Blossom, too?" he said, watching Thunder return to the stance he'd taken after the bow.

At the sound of her name, Blossom walked up beside Thunder and took a strikingly similar stance.

"You want me to bow to Blossom now?" Higant said, looking to Vandrune as if he'd lost his mind. "I thought I was the one going crazy."

With a sigh, he walked around to the back of Vandrune to stand in front of Blossom. He bowed as low as he'd done the last time with Thunder, and to his surprise, Blossom didn't bow ... but she did lower herself to the ground, curling both of her forelegs underneath her before standing back up.

"Was that a *curtsy?*" Higant exclaimed.

"I believe it was," said Vandrune, a new look upon his face. "Perhaps you should try to brush her?"

Higant threw up his hands and walked to Blossom's side. Reaching out with the brush again, she too sidestepped his advance. Stranger still, Thunder moved with her in complete unison to avoid getting bumped into.

"This is getting weird," Higant said, a scrunched-up look on his face.

He moved back to stand alongside Vandrune, and the two-horse returned to its place in front of them.

"Higant, I will move back, and I want you to stand between them so they can both see you," said Vandrune. "Then, I want you to bow again—but this time, take it seriously. After that, I want you to ask them a question."

Higant looked up at Vandrune with an eyebrow raised.

"Trust me," Vandrune said with a smile.

"What do you want me to ask?" Higant said, and Vandrune whispered in his ear. Higant scrunched up his nose at the question, but proceeded nonetheless.

Following Vandrune's instructions, Higant said, "Thunder and Blossom, you've been so generous to take us on this long journey. You graciously accepted the new names we gave you, and have been wonderful companions. I have but one question for you. Do you think of me as your leader?"

Thunder and Blossom both stepped back and dropped their hindquarters, their forelegs remaining where they were. The image was reminiscent of a deep reverse bow, their heads dipping to a similar depth as Higant had with his bow. As they returned to their original position, they both gave a neigh that could only be interpreted as an affirmative answer to his question.

Surprised by the instant response, Higant took a step back. Vandrune, who was now smiling from ear to ear, had heard tell of stories from long ago about horsemasters—individuals with an innate dominion over horses. This was yet another mystery about Higant that Vandrune could not stitch together. Again, this was a skill thought lost to the centuries, and yet here they were, with each of their horses regarding Higant as their leader.

Vandrune relayed this information to Higant, and he was not sure how to react to the idea.

"I don't even ride that much," he said, turning to Vandrune.

Vandrune shrugged. "They don't seem to mind."

Resigning himself, Higant walked over to Thunder and patted his head, then scratched his chin. Both horses seemed to have returned to their normal behaviour—no bowing, and no stopping him from brushing them, either. Thunder leaned into the brush with as much enthusiasm as he usually did, if not more.

Eventually, Higant finished brushing and feeding his friends, then returned to sit on his bedroll. Vandrune had finished cooking their early morning 'dinner', and both of them were starting to feel the tiredness of the ride catch up with them. Shortly after their meal, they each lay down on the bedrolls and were fast asleep.

Higant especially had been exhausted. Almost as soon as his head rested on his bedroll, he was out. His dreams came and went, trying to make sense of the events of the day, but his subconscious mind could not unpack it.

As he drifted through the void of dreams, he slipped into something akin to a trance. There, he came across a noise. Hard to hear at first, it slowly grew in intensity and vibration. His mind started to clear the mess of thoughts around his dream until just one image was constant in his mind's eye: Marcus. His friend was standing there, unmoving, enveloped in a faint blue light. At the centre of his chest, a little blue pebble glowed brighter than any part of his body.

The noise continued to grow in strength and rhythm, and as Higant looked at Marcus, he could feel himself calling out to him, but his words were lost in the noise. Marcus slowly turned to face the source of the noise.

It was Neleuwan. Their home.

Higant's subconscious was hard at work. What did the noise represent? Why was it so loud, and why was Marcus glowing?

Before he was able to arrive at a single answer, Marcus turned back to Higant and looked intently at him, mouthing some words that were again lost to his ears.

Slowly, Marcus started to drift back to the location of the vibration and the noise. Faster and faster, he picked up speed until Higant could not see him anymore. All that remained in his vision was Castle Neleuwan, and the glowing pebble Marcus had in the centre of his chest. Soon, it came to rest at a location inside the castle, but the noise was so loud now that it hurt Higant's ears, consuming all of his attention. It was so loud that he had to hold his hands over his ears, his body reflexively curling into a ball in an effort to resist the sound.

All of a sudden, the noise stopped. Higant opened his eyes to find himself curled up in his bedroll. Dusk was upon them now, and Vandrune was sitting once again, looking at Higant intently, a look of concern upon his face.

"Tell me what you saw."

CHAPTER TWENTY

THE CITADEL

The Citadel was quiet. Echoes of insects filtered in through the air from out in the mountain range beyond the archway. The living quarters where Crimson had washed and changed her clothes were solitary, and devoid of any people.

The family of truants that resided there, if you could call it that, had worked together as a community since well before Crimson was born, surviving by staying out of history's way. Since the Lolariane War, in which the truants' numbers had dwindled to near extinction, those who were left had thought it important to let the world think they no longer existed—that their fanaticism was lost to the throes of time.

Instead, they had bided their time, waiting in the shadow of a world that had moved on. They found solace and safety in anonymity and isolation, growing in numbers and strength. The Citadels weren't just their home—they were their refuge, their shield against the terrible world beyond.

Crimson now sat on the cushions upon the central dais that made up the unusual-shaped room that served as a place to perform many rituals. The dais had steps that surrounded the main structure, and at every third step down and across was another place for someone to sit. The stairs curved like a bowl down and up the opposite walls, with similar seating areas within.

The deep red rock of the mountains, lit by the glow of lanterns that hung from metal brackets positioned around the chamber, gave a solemn glow to the place. Crimson surveyed the room, acknowledging those who sat in each of the alcoves, as well as those who sat on the stairs below her dais. Turning her thoughts inward, she sought the frequency she had connected with when she'd seduced Marcus back in Neleuwan for sport, revelling in the good fortune it had brought. A sinister look came across her face as she recalled the death of the baron, the pleasures she took from the young boy, and that she'd been able to make use of having attuned to his frequency at the height of his ecstasy.

She now started to look inward, resonating with the frequency she needed to find. She connected herself to the depths of the mountains, seeking the source of the earth's power, drawing it into her body and letting it flow through her cells and across her nerves. Guiding the power's course with her mind, she caused a vibration that was subtle at first, emanating through the air around her with increasing strength.

As she started to fill the air with the vibration, the first row of truants sitting around the dais did the same, connecting and adjusting to the frequency of the vibration. This type of connection took concentration and strength, both of which the Ladies Truant had been training for all their life. The process extended all around the room, row by row until the room itself felt like it was a beating heart, vibrating rhythmically, coursing through the earth.

Whatever this chamber and Citadel had originally been created for, it was clear that this room had been specifically designed to focus power, and to combine the efforts of many to achieve something greater. Today, that something was the resonance rite.

The room started to unify, and Crimson let her mind drift towards the frequency at which she was resonating. At first, she found in her mind's eye the ruins at which they'd arrived after the truant calling. It was here she started to trigger the first connection.

The bowl in which they'd landed began to vibrate, the small stones on the ground bouncing around as the power seeped through the ground from the chamber and into the bowl, even from hundreds of miles away.

No matter how many times she performed the rite, it always made her marvel at how the power and resonance could be used in this way.

Crimson released a small amount of the resonance to see if it reacted with the surrounding area. In her mind, she saw waves of frequencies bouncing around the bowl, looking to resonate with similar residual frequencies. As she expanded the resonance to a further and wider circle, she found the spot where Marcus had struck the earth. It was a number of days old now, but there was still a residual resonance that could be seen.

Now that she had a starting point, she brought herself back to the chamber and opened her eyes, looking around at the others.

"Prepare," she said simply.

The room's vibrations grew in intensity, ebbing and flowing with the frequency that Crimson now led, its rate and pace increasing. The truants sat silent and unmoving, but their clothes billowed in time with the rhythm of the vibrations.

Crimson once again closed her eyes. In the quiet centre of her mind, she felt each and every person around the room, then started to pull at the threads of their power, drawing them into her own. It was like a spider tugging on its web, not to catch a fly, but a person.

She felt her power grow with every thread she pulled, connecting to the others in the chamber and allowing the power they'd pulled from the earth to feed her own. The vibrations of the frequency grew and grew until there were no more threads to take. She knew well her maximum capacity for power, and the exact number of people in the room reflected this. Upon connecting to each of them, she let her power explode outward.

In the room itself, there was no visible change, but the power was amplified and projected out through a small pinhole channel located above her head in the centre of the chamber. It resonated up and out into the sky above, so powerful that it hit the lower atmosphere and reflected back across the land below. Once it came back down, it spread in all directions across the landscape, seeking the same frequency that it was vibrating at.

In Crimson's mind, she was free to see where it went. She moved towards the ruins and followed the changes in resonance from there. Gradually, she saw the light in her mind shift, moving to a small house upon a cliff above a coastal town. It glowed there for a moment, then moved down into the town into what looked like a harbour.

Either he had boarded a boat, or he was hiding out in the harbour. Resonance was often lost over water, whose subtle vibrations helped to obscure and disperse resonance vibrations.

Undeterred, she took herself back up to a height in her mind to look over the land once more, just in case he'd come ashore elsewhere. As she scanned the landscape in concentric circles around the harbour where she last found Marcus's resonance, her hope began to dwindle. If he'd sailed out into the open ocean, then he was lost to her.

The power starting to wane, and fatiguing from channelling the power, right before she was going to sever the rite, she caught sight of the resonance once again, this time in the sands far to the northwest, of all places. It was only a small collection of resonance ... but how had he arrived there from the ocean? And how had he moved so far in such a short time? It wasn't possible.

Noting the location in her mind, she slowly severed herself from the power she was drawing from the earth and returned to the chamber.

She opened her eyes and looked around the room. Her truant colleagues had passed out from the power required to feed the resonance rite, and Crimson was nearly as exhausted. Still, she'd been able to keep her mind and consciousness intact, and those who lay around her would soon return to themselves.

She couldn't make sense of it. How could Marcus have arrived there without leaving a track or trace of his movement? There were no ports in the hotlands regardless, surrounded by cliffs as it were, so arriving there after departing from a harbour didn't make sense.

Checking over each step in the process, she confirmed that they'd performed the ritual correctly, nodding that she had and assuring herself that what she'd seen was accurate.

As uncertain as the information was, she had to make a decision, and so decide she did. She and her Ladies Truant would ride back to Cantaloria to confirm Marcus's presence or departure, and if he was not there, then they would move south towards the resonance in the hotlands.

They would rest tonight, regain their strength, and ride out at first light.

In a matter of days, they would have their answers, and hopefully have Marcus back in their grasp, bringing them ever closer to breaking the seal on Higant's mind.

CHAPTER TWENTY-ONE

LOSS

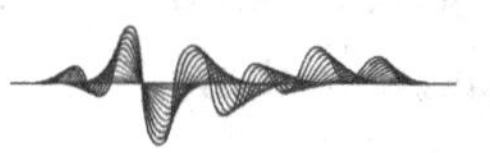

Frederick came around the corner and found William and Katarg standing guard, turning as he stepped into the light just outside the archway.

"Thank you, my friends. There is much to discuss—much to do, and not much time to do it. Send word to the stables that we need fresh horses ready to ride by daybreak, then join me in my office."

The king did not break his stride across the courtyard, and William and Katarg were pressed to keep up. Passing one of the guards stationed at the entrance to the great hall, Katarg paused to speak with the man in hushed tones, and he immediately took off at pace in the opposite direction and out into the night.

Frederick continued to move with purpose towards his office at the back of the dais, Katarg rejoining him and William just as they were heading through the tapestries at the rear of the throne. As the king entered his office, both William and Katarg instinctually took up their places guarding the door.

Frederick, who hadn't said a word since his last instruction, turned and said, "Both of you, enter and close the door."

The two of them shared a glance at the unusual request. At no time had they ever been requested to enter the room when the king was in his office, and certainly not without anyone else to guard the door. Their king had given them an order, but that order conflicted with their duty to protect him from harm. For a moment, they stood paralysed, uncertain which of their duties should take precedence.

"Sire," William said tentatively, "it would not be appropriate to leave the door unguarded while you are in your office alone. If you'd have us enter, might I suggest we call upon the Home Guard to take up station in our stead?"

"That is precisely why I need you to enter, gentlemen," said Frederick, his voice dropping to nothing more than a whisper. "The Home Guard have been relieved of duty."

The eyes of both William and Katarg went wide. They moved to speak, but Frederick raised a hand.

"The castle and kingdom are vulnerable," Frederick continued, a look of concern on his brow. "We need to discuss how we're going to change that."

With that, Frederick walked into his office and sat on the lounge off to the side of the room, reaching into his pocket and pulling out a blue stone while he waited for the guards to decide what they would do. They were discussing the matter, he could see, but couldn't hear what they were saying.

After a time, Katarg took up station at the door and William entered the office, closing the door as Frederick had requested. Frederick smiled at the commitment they had to his safety. He couldn't have asked for better protectors.

"Will Katarg not be joining us, William?" Frederick said, amused.

"Forgive us, sire, but we simply couldn't allow the room to remain unguarded," William said, his manner excessively formal. "We discussed the best course of action considering your ... comment, and this was the most we could agree to."

"At ease, William. Please, take a seat. I must tell you what has happened, and what I believe we must do to ensure continued protection for the people of Neleuwan. I would like your counsel."

William was humbled that Frederick wanted his opinion, but was also wondering why he, a mere guard, was being included in this discussion while the king's advisors were not. Why not Vandrune or Portlief?

Setting his misgivings aside, William sat down and placed his battle axe against the chair as he squeezed into it. His weapon was always within arm's reach, and he was always at the ready.

"You have my ear, sire."

"Tonight, the Fountain of the Dragon called to me," said Frederick. "I felt pulled to meditate by its waters, and as I did, I had a sort of vision that compelled me to release the Ku-Da-Ru from their service."

"I'm not sure I understand, my lord," William said, frowning as he spoke. "Though to be fair, the Home Guard have ever been a mystery to me."

"As they were to me before tonight," said Frederick, placing the blue stone on the table. "Allow me to tell you their story—a tale from when my great grandfather was king, so you can understand the gravity of what has occurred this night."

In a time when roving barbarians and lawlessness plagued the lands of Neleuwan, a powerful mage came to the castle at the king's request. The king asked this mage what could be done to protect the kingdom of Neleuwan—to secure it from outside influence and attack, now and into the future. The mage agreed to help the king, taking up chambers in the castle to study in search of a lasting solution.

For many moons, the mage read day and night, deep into ancient stories and accounts left by great thinkers of the past. Then, late one night, the king heard a knock at his door while reading in his study. Seeing the mage at his door, the king was hopeful that he'd chanced upon an answer.

"In none of the texts have I found any existing solution that would give you confidence in the protection of your kingdom," said the mage. "I have, however, had a new idea."

Despite this development, the mage did not appear enthusiastic.

"And what might that be?" asked the king, his interest piqued.

"Frustrated by my lack of progress, I took a stroll through the town to clear my head a number of days ago, and soon found myself by shore near the harbour," said the mage. "There, I came across a woman who was down on her luck, and decided to sit and speak with her for a while. After offering her some food and drink, I asked how she'd come to find herself there, and she explained that her husband had had an accident that had left him unable to work. She'd tried to keep them afloat in his stead, but struggled to make ends meet, and his health continued to deteriorate. Finally, naught but a few days ago, he succumbed to illness … and after that, she'd simply given up. They'd never had any children, and she saw no reason left for her to continue. I offered what coins I had, and while she was grateful, the light did not return to her eyes."

"A regrettable tale," the king said solemnly, "but how does it relate to the protection of the kingdom?"

"Whilst talking with the woman, I couldn't help but think of her husband. Faced with his own powerlessness, having to watch his wife work herself to the bone in his stead, it's a small wonder he fell ill. It was then I had the thought that death and infirmity, while tragic, are things that no one can stop—only delay … and thence came an idea that is not what I would call morally sound," the mage responded grimly, leaning forward to the king. "I can only imagine that, even on his deathbed, the husband would've given anything for a chance to regain his capacity and provide for his loved ones. What if we could've given him that chance?"

The king, who had leaned in to meet him, sat back with a look of confusion.

"Are you suggesting we put some sort of a stopper in death? Is such a thing even possible?"

"I believe I've come up with a way to do just that," said the mage, his eyes shining with intelligence and a strong conviction.

"What exactly are you proposing?" the king asked hesitantly.

"I will speak plainly. The ritual I've devised involves separating the spirit from the body, so that it may continue to serve after the body's death. To suggest we perform such a thing on a healthy individual would be heresy—but if we were to seek out those who are not long for this world and offer them a choice ..."

The king rose from his chair and started to pace the room.

"I'm not sure if this is madness or pure genius, but either way, I'm conflicted. Yes, they might be due to die, but the spirit is not something to be tampered with lightly. What would the process involve?"

"For better or worse, much of the spirit is inseparable from the body before death ... and so, in order to accomplish what I propose, parts of the spirit must be severed and left to die with the body. If my theory is correct, the spirit that is removed would retain its intellect, core functions, and form ... but would lose much, if not all, of its emotional capacity. In order to focus such an entity, they would have to be bound to refer to a specific person for instructions—in this case, the current monarch of Neleuwan. In exchange however, not only would they gain special traits and abilities, they would effectively be undying, and therefore able to continue to watch over and provide for their loved ones in defence of the realm.

"There's no denying the price they'd pay would be great … but between that and what befell that woman and her husband, it's difficult to say what's worse. Once we have a candidate's choice, and a choice it must be, for they must be completely committed to the next step or it won't work. That way, there will be some assurance that the decision is made after appropriate consideration."

For a while, the king was silent. The weight of the crown upon his head felt heavy.

Eventually, he asked of the mage, "If we do this, do you believe the land might be free from tyranny, and its people might enjoy peace?"

"It is conceivable that Neleuwan would have many golden years ahead," the mage suggested.

And so it was agreed.

After perfecting the ritual over the next few weeks, the mage came upon the first person he would offer the fateful choice: a young man of about twenty summers named Kai. Kai had been ill for most of his life, and was not getting any better. His family had used up all of their resources on healers, mages, and even barbarian mystics, but nothing had helped. Having recently taken a turn for the worse, the family was preparing for his death.

When the mage chanced upon Kai, the young man was nothing more than skin and bone. His body was a shell, and the poor boy was in agony. He had days left at best, and seemed to have long since resigned to his fate.

The mage first spoke with the family, and then to Kai himself.

"Though I cannot grant you the life you should've had, I can grant you the opportunity to do more than simply be born into this world only to suffer and die. You will be part of something greater, and will be able to protect and provide for the ones you love. Know, however, that though you will suffer no more, no longer will you be the person who your family loves and hopes for today. What's more, you may be denied whatever peace awaits after death for a long, long time."

"Will we still be able to see him?" Kai's mother asked, eyes red with tears.

"It would not be impossible, but I would advise against it," said the mage, his heart like lead. "There would be little left for you to recognise. His body would live on for a short time after the process, though it would be unresponsive. It would be best if you mourned the passing of his body as if he himself had passed, because in all but the most abstract sense, he will have."

The mother began to weep, and it was heart-wrenching.

Before continuing, the mage pursed his lips.

"If you were to decide amongst yourselves that you wanted to see his new form before we depart, I would not deny you. As confronting as the change in personality may be, Kai's spirit would appear as he would have at the height of its strength, giving you a glimpse at the man he might've grown into. On the other hand, the truth of what he'd have become would be its own burden to bear."

The mage turned his attention back to Kai.

"In the end, the choice is yours, Kai. You have every right to choose a peaceful passage among family and friends. What I offer is an alternative, but it is not without cost."

Kai and his family pulled together in a huddle around the bed.

After several minutes, the family pulled back, tears running down their faces.

At the centre of his family, Kai looked up at the mage with a strength in his eyes that belied his frail body.

"I choose to be more than death."

The mage then asked everyone to say their goodbyes, and after a long, emotional farewell, they eventually left the room.

The mage had been prepared for this outcome, so he'd brought everything he needed with him. He reached into his sleeve pocket and retrieved some herbs and a small, grey pebble on a leather thong that he placed around the neck of the frail Kai.

"This will carry your spirit to where it needs to be," said the mage.

Kai nodded stoically in acknowledgment.

The mage sat beside the boy, placing one hand over his heart and the other over his head. He closed his eyes and let his energy flow between the two. Normally, this would allow the mage to map out the young man's vitals, but with the pebble in place, it did something wholly different.

The stone resting upon Kai's skin started to glow an ethereal blue, the light growing in intensity almost to the point of being hot and piercing, as though it might blind someone if they were to look directly at it. The mage's energy coalesced at the base of the pebble, drawing the boy's spirit away from his physical form to be held within the pebble.

Eventually, the thread of Kai's spirit energy grew taut between his body and the pebble, and would draw no further. Grimacing, the mage sharpened the flow of energy, then severed the spirit as close to the body as possible, drawing the tail end of the thread into the pebble. Immediately, Kai looked even more frail than he had before.

All too quickly, the ritual was over. The mage looked over the young man's body, no longer contorted into a grimace of pain and anticipation of the end, but at peace. As the mage stood up, the little pebble's glow had started to diminish in its intensity, but retained some of its blue glow. The mage removed the stone from Kai's chest and held it gently in his palm.

After taking a moment to steel himself, he opened the door, where the family was waiting just beyond.

"It is done," he said softly, a question in his eyes.

"We've decided," said Kai's mother. "We want to see him."

"... Very well."

Still holding the pebble, the mage uttered the word, "Ku-Da-Ru."

In an instant, the form of Kai appeared as if from nowhere—but instead of the frail boy he'd been, he stood before them fully grown, his body strong and vibrant in stature, now wearing the colours of the castle of Neleuwan. It was as though he'd been reborn.

"My boy," said his mother, cupping his face with a hand. "How do you feel?"

"I don't feel anything," said Kai. "I'm ready to begin."

Then, as suddenly as he'd appeared, he was gone.

It was a simple statement, delivered with no emotion.

He'd become exactly what the mage had said he would.

"From that day forward, the numbers of the Ku-Da Ru grew in much the same way," said Frederick. "The kingdom began to thrive, and in exchange for the Ku-Da-Ru's service, their families were cared for … but as a cruel irony, there was very little left of them to appreciate it. Worse, the families they'd given everything to protect are now long dead, and yet they'd remained trapped here, unable to cross over and join them in death."

Pausing, he gave William a moment to process everything he'd said.

"If I may speak freely, sire," William said eventually, "it was compassionate of you to release them from their service, and I have the utmost respect for it … but you said it yourself—without them, the kingdom is vulnerable. They were the heart of our military, and their existence alone was a deterrent to any foreign powers that might seek to invade. Not to sound callous, but they'd already been serving for a long time. I fear it may have been wiser to wait until we had a replacement for them before releasing them."

Frederick smiled. "Perhaps you've missed your calling, William. I'd sooner have you as my advisor than some of those stuffy nobles." His expression turned sombre. "But if you'd seen what I saw in my vision, I think you'd understand why I had to release them. It was well past time for the Ku-Da-Ru to be whole again ... to reunite with the rest of their spirit and leave this life behind. Knowing what I knew, with the key to their way home in my hands, unlocking the door and helping them to walk through it was the only choice I had."

William looked on at the king he served with pride.

"Well, no sense in dwelling on it now," he said. "Best to focus on what we're going to do about it. I don't suppose you have any ideas, sire?"

"As a matter of fact, I do," said Frederick, standing.

"Tomorrow, we ride for the Council of Chieftains."

CHAPTER TWENTY-TWO

PEBBLE

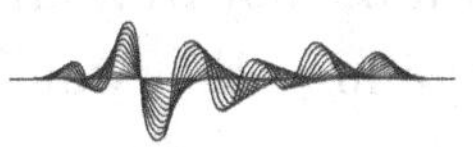

When the pebble on Marcus's chest began to glow that distinct iridescent blue, Kyruarth's second thought after his vision below the cliffs had been of the Ku-Da-Ru—both for the colour, and for the use of the pebble. Having witnessed separation after painful separation in the process of creating the soldiers who would go on to become the Home Guard, it was a time he looked back on with a heavy heart.

The Ku-Da-Ru had been more than successful at fulfilling their purpose, and had ultimately been the ones to choose their fate … but even centuries later, he wasn't certain that choice was one that anyone should be given, much less be the one to offer it.

Forcing himself to return to the matter at hand, he wondered what it all meant. How was this young man connected to the fabled Guardian Accord?

Whatever the answers were, he would not find them here.

"Pip, something tells me there's more to this young man than anyone knows ... perhaps even himself," he said. "I regret that my visit will be cut short, but I must leave to seek guidance on the matter. I also believe that you and this boy may be in danger."

"You think they'll come looking for him?" said Pip.

"I may be a prophet, my friend, but there is something larger at work here than even I can foresee. The present is a mystery to me, and the few visions I've had lately have only left me with more questions. What I *do* know is that if the boy truly arrived in a truant calling, they will come looking for him. They would not have brought him through the breach unless he were someone of importance.

"When he regains consciousness, you need to be prepared to travel. Explain to him all that has occurred, but do not mention my role here."

Pip frowned at this last request, but let it pass by. Mages and their secrets.

"You must take him to your boat and head out to sea," Kyruarth continued. "The safest place for this boy is with King Frederick of Neleuwan. I will give you a map to the port of Sonder, a hidden cave port off the coast used by those who prefer not to have the port authorities looking over their shipment. It's not the safest place either, but as long as you don't carry anything of value, it shouldn't pose too much of a risk."

Pip gave Kyruarth a lop-sided grin. "You can keep your map. Believe it or not, I've seen my fair share of Sonder. Might even be able to call in some favours from back in the day and get the old boat back over here. Would hate for her to end up being used for piracy," he said with a wink.

Kyruarth raised an eyebrow, then smiled.

"That is a story I look forward to hearing," he said, shouldering his pack and heading for the door. "There's someone I must meet with along the way, so I will take the overland route and meet you in Pillton to take you the rest of the way to the castle. Once this business is behind us, my friend, let us return here for talk of our travels and more of your wonderful tea."

Pip smiled. "Looking forward to it."

Two moons later, the boy woke up, and Pip did exactly as he'd been asked.

The boy, who he soon learned was named Marcus, was sad to leave Pip's home upon the Pinnacle of Osciros, even though he'd really only had a chance to see it for a few short hours. As soon as he'd been able to walk under his own weight, the two of them had headed out the door, and down towards the boat in the harbour.

By the time they'd hopped aboard the small vessel, Marcus had been exhausted. Still recovering from his recent ordeal, his body was clearly still regaining its strength, and had not quite been ready to descend the cliff. Pip had made short work of the moorings, casting off with wind in their sails, heading out and around headland to the south.

Several days of hard riding later, a group of red-robed women stood on the docks, inspecting the different moorings and boats for any sign of Marcus.

Crimson stood out in the daylight, her dark-red travelling robes ablaze in the sun as she stood in the middle of the dock. She closed her eyes and sent out her energy with the distinct resonance vibrations she knew to be Marcus. The image returned to her mind's eye, highlighting once again this location and its faint collection of blue light.

His unique signature ended not far from where she stood … but there was no sign of him.

"He's taken to water. This trail is cold," she said, turning to move through the Ladies who'd gathered at her back. "It seems we're bound for the sands."

Change of Direction

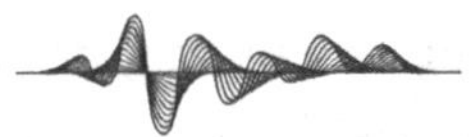

Higant sat up from his bedroll, still reeling from the dream, trying to gather his thoughts. He sat facing Vandrune, who'd handed him some tea he'd prepared while Higant had slept. The tea was warm and comforting, which were welcome sensations after what he'd just seen.

Looking out from under the shelter's overhang, Higant saw that night was falling. They would soon be on the move again. There was a faint breeze picking up, and the early evening temperature was slightly cooler than the previous nights had been, indicating they were closing in on the other side of the hotlands. It felt like it had been many moons since they'd crossed the Yuill Ion Pass into the hotlands, but in truth, there had only been seven moonrises—seven long, hot rides through the night.

Both Thunder and Blossom were now showing their dislike for the heat. They'd shared their water generously with the horses, but beasts of such a size needed far more than the travellers had to share, so their moods had begun to sour. In recognition of this, Higant had brushed them both before bed every night, making sure to find enough shelter for them to stay out of the sun during the day.

It was a good omen that they now felt they were coming to the end of the hot ride. They hadn't seen a soul in all the days they'd been riding, and even with company, it had been a solitary journey. Both of them had been focused on reaching their destination as soon as possible, and had spared little time for talk.

The dream—or vision—Higant had just awoken from remained firmly in his mind's eye. To Vandrune's eyes, the look on the boy's face was nothing short of despair.

"Higant," Vandrune said softly, bringing the boy out of his thoughts. "What did you see?"

"It was Marcus," he said, his voice strained.

He went on to describe what he'd seen—the blue glow, the noise, the map of Neleuwan, and the glowing blue stone that had landed somewhere in the castle.

"A stone, you say?" mused Vandrune.

"Yes. Marcus had been wearing it around his neck, and when he faded away, the necklace remained. Then, the map of Neleuwan appeared, and the stone landed on the castle."

Higant shrugged. None of it was making any sense to him.

Vandrune, however, was tense.

Without warning, he stood up and started to roll up his bedroll.

"Pack up your things, Higant. There's no time to lose. We must make it to Kyruarth with haste."

"Because of the dream? What part of it? What does it mean?" said Higant, his voice rising in pitch as Vandrune packed up his gear.

"The blue stone is an omen of sorts, and indicates that time is against us. Kyruarth will know what to do. Hurry, lad!"

Higant jumped into action and started to pack up his gear. He still had questions, but he knew that he would get no more out of Vandrune. He'd seen the mage like this before, hard at work trying to piece together some impossible puzzle, and he would simply have to wait until he was ready.

He only hoped that his dream did not mean something was wrong with Marcus.

Walking over to Thunder, Higant scratched the friendly horse under his chin. Thunder nudged the boy as he walked around to affix the saddle and bedroll onto his back, then huffed as Higant turned to Blossom, who'd approached to receive a scratch as well.

The travellers mounted their horses, and instead of starting at a trot, Vandrune immediately brought Blossom into a gallop, leaving Thunder and Higant at his back, surprising them with the speed he was travelling. Higant leaned over Thunder's neck, encouraging him to keep pace with Vandrune and Blossom.

After a few hours of hard riding, the land started to change. The ground was no longer covered in red rock, and there were signs of shrubs and grasses growing on the hills to the east. Vandrune started to veer towards them, and as they started up the incline, a change in the air temperature came as a welcome surprise. With a cool breeze coming down over the hills, no longer were they sweating with every stride, even at the pace they were travelling.

The further into the hills they went, the cooler the air became. They slowed up for a moment when they came upon a small stream, stopping only to allow the horses to drink the fresh water, splash their faces, and fill their waterskins before continuing on without a word.

Along the way, they passed a number of abandoned old shacks until they eventually found a road, which they now followed to the north. It seemed to Higant that Vandrune had found his direction, and now knew exactly where they were going.

The sun began to crest over the horizon, and Higant thought they should be stopping soon to rest and let the horses get some of their strength back, but Vandrune showed no sign of slowing. Just as the sun came over the hill before them, it caught the image of a rider coming down the road, heading right for them.

Higant spotted the rider first and called to Vandrune, who looked up and slowed his pace to let the horses come alongside each other, each of them slowing to a trot so as not to be seen to be in a hurry. As the lone rider got closer, Vandrune became more wary, as the rider was moving at pace themselves.

No more than a hundred yards away from them now, Vandrune realised that the rider had not lifted their head, and likely had not yet seen them. Vandrune instinctively started to veer off the road, and Higant followed.

Just as the rider was about to pass them by, his head rose, and Vandrune would've recognised those piercing green eyes anywhere. They belonged to a legend—a man he'd seen only in prophetic visions, around which the world's centre of prophecy was built.

The true prophet, Kyruarth.

A smile came across Vandrune's face. Recognising Vandrune from visions of his own, Kyruarth slowed his horse to a trot, then rode back up the road to the two of them.

"Time turns for no man but the one true prophet," said Vandrune.

Kyruarth smiled at the old words.

"Time has no master but time itself."

Both mages dismounted their steeds and greeted each other, clasping their forearms.

"It is good to finally meet you, Kyruarth. I only wish it were under better circumstances."

"And you, Vandrune," said Kyruarth. "Your master has been well, I trust?"

Vandrune gave a slight chuckle. "He remains as serious as ever, but is well enough."

With a knowing nod, Kyruarth said, "Some things never change. Come. Let us find a place to talk."

Looking around for some shelter away from the road, they saw a small group of pines clustered about a hundred yards up the slope of a hill that would provide shelter and cover from prying eyes. Kyruarth acknowledged Higant with a smile, beckoning for him to follow, which he did without a word.

When they came to a stop, Higant took the horses and picketed them nearby, including Kyruarth's. He gave them more water from the skin he'd filled at the creek, and immediately set about thinking of a name for Kyruarth's horse, a strong, grey stallion.

Upon returning to the two mages, he had the sense that Kyruarth had been watching him the entire time.

"Who is this young man here, Vandrune? We haven't been properly introduced."

In truth, Kyruarth had felt Higant's presence in the Reaching Vandrune had performed a number of days earlier, and had been infinitely curious as to his identity.

Vandrune smiled. "This is Higant, squire to King Frederick of Neleuwan."

"Hello and greetings, Squire Higant. It is a pleasure to make your acquaintance," Kyruarth said with as much formality as he could muster. "Tell me, Higant. If you are a squire to the king, how is it you find yourself in the wilderness with a prophet?"

"My friend is lost, sir," said Higant, the worry on his face plain. "Vandrune and I are trying to find him. He's in danger, and I'm worried he might be hurt."

"Lost, you say? How did he get lost?"

Vandrune had seen this type of questioning before. Already, he could sense that Kyruarth had a way about him—a presence that put people at ease, and encouraged them to reveal more than they wanted to.

"After our master was killed, my friend went to bring the person to justice, and was kidnapped for it. Forcibly taken away from our home of Neleuwan."

Higant looked to Vandrune as if asking for permission, and the mage just smiled back.

"He was put in a wagon, tied up, and taken by a truant!" he added matter-of-factly.

"A truant? How is that possible?" said Kyruarth, his voice laced with curiosity.

Higant went on to explain the truant calling, the resulting truant mound, and the mechanics of truant magic. Vandrune looked on with a wry smile as Kyruarth continued his game of cat and mouse, always giving the impression he knew less than he really did, teasing out every last bit of information Higant had to offer. At some point during Higant's tell-all, his eyes flared blue, as they did whenever he was accessing his hidden knowledge. If Kyruarth noticed it, he did not let on.

Eventually, Kyruarth's enquiries became more pointed.

"How is it you know so much about these things, Higant?"

Higant shifted on his feet. "I have knowledge of things I should have no way of knowing—some reservoir of information that I only have access to, but only in times of need. I fall asleep shortly after accessing it, and wake with no memory of the incident. The only reason I even know about it is because Vandrune tells me about it afterward ... except for that one time."

"What time might that be?" asked Kyruarth.

"When I heard your conversation in the Reaching," he said aloud before he could stop himself.

Kyruarth looked long and hard at Higant, then turned to Vandrune.

"This is the boy whose mind is locked," said Vandrune. "The prophecy identifies him as a twin, with mysterious knowledge sealed away in his mind. I believe his friend was taken as a means of stressing his mind, and thereby breaking the seal."

Kyruarth paced among the pine trees for a moment, thinking and talking to himself. After a while, he stood before them and said, "Your friend is safe, young Higant. The truant calling deposited him near the location I set as our meeting place, and though he arrived injured, an old friend of mine gave him shelter. Together, we were able to heal him, and he now makes his way to Pillton by sea."

"Marcus is alive, then?" said Higant, hope returning to his voice. "He's really okay?"

"Indeed. So Marcus is his name," said Kyruarth, smiling. "However, much like yourself, there is more to young Marcus than there appears."

Higant frowned. "He is my friend, sir, and a squire. What more can there be to him?"

Kyruarth recounted the details of the vision he'd had involving Marcus, including the blue glow he'd seen about him. He also told the story of Pip's wife, the necklace she wore, the pebble set within it, and the possible connection between Marcus and the Guardian Accord.

"The Guardian Accord are a myth," said Vandrune, flabbergasted. "Phantoms of a time long forgotten."

Kyruarth smiled. "Some say the same about me, my friend. Stranger things have happened." He turned his attention to Higant. "Perhaps our squire here might tell us more of the Accord?"

Higant's eyes flashed once more, and his confident, scholarly demeanour came to the fore.

"The Guardian Accord are a sect created in a time long forgotten, their purpose to safeguard the timeline and help prepare the world for the return. Their knowledge and skills are passed on from generation to generation in the form of a power that manifests in female-born children. When a male child presents with this power, he is heralded as the Guardian Dracco, and the time of the return is close at hand.

"The return of *what?*" asked Vandrune.

"Of dragons," said Higant, as though it were obvious.

Strangely enough, this time, Higant didn't fall asleep. He didn't even appear tired, and the words he'd spoken remained in his mind. Vandrune looked at Kyruarth incredulously, and the legendary prophet just smiled.

"Speaking of the stone," said Vandrune, remembering his urgency, "last night, Higant here had a vision featuring the blue pebble, worn upon Marcus's neck. It seems you were already aware of the omen ... but it's not the only thing about Higant's vision that concerns me. In it, a noise pulled Marcus away, leaving only the stone and a map of Neleuwan. It seems the pebble was drawing attention to a location in the castle."

For the first time in the conversation, Kyruarth seemed surprised. The stone he'd used to create the Ku-Da-Ru had been lost to him, and now Pip had another one, one that was appearing at the heart of several prophetic events.

"This noise. What did it sound like?"

"It was like a humming sound," said Higant. "A vibration that grew louder and louder. It got so loud that I had to cover my ears."

Kyruarth held his composure, but his insides were churning.

"How many hours have passed since the dream?"

Higant looked to Vandrune for confirmation.

"A little over twelve, I'd say."

"We must hurry to Pillton," he said, moving for his horse.

Nothing could've made Higant happier, but Kyruarth's reaction bothered him.

"What's wrong? Do you know something about the noise?"

"What you've described is a resonance rite," said Kyruarth. "It is an ancient art that reveals the location of a known target. Your vision suggests they performed one to locate Marcus, and have been on his trail for at least twelve hours. We must get to him before they do."

Vandrune and Higant mounted their horses, expecting Kyruarth to head back down to the road. Instead, he headed towards the top of the nearest hill at pace, and they followed closely behind.

When they came to the crest, Kyruarth slowed to a stop and looked back the way they'd come. On the road just by the cluster of pines were a number of horses galloping down the road at impossible speed, screaming along the road into the hotlands.

Upon each of the horses sat riders with dark hooded cloaks—with the exception of their leader at the head of the formation, who wore a cloak of deep crimson.

Kyruarth signalled to the others, and they looked down over the hill to see the horses tearing across the landscape.

"Who are they?" asked Higant. "How can their horses move with such speed?"

"Truants," Kyruarth said grimly.

"It seems Marcus is not the only one they're looking for."

CHAPTER TWENTY-FOUR

RESONANCE

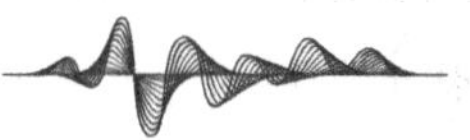

Crimson and her troupe had been riding from Cantaloria for two full days, constantly drawing power from the earth to push their horses to an unnatural pace. The horses likely wouldn't survive such a brutal journey, but she wanted to be sure they caught Marcus on the road, and saw it as a necessary sacrifice. The location she'd seen in the resonance rite was about a day's ride into the hotlands, and it was conceivable that Marcus had been heading further south and away from them, so they had to be swift.

What she still couldn't understand was that not one, but two locations had resonated during the rite. Resonance was lost over water, that much was true ... but for the boy to have travelled that distance in such a short amount of time was unfathomable. For the residual frequency at the harbour to have been so strong, he would essentially have to have been there one minute, and in the hotlands the next. There should've been no way for him to get that far inland from any of the surrounding bodies of water.

In all the time she'd been performing the rite, she had been doing it the same as her mother had before her, and had never had an issue ... yet here, she had been presented with an anomaly, something thought to be impossible.

It had been gnawing at the back of her mind from the moment she'd performed the rite ... but finally, it hit her. She signalled for the others to pull up their horses, then brought her own to a stop.

"How could I have not considered it?" she said to herself, not realising that she had spoken aloud. Her Ladies Truant started to encircle her.

"What is it, Lady Crimson?" asked the young Lady Heart.

"Have any of you ever heard of a resonance rite producing more than one signal?" she said, turning her head to look at each of them.

The Ladies Truant looked at each other and thought about the request. Each of them shook their heads in turn.

"It is impossible," Lady Hytern said with authority and experience. "Each resonance is unique to the individual. No two have ever been alike."

"Then why, Lady Hytern, did my resonance rite pick up two signals?"

It took a little while before Lady Hytern spoke, and though her words were brash, she spoke them cautiously.

"I cannot speak for what you did or did not see in the resonance rite, but I can think of one possibility."

"And what is that?" asked Crimson, looking at her with threatening intensity.

"Perhaps there was an echo due to an overload of power sent through the resonance rite."

"An echo, you say? Interesting," she said, her lips curling. "How would such a thing occur, given that resonance only travels in one direction? The vibrations we emit as part of the rite are twin to the resonance of the target alone, and none other. Your theory is nonsense.

The answer is as simple as it is unfathomable—there are two people with the same resonance," she said with conviction. "If we analyse the process and the outcome, it's the only explanation."

One of the ladies, a shy and unassuming truant, spoke up.

"I don't disagree, my lady, but it goes against everything our teachings tell us. Even identical twins are unique in their resonance. If there's another explanation we're missing, and we chase after this notion instead, we could lose him."

"We could just as easily lose him in the process of trying to confirm it," said Crimson. "Better to act under the assumption that Marcus departed from Cantaloria by boat, and whoever we're chasing here is someone else entirely."

Crimson rode out of the circle, turning to each of the ladies as she spoke.

"The time of the truant is upon us. It is almost time for us to come out of the shadows," she announced proudly. "You are my generals in this next step, and each of you has a purpose. It's time we parted ways. Make your way to the Citadels and prepare for the Cascade. I will send the signal at the appointed time. Once it starts, it cannot be stopped until we regain what is rightfully ours—a place in the world that accepts us for who we are, not for what our ancestors determined was our role. A place where our loved ones are not cruelly taken from us without reason. Thank you all for your service. Hold all those you lead into this next stage close to your hearts ... and once this is done, may we all find the world we are looking for."

Each of the Ladies bowed their heads and turned their horses, setting off in different directions as they went.

Once they were all gone, Crimson pulled a small blue stone from her pocket.

"Fanton."

It took a moment, but soon after, the small head of Fanton appeared just above the stone.

"Milady," he said with a bow, translating through the stone as a slight decline of the head.

"I have a feeling you may be needed after all," she said. "Are you in position?"

"I arrived late last night. Rest assured, I will be watching the harbour closely. Not many fishing boats in these parts," he said, a knowing smile on his face.

She hadn't expected anything to come of it, but back at the docks, Crimson had considered where Marcus might have fled to if he'd travelled conventionally by sea. Her conclusion had been the one place that was close enough to Castle Neleuwan, had a hidden port, and pursuers would be unlikely to predict: Sonder.

"My pet wants to go home, does he?" she said with a wicked smile. "I'm afraid I have other plans for him. Fanton, I will arrive there tomorrow."

Fanton's head bobbed. "I will make the arrangements."

The image disappeared, and Crimson returned the stone to her pocket.

As she did, she had the strangest sensation that she was being watched. She looked around at the surrounding hills, trees, bushes, and the wooded area up the hill to her right ... but she didn't see anyone.

If there was anyone there, let them watch. It wouldn't change a thing.

Now that she was alone, she could set her own pace, and that she did. She took off as fast as the horse would take her, faster than any creature should ever be able to move, determined to get to Sonder before sunup the following day.

When Marcus arrived, she would be there waiting.

CHAPTER TWENTY-FIVE

RETURN

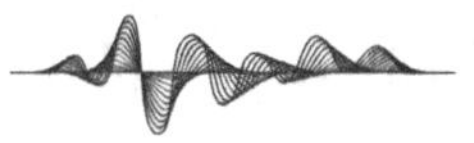

Pip and Marcus travelled out onto the ocean in Pip's fishing boat, heading down the coast towards Sonder. In his youth, Pip had travelled far afield, and understood the need to occasionally find shelter in places less than savoury. Sonder in particular, he knew extremely well—in fact, he even had a second home there.

Well before settling on the Cantalorian cliffs, and over the years since, he had travelled there many times. When one sails the seas and visits many ports, they get to know the locals, and Pip had made a number of good friends—some would call them pirates, thieves, and scoundrels, but he found that most of them were simply trying to get by, and were not without principles.

It had been some time since Pip's last visit to Sonder, but he'd kept in touch with his friends, and knew exactly who to talk to and where to go to get Marcus safely through the port.

An expert sailor, Pip bent his old fishing boat to his will. Marcus, however, was having trouble keeping down the food he'd eaten that morning. He'd never seen the ocean before today, and here he was on a boat, headed to a location he hadn't known existed until Pip explained where they were heading. So much had happened in such a short time. He'd found the baron murdered, had his first experience with a woman, been kidnapped by members of a lost civilisation, arrived on another continent on a bolt of lightning and almost died … and now he was with a stranger out at sea, travelling to a place full of thieves and pirates.

Before now, he'd led a very simple life as the baron's squire.

What a story he had to tell Higant when he returned.

"Marcus, help me with this sail," Pip called out from the front of the boat.

Raising his head, having lowered it earlier in an effort to suppress the nausea, he saw the boat rocking on the ocean as it went with the swell. The bow of the boat bobbed up and down, up and down … and in an instant, he was leaning back over the edge of the boat, releasing what little remained of his stomach contents.

"Come on, my boy. It's only the ocean. It won't hurt you!" shouted Pip, chuckling to himself.

"Says the hundred-year-old sailor! This is my first time!" Marcus hollered in a lull between retching.

As soon as he got the last word out, his head was again over the edge, emphatically expressing his dislike for the ocean. It seemed a long time since he'd looked upon the ocean and felt he was at home. Now, he despised everything about it … though he might've felt differently if it weren't making him so sick.

Pip moved towards the back of the boat to check on the steering and see how Marcus was doing.

"You look a little pale, lad," he gibed, shaking his head with a smile.

Marcus glared at him, then returned to his heaving.

Pip entered the cabin—which was more like a shanty with a

couple of hammocks strung up—and reached for a small cloth pouch hanging from a hook. He reached in and pulled out a small handful of shavings, then returned to Marcus, holding them out to him.

"Chew on these. It'll help."

Marcus took the shavings reluctantly, then placed them in his mouth and chewed. It took a couple of minutes, but colour started to return to his cheeks, and the feeling of sickness dissipated.

He looked at Pip, who'd since moved to the helm.

"What *was* that? I—I feel fine now."

"That, my young friend, is a secret. All you need to know is that I worked magic today," Pip said with a satisfied smile.

Now that he was feeling better, Marcus asked, "What did you want me to do with the sail?"

Pip slapped him on the back. "Nothing, really. I was trying to get you to forget you were sick. Turns out that was harder than I first thought," he said, chuckling. "Enjoy the ocean, Marcus. If this is your first time, let it be a good experience."

Now that they were around the headland, Pip sailed them quite a distance from the shore, wanting to make sure they kept out of line of sight and were not followed. It was a three-day journey to Sonder, and they were making good time. It looked like there may be another storm brewing at their backs, so they may even pick up some more speed with the oncoming winds.

Marcus found his way to the bow and sat looking out at the vastness of the ocean. Continuing to chew on the shavings Pip had given him, his sickness had been left far behind. He looked down at the ocean and noticed there were fish gliding along with the boat, using the hull and the water being displaced as a way of propelling themselves through the waves. He hadn't realised that something so big and vast could be so beautiful, so full of life.

For hours, he just sat there, mesmerised by it all.

Soon enough, Pip called out to him to come to the cabin for

a meal. Marcus was not sure eating was the best idea, considering his digestive system had found the beginning of the journey less than welcoming, but it had certainly left him hungry.

At the back of the boat, Pip had some broth waiting for him. Marcus wasn't sure when he'd brewed it up, or how for that matter, but he was thankful it was mostly liquid and would be easy on the way up if it came to that.

As soon as it hit his lips, he recognised it had a similar flavour to the shavings. What in the world were they?

"It's delicious. What's in it?" Marcus asked innocently, angling for an answer.

"My secret recipe," Pip said with a wink that said, *nice try*.

"Are you ever going to tell me what they are?" Marcus said, pouting.

"Let's just say it's full of sugar, spice, and everything nice."

With a laugh, Pip went over everything that was in the broth … except the shavings, of course. Marcus just dropped his head and shook it, hiding the smile on his face. He didn't want to give Pip the satisfaction of knowing he'd succeeded in making him feel better.

The two of them were fast becoming friends. Having lost his own child, Pip never missed an opportunity to enrich the life of another young person. While even he would admit it was partially a salve to fill the void of the loss of his little girl, he was a caretaker by nature, and there was genuine compassion in his actions.

They sailed into the night, the storm at their backs indeed putting more wind in their sails. Thankfully, it also passed them by without issue, heading further out to sea and allowing them to doze off and on during the night.

The next morning, the tailwind kept them moving at pace, cutting across the gulf between Gyrockgenci and Neleuwan. Right as the sun was hitting it's zenith, Pip caught sight of Yugen Point, a protruding rock face on Neleuwan's west coast that was an indicator that they were less than a day away from Sonder. It seemed the wind had driven them even faster than Pip had realised. With the pace the storm had given them, they'd made up for almost half a day's worth of sailing. He was quite pleased with this outcome, as it would allow them to dock at Sonder long before they—and any of their pursuers—would've thought possible for the little fishing boat.

After another day of sailing and playful verbal sparring, they sailed into the mouth of the hidden cove right on twilight. The cove was hidden behind outcroppings on both sides that blended so well with the rock face that unless one knew what they were looking for, they would imagine it was a solid wall and not give it a second thought. When one came around the bend and headed on through the gap, however, they would discover a natural cavern that would hide any vessel from sight. This was no small cavern, either. It was a large natural chamber, capable of docking even the largest vessels from far across the ocean.

For Pip and Marcus in their small fishing boat, the entrance was cavernous, the vessel feeling tiny in comparison to the size of the chamber. Interestingly, despite being fully enclosed, the inside of the cove was fairly well lit—and the reason for that became apparent when Marcus saw the giant mirrors lining the entrance into the cavern, positioned strategically around it in order to reflect the light of the sun. Even in this twilight, there was a set of reflectors positioned to catch the last of the sun's rays. It was genius.

The dock was located on the far side, with small huts and buildings extending further into the chamber heading inland. Once docked, Pip tied the boat off to the dock and secured it with a canvas sheet over the top, keeping it tied down and watertight. Taking only a handful of things with them, they headed along the gangway up towards Sonder proper.

Before leaving the dock, Pip turned around and looked longingly back at his vessel. Marcus stopped when Pip paused, knowing all too well what it was like to leave something behind. He hadn't had a choice when he was taken, but he'd left behind all that he loved nonetheless—Neleuwan, Higant, the other squires ... and none of them knew where he'd gone. All he wanted was to get back to them, and here was Pip, leaving all he loved behind to make that happen.

He patted Pip on the back, bringing him out of his reverie.

"Time to go," he said gently.

Pip nodded, and they turned onto the street just off the docks, heading into the heart of Sonder.

Pip weaved through the mass of huts and buildings like a local, turning this way and that, up the alleys and down the passages until he came to a small door off to the side of one of the large buildings.

He handed his bag to Marcus and proceeded to unlace his shoe. Marcus, who thought what he was doing looked extremely suspicious, looked around to see if anyone might be watching, but saw no one. Pip then proceeded to untie the other shoe, and after he'd done so, he retrieved a small metal pin from each shoe. He then tied his shoes back up and stood up straight, retrieving his bag from Marcus.

"Good thing I've got a key, eh?" said Pip, smiling.

"You really are full of surprises, old man," Marcus said with a grin. "Let me know if you need a hand."

Pip's eyes flashed, giving the impression of someone far younger.

"Watch and learn."

With a motion so deft that Marcus couldn't hide his amazement, Pip released the lock on the door, pushed it open, and stepped inside.

"You coming?"

Shaking his head, he followed Pip inside.

The room was dark and dank, smelling like it had not been lived in for a very long time. Marcus immediately set about finding a way to get some air in the room, feeling around the edges of the room for a shutter or a window. Before he had a chance, the room started to glow. The room gradually became brighter, almost to the point of being able to see as clearly as if direct sunlight was filtering into the room.

"This better, Marcus?" Pip asked, still smiling like a Cheshire cat.

"It is ... but how is it doing that?"

Marcus pointed at the round stone upon a small table in the middle of the room, apparently the source of the light.

"My wife was a mage, my boy," he said proudly. "She made things that made life easier, and this is one of those things. She called it a sunstone."

"What is this place, Pip?" Marcus asked.

"This was a home away from home. My wife and I came here many times before our daughter was born," said Pip, suddenly wistful. "We would come to Sonder for holidays and sit by the nearby beach, enjoying each other's company. We would laugh, and giggle, and swim ... living life to the fullest. It was a wonderful time in our lives ... and I suppose that's why it's been so long since I returned.

"We'll be safe here for the rest of the night. Tomorrow, I will call upon an old friend for horses and supplies, and we'll make a start towards Pillton. You'll find a room through that door, and a bed on your right. Get some rest. We have a long ride ahead of us, and we'll need all the energy we can get."

Marcus paused in the doorway.

"Thank you, Pip. For everything. I'm grateful for all you've done for me."

Without waiting for a response, he disappeared into the room.

Smiling, Pip looked around the shelter, and happy memories of his wife came back to him. A single tear rolled off his cheek.

He headed for the small armchair at the far side of the room, where he sat down and then retrieved the pebble on the leather thong from his pocket, still glowing a faint blue.

"Who are you, Marcus?" he pondered quietly.

ESCAPE

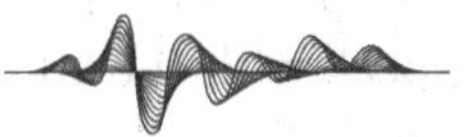

Upon entering the room, Marcus had found a small bed stacked high with a pile of blankets and pillows. Next to the bed was a small hutch with some toys on it, including a doll and some figurines. Dust had begun to form on top of their heads, giving the impression that they'd been placed there a long time ago.

He looked up and noticed a small, round window at the top of the room near the roof. It seemed a strange place for a window, but he soon realised why it was there. As the moon continued to rise, the moonlight came beaming into the room via the reflectors, bathing it in peaceful and comforting light. Judging by the configuration of the surrounding houses and alleys, it must've been the only part of the building that got any light.

He removed his boots and the clothes Pip had given him to replace his squire's outfit, which would quickly have given his identity away. Only now that they were off and he felt the cool air on his skin did he realise that he hadn't changed in days. Conscious of this fact,

Pip had left him a bowl with some water and a fresh pair of clothes behind the door, and as he bathed himself, the water turned from clear to dark very quickly. Refreshed and ready for a good sleep, he fell upon the bed, and was out in a matter of moments.

It was early morning when he woke. A little unsure of where he was at first, he slowly recalled the chaos of the last few days since the baron's death, then laid back and stared up at the ceiling. He thought of what was to come next. They were to make their way back to Neleu-wan, where they would speak with the king. It seemed so simple ... but something told him it would not be anywhere near that easy.

Marcus sat up on the side of the bed, looking around for the clothes he'd discarded by the bowl of water the night before. Surprisingly, he found that the bowl had been refreshed, and his clothes sat cleaned and folded to the left of it. After getting dressed, he splashed some of the fresh new water on his face and gathered up the rest of his things before heading out the door.

In the main room, he found Pip drinking a cup of tea, reading a small book and smiling to himself with some breakfast already prepared on the table.

"Good morning, Pip," Marcus said with a yawn.

"Good morning, Marcus," he said cheerily. "How did you sleep?"

"Like a stone. Thank you for the water and clothes," he said sincerely. "It made all the difference."

Pip, who was no stranger to the thanks of others, found himself lost for words. With every passing moment, Marcus reminded him more and more of his daughter. She too had been pleasant, polite, and in love with life. He felt a similar feeling from Marcus.

"Sit," he said, looking away. "Have some breakfast."

Marcus didn't need to be told twice.

"So, where are these friends of yours?" he asked through his food.

"Actually, they've already been and gone," said Pip. "They caught wind of me being in town—goodness knows how they do it—and turned up on our doorstep some twenty minutes after you'd fallen asleep. The arrangements have already been made."

Marcus was baffled.

"Those are some efficient friends. Why would they go out of their way to help me?"

"Any friend of mine is a friend of theirs," Pip said, smiling.

"Will I get to thank them?"

"Unfortunately not. In their line of work, they're the type to remain anonymous, especially when strangers are involved. However, they did say it was nice meeting you while you slept."

Marcus raised an eyebrow, and the two of them laughed.

After finishing the morsels that were left on his plate, Pip stood up and began tidying. He walked back to the chair he'd been sitting in the night before and placed the book back on the small table beside it, closing his eyes and resting a hand on the book for a short minute before turning away. Finally, Pip started for the door, and Marcus fell in step behind him.

The alley outside remained empty and quiet. It was one of the reasons Pip had liked this placed when he'd first found it—it was private, and no one would disturb him here. Closing the door behind them, Pip turned his 'key' in the lock once more, quickly resulting in a satisfying locking sound.

They soon emerged from the maze of alleys and lanes onto a small street that headed to the right, away from the port. After a few minutes of walking casually along it, Pip suddenly stopped, then turned down another alleyway. This alley was strange, on a slant that headed downward. Marcus found it a little off-putting. Surely they should be heading up and towards the plateau above?

Whatever the reason for it, Marcus trusted Pip, and decided not to say anything.

Halfway down the alley was an intersection and a series of shadowed alcoves. Quickly, Pip slipped behind a bit of fabric that had been drawn across one of the alcoves and ushered Marcus inside. There, they waited in the shadows where they would not be seen, but could see everything else. It turned out this was not an alley at all, but a spy hole with a good view of the street beyond. A mesh lace had been strung across the opening, allowing those on the inside to see out, and preventing those on the outside from seeing in.

It was quite ingenious, really—a simple yet effective way to watch for enemies without them seeing you. There was a network of them throughout the town, and Pip knew it like the back of his hand.

Marcus, who was still not sure what was going on, leaned into Pip.

"What are we doing?" he whispered.

Pip reached a hand up and signalled for Marcus to be quiet, then pointed out through the mesh to two figures standing not far away.

"Those two. They've been tailing us."

The colour drained from Marcus's face.

"That's them. The ones who kidnapped me."

Sure enough, there was Fanton, the short man who'd held him at knifepoint and tied him up ... and beside him, Crimson, the woman who'd orchestrated it all. Even with her face obscured by the hood of her dark red travel robe, her piercing eyes were unmistakable. Now shining a dark shade of grey, Marcus could only guess at what emotion this reflected.

Pip watched them intently as they moved past and away from both of them. Once they were out of earshot, Pip turned to Marcus and pointed back up the makeshift alley. Before they got to the far side of it, Pip lifted a metal panel and slid into the space beneath, indicating for Marcus to do the same.

On the other side of the short tunnel was a stable full of horses and gear. Standing in front of one of the horses was a small boy, not at all alarmed to see them emerge in such a strange way.

"Wyverns tell the best stories," the young man said.

"They only tell the truth," was Pip's reply.

He then shook the boy's hand in a fashion that Marcus had never seen, consisting of a series of complex hand movements that Marcus didn't think he'd ever be able to decipher.

"Thank you, Sindar," said Pip. "Please, thank your father for me as well, and tell him our debts are settled ... *after* he returns the boat in one piece."

At that, Pip raised his eyebrow to accentuate the need for the boat's safety. Sindar's father was generally reliable, but Pip had been caught out before. Still, a debt was a debt, and such things were taken very seriously around here.

"He assures you, he will keep it safe and sound."

"I trust that he will. Dragon's blessings go with you."

Marcus was deeply curious about this greeting, but sensed that now was not the time to ask questions. He made a mental note to ask Pip about it when he had the chance.

They mounted their horses, and Sindar opened a large set of double doors at the back of the stable. On the other side of it was a dimly lit tunnel that seemed to continue straight for a long distance. Pip put his boots to the flanks of the horse, and the two of them took off, Marcus's horse in tow.

They must have ridden for a mile or two in silence before they started to see some rays of light up ahead. They slowed the horses to come around a few tight bends, and the tunnel got brighter and brighter. Finally, they emerged from the tunnel, their eyes taking a moment to adjust to the bright daylight. The tunnel, it seemed, ran right out into an outcropping of rocks in the middle of the plains. They'd made good time, and seemed to have avoided the interest of any parties of an unsavoury nature.

"Let's get some distance between us and the port," said Pip, smiling back at Marcus.

Once again, he bounded away on his horse, who was eager to run. Marcus followed suit, and soon they were heading to Pillton at pace, where they would meet with Kyruarth.

A smile crept upon Marcus's face.

Soon, he would be home.

CHAPTER TWENTY-SEVEN

SONDER

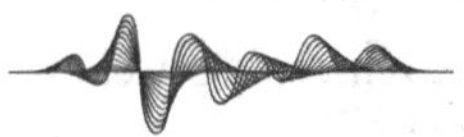

C rimson had arrived just as the sun was cresting the horizon to the east. The giant ball of fire's reflection off the ocean beyond the cliffs was a sight to see, giving light to a new day. The ripples across the water gave the light a diffused look that came with hues of pink and orange in the early part of the dawn. Birds had started to move about, their morning calls growing in frequency and abundance.

Crimson and her supernaturally fast horse had blazed their way through an opening in the cliff's walls and through a tunnel, eventually arriving at a gate that led through to a stable. She'd been here a number of times, and knew its secrets well. As she rode up to the gate, she found Fanton there waiting, as if he knew she would arrive at this very moment. He stood holding the gate open, allowing her to ride straight through.

The minute she dismounted the horse and released the energy she'd forced through its body for hours on end, the beast collapsed in its corral, heaving as though it hadn't taken a breath in hours.

Fanton dropped some coins into the stable hand's palm. "Take care of it."

The stable hand nodded and slipped away.

"Where is he?" said Crimson, ignoring the poor horse and barely acknowledging Fanton himself.

Crimson had encountered Fanton for the first time during her first visit to Sonder. At the time, he'd been nothing more than a pickpocket. Since then, she'd made him her colleague, bringing him into the fold and helping him to find purpose. He was more than loyal—he was downright fanatical about being her best spy, thief, deliverer of things, and supporter in her goal of creating a world where truants no longer kept to the shadows.

And though she'd never admit it, she had grown to depend upon him.

"He arrived with an older man and quickly found lodgings for the night," Fanton reported as though delivering a military report. "They haven't left the domicile since, but others came and went through the night."

"Others? What others?"

"Seasoned curators of illegal merchandise. Locals." Fanton hesitated. "There is … something else. The man he travels with is none other than Pip."

Almost reflexively, Fanton took a step back. Having lived in Sonder for most of his life, he'd known of Pip, though it wasn't until much later he'd made the connection between the man and the one who'd injured his lady in her youth.

"Pip?!"

Crimson's face went red. She instantly closed the distance Fanton had created and grabbed his collar.

"I'm afraid so, my lady."

"How did *he* get involved in all this? Surely he's too old to be out and about. I had thought him long dead," she spat.

Crimson's mind was racing. Pip being here now was no coincidence, and it would explain how Marcus had been able to get away at the wharf.

How in the world was Pip involved in all this?

Before settling down on the cliffs of Cantaloria, Pip and his wife Ally had travelled together to all the corners of the world, and were well known for helping folk along the way. In particular, Ally was recognised as a powerful healer, with skills that went far beyond that of the average mage. Not long after having their daughter, however, it became clear they needed somewhere to come home to ... even if only occasionally. And so it was that they built their home upon the Pinnacle of Osciros.

Still, their reputation was such that they were often called upon, and their tasks were not always safe for a child of only a few summers.

On this occasion, the request had demanded that they travel across the hotlands. Leaving their daughter in the care of a trusted friend, they made the trek across the arid desert, and soon came to make camp in the depths of a forest to the west.

In the dead of night, a young lady stumbled into their camp.

"Someone, please! She needs healing!"

No more than fifteen summers old, the girl had a companion of a similar age leaning heavily on her shoulder, bleeding from a deep wound to her stomach.

"Set her down over here," said Ally, her voice calm and soothing. "I'll do what I can."

"What happened to her?" Pip asked as Ally set about removing the clothing around the wound, gathering energy in her hands.

"She was thrown by her horse, and it trampled her as it ran," said the girl, tears streaming down her face.

Suddenly, Ally gasped. Upon the injured young woman's hip was a tattoo—the symbol of the truant.

"I'm truly sorry," she said to the distraught girl. "I can dress the wound, but no more."

"What? But—but that's not enough! You're a healer, aren't you? I saw the energy!"

The girl's eyes fell to her injured friend, and she saw the exposed tattoo.

"Oh. So that's it." The girl's despair quickly turned to rage. "You know what we are, don't you? Are we not worth saving to you?!"

"Please, calm down," Ally said softly. "It isn't that. I know you are truants, that much is true, but it's not that I won't heal her—it's that if I tried, it would kill her. Healing takes more than just my power. It requires the natural reserves of energy of the injured, and in the case of the truants, you have no energies of your own. Your power is pulled from the earth. Healing her would only diminish her life force even further. If I could change the nature of things, I would, but I can't. I'm sorry."

Lost in her fury, the girl wasn't listening. All she heard was further proof of the prejudice against her people. She began to pull vast amounts of power from the earth, drawing it up into herself with every step she took towards them. Her eyes began to glow red, flickering with the power that was being accumulated.

Ally held up her hands in defence, taking a step back, pulling Pip with her.

"Please, I'm telling you the truth! Let me treat your friend's wounds as any other healer might, and she may still have a chance!"

The girl was lost to the surge of power and hate. The air started to crackle around her, sending ribbons of red power travelling up her legs. The output of such vast amounts of power would be devastating.

Cursing, Pip dove to the right and grabbed his bow. The young lady was well beyond reason, and he had to do something to stop the situation from getting any worse.

He nocked an arrow and aimed it at her.

"I don't want to do this, but if you move any closer, I *will* send this to you!"

It was as if she hadn't even heard him. She continued her advance, drawing more and more power up through her feet, the air around her warping and tearing with the sheer volume of it.

Ally moved into Pip's path, and the stone around her neck began to pulse with a spectacular blue light. Weaving her energy through the air, she set about creating a shield of protection, so as to deflect the attack that was about to be released. The blue hue quickly enveloped her, rapidly building to such a degree that it seemed to match the opposing force.

Seeing the strength and resolve in Ally's eyes, the girl swathed in red stopped her advance and squared off with her. To anyone passing by, the sight would have been awe-inspiring: two formidable women emanating vast amounts of opposing energy, red against blue, to determine which was stronger—the will to attack, or the will to defend.

The injured young truant, whose wound had not yet been tended to, was starting to bleed out. She moaned with pain, causing Ally to look down at her for a split second.

That split second was all her opponent needed.

Sensing the attack, Pip sidestepped Ally's bubble and released his arrow. Sure enough, the girl released her power with such anger that the air itself seemed to explode.

Ally had miscalculated. She would be safe inside her shield, but the attack was too large to deflect. Pip would be annihilated.

"Pip, no!"

In that instant, she did the only thing she could think to do to save him. She pushed her shield over to protect him, and took the brunt of the strike into herself. It threw her back hard against a tree, and she crumpled to the ground. At that same moment, Pip's arrow struck the girl in her right shoulder, taking her down.

The wounded truant was quiet now.

Ignoring the girl his arrow had struck, Pip raced to his wife's side. He lifted her head and cradled it in his lap. Her breaths were very shallow. Tears flowed down his cheeks like waterfalls.

"My love ... what did you do?"

"I had—to keep—you safe," she whispered, trying her hardest to smile. "Look—after our—girl. She'll need—her dad ..."

With eyes of purest blue, she reached up to her necklace with a shaky hand and gave it to Pip ... and then her last breath escaped her lungs. The stone's glow, which had been steady for as long as he'd known her, dimmed to a pale grey.

Pip held her to his chest and sobbed, holding her there for a long time.

By the time he looked up, day had broken, and the truant he'd injured was long gone. The earth had already begun to reclaim the body of the one who'd expired the night before, and Pip felt there was a sort of justice in this, given the way their power ravaged it.

When he was ready, he lifted Ally up and placed her on her bedroll, smoothing out her clothes and holding her necklace tightly in his hand.

"I will give this to our girl, my love," he said, his voice hoarse. "She will cherish it forever, knowing she had the most amazing mother in the world. Thank you for being mine."

He leant forward and kissed her forehead.

At that moment, her body started to glow the same shade of blue it often did ... but this time, the strength of it was far beyond anything he'd seen before. The glow started to feel hot, and he had to step away, shielding his eyes from the light.

The event lasted for no more than twenty seconds, but when the light dimmed and the world around him returned to darkness, her body was gone. All that was left of her now was her bedroll, and the pebble necklace he held in his hand.

He stared at the bedroll for a long time, hoping that he would see her again someday ... but he knew it for a fool's thought.

His mind turned to the one who had taken her away from him.

It was an unpleasant feeling, and one he knew Ally wouldn't have approved of ... but in the wake of her absence, he couldn't help it.

One day, he would have his revenge.

"I trust you've readied a bath?" said Crimson

"Yes, my lady. Right this way."

Fanton bowed before his mistress, directing her to a far door in the stables.

In the room beyond, there was another door at the end of a corridor. Through it, they exited the barn and found themselves in a side street. It was still dark in this part of the town, and the light of the dawn sun was only just now hitting the port. It would be a number of hours before the reflectors leading into the cove would get the sun's rays this deep into the cavern—a fact that would prove useful for those who didn't want to be seen passing along the narrows, as the roads were called here. They turned right and headed up the narrows towards a large, well-established residence, larger than any other in the area.

This was Fanton's home. He had bought the place after Crimson had taught him how to grow his wealth and rewarded him well for his service.

Fanton showed Crimson to the room he'd prepared for her, to the left and through the gabled hall towards the rear of the home. He opened the double-doored entry to the room, revealing a four-poster bed with golden sheets and drapes hanging from the banister. Across from the bed on the right wall was a dresser with an ornate mirror and washbasin, the room smelling of roses and jasmine.

On the bed were fresh clothes to Crimson's size and taste, as well as shoes that were designed for riding.

"I will leave you to refresh yourself, and return within the hour. There'll be a meal waiting for you in the kitchen. If it pleases you, and you're ready to ride, we may depart after that."

"A slight change of plans, Fanton," said Crimson, looking at him with eyes ablaze with orange and rubbing at her right shoulder. "I've an old score to settle."

BETWEEN WORLDS

The morning after the Ku-Da-Ru were released from service, Frederick, William, Katarg, and a number of soldiers from the castle gates had made for the barbarian lands with haste—and now, four days of hard riding later, the party made its way into the foothills and down towards the Lunar River.

In the years following his inauguration, Frederick had spent many nights riding long and hard across the lands now known as the Lunar Ranges, helping the disparate barbarian clans to become a unified land with a council of voices working together. It had been a number of years since that time, and now that he'd returned to ride the plains once more, the fruits of that labour were easy to see.

In the settlements along the river, weapons no longer hung at the people's hips, and instead of hiding in huts and caves, their children ran around and played in the open. It was freedom that Frederick had advocated for in his barbarian neighbours, and as he worked his way towards the Pillars, freedom was exactly what he saw. It made his heart swell with pride.

Upon arrival before the stairs leading up to the central chamber, Frederick's group was met by the outer guards, who recognised the broker of the peace they now enjoyed, and greeted him warmly. The guards summoned stable hands for their horses, then began to lead them up the path. At the top of the stairs was an opening that looked like nothing more than an entry to a small cave, but as they crested the rise and turned into the opening, it opened up into a staggeringly large chamber, greater than any other they had ever seen. Having been here before, Frederick looked on at the others' reactions in amusement, the sight stopping them in their tracks.

The entry was a low overhang, and as they proceeded inside, the roof disappeared almost instantly, the internals of the Lunar Ranges opening up as if hollowed out. In the far reaches of the cavern was a brilliant blue glow that emanated from the walls themselves, shedding light to the far reaches of the cave and bathing everything within it in a wonderfully calming glow.

Making further use of the natural glow, the path had been covered with colourful stones that helped to reflect the light. Made up of every colour one could imagine, the stones were charged by the surrounding glow, giving the impression of a patterned rainbow leading the way to the central chamber and the council hall. Off to the left and right were bundles of weaved baskets filled with food of all types, stockpiled for when winter was upon them to sustain their people during the colder months when food was scarce.

As remarkable as it all was, more than his surroundings, Frederick was looking at the warriors. He had come with a purpose—to call upon his allies for help in securing his borders and his castle.

Calling for the Castle Neleuwan guards to hold their position outside, Frederick, William, and Katarg moved forward into the final part of the chamber, the Council Circle. In a smaller chamber at the end of the path lay a circle of hewn stone seats, covered with pelts and skins to make them soft and supple. Since the request had come from the King of Neleuwan himself, all of the clan's chieftains were in attendance.

The three men approached the circle, and were invited to take a seat at some of the vacant seats by the entrance.

The first to speak was an older man—the first chieftain Frederick had entreated on his initial tour across the Ranges, the chieftain of the Qhillip clan, a man who'd commanded the respect of all the clans even when they were still at odds. With dark grey hair braided on both sides of his head, bound tightly towards the back of his skull, his muscular form was intimidating despite his obvious age.

"Welcome back to the Setilim of Peace, friend," said the chieftain.

"It is good to see you well, Yetingi," said Frederick. "It warms my heart to see the people of the plains in such good spirits."

"For that, we have you to thank. Without your wise words and your show of strength, we may never have understood that our differences were not differences at all. I welcome you and your guards to the Council of Chieftains."

"It is an honour, my friend," said Frederick, addressing the room. "I thank you all for allowing me to walk among you in your sacred spaces once more."

Smiles and nods of acknowledgement spread around the circle.

"I must say, your summons came as a surprise," Yetingi continued. "What brings you before us this day?"

Frederick looked around the room tentatively, and with each face he saw, his fear that what he was about to say would cause all sorts of misunderstandings grew ... but he could think of no other option.

"Chieftains of the Lunar Ranges, I sit here under the Pillars of Kamiditra with a heavy heart. A number of days ago, my personal guard, the warriors known as the Ku-Da-Ru, were released from my service. Without anyone to replace them, my kingdom is vulnerable. I come seeking your guidance on the matter ... and with a request for you to consider."

He let the air stay silent a little longer than most would be comfortable with, intentionally building the tension in the air to bring his points home.

"We are well aware of the Ku-Da-Ru's strength," spoke one of the chieftains. "Were it not for them, I daresay we'd have overrun Neleuwan a generation ago. And you say you dismissed such warriors? Why?"

Frederick went on to explain everything he'd come to understand about the spirits who'd made up his Home Guard, and the reasons he'd felt it necessary to free them, regardless of the consequences. His explanation seemed to garner a great deal of respect from the barbarian chieftains, whose culture saw them conferring with the spirit world often.

Strangely enough, each of them seemed to react to Commander Kai's name.

"It is a well-established fact that these plains, now known as the Lunar Ranges, are home to some of the greatest warriors ever to exist—warriors forged in the fires of brutal conflict and great need. Among those, there are few more lauded than the legendary Avarie," Frederick continued carefully. "It pains me to come before you after helping your people to find peace, only to ask you to take up your weapons once more ... but if there are those among you who still lust for battle, then perhaps there might be an opportunity for them to regain their honour as the new guardians Commander Kai spoke of, and to further unify our peoples. I once faced the Avarie's ferocity firsthand, and can think of no finer allies to have at our side."

Without a word, every one of the chieftains stood up. Yetingi walked to the middle of the circle and took a knee, his back to

Frederick, and the remaining chieftains gathering around him, each of them placing a hand on his back and shoulders.

Though unnerved by the reaction, Frederick trusted the chieftains, and did not move a muscle.

A low hum started to emanate from the chieftains, resonating off the walls of the chamber. As the humming grew more rhythmic, the undulating blue glow of the walls and the stones reflecting it started to pulse. The warriors' hum waxed and waned in intensity, and with each rise, the glow would flare. William and Katarg scanned the room back to back, circling Frederick, making sure he was not in any danger.

The group of men started to move like a wave every time the humming grew in intensity, and Frederick realised that the waves were generating the pulsing light—with every wave, the light grew in strength, and the pulses became more frequent. It was as if the hum were generating some kind of esoteric power, rising in volume until it reverberated through every cell in their bodies. It felt as though they were being pulled into a void of light and sound ... and then suddenly, it stopped.

Opening the eyes they'd closed to ward off the light, Frederick and his two most trusted men found themselves in the middle of a white expanse, pulsing and thrumming with unknown power. Of the chieftains who'd been present in the council chamber, only Yetingi remained.

Rising from his kneeling position, the elder chieftain indicated for Frederick to stand, then motioned for them to follow.

The three followed Yetingi towards an iridescent blue light glowing in the distance, and as they approached, the light became bigger and bigger. When the blue light was almost upon them, Yetingi indicated for them to stop, then reached out to touch what appeared to be the source of the glow. Upon contact, the source descended in a slow drip down to whatever floor there was in this place, then dissolved to a puddle.

A moment later, the puddle started to reconstitute itself into a feminine silhouette.

The voice that spoke was subtle, lilting, and beautiful. Rather than arriving like spoken words, it emanated out from the being like waves, enveloping each of the men's bodies with pure love and care.

Yetingi just smiled, bowing his head to the figure before them.

"I have been waiting for you, young king," its voice echoed. "Frederick, king of Neleuwan, holder of the Bands of Awe … and carrier of a burden yet to be understood." She turned to William and Katarg. "William, warrior at heart. Your prowess in battle is unmatched, though you are yet to discover your true strength. Katarg … you are duty bound, but you too have a heart that yearns only for one thing: the safety and wellbeing of your king. Your mind is your armour."

Compared to hers, in this place, Frederick's voice seemed feeble, hoarse.

"Who … who are you?" he managed.

Frederick felt her smile, more than he saw it.

"In life, my name was Ally. I am but a shadow now, fulfilling the last of my purpose before continuing into the world beyond. I come before you to prepare you for what is yet to come—to do my part in returning the world to its rightful place among the stars. The words I speak to you now will not be familiar to you, but their meaning will become clear in time. The Guardian Dracco has been found, and with him, the new Fellowship of the Accord. Above all, you must understand that the Avarie you came here for are not the guardians you seek."

Frederick's expression grew pained.

"If not the Avarie, then who? I've no one else to turn to."

After speaking those words, William and Katarg vanished from sight.

"Dragons, young king. The Accord are a society formed when they yet roamed the land, imparted with the dragons' secrets and the power to match. They have been here for thousands, if not tens of thousands of years, watching and waiting for the return of the Guardian Dracco, the one who will lead the dragons back to the light."

Immediately, Frederick's mind turned to the fountain.

"There is more you must understand," Ally continued. "The Guardians are young. They have not yet come into themselves, but they will, and will grow into their abilities at pace. They are the key to the dragons' return. They *must* be protected, so that the dragons become your guardians in Neleuwan as the Fountain of the Dragon has foretold."

"Who are these guardians?" asked Frederick.

"Seek out the boy named Marcus, and all will become clear."

Marcus? The squire he'd set out to find?

Suddenly, Frederick understood why the truants had taken him.

Yetingi, who'd been standing back, moved forward towards the spirit, the two of them exchanging words Frederick couldn't quite hear before turning and starting back the way they had come.

"I understand," said Frederick, watching as Yetingi departed. "There is one more thing I must ask. Commander Kai spoke of a Chamber of Life, but in all my reading, I've never heard of such a thing. I'm beginning to suspect I know to whom the Bands must go, but I'm not sure when, or where."

Again, he felt Ally's smile.

"You needn't worry. When the time comes, you will know what must be done."

"Very well," he said, resolute. "Is there anything else I must do?"

There was a hesitation, almost a shyness, from the ethereal figure.

"If you can ... tell my husband that I loved him, in life and in death. I await him here, so that we might cross over together. He was my life ... my love ... my everything. Above all ... tell him our daughter yet lives, and will return to him soon."

The words carried such emotion that Frederick could not help but shed a tear.

"What is his name, milady, that I might deliver your message?"

As the name passed her lips, her features began to clarify.

"His name is Pip."

And then, the world went black.

CHAPTER TWENTY-NINE

CHANGED

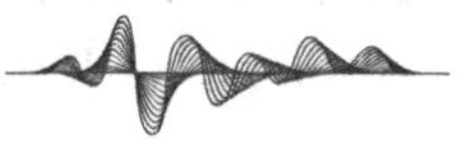

Slowly, Frederick opened his eyes to find himself lying on the floor, the group of chieftains crowded around him. Sitting up and straightening himself out, he saw William and Katarg lying on the ground just behind him, yet to awaken. He took a second to get his bearings, looking around himself and then up into the waiting faces of the chieftains, all wearing smiles.

"My men," said Frederick, still a little dazed himself. "Are they alright?"

"They will rouse shortly," said Yetingi, who stood in the middle of the group. "How do you feel?"

"Strange," he replied. "Like I've awoken from a dream ... but that was no mere dream. I feel a clarity of purpose in the things I must do. What *was* that?"

"We simply guided you as you walked the space between worlds, where each of us has walked before and returned with purpose of our own. You came to us because the loss of your protectors and friends was hard to take, but above all, it was duty that compelled you to seek our counsel."

"In truth, we have known of your coming for several moons," said another of the chieftains. "Your Commander Kai came to us in a unified vision, asking us to prepare you for a crossing so that one of the Accord could speak with you. He also anticipated your request for the Avarie to be re-established ... and though there is wisdom in this, the commander made it clear they are not the best way to manage the safety of your people long-term. Instead, he spoke of another. The Guardian Dracco."

Frederick was astounded. Even after crossing over to the spirit world, Kai was still serving his king. The compassion he held in his heart for the Ku-Da-Ru and their dedication and love for Neleuwan brought him to silent tears.

Yetingi offered him a hand, and helped him to his feet.

"Thank you," said Frederick, wiping his eyes. "The lady of the Accord mentioned the Guardian Dracco and her order, but said little about their nature. Do you know of them? Is there anything you can tell me about who or what they are?"

Before the chieftains could answer, Frederick heard groans coming from behind him. William and Katarg slowly lifted themselves off the ground, standing a little wobbly on their feet before regaining their balance and orientation.

"What happened?" said William, shaking his head like it was foggy.

Katarg did the same, then looked to William.

"My mind is my armour," he said, as if repeating a whisper.

"Warrior at heart, yet to discover my true strength," William echoed.

Frederick smiled. "An accurate assessment, I think."

"Come," said Yetingi. "Let us rejoin the circle."

Moments later, all present had returned to their respective seats.

"The knowledge of the Accord was passed down to me by my father, and by fathers in my family going back generations," said Yetingi. "The Guardian Accord are a group of warrior mages formed in a time long forgotten—a time of great flux, much like this one. Their role in history is to guard the lives of those who are necessary to ensure that the delicate balance of the world is maintained ... a balance that is currently under threat. Only when a Guardian Dracco is named will the balance be assured."

"All of that makes sense," said Frederick, "but where are they? How have they managed to remain even more out of sight and absent from the history books than the truants we now face?"

"Alas, that detail was not preserved in the stories of my ancestors. What we do know is that for the first five years of their lives, the females of the Accord bloodline grow up with their families, and are then taken somewhere to grow and learn the ways of the Accord. After that, they are returned to their families to live out their lives as normal, preserving the knowledge of the Accord and awaiting the return of the Dracco."

Frederick's brow furrowed.

"It appears my path is entwined with this Guardian Dracco, but as much as I've learned, I still haven't the faintest idea where to begin the search for him. I suppose I shall have to trust he will show himself in time."

Yetingi smiled.

"There is no need to search, my friend. The Dracco has already been found."

CHAPTER THIRTY

GUARDIAN REVEALED

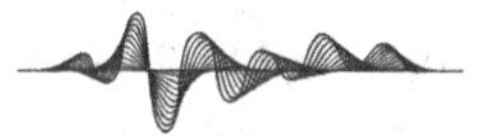

Pip and Marcus had ridden hard all day, hoping to get to Pillton by nightfall. It would be a near thing, and would test riders and steeds alike, but they would be far safer in Pillton proper than anywhere on the outskirts. By the time the sun began to fall, they had ridden across most of the green pastureland that lay beyond the borders of Sonder and across the Hills of Lomi, an undulating mix of small hills that rose and fell like frozen waves on a green, grassy ocean.

Finally beginning to turn his mind away from the danger at his back, Marcus spared a thought for the landscapes he'd witnessed over the past week. It was incredible to think that the land had such diversity across such vast distances … and that it had taken him getting kidnapped to see any of it.

Ironically, for the first time in his life, he felt free, and he relished the feeling.

Pip had taken the lead, and was setting a fast pace for an older man. Of course, he'd ridden horses all his life, and knew how to handle them. That said, Marcus also had a lot of experience with horses from running errands for the baron. As much as his friend Higant loved horses, he'd never quite taken to riding, and so he'd always been happy to pass errands that called for horseback onto Marcus. As a result, he'd become fairly adept at it, and it didn't hurt that this particular horse enjoyed the freedom to run.

Thinking back, Marcus recalled it was their shared love of horses that had brought them together in the beginning, and what had allowed them to become fast friends.

After his time on the open road, with the loss of the baron, Higant was really the only thing calling him to return home.

It was late in the day when they arrived atop of one of the last hills, and as they crested it, they could see a settlement in the distance. Pip, who had come over the top of the hill first, slowed his horse and waited for Marcus to catch up.

"Looks like we made good time. Marcus ... I give you Pillton."

Pip delivered the line with as much fanfare as he could muster, not to mention a big smile on his face. Seeing his own budding sense of adventure mirrored back at him, the look made Marcus smile ... but there was a sadness in it, too. They had grown fond of each other, and knew that their time together was coming to an end.

They headed down the hill at a slow trot, enjoying the last of the sunlight as it settled beyond the mountains far off in the distance. For all the sights they had seen, the humble sunset remained one of the most captivating to witness, transforming even the most mundane scenery into a thing of wonder.

Just before it disappeared behind the mountains, Pip thought he saw a shape coming their way at speed. Could it have been a trick of the light, or had he really seen something? Either way, it was fleeting and far off in the distance, so he shook it off and nudged his horse into a canter towards Pillton.

As they descended the hillside, they came across a road that passed through the base of the hills. They hadn't had any issues with their ride thus far, with no sign of their pursuers. Having made it this close to where they were set to meet up with Kyruarth, they figured there was no harm in taking the road the rest of the way into town.

After riding it for a while, they saw some dust kicking up from the road in front of them. It was hard to see what was causing it, but to be disturbing that much of the road, it must've been moving quite quickly.

Pip and Marcus slowed their horses as a caution, then moved off the road to avoid a confrontation. No sooner had they done that than a horse bolted past them at breakneck speed, perplexing them both.

The horse had no rider.

Looking at each other for an explanation, they shrugged and moved back towards the road ... to find that in the direction the horse had come from, a lone red-robed figure stood in the middle of the road.

The two of them froze.

"It's her," said Marcus. "Crimson."

Then, to Marcus's surprise, Pip stepped out into the middle of the road to face off with the robed figure, signalling for Marcus to stay behind him.

Behind them, another figure appeared. Short and well dressed, the figure held a sword that matched his stature, which to Marcus seemed more like a dagger than a sword. Some ten feet behind Marcus, he too stood directly in the middle of the road.

Turning his back to Pip, Marcus murmured, "Fanton is behind us. I'll keep watch."

Pip nodded, keeping his eyes on the figure before him.

Crimson pulled back her hood, revealing a twisted smirk.

Pip's whole body went rigid, the breath escaping his lungs.

"It's you. The one who took Ally from me," he said, shaking. "You have a debt to pay."

"Interesting," said Crimson, rubbing her shoulder. "I was about to the say the same to you. For the record, however, I have no debt. It was your foolish wife's choice to place her shield over a nobody like you. Had she healed my lady as I'd asked, there would've been no need for any of this."

Marcus could do nothing but listen to the exchange and eye off the small man before him, baffled that his kidnapper and his rescuer were acquainted.

"Her name was Ally, and she should not have paid for your misdeeds with her life," said Pip, his voice just barely tempered by his wisdom, age, and calm. "She offered you nothing more than the truth, and the only healing your companion would've benefited from, yet you rejected that which was right in front of you. In all likelihood, had you simply listened, your lady would've survived, and the crossing of our paths today would've been a happier one … yet here we both stand, with pain in our hearts at the loss of the ones we've loved. That burden falls upon your head."

Crimson eyed him carefully, but did not make a move.

"Why are you here, Crimson?" said Pip, using the name he'd just learned from Marcus. "Why do you seek this boy? What could he possibly mean to you?"

Her eyes flared a deep red, her anger starting to rise.

"None of your business, old man," she spat. "He is my property, and you will return him."

During the exchange, Marcus felt a tap on the hand he held behind his back. Opening his hand, he felt cold steel being pressed into his palm. Feeling around for the grip, he grasped the dagger Pip had handed him and kept it hidden, just in case Fanton made a move.

Marcus kept his eyes firmly locked on Fanton's position, but even at such close range, with the sun's rays disappearing over the ranges, it was becoming hard to see him clearly.

Crimson took a step forward, but Pip stood his ground.

"I warn you, Crimson. Come any closer to the boy and it will be your undoing."

"You are no threat to me," said Crimson, her voice thick with vibrato. "You're nothing more than a peasant who got off a lucky shot. I've already gathered more than enough power to finish you where you stand."

"You have nothing," said Pip, goading her. "You claim to be all-powerful, yet you couldn't even stop an arrow. You're nothing more than a spoilt little girl who throws a tantrum whenever she doesn't get her way."

Crimson's eyes ablaze, she screamed and lifted an arm from her side, palms facing upward. In that instant, she pulled so much power from the earth that the land beneath her feet withered and turned as black as charcoal. She turned and twisted her hands together, calling more and more power from the earth and into the centre of her hands, taking shape and coalescing into a fiery gathering of power.

To Pip, it felt as if time had slowed. His hands still behind his back, he looked at where she was, knowing what was to come. In focusing on her hands, the world had slowed down so much that the small specks of dust in the air almost seemed suspended there, waiting for the change to come.

In an instant, the world righted itself, and time came back in a rush. Pip spun around, grabbed Marcus by the shirt, and leapt with him off to the right.

The power that Crimson had released ripped past them so fast that it almost collected their clothes. Thankfully, Pip had timed it right, moving just enough to get out of the way of the mass of power and energy. It was so strong that both Marcus and Pip felt the hairs on the arms shrivel as it passed them by.

When they hit the ground, they heard an almighty thud. They scrambled back up to the side of the road to see what it hit, and stood up to see Crimson running past them. There, some twenty feet from where he'd stood, was Fanton, having taken the full force of the energy to his chest and fallen in the middle of the road.

With a surprising amount of emotion, Crimson ran up to him and lifted his head.

"Fanton? Fanton! Stay with me. I'll heal you, okay? Just hang on!"

Pip ran to his horse and was just about to mount it when Marcus grabbed his arm.

"Pip, we have to help!"

Pip, who was not expecting this, looked back at Marcus, then up the road to Crimson frantically trying to heal Fanton.

Upon seeing the scene, he just nodded and let go of the horse's reins, heading back towards Crimson and Fanton.

"Crimson," Pip said softly, reaching down to place a hand on her shoulder. "I was a healer for many years. I can help."

No longer was it anger he saw in her eyes, but the little girl she'd been the night she'd approached their camp.

"I used up all my energy," she said, tears streaming down her face. "If you can help him ... please ..."

Marcus stood back while Pip got to work, laying out the healing supplies he'd pulled from his horse's pack.

Pip removed Fanton's shirt to get a better look at what the impact had done, revealing burns and cuts across his chest where the energy had hit him. He placed salves and compresses across the wounds to ease his discomfort, binding them with bandages across to hold it all in place, but there was only so far it would go. Crimson had meant for the attack to kill.

"This will help, but he is severely injured," said Pip. "The wound is more than physical. He needs the help of a mage to remove the energy that was released."

She nodded with finality.

"I know what went into that blast. There is nothing that can save him," she said, her eyes empty. "Leave us."

"I'm sorry," Pip said sorrowfully, thinking of his wife.

He stood and walked away from Crimson and Fanton, moving back to his horse.

Marcus, who was still standing a little ways away, felt compelled to move closer to Fanton. He wasn't sure why, but his legs moved almost of their own accord. He found himself kneeling next to Fanton, reaching out his hands—one over his head, and the other over his heart. His eyes closed, and the air around them changed. It felt cooler somehow, like the heat had been pulled out of the air.

Pip was leaning against his horse, head resting against it, trying to hold back the tears that flared at the memory of the loss of his wife. Suddenly, a light started to come from behind him. It was a glow and a feeling he hadn't felt for a very long time.

It was so like Ally's that he turned as if he would find her standing there.

Instead, he saw the iridescent blue glow emanating from Marcus, pulsing with such rhythm and strength that he was stunned. Could such mastery of that power truly exist? He felt his sorrow fall away, only to be replaced by peace.

Crimson, who was still holding Fanton, felt the power surge through him and into her. Her pained expression went slack, and the pure calm she felt was like no other she had felt before. It was brought about by power in the extreme, yet its source was unknown to her, and foreign in every way. She looked down at Fanton and realised that his wounds, blackened and bleeding as they'd been just moments before, were now starting to heal. His shallow breaths, which seemed to be rapidly approaching his last, were slowly returning to normal.

She looked up at the face of the young man she'd been chasing—the young man she'd made love with on a whim and then held prisoner, amazed at the sheer power emanating from him. How was this possible? He was but a squire, and yet here he was, commanding power beyond measure.

As Fanton's breathing stabilised and his wounds finished healing, Marcus opened his eyes. They now held a ring of iridescent blue glowing around his irises, giving him an otherworldly look.

"Sleep," he said gently, and Crimson immediately lost consciousness, slumping to the ground.

Marcus removed his hands from Fanton and stood, the light blue glow still pulsing around him. He turned his palms up and raised them in an upward motion, causing both Crimson and Fanton to rise from the middle of the road float into the air. They continued to ascend until they were hundreds of feet up, and he pointed into the distance, back in the direction where he and Pip had come. As if bending to his will, their bodies moved off in that direction, coming to land softly over the hills in the distance.

He then walked slowly towards Pip, and once he stopped in front of him, he looked up into his eyes.

"The Guardian Dracco is with you," he said. "Protect him at all costs. She will return to you ... but only if the Guardian Dracco makes it to his destination."

Pip's eyes overflowed with tears.

"Ally? Is that you?"

At this, the glow dimmed and then plunged into darkness.

Marcus's body fell forward, and into Pip's waiting arms.

CHAPTER THIRTY-ONE

FOUND

Kyruarth, Vandrune, and Higant had been riding hard to make it back to Pillton. Since seeing the group of truants venturing into the hotlands, they'd tried to make sense of why the truants seemed to have changed tactic, going after Higant directly. What could that mean for Marcus? Whatever the reason, it was hard not to imagine that had Vandrune and Higant not crossed paths with Kyruarth, they could've ended up in a very different circumstance, and all of their fortunes would've taken a turn for the worse.

In the few riding breaks they'd taken to rest their horses, the three exchanged what information they'd learned about their situation. During this, Higant had had another couple of episodes in which he'd recited large amounts of unexpected knowledge ... and again, though he didn't retain any of what he'd said in response to Vandrune's musings, he could recall everything when the event was prompted by Kyruarth. None of them knew quite what to make of it.

At the end of the second day, when they could ride no more, the group set up camp. Higant's first order of business was to tend to the horses, who'd been ridden almost non-stop for days now.

He'd come to be very fond of Blossom and Thunder, and ever since he'd bowed to them and they'd returned the gesture, they'd coveted their time with him. With everything else that was going on, he still couldn't put the idea of him being a horsemaster together. He simply brushed them every morning and night to make sure they had no burrs or dirt that could rub under the saddles, and they enjoyed the affection and the tending, showing their appreciation by way of hugs with their long necks.

Kyruarth's grey horse was a whole different story. Horsemaster or no, Higant had tried many times to tend to the horse and befriend him, but to no avail. He'd thought up many potential names for the beast, only to find that none of them fit, and the horse would turn away at the mention of them.

As they were making camp, Higant asked Kyruarth, "What do you know of your horse?"

"He was at a stable in Cantaloria, and I paid a fair price for him ... but other than that, I know nothing of him," Kyruarth admitted. "That said, he is a unique horse, to be sure. He has a way about him that other horses do not possess. It's almost like he knows more of this world than we do. You can tell by the way he holds himself, and how freely he rides through the landscape. I rarely have to lead him. It's as if he already knows where he's going."

Higant became borderline obsessed with trying to come up with a suitable name for the beast, one that would express his grandeur and nobility, yet every name was met with refusal.

The next night, Higant had a dream of a landscape he didn't recognise, finding himself standing on a shore lined with cliff faces. Echoing in the distance was a voice that struck him as somebody shouting from the top of the cliffs, and though their elevation helped their voice to travel down to him, he couldn't make out what they were saying. Gradually, the voice grew in depth and volume until it was almost booming, and it became apparent that it was repeating the same word over and over.

Waking with a start, he climbed out of his bedroll and headed towards the string line the horses were secured to, stopping just feet away from the grey steed of Kyruarth. The stallion had seen him approach, and was observing him with eyes of interest.

Higant looked at him for a long moment, then dropped to a knee and knelt before the horse. Thunder and Blossom, who'd been through this before, moved alongside the grey horse, and as one, they all returned the bow.

Higant stood, and the horses stood back up as well.

"My name is Higant, squire to the king of Neleuwan," he said. "I have found a name I believe suits you. It has travelled a long way through a dream to get to me. As horsemaster, I call your name: Numinous."

All three horses stood staring at him, as still as stone. The grey horse, who now was named Numinous, stepped forward and bowed even deeper than before. Thunder and Blossom did the same.

It was an acknowledgement that he'd found a name that the horse was happy to accept, and that he too acknowledged him as a horsemaster, though Higant was still not sure how to process this.

The next morning, after Higant had informed Kyruarth and Vandrune of the horse's new name, they set out on what was to be their final day of travel before arriving at Pillton—and, in theory, Higant's long-awaited reunion with Marcus.

Not wasting any time, Higant was up with the sun and ready to ride.

After yet another hard day of riding, right as the sun was vanishing over the Hills of Lomi, the town of Pillton came into view. Now that it was in sight, Higant was so focused on his destination that he didn't even notice the pulsing blue light emanating off in the distance.

"Higant? Higant!" Vandrune yelled, bringing him out of his reverie. "Over there!"

Instantly, he knew that light was the same he had seen in his dream about Marcus. Without hesitation, he wheeled Thunder to head towards the light.

"Slow down, Higant!" Kyruarth called after him, catching up to him on Numinous. "I understand your eagerness, but we don't yet know what it is or what it means. We must approach carefully."

Reluctantly, Higant slowed his pace so as to be more wary as they approached the crest of the hill above where the light was coming from. Just as they were about to catch sight of its source, the light vanished, plunging them back into the darkness of twilight. They pulled up short of the top of the hill and hopped off their horses, crouching low to the ground.

Peering over the hill's edge, they could see shapes down on the road below. In the low light, it looked like a couple of horses, and someone struggling to lift something onto one of them.

Kyruarth and Vandrune both cast out some of their energy to feel what was below, a trick of mages that allowed them to find the lay of the land when visibility was low. When the invisible energy hit the figures down below, Kyruarth stood immediately and mounted his horse, which was Higant and Vandrune's cue to do the same.

It didn't take them long to get to the base of the hill and slowly work their way up to the figures in the roadway. As they got close, Vandrune used some of his power to ignite an orb of white light above his hand, giving off more than enough light to illuminate the figures.

There, an older man was trying to lift an unconscious boy onto the back of a horse, and not doing a very good job of it.

Responding to the brightness of the light, the older man slowly brought the body back to the ground and turned around.

"Pip!" Kyruarth exclaimed, bounding off his horse and walking to greet his friend.

"You are a wonderful sight, Kyruarth," said Pip, panting from the effort.

Vandrune and Higant had both dismounted by now, and while Vandrune was looking back up the road towards to see if there was anyone coming, Higant only had eyes for the young man on the ground.

"Marcus!" he shouted, running to his friend's side. He looked up at Pip. "What happened? Is he okay?"

"He'll be fine, but here is neither the time nor the place to explain," Pip assured him, then turned to Kyruarth. "We've been lucky enough to survive an encounter with a truant, and though the immediate danger has passed, we should move on to Neleuwan as fast as possible. They won't be far behind."

Kyruarth nodded. "Let me give you a hand with the boy."

Together, they leveraged Marcus up to his saddle. Both of them breathing heavily with the exertion, Pip smiled at Kyruarth with thanks.

"I don't think any of us can take much more travel, but we can't stay in Pillton either," said Pip. "We should skirt around the walls and find a place to camp for the night in the forest beyond."

After securing Marcus to his horse, the three of them mounted their own and set out for the other side of Pillton. Higant took it upon himself to lead Marcus's horse, holding its reins and riding closely alongside it, barely taking his eyes off his unconscious friend.

This had not been the reunion he'd expected.

He only hoped that Pip was right, and Marcus would be okay.

CHAPTER THIRTY-TWO

EINFALL

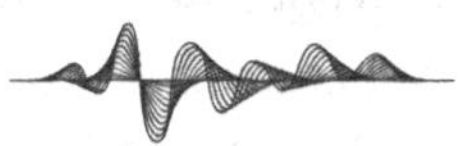

Their business in the Lunar Ranges complete, Frederick and his attendants had begun the return journey to his kingdom. For all the information they'd gained, while he was certain it would be of use, Frederick still couldn't quite wrap his head around the fact that the solution to his kingdom's lack of defences was dragons. Would they really be willing to serve him? And would they arrive in time to guard against the truant threat?

Shaking the doubts from his mind, he set about the task at hand.

It had been some time since Vandrune and Higant had set off after Marcus, who at that point was only a friend dear to the young man. Frederick didn't think even Marcus knew who or what he was. The Guardian Accord ... protectors of those who return the world to balance. But of what balance did they speak? Doubtless, the truants were a threat, but the land had been prosperous and growing for some time.

If there was some sort of an imbalance, he couldn't imagine what it was.

It seemed odd to Frederick that he hadn't heard of them before, and that he'd never been alerted to any of this, by prophecy or otherwise.

He tried to recall the exact words of Kyruarth's prophecy, and measure it against the information he had gathered.

Two boys, one lost and one found, hold truth.

If the boy lost was Marcus, then the one found must be Higant. Was Higant the other guardian that Ally had alluded to? If he was not a Guardian Dracco, then what manner of guardian was he? As for the truth the boys held ... he wasn't quite sure.

Seek that which is lost. Keep that which is found.

Higant had chosen to follow his lost friend, and Vandrune had gone with him to make sure he didn't end up lost himself.

Both will reveal their core.

Marcus had not yet come into his own as the Guardian Dracco, and Higant was yet to fully unlock his mind. This assessment of what was intended seemed fairly clear.

When the rune flares and the spirit calls, send them home.

Frederick could only imagine that this referred to the rune in the fountain flaring, and the Ku-Da-Ru's passage to the spirit world. But why was that line alone unrelated to the boys?

Frederick was at a loss.

It was William who brought him out of his thoughts.

"Sire ... we have riders approaching."

William and Katarg took up defensive positions at the front and back of the king. The two had taken on a different demeanour since the event between worlds. They now knew they each had a purpose to discover and uphold, and it was almost like it had given them a confidence boost—something they now wore as a mantle on their path to finding their true selves.

The riders approached over a ridge ahead of them, making a line towards the king. As the riders came closer, they slowed and spread out in front of them like an arrowhead. There were layers upon layers of them, at least fifty riders strong.

Frederick sat atop his horse and waited. If he dismounted to greet them, they might consider him to be less than them in stature, and he would immediately be at a disadvantage. As the company came to a halt, the front rider held their ground a moment before walking their horse forward until it was almost nose to nose with William's horse.

"I will speak with your king," said the rider.

The voice was feminine, yet powerful. The woman wore hide armour upon her body, but it was shapely and becoming, leaving nothing of the beauty beneath it to the imagination. The strength of this rider and her entourage was not lost on the king—these were seasoned warriors.

"It's alright, William."

Begrudgingly, William brought his horse around to stand beside the king's, remaining ready for anything. Now, Frederick and the woman stood face to face.

"Greetings, Peacebringer," said the woman, giving a slight bow.

It was a formal greeting, and a name he hadn't heard until now. It seemed his successes abroad had granted him an informal but pleasant title.

"You honour me with such a title. Thank you, milady. May I ask to whom I speak?"

"I am the Einfall of the Avarie," she spoke. "We have been charged with the protection of your lands while we await the coming of the Guardian Accord. Now that the Guardian Dracco has been identified, we will do as the stories have ordained. In the time of the Becoming, the Avarie will spread its wings and alight to protect the kingdom of the spirit."

Frederick was surprised by a number of things the Einfall had said, but didn't show it on his face. He would save that for another time. First and foremost, he was stunned that the Council had sent the Avarie to support the kingdom. Only now did he notice that all of the warriors before him were women. Hadn't the Council said the Avarie were not the answer?

Then, it hit him. Thinking back on the conversation, he was never actually given a clear answer to his request. Yetingi had simply said they were not a long-term solution ... but that didn't mean they weren't a part of the plan, and based on what this Einfall had said, this was always going to happen.

Frederick smiled ruefully. It seemed the chieftains were as cryptic with their wisdom as prophets.

"It is a great honour to be supported and protected by the elite of the Lunar Ranges," he said, bowing his head. "I welcome you as though you were family, and only hope your protection does not require battle."

At this the, warrior woman turned to return to her formation, but Frederick raised a hand, stopping her in her tracks.

"Einfall ... might I know your true name, that I might address you correctly?"

The woman seemed taken aback, as though he'd asked something strange. For a moment, Frederick was concerned he'd offended her, but her lips soon curved into a smile. She turned her horse back around to speak to him directly, bringing it close to his side so they were only an arm's length apart.

"I am a warrior first, a lover second, and a woman third," she said. "To those who fear me, I am death. To those who know me, I am love. To those who meet me in battle, I am scorn ... and to those who ask my name in friendship, I am Seren."

Frederick was struck by the name's softness.

"It is wonderful to know your name," he said, smiling back at her, and she bowed her head in acknowledgment.

With that, she turned once more and headed back to her warriors. The Avarie formed a circle around the three of them, and together, they all rode out of the Lunar Ranges and back into the lands of Neleuwan.

Continuing to ride for most of the day, they crossed much of the land between the ranges and the capital. Eventually, the day started to wane, the sun at their backs beginning to dip behind the mountains. There was still a number of hours' worth of riding before they arrived back at the castle, and so Frederick decided to find a place to stop and have some refreshments while they let their horses rest. Sure enough, with the last of the day's light, they found a stream meandering through the plains, offering a place for the horses to drink.

The warriors tended to their horses and continued to be on guard. To them, who were not accustomed to such level ground and verdant plains, it was a strange and unfamiliar landscape. As they explored the grasses that grew to hip height and the rise and fall of the earth's mounds, a child-like wonder came over their faces. They began to talk in strange tongues to each other, examining the elements of the world around them and how they differed from their own.

Though the display warmed him, Frederick was anxious to get back to the castle, considering all the things he'd seen and the way his world had been tipped on its head. How was he ever going to explain everything that had happened? He desperately needed Vandrune's counsel. It had been weeks since he'd heard anything, and he was starting to worry.

William had been standing not far from the king, and Katarg did the same from the opposite side. They both watched as Frederick paced back and forth, something he did often when trying to solve a problem. Though they did their best not to interrupt him when he got like this, he would sometimes get lost in it, and needed a gentle nudge to get back on course.

The longer they stayed out here, the later it would be when they returned to the castle.

"My liege?" William said softly.

Frederick raised his head, then smiled.

"I'm doing it again, aren't I? Thank you, William. Let's go."

He quickly mounted up and set off with William, Katarg, and the Avarie right on his heels. The warriors, with Seren at the lead, kept their wary eye even during the dark. Courtesy of the large cave systems of the Lunar Ranges, they'd trained from an early age to be just as effective in the dark as the light.

The party rode for a few hours without any incident or interaction with anyone. As they came closer to the capital, farms and huts started to spring out of the ground like ghosts in the night. Being quite late now, most had called it a night and gone to bed, and so Frederick decided to slow the pace, not wanting to disturb his people with a large group of warriors coming into the city.

They passed through a few small villages and were about to come around the far side of the last village leading up towards the castle when the warriors out in front came to a sudden stop.

In the middle of the road were soldiers of Neleuwan, heavily armed and ready for a fight. Frederick made his way through to the front, nodding at Seren as he moved past, who was equally poised for battle.

"Both of you, stand down," he said calmly.

Seeing Frederick, the soldier at the head of the formation, Guard Captain Sabr, yelled back to his men.

"King Frederick," said Sabr, moving forward to greet him. "It is wonderful to see you back with us."

"It's nice to be back, Sabr. How fared the kingdom in my absence?"

"The kingdom holds strong as ever, my liege. Allow us to escort you to the castle," he said, turning about to leave and expecting him to follow.

"That won't be necessary," he said, knowing full well this would be an unwelcome change in protocol. Nevertheless, he considered it a necessary step towards acceptance.

"But sire—"

"Today, the Avarie of the Lunar Ranges are to be my escort. I ask that you fall in with them, and that you both see me through the city and back to the castle. Furthermore, I would have you join me in my office with the Einfall of the Avarie to discuss the next steps regarding their boarding and support over the time to come."

To hardened soldiers as much as advisors, tradition was a hard thing to break, but Frederick had offered the man a compromise by having his retinue join the escort, that he might accept his king's instruction without losing any face.

Sabr nodded tightly, returned to his horse, then spoke to his men. The guard dispersed to the side streets and interspersed with the Avarie, taking up positions around the lines of horses now making their way through the city this late at night.

Soon, they arrived back at the castle courtyard and dismounted, met by a number of stable hands who had come from out of the night to stable the horses. The warrior women, who were closely bonded with their mounts, refused at first to part with them until Frederick explained where they would be going, and that they would be well cared for. They agreed, if reluctantly, and Katarg showed them to their billets, leaving Sabr, William, and Seren to join him in his office.

As they entered the office at the back of the dais, Frederick took off his coat and walked to the washbasin, splashing some water on his face. He had been too deep in thought to refresh himself whilst at the stream, and the ride had been long.

He turned to the others while wiping his face, indicating for them to sit.

Instead, Sabr stood next to his allocated chair, as did Seren. Both were unaccustomed to sitting in the presence of someone of important, and were always on alert.

"Very well," Frederick said with a smirk. "Then I shall stand as well."

He took his place in front of his seat and addressed the room.

"Sabr, this is the Einfall of the Averie, the elite guard of the Lunar Ranges," he said with great formality. "They are here because a number of days ago, circumstances led me to release the Ku-Da-Ru from service, leaving our lands more vulnerable than ever."

Sabr tried not to show it, but he was quite shocked by the news.

"Sire. My men had thought it strange they'd been asked to take up posts usually reserved for the Home Guard."

"I will explain the matter fully in the days to come, but for now, let it be known that you and your men are a formidable force, and I respect your sacrifice to the man. In recognition of your service, I propose that you and your men are elevated to the position of Home Guard in the Ku-Da-Ru's absence, to serve alongside the Avarie in their stead until such a time as a way forward can be found."

Sabr bowed his head deeply. However he might have felt about the Avarie, being counted among the ranks of the Home Guard was a tremendous honour.

"We will serve you to the last, my king." Then, Sabr turned to Seren and said, "Einfall, it is an honour to have you join us in defence of our kingdom and the people therein. Anything you require, you shall have."

"To that end, Sabr ... if you could show the Einfall to her quarters in the west wing, I would be grateful," said Frederick. "We are all in need of some rest, and will convene again in the morning."

Sabr acknowledged the request with a nod of his head and headed for the door, indicating for the Einfall to move with him. Instead, she stood her ground, keeping her eyes fixed upon Frederick.

"May I have a moment in private, Peacebringer?"

"Of course. Sabr, if you and William could please wait outside."

Sabr appeared uncertain about the idea, but did not question his orders. William, who'd been standing just inside the door, proceeded to exit the room and closed the door behind them.

After the two men had left, Seren visibly relaxed, moving around the seat she'd been allocated and sitting down, hands falling her into her lap. It seemed odd to Frederick that the stoic warrior who'd been before him moments ago now appeared as a lady, sitting delicately in his chair. Nevertheless, he took the cue, and so proceeded to sit in the opposite chair.

"Thank you for not repeating the name I spoke to you," Seren said softly. "I ask that you continue to use my title in all other company. That name is for you, and you alone."

"I know full well the benefit of titles, and the weight of personal names," said Frederick, a little taken aback by her words. "I must confess, however, I don't quite understand why it is reserved for me."

"When you asked my name when we first met, I explained that I was many things ... but the name I shared with you is one that is most personal to me," she said, suddenly looking extremely vulnerable. "As a woman of the Avarie, we are trained in battle and the art of defence—trained to be strong, and to show no vulnerability. We forsake our names, only to be granted a title when we become a fully-fledged Avarie. At that time, we are also taught one final lesson: that the name we once forsook is the name that we use to unlock our femininity. It is to be shared only with those in whom we hope to find love, affection, care, and freedom."

Frederick was utterly speechless, held captive by her unerring gaze.

"Since I was a little girl, my mother has told me the story of the day the King of Neleuwan would come seeking the Avarie ... and the day the Einfall would find love in another land," she continued quietly. "Even when I became the Einfall, I didn't believe it ... until I met you, and you asked for my name. No one has ever asked me my name."

"Seren," said Frederick, the name like honey in his mouth, "the moment I heard it, I felt it was special, and something to be treasured. Thank you for entrusting it to me. I will protect it as though it were my own heart."

She kept her eyes locked on him, her chest rising and falling with the deep breaths she was taking.

"If you are willing," he said, "I would like to hear more about you and your life, that I might understand you better."

They held each other's eyes, and it was a touching and heart-felt moment—one that Frederick certainly hadn't been expecting. The woman before him was both out of reach, and right in front of him, and that was incredibly enticing. She was smart, beautiful, and knew who she was and what she wanted. It made his heart race like no other had before.

Seren rose from her chair, and Frederick followed suit. She reached out a hand, and he took it gently. Their skin was warm against each other's, and they let it linger a moment before Seren turned and walked to the door, shoring up her vulnerable state with her upright and strong veneer.

Before she opened it, she looked back and held his eyes ... and with the most beautiful smile he'd ever seen, she turned and walked out of the room.

As the door closed, Frederick flopped back into his chair and let out a deep breath.

"Seren," he said aloud, savouring the name one more time.

REUNITED

Skirting the edges of Pillton, Kyruarth rode out in front of Higant and Marcus, with Pip and Vandrune guarding the rear. After arriving on the other side of town, they travelled for about another hour into the forest, coming to a stop not far from where the truant calling had swept Marcus away initially. There were only a number of hours remaining between them and the castle, but Marcus's condition prevented them from riding at a decent clip, and every one of them was deeply exhausted.

The group dismounted, coming together to pull Marcus off his horse and lay him down on his bedroll. By all appearances, he was alive and well, and had simply exhausted himself by healing Fanton with a power he'd not yet understood. Higant stayed right by his side waiting for him to wake up, and in the meantime, Kyruarth, Vandrune, and Pip moved off a ways to recount their stories.

"The initial theory was that Marcus was simply a means to

an end—a way to unlock Higant's latent knowledge and power," said Vandrune.

"And yet Marcus exhibits abilities of his own, and has presented himself as the Guardian Dracco," Pip added. "Are the truants aware of his power? Which of the boys is their real target, and what do they hope to achieve with them?"

"Given how many prophetic events are aligned with their scheme, I can only think they intend to attempt another Cascade," said Kyruarth.

"What exactly is the Cascade, Kyruarth?" asked Vandrune. "The only thing the limited history of truants tells us is that their previous attempt to ignite one failed."

"The only thing we know for sure is that it involves a large number of truants resonating together to channel their stolen energy into a single point. Imagine the truants as links in a chain: in order for the Cascade to succeed, all of their energies must connect, thus completing the circuit and allowing the energy to be focused correctly. If even one link in the chain is broken, the circuit cannot be completed, and the energy loses its focus. That's how their plan was foiled the last time, and how the truants nearly went extinct, destroyed by the backlash of their own power. If they succeed in gathering that much energy in one place, what they might do with it is anyone's guess."

"If they're attempting it again, they're certain to have refined the process somehow," said Pip. "And whatever they intend, it seems to involve these two young men."

Higant, who had been sipping on the soup Vandrune had pulled together for them, did not fail to notice the three men glancing over at him.

As he went to put his cup down, he noticed that Marcus was starting to stir.

"Marcus? It's me, Higant! Marcus, can you hear me?"

Marcus opened his eyes slowly, only to see his friend sitting there watching him.

"You look terrible, Higant," he said with a smile. "When was the last time you took a bath?"

Higant started to laugh, reaching down to his friend and pulling him into a hug. It was the greatest, most reassuring hug that either of them had ever had.

Witnessing the scene, the three men moved towards Marcus to see how he was doing. Vandrune knelt down and placed his hand against Marcus's forehead to see if he had any fever.

"How are you feeling?" he asked.

Higant released Marcus from his hug and let him lie back down.

"Honestly? I feel energised," said Marcus, sitting up on his elbows. "Not tired, nor ill, or even fatigued."

The three men looked at each other, then settled on the ground around him.

"What happened?" he asked.

"Well, what do you recall?" said Kyruarth.

"I was standing near Pip, who was trying to save Fanton. Crimson was crying for him ... and after that, I'm not sure. Next thing I knew, I was waking up here."

"If I may, Marcus ... are you aware of your heritage? Where you came from? Who your family is?" asked Vandrune.

Higant listened to this conversation intently, wanting to know the answer as much as any of them. Marcus had never spoken of his family, if he'd had any.

"I've lived with the baron since I was very young," said Marcus. "He raised me as one of his squires, and was like a father to me. I have no idea who my real family are."

"Have you ever heard of the Guardian Accord?" said Kyruarth.

Marcus shook his head in the negative, looking at Vandrune and Pip and then back to Kyruarth for clarity.

"The Guardian Accord is a group of warrior mages who protect both the balance and the legacy of the dragon," said Pip. "They—"

Before Pip could continue, Higant's eyes flashed blue, and he began to speak. Tapping into his hidden knowledge, he gave a full account of their understanding of the Guardian Accord to date, astounding his friend Marcus with how much he knew on the subject.

Of particular interest to Pip in this explanation was a detail previously unknown to him—that at the age of five, the females of the Accord were spirited away for training, to be returned to their families once their training was complete.

Pip's eyes shone brightly, and he dared to let himself hope.

"Higant, did you say they will be returned to their families?" he said. "Where are they taken? When do they return?"

But Higant had already started to lay down next to his friend, his eyes closing of their own accord.

"Higant? Higant!"

Kyruarth walked to his friend's side.

"The window is closed, old friend. When he wakes, he will not recall what he said. For now, let us weigh his words, and consider what comfort we may take from them."

Pip turned to his friend and nodded, lost in his own thoughts. The notion that his long-lost daughter might still be alive and well, with every intention of being returned to him, was a lot for his wounded heart to digest. If there was truth to Higant's words, then where was she? Who was she with, and how could he find her?

While he pondered these questions, Higant had fallen fast asleep, and the three gents were not about to wake him. Vandrune placed his blanket on top of him and let him sleep.

Marcus, however, was wide awake, and had many questions.

Marcus asked many and varied questions about where Higant had been, and what to make of the Guardian Accord. Vandrune and

Kyruarth told him everything they knew so far, with Pip chiming in occasionally when not lost in thoughts of his daughter.

Many hours passed as they spoke, and when the crescent moon crested the horizon, they took it as a sign to get some rest.

The travellers, every one of them exhausted to the bone, were asleep within moments.

CHAPTER THIRTY-FOUR

It Begins

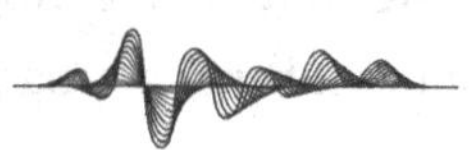

As the light streaked across the morning sky, the clouds turned bright colours of yellow and orange. The winds blew a soft breeze that made the green grass move and sway as if rolling upon an ocean wave, brushing against the bodies of Fanton and Crimson where they lay.

Crimson's eyes opened sleepily as she stirred, disoriented and confused. It took a minute for her to remember what had happened, realising that it was morning, and that the whole night had been and gone. She sat up and rested her arms behind to hold her torso up, looking over to her left, where she saw Fanton whole and sleeping soundly.

A feeling of relief passed over her. She was certain she had lost him. She held her gaze upon him for a few moments more, watching his chest rise and fall with each breath. It comforted her to know he was alright.

In her recollection of the events of the night before, Crimson remembered releasing her power at Pip and Marcus after her anger got the better of her, and the blast slamming into Fanton, sending him reeling away down the road ... but after that, it was hazy. She wasn't sure how she'd ended up here, nor how Fanton had been healed so completely. Pip was no mage. She must've healed him herself, somehow. But where were Pip and Marcus? And how had the two of them come to be lying in the grass, so far away from the road?

Rising to her feet, she saw the horses they'd ridden from Sonder just down the slope, milling about and eating grass.

Sensing her movement, Fanton groaned as he too stirred and staggered to his feet.

"What ... happened?" he said, looking around.

"I'm not entirely sure," said Crimson, frowning. "I'm still piecing it together myself."

When the memory would not return, she decided it wasn't important. What mattered was that they'd lost an entire evening. She reached into her pocket and pulled out a small blue stone, then held it in her hand.

"Lady Sorten," she spoke into it, and a hooded head appeared above the stone.

"I am here to serve," said the Lady.

"How are the preparations? I draw near to the Chamber of Life, and all must be in hand before I initiate the Cascade."

"All the Ladies are in place," said Lady Sorten. "The tendrils are nearing connection, and will lock in place very soon. We await only the final pulse."

"Tell the ladies that the final signal will be felt after the tendrils are given tension," said Crimson. "This will be the last time I speak with you all before that time. Please give the Ladies my love. The new world is almost upon us."

"Your parents would be proud, my lady."

The blue head disappeared, and Crimson returned the stone to their pocket once more.

Fanton reached a hand to rest in Crimson's, hanging by her side.

"I'm with you to the end, my love," he said.

Crimson looked down at him and smiled that special smile she only rarely allowed him to see.

"We've wasted enough time on Marcus," she said. "We must head straight to the heart of Neleuwan—to the entry of the Chamber, and to the boy named Higant."

She started down the slope towards their horses, and Fanton followed.

"To think the Chamber has been beneath the castle the whole time ... fitting, really," said Fanton. "What better place to initiate the reset? Now all we have to do is find the entrance."

"We're close to the endgame now, Fanton ... and for me, it's been too long in the coming. Since I found out about the Chamber, and that the Cascade could be used in such a way ... the future has never looked so bright."

At about the same time, not too far to the north, Higant stretched as he got out of his bedroll and stood up. He'd slept solidly all night, and the light of the morning made him feel hopeful for the day to come. He couldn't recall when he'd fallen to sleep, only that he'd needed it desperately after riding at pace for what felt like an eternity.

The rest of the camp was quiet and still. Noticing some dried meat and fruits sitting on a rock, he made his way over to it and started to eat some of the delights, washed them down with some water from his skin. With no one else awake, he decided to go check on the horses.

He walked up to Numinous first, who welcomed the scratch underneath his chin. Next, it was Blossom's turn, and then finally his own horse, Thunder. By that point, they'd all surrounded him, and were taking turns getting scratches and rubs.

"Thank you for looking after us all this time," said Higant. "We couldn't have done any of it without you."

In a gesture that was becoming all too common, the horses stepped back and leant towards the ground as if bowing towards him. Within moments, the unnamed horses belonging to Pip and Marcus walked up to fill the void between the horses, joining in the gesture. He didn't understand why this kept happening, but he took the lead from the horses and returned the bow.

After straightening his back, Numinous rose back up, while the rest remained. The grey stallion stepped closer to Higant and rested his head against him.

"Master, we are close to the time of the release," said Numinous. "Our lives are yours to command. We will stand with you when the time comes, standing fast and holding strong until the return of the Dracco."

Numinous moved back and rejoined the other horses, who had since returned to their standing positions.

Higant, who was still waking up after his deep sleep, was absolutely dumbfounded. Had he truly heard Numinous speak to him? Was it simply a dream, from which he was about to wake up?

Whatever was going on, the world around Higant had grown terribly strange. All he wanted to do was go back to being a squire, living his life in the service of the king.

Higant returned to his bedroll and sat with his head hung low, looking down at the grass underfoot, waiting for the others to wake. Thankfully, he didn't have to wait long, as Marcus soon came to and lifted himself onto his elbows.

"You're a sight for sore eyes," he said, looking at Higant. "Not going to fall asleep on me again, are you?"

Higant's head instantly popped up, and he launched himself at his friend.

"Marcus, you're found! I am *so* happy to see you. I've been looking everywhere for you." Tears started to roll down his eyes. "I was so worried."

"It's alright, Higant," said Marcus. "I'm fine. I'm happy to see you too, my friend. You won't believe some of the things I've seen."

The two boys spoke about their adventures at length, and all they'd experienced since being separated. They laughed and cried about how they'd felt at times whilst trying to get back home, and how strange their fates had become.

Caught up in the whirlwind of reunion, they had not even noticed that the rest of the party had woken and started to organise themselves to travel again. It wasn't until Vandrune tapped Marcus on the shoulder that they realised everyone else was ready to ride.

"Come on, gents," said Vandrune. "Let's get you squires back to your king."

The boys smiled up at Vandrune and quickly stood up, gathering their gear and climbing upon their horses.

In no time at all, they set off at pace towards their destination: home

CHAPTER THIRTY-FIVE

ENTRY

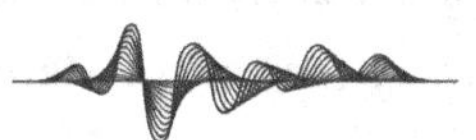

Removing the small, leather-bound parchment wrapped around the leg of the messenger bird was proving to be a challenge. Fanton had sent word to his contacts in the castle, and they'd sent the return bird back to him that very morning. They'd stopped their advance towards Castle Neleuwan as the sun was reaching its zenith to await the reply—they needed to make sure they were heading to the right location to gain entry to the castle, and to reach the Chamber unimpeded.

Fanton finally got the message off the leg of the bird and let it fly off, knowing that it would follow him until it was released from its duty.

"We must make our way to the small stream that runs out of the mountains to the east of the castle walls," he said, summarising what the note had said.

"No more than a couple of hours until we arrive, then," Crimson stated.

From the moment she'd awoken, she couldn't shake the feeling that she was missing something. How had they gone from attacking Pip and Marcus to sleeping in the grass overnight? It just didn't add up. It shouldn't have had any bearing on the plan, but something about it made her feel unsettled, though she couldn't understand why.

Fanton handed her a cup of tea, and she took it without a thank you, or even a nod. For the most part, this wasn't unusual behaviour for her, but something was clearly bothering her. He knew her well enough to know there was no point in asking her about it, and that she would bring it to him if and when she was ready. Leaving her to her tea, he just turned and walked back to the little fire he'd started and put it out, preparing for the ride to continue.

Soon enough, Crimson finished her tea and silently mounted her horse, riding into the plains with Fanton at her side.

It took several hours for them to make their way through the fields and navigate the landscape where farms and houses resided, being careful not to be spotted during the daylight hours. By the time they arrived near the stream, it was dusk, and the light was fading.

They dismounted and walked to the stream's edge, where they put their hands in and cupped water to their mouths. The water felt cool and fresh.

"That's glacial water, that," said a gruff voice, coming from out of the tunnel the stream had been heading into.

"Kabi!" said Fanton, running towards him and giving him a big hug around his legs.

"It is good to see you, my boy," said Kabi, returning the hug he was given.

Crimson smiled to herself at the affection they both had for each other.

"Kabi, let me introduce you to a good friend of mine," said Fanton, looking back towards Crimson.

Crimson stood at the stream's edge, her eyes a smouldering purple as Kabi made his way up to her.

"You need no introduction, my lady. I know who you are."

Unsure of how to respond, she remained quiet, frowning slightly.

"The truants have not been as silent as you think," Kabi went on. "When I heard about the truant mound near the castle, I knew it wouldn't be long before Lady Crimson of the Whistling Sailor showed more than just her skin," he said, laughing cheerfully.

This man knew enough about her to know she'd been a truant masquerading as a prostitute. What else did he know?

"I understand your hesitation, my lady, but we can trust Kabi," said Fanton. "He's been keeping tabs on people and places in the castle and keeping trouble off your back for many years. He's as much of a supporter of the cause as I am ... well, almost."

"And now I get to meet you in the flesh," said Kabi, bowing his head. "It is truly an honour."

"Thank you, Kabi, for helping me in my time of need. I did for a moment think you were here for other reasons, but I trust Fanton, and he apparently trusts you. I can't say I've ever seen him hug another person," said Crimson, smiling down at Fanton.

Fanton blushed at the telling, quickly shuffling away towards the horses to remove their gear and let them roam free.

"So? Where to?" he said, waiting until after the moment had passed.

"This way," said Kabi, proceeding back into the tunnel.

They walked into the dark opening and followed the water flow. The tunnel bent and sloped over wet, undulating ground before opening up into a small chamber. It was as though the current had once been much larger and much stronger, having worn away at the walls over countless years and forming these natural passages.

In the chamber, Kabi pointed to a passageway about thirty feet across the chamber.

"You're in for a treat," he said, grinning.

They walked through the entry and into another world. The tunnel was lit by glowing blue creatures, attached to the roof and walls of the tunnel by the hundreds.

It would've been a spectacular sight, had their lustrous blue glow not reminded Crimson of her encounter with Pip's wife. The colour also felt familiar for another reason, but she couldn't quite place why.

They made their way forward through the brilliantly lit cavern for a number of minutes before it started to move in an upward direction—and interestingly, so too did the stream. It seemed that the slope worked like an aqueduct, moving the water upwards towards the next opening.

As they came to the opening, things were much different again.

A small amount of natural light filtered in through an opening in the roof, which appeared to be coming in through a sort of man-made funnel leading up to the sky above. Below it was a deep pond, where the water came to settle after its journey up the slope. Off to the right was a makeshift ladder that Kabi grabbed and leant up against the funnel wall.

"Now, we climb," he said, looking at them both.

Kabi led off up the ladder, followed by Crimson and then Fanton.

At the top of the makeshift ladder, they found a more substantial ladder made of metal attached the to the side wall of the funnel. They transitioned to this ladder and climbed, not sure where they were headed, but hoping they would emerge soon.

All of a sudden, they reached the top of the funnel.

Kabi climbed out over the lip, then stuck his head back over the top of the funnel and reached down a hand to help Crimson out, with Fanton following just behind. When their eyes adjusted, they found they had climbed out of the funnel ... and into a shrub.

Turning in place, it seemed they were surrounded by dense shrubs arranged around the funnel like walls, creating a space almost the size of a small room around the funnel. Furthermore, the funnel they had climbed out of was, in fact, a well.

"How does a well get surrounded by a plant?" said Fanton, echoing what Crimson was thinking.

"That's how I hid it from everyone," Kabi said with a wink. "Spent years cultivating it, keeping this hidden. The bushes are thorny and harsh, so people left it well enough alone. Makes for a bit of a scratchy exit, but I'd say it's worth the trouble."

"And this is inside the castle walls?" said Crimson. "Did they not notice one of their wells disappearing?"

"They updated the aqueducts decades ago. This old well had been nothing more than a decoration for years before I got to it."

"Amazing, Kabi," said Fanton. "Where to now?"

"My home is just over the way," he said. "Mind the thorns."

CHAPTER THIRTY-SIX

CORRELATION

A number of days had passed since Frederick had returned to the castle. Since then, the Avarie and the newly appointed Home Guard had kept watch upon the walls and at key locations around the castle. It hadn't taken long at all for the Avarie to become part of the new look for the warrior guards who watched over Neleuwan. They'd made a good first impression with the people, interacting and engaging with them whenever they were on watch ... but always remaining vigilant, ready for whatever threat might arise.

On this particular morning, the sun had risen to paint the sky a brilliant orange, the clouds reflecting the sun back down upon the land below. The landscape's orange hues ranging from bright and lively to muted and earthy, few things put the beauty of Neleuwan on display quite like the early morning.

The division of duties for the day saw the Avarie keeping watch from outer towers hidden by the landscape, while the Home Guard were positioned across the walls and gates of the city.

Given their positions, it had been the Avarie that had first seen the riders approaching upon the road—five in total, and moving at pace towards the main gate into the city. The Avarie moved in silently behind the approaching party as it rode past, keeping just enough of a distance to avoid alerting them as they made their way towards the gate.

It seemed the riders were made up of two young boys and three older men, but the Avarie knew better than to judge by appearances.

The riders did not appear to notice the Avarie moving in behind them, and so they proceeded towards the gate undeterred. As they came to the gate, the Home Guard posted there held up a hand to stop them as they came forward, causing them to slow their horses.

"State your business," the guard said warily.

As they'd agreed, Vandrune had been at the head of the riders, and approached first.

"I am the prophet Vandrune, advisor to the king. We have important business with His Majesty."

The guard got a closer look at Vandrune and then bowed apologetically.

"Master Vandrune. A pleasure to see you again," he said, then leant out past him to take in the rest of the riders. He noticed the young boys on the horses and a smile came across his face.

"Marcus? Is that you? I haven't seen you in ages," he said, walking around to the side of Marcus's horse. "Where have you been? And what on earth were you doing outside the walls with one of the king's advisors?"

"Jerry … wow, it has been a while. Good to see you," said Marcus, shaking hands with the guard. "It's a long story, and I'm afraid it'll have to wait. It really is important we see the king as soon as possible. Any chance we could speed this up?"

"For you, my friend? Anything," said Jerry. "A—and you, of course, Master Vandrune. The Avarie will see you through to the castle."

The guard walked back towards the gate and raised a hand to

indicate to the rest of the men to allow entry, then turned and watched the horses advance through the gate along with the Avarie.

The party made their way up through the town and into the castle proper—to the main yard, from which they'd set off in search of Marcus all those weeks ago.

"It feels strange to be back," said Marcus. "Especially to be seeing the king ... I still can't believe he'd cared enough to personally give chase when I was taken."

"Oh, that's right," said Higant. "I forgot to mention that with everything else that's been happening, but ... we're the king's squires now."

Marcus's jaw dropped, then he just shook his head.

"You know, that's actually one of the least crazy things to happen lately."

Vandrune dismounted first, and Kyruarth followed. The two walked over to Pip and assisted him off his horse while the boys dismounted, taking the reins of their horses and walking them to the waiting stable hand.

Before handing the young stable boy the reins, Higant bowed before the horses.

"Go with this boy. He'll take good care of you," he said. "I'll visit you soon."

The horses all nodded their heads as if they'd understood him perfectly, leaving the stable hand looking at Higant very strangely as he led the horses away. As he turned, he found a similar look upon Marcus, Pip, and Kyruarth's faces. Vandrune just smiled.

"What?" said Higant.

"How long have you been a horsemaster, young Higant?" said Kyruarth in his deep, resonant voice.

"I, uh ... I'm still not sure about this horsemaster business, but I found out I could communicate with them recently," he said rather meekly.

Kyruarth looked upon the boy for a moment with interest.

"The times we live in are strange indeed," he added, then turned and followed Vandrune into the castle.

Before Higant could follow, Marcus grabbed his arm.

"I'm sorry, but *what was that?*"

"I can sort of talk to horses now?" he said, shrugging his shoulders. "Like you said, stranger things have happened."

Higant continued after the group, and Marcus followed close behind. Pip, who had been watching the exchange with a smile, took up the rear.

None of them noticed that among the number of people drawn to their arrival were a lady, a short man, and their unscrupulous associate.

"They've arrived, my love," Fanton said to Crimson.

"Yes ... which means we have work to do."

The three of them walked away from the entry and out into the crowd.

At the rear of the dais, Vandrune knocked on the door to Frederick's office and waited. William and Katarg were standing watch outside the office, which meant that the king was inside working. Vandrune had greeted each man with warmth and thanks for looking after the king in his absence, and they'd looked at him a little strange, but said nothing.

The doors swung open, and standing before them was King Frederick.

"Vandrune! Oh, my, it is wonderful to see you back. Come in. We must talk. I have so much to tell you about—"

Frederick looked past Vandrune and noticed the number of others at his door.

Vandrune stepped aside to allow the king to move out into

the doorway and see who was there, and his eyes fell upon Marcus and Higant.

"Marcus, you are well! It is so good to see you returned," he said, reaching for the boy and hugging him tightly. I'm sorry for sending you on such a fool's errand. If I'd exercised better judgement, you may never have been taken. Welcome home, my squire."

As kind as the baron had been, he'd never been much for affection. Marcus, who'd never been greeted in this way by anyone other than Higant, and certainly not by an authority figure, felt a wave of emotion come over him. He was finally back in a safe place, surrounded by people who cared about him. Tears streaked down his face as the hug lingered.

Frederick eventually pulled back, then turned to Higant.

"You chose wisely, young Higant. I hope the journey was not too arduous, and the world treated you well?"

"I found more questions than answers outside the castle walls," said Higant, placing a hand on Marcus shoulder, "but the goal was to find my friend, and find him I did."

King Frederick smiled and then stood up, taking in the remaining two people in the room. Finding Kyruarth's eyes, his breath caught in his chest.

"It's you. The one who brought me the prophecy."

"So it is, King Frederick. I am Kyruarth, and I'm here with Vandrune and the others to see this through."

Frederick nodded in affirmation.

"This is a good friend of mine, it was he who kept Marcus safe on his journey back to his home." Kyruarth explained

"You have my thanks, and my debt of gratitude, sir. You are welcome to stay as long as you need."

Pip smiled. "Thank you, my liege."

Frederick turned and headed back into his office.

"Come. Sit. Have some refreshments. We have much to discuss."

He gestured for William and Katarg to join them inside the room and they nodded, quickly to be replaced by the Avarie who'd escorted Vandrune's party. Not for the first time, Frederick and his guards marvelled at the Avarie, who were every bit as efficient and disciplined as the Ku-Da-Ru. William closed the door as he came in, and as a compromise, he and Katarg stood guard at the other side of the door.

Shortly after, a young lady brought in food from a small passageway to the left of the room, where a hidden staff corridor existed for such things. She laid food and drink upon the table and returned to the hidden door, disappearing as though she were never there.

"Please, eat, drink," Frederick insisted.

They all took advantage of the food and drink, proceeding to take their fill. Frederick, on the other hand, had simply sat and watched them move about, taking in information about their tastes and preferred drinks.

Finally, once they'd all settled, he delivered the news.

"The Ku-Da-Ru have left my service, and returned home."

Higant and Marcus continued eating through the conversation, as they were famished, and hadn't eaten a hearty meal in what felt like a very long time.

"Then the prophecy has begun," said Kyruarth.

Frederick gave the room an in-depth summary of all that had occurred in their absence, from his experience at the Fountain of the Dragon to his walk between worlds at the Council of Chieftains. To emphasise his story, he pulled the Bands of Awe out from his coat pocket, and all the people in the room leaned in to see.

Enraptured as they were, of all the details he had shared, there was one that was of more interest to one of them than any other.

"You said the spirit's name was Ally?" Pip breathed.

"I did," said Frederick, pointing at William and Katarg. "We returned from our meeting with her changed—different somehow, and yet the same. We felt her words deep in the depths of our souls."

Pip began to tear up, and somehow, Frederick knew.

"You ... you're Pip, aren't you?"

Eyes wide, the old man nodded.

Frederick smiled. "Your wife had words for you, dear Pip."

The king relayed Ally's message, along with her promise to meet him in the world between so they might cross over together ... and, perhaps most significantly, the promise of the imminent return of their daughter.

Combined with Higant's assertions of Accord children returning to their families after their training, Pip's reunion with his daughter now seemed more possible than ever. His emotions got the better of him, and the room could do naught but give him the space to process what he'd heard.

"Thank you, sire. I cannot tell you how much this means to me."

After the air had cleared, Vandrune was the next to speak.

"We have much to share ourselves, my liege."

He informed Frederick of all they had learned—of the knowledge locked in Higant's mind, Marcus's status as the Guardian Dracco, and the looming threat of the Truant Cascade, as unclear as its nature remained.

"There's still so much we don't understand," said the king. "What does this Crimson hope to accomplish with the Cascade, and what do the boys have to do with it? What role do the Bands of Awe play in all this, and how in the world are dragons involved?"

"There are more moving pieces on this board than even we can see," said Vandrune. "One thing is certain. We stand on a precipice, waiting for the fall ... but what form it will take, and where the pieces will land, are all yet to be determined."

The room fell into a contemplative silence.

"Kyruarth," Frederick said eventually. "I would like to go over the last line of your prophecy, if I may. *When the rune flares and the spirit calls, send them home.* It seems a fairly clear reference to the freeing of the Ku-Da-Ru ... but it's the only line that doesn't directly relate to Marcus and Higant. Is it possible there might be another meaning? One that applies to them more closely?"

Kyruarth smiled. "Personally, I believe it hints at the boys' entanglement in the events to come. Unrelated as it may seem, it was necessary for you to hear it in order for things to progress to this point, and for the stage to be set for the parts they each have to play."

At that, Marcus stepped forward, clearly unsure of himself.

"I've been told of what happened on the road to Pillton, but I have no memory of it. It's hard to believe I have anything to do with dragons," he said. "As far as I know, I'm just a squire. I don't know what I'm supposed to do."

"I understand it's a lot to take in," said Kyruarth, "but the proof lies in this necklace. Pip?"

Pip retrieved Ally's necklace from his pocket, beckoning for Marcus to approach.

"Marcus ... my wife treasured this stone, wearing it from the day I met her to the day she was taken from me. It glowed the same blue the entire time she lived, only turning grey when she passed. It has only ever shone blue again once since that time—when we placed it upon your neck."

"What is it, exactly?" Marcus asked. "How does it prove anything?"

Kyruarth stepped forward to answer.

"It is a bone nodule of an elder dragon, given freely at the moment of its death. The dragon kin are uniquely connected to the spirit world, and offer these stones to members of the Accord, that they might draw upon their power after their passing. I once made use of one to create the Ku-Da-Ru, but even for me, it never glowed as it does in the presence of a true member of the Accord bloodline. Observe."

He gestured to Pip, and Pip slowly lifted the thong on which the pebble had been strung and placed it over Marcus's head, allowing it to come to rest on his chest.

And yet, as it came into contact with Marcus's skin, no light emitted from it. It simply sat there, grey and unmoved.

"Kyruarth?" said Pip, looking to his friend for answers. "What does this mean?"

The prophet simply frowned with consternation.

"Is he not the Guardian Dracco after all?" said Higant.

Marcus turned and shrugged at him with a look that said 'I told you so'.

"I don't know what to make of the sudden change," said Frederick, "but Ally herself confirmed that Marcus is the Guardian Dracco."

"Then why does the stone not glow?" said Vandrune, stroking his beard.

"I was unconscious when it glowed last time," said Marcus, addressing Kyruarth. "Could it have been sensing your residual energy after healing me?"

"The power of a mage does not linger," Kyruarth said finally. "It is used, or it is lost. It is pulled from the mage himself, from the fundamental powerhouse of the body: miniscule cells called mitochondria. As mages, we pull energy from them, as they pull energy from us. It is a symbiotic relationship. Once their power is expended, no trace of it remains."

None of them seemed to know what to say.

"I don't know if it means anything," said Pip, "but after Marcus healed the truant's companion, when he told me the Dracco was with me, I—I felt as if it were Ally herself speaking to me."

Vandrune leant in a little, an inquisitive look upon his brow.

"What gave you that impression?"

"It just ... felt like her," Pip said slowly. "When my wife healed people in the past, it was in exactly the same way that Marcus had. She would put a hand on their head, another on their heart, and ignite with power ... but there was more to it than that. It had a feeling—a certain vibration to it. It was like ... a resonance they shared somehow."

Kyruarth and Vandrune shared a look at the mention of that last word.

"Such an event brings to mind the events of the night you saw Marcus in your dream, Higant," said Kyruarth. "It's something that's bothered me since the day we met out on the sands: why would the truants change their tactics at the last, abandoning their search for Marcus and seeking you out directly? Furthermore, the resonance rite requires an intimate understanding of the target's frequency. We've since learned the means by which they obtained Marcus's frequency ... but how could they possibly have discovered yours?"

Vandrune looked alarmed. "You don't think they—"

"There's nothing for it but to confirm," Kyruarth interjected.

Vandrune nodded slowly, and the two mages closed their eyes, relaxing their breathing and leaving the others guessing as to what was happening.

Moments later, both Higant and Marcus began to hear a noise much like the one they'd felt in their respective dreams—that same insect-like hum, soft at first, but growing in intensity until it was loud and vibrant.

Vandrune and Kyruarth's eyes flew open, a look of pure confusion upon their faces, and the vibrations faded from the boys' minds.

"Their frequencies," said Vandrune. "They're identical."

"I don't know how such a thing is possible, but they are," Kyruarth confirmed. "That explains how the truants caught wind of Higant. They weren't looking for him at all—they thought they were still on Marcus's trail. No wonder the prophecy regards them as twins. But what does it mean?"

Higant, however, was not listening.

After being exposed to the vibrations of the resonance ritual once again, he'd seen another flash of the pebble he'd seen landing on the map of Castle Neleuwan in his vision—only this time, the location it pointed to was much clearer.

He looked over at Marcus, and to his surprise, he saw recognition in his eyes. Had he seen the same thing?

"What is it, boys?" said Vandrune, noticing their alarm.

"I know where we must go," the two of them said in unison. "The Fountain of the Dragon."

CHAPTER THIRTY-SEVEN

The Path Opens

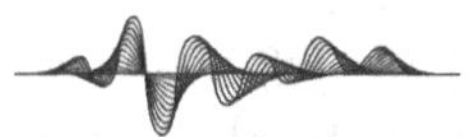

Having delivered the meal to Frederick's office, the serving girl returned through the servant door and took a deep breath.

It was always nerve-wracking bringing food to His Majesty, especially when he had guests, and today there had been many. Walking through the corridor, she rounded the corner and began to descend the stairs to the kitchen—when all of a sudden, an arm shot out from the shadows, locking around her throat and incapacitating her in seconds.

Crimson lowered the girl's unconscious body to the floor, then snuck around the corner to the servant door, keeping her body low and an ear to the slight crack in the doorframe. With contacts like Fanton, who had access to the castle, it was not that hard to find her way into this hidden hall, which was just one of the many secrets she'd come to learn.

The conversation happening on the other side of the door revealed a number of new things to her, as well as confirming there was still a lot her enemy didn't know. She smiled silently to herself.

They had no idea what was coming.

Her initial plan to ignite the Cascade had been thrown into complete disarray, and yet all the pieces had effectively assembled themselves. Higant, Marcus, and Kyruarth were all in place, they had the Blade of Ki, and if her guess was correct, this fountain that had appeared to them in dreams and prophecies held the key to the Chamber, the scrolls lead them all to here.

Ignoring the serving girl, she headed back down the hidden stairs of the servant passages. By the time the girl awoke, even if she had some indication of what had happened, it would be too late to alert anyone.

Weaving her way through the passages, Crimson stepped through a gate and out into a bustling alleyway near the marketplace at the castle's outer walls, blending in with the crowd and heading back to The Whistling Sailor.

As she entered the inn, she headed towards the bar and addressed the innkeeper.

"I'll have a Crimson Fire and two meads at the table in the back," she said. "Bring some meats as well."

The man behind the bar nodded, and she proceeded to the edge of the bar, then through a hanging blind and into the dimly lit booth where Fanton and Kabi awaited.

"They move for the Chamber," she said. "We must make for the Fountain of the Dragon immediately."

"The Fountain of the Dragon? What does that have to do with the Chamber?" said Kabi.

"I admit, I don't know for certain, but the fountain has appeared at the centre of a number of prophetic events. Not even they seem to have made the connection. If the fountain is about to lead them all to the Chamber without them even knowing it, we won't get a better chance than this to take back what we've lost."

Both men sat back in awe, lost in her passion and desire to see this done. Even after she stopped talking, both men remained transfixed. It was only then that Crimson realised she had been pulling power from the earth below her feet, extending her will to both men unintentionally.

She took a breath and they both relaxed visibly.

Crimson smiled to herself, then shook her head. Released from her influence, the men continued on as if nothing had happened.

"It's time," she said. "Let's see it done."

William and Katarg flanked Frederick as the group marched down the dais and across the floor of the presentation hall. When they approached the doors through to the public gallery, out of the shadows stepped a beautiful warrior, standing tall and strong. Her posture and the way she carried herself demonstrated her confidence and capability, her intellect evident in her piercing green eyes.

"My king," said Seren, though her demeanour was very much that of the Einfall. "I'd heard you were receiving guests. Whom might I find you with?"

"My advisors, Einfall, and my squires returned," said Frederick. "This is Vandrune, the prophet Kyruarth, Pip, Marcus, and Higant. It is well you have arrived. Would you join us? Something tells me we are about to bear witness to history, and I would have you at my side."

"Greetings to you all," she said, acknowledging each of them warmly. "It would be my honour."

Frederick met her eyes and nodded, and she fell into step with him. Familiar with her presence among them and having come to trust her with their king, William and Katarg took up leading positions, leaving the Einfall to guard his rear.

The party continued through the corridors until they emerged through the halls to the Dome of Lillifor, where they were struck by a strange sight. The light from outside was making its way in and projecting the map of Neleuwan onto the floor as it ever had ... and yet as soon as they set foot on it, in defiance of the colours of the stained glass on the ceiling, the map began to glow a familiar iridescent blue.

"Has the map ever done this before?" Kyruarth asked of the king.

"Not that I've ever heard of," said Frederick.

Marcus, who'd been towards the back of the group, made his way through the throng of people to get a better look. Oddly, wherever his feet landed upon the map, the blue began to fade in a small radius around him, only regaining its light after he moved away. Everyone present noted the phenomenon, but Kyruarth's attention was reserved for another.

"Higant," he said, "could you tell me what this might indicate?"

At first, Higant looked up as Kyruarth with a frown, probably wondering why the prophet had asked him ... however, after a flash of his eyes, that look soon turned to one of intrigue, and then to speech.

"It is common knowledge that the blue light has ties to the spirit world," he began, "which is why it features heavily in matters relating to the Guardian Accord, whose members draw their power from there. The map room's purpose was always to ignite in this way when it comes into contact with the named Guardian Dracco's resonance, thus confirming that the return is upon us."

He finished speaking and looked back at Kyruarth, awaiting his response.

"Thank you, Higant," he said. "It is good to have further confirmation of Marcus as the Guardian Dracco ... though I'm afraid that doesn't shed much light on the phenomenon of the dimming map and bone nodule."

Higant lowered his head, dejected. It seemed that was all he had to share on the subject.

"Worry not, Squire Higant," said Frederick, placing a hand on his shoulder. "Perhaps we'll discover more at the Fountain of the Dragon, as you and Marcus suggest."

Higant offered a smile.

"I certainly hope so," said Marcus. "Even now, the more we learn, the less we understand."

They moved as a group towards the far exit of the map chamber, and towards the final corridor before the fountain.

Crimson, Fanton, and Kabi had made their way ahead of the group, where they now laid in wait in the dark corners of the fountain room. Again, they'd made use of the servant's corridors running parallel to the main thoroughfare, designed both to keep the serving staff out of sight and so they could move through the castle more efficiently.

The three of them held their breath, hoping the sound of the fountain's endless cycle of water would hide any noise they might make.

When the party entered the fountain hall, another strange thing happened. The fountain, which had been the same as they'd remembered it only moments before, started to change. The rune at the foot of the soldier flared as it had the night of Frederick's vision, sending the familiar blue glow emanating throughout the water ... and this time, the dragon's eyes started to glow as well, along with the claws at the end of its feet and the ridged fins on its spine.

"Another effect of the presence of the Guardian Dracco, perhaps," said Vandrune, looking on curiously. "Marcus, Higant ... have you any idea what happens next?"

The boys simply looked at each other and shook their heads.

Einfall stood apart from the main group, remaining utterly vigilant in her protection of the king while William and Katarg took up stations at each entrance to the fountain room. Frederick himself moved towards the fountain, withdrew the Bands of Awe from his coat, and then turned to face the group.

"As you know, the Bands fell from this very fountain," he said, gesturing to the arms of the soldier. "I was told they would be needed in a place called the Chamber of Life, to be used by one to who is twinned by prophecy ... and also that when the eyes flare, they would unlock the knowledge in the barred mind."

All eyes turned to Higant.

"I know not of this Chamber of Life ... but Higant, your eyes flare blue every time you access your untapped potential," said Vandrune. "However, if 'when the eyes flare' referred to your eyes, it could indicate any of a hundred moments."

"The eyes of the dragon, however, have never done this," said Frederick, coming to kneel before Higant. "Perhaps now is that time."

Higant looked at Frederick with uncertainty, then over to Marcus, who gave him a reassuring nod.

"Alright," he said, mustering his courage. "I'm ready."

Frederick clasped the bands on Higant's wrists and upper arms, as he'd seen them configured upon the statue. They were a little loose on him at first, and the bands and their chains felt cold and foreign upon his skin ... but they slowly started to get warmer, growing more firmly upon his skin, shrinking and adjusting to the size of his arms.

Before he realised it, they felt comfortable, as though they belonged there. It felt odd for him to think that, but that was just how they felt to him.

A tingling sensation began to crawl up his arms, ascending from the lower bands to the upper ones ... and though the sensation was strange, he didn't feel any different overall, and had no sense that he had any more access to the knowledge than he usually did.

"I don't think it's working," said Higant, frowning.

The others, however, were stunned.

Higant had started to radiate a subtle golden glow, pulsing in a way that none of them had ever seen. Feeling the sheer amount of energy emanating from Higant, each of them instinctively moved back a few steps.

The glow built in strength until even he could see it, looking down at his hands in amazement.

"How do you feel, Higant?" said Kyruarth.

"I feel great," he said, grinning broadly. "I feel like I've jumped into fresh summer water. I feel ... alive."

All of a sudden, his head snapped back, and a beam of intense golden light shone from his eyes. His arms formed a cross upon his chest, and each of the bands touched their counterparts on the opposite arm. Higant slowly started to lift off the ground, levitating a few feet in the air as the pulsing golden glow created a field of energy around him, magnetic in its gravity. Forced to shield their eyes, the others couldn't approach him even if they tried.

Some thirty seconds later, Higant gradually descended to the floor, his head and arms coming to rest in their original positions. The glow had dissipated slightly, but never disappeared, coming to outline him like a barrier an inch above his skin.

Vandrune was the first to uncover his eyes. Now that Higant's eyes were clear of the beam, they could be seen clearly—and his irises, once blue, had transformed into a striking gold.

"I remember it all, Vandrune," Higant said calmly. "I understand why I was given this knowledge ... and I mustn't reveal it to anyone. That knowledge is for me, and me alone."

Before anyone could react, the glowing portions of the fountain flared with intensity … and so too did Marcus, who'd been standing at Frederick's side, igniting as he'd done just outside of Pillton a number of moons earlier. He walked over to the fountain and stood in front of the soldier and the dragon.

"The soldier lay down the Blade of Ki before the dragon," said Marcus. "It must be returned to the fountain in order to open the Chamber."

Within the servant's corridors, Crimson grinned. The scrolls had been right: the Blade was required to open the chamber. She needed the Chamber of Life open as much as they did, and so she had risked parting with the Blade in order to set things in motion with the baron's death.

"Vandrune," Marcus continued. "The Blade."

The old mage walked over to him, face pulled taut, withdrawing a blade wrapped in cloth from his robes.

When the cloth fell away the blade that he had kept since the death of the baron was revealed.

Crimson spoke softly to herself, reciting the words as written.

"Upon the stone in water blue, the Blade of Ki will answer too. Do what you must to deliver the Ki, to the enemy's lair and destiny. Bands and Blade are twins of a kind; upon the seal they must combine. Unlock the seal to release time's charm … realign the stars to move afar."

CHAPTER THIRTY-EIGHT

The Chamber of Life

Fanton, Kabi, and Crimson all leaned in as Marcus took the Blade from Vandrune. Crimson could hardly believe she'd been able to get this come together so well. All that she'd worked toward - all that she'd promised to herself all those years ago - was all for this moment, and what was to come.

Fanton and Kabi looked on with great interest. Amazed as they were by the glow of the Fountain and the two boys, but they knew they had to be ready to act when Crimson indicated. They both drew their blades and held them in hand.

"We do this together," said Marcus, looking over at Higant.

His friend gave him a nod.

Still wreathed in gold, Higant moved towards Marcus at the fountain.

Side by side, their resplendent energies were a sight to behold—one a brilliant blue, and the other a vibrant gold. Holding the Blade of Ki with the cloth, Marcus stepped into the water of the fountain, and Higant followed closely behind.

Kneeling down next to the stone soldier in a similar pose, Marcus began to lower the Blade into the recess, cloth and all. Higant placed a hand on his shoulder, and the connection of the energies emanating from each of them flared at the touch, responding to one another in harmony.

As the blade nestled into the relief, both of the boys started to glow ever brighter, the iridescent blue merging with the pulsing gold. With every pulse, a shockwave was sent out in all directions, pushing the rest of the group further and further backwards. In the inner sanctum of their power, the lights continued to feed into one another, and the connection the two boys felt grew stronger than ever.

All of a sudden, the room went dark. The boys stopped glowing their respective colours and stood still for a moment before retreating from the fountain, coming to stand behind the kneeling soldier.

Vandrune, Kyruarth, and the others looked back to where the fountain was, and suddenly there was a thud, and a click of a mechanism. The stone statue at the heart of the fountain bisected and spread apart, separating the soldier and the dragon, leaving an opening in between them. A set of stone steps rose up from beneath the water, paving the way to the centre of the fountain.

The party gathered at the boys' backs, with Vandrune and Kyruarth placing a hand on Higant and Marcus's shoulders respectively.

"The Chamber of Life, no doubt," said Frederick. "I've no concept of what awaits us, but whatever it is, we face it together."

Seren joined Frederick at his side, giving him a nod that said she was with him. He didn't even need to look to know William and Katarg were at his back.

"Together, then," said Higant, smiling at Marcus.

Marcus grinned. "You're hopeless without me, after all."

With that, the two boys led the way down the stairs.

"Just a little longer, Ally," Pip whispered to himself.

After the last of them disappeared down the opening, Crimson, Fanton, and Kabi approached the fountain.

Reaching down for the Blade of Ki, still resting at the foot of the soldier, Crimson's lips peeled back into a wicked grin. She lifted the blade and the hilt flared red, the markings on the handle responding to her truant power. She put the knife in its sheath between her shoulder blades on her back and turned to the others.

"Stay here and contact the Citadels. The Cascade begins now."

Inside the opening, a series of stone-hewn steps spiralled around the edge of a gradually widening cavern, descending deep into the bedrock below the castle fountain and into the mountain behind. By all rights, the cavern should've been pitch dark ... but the walls and steps were covered with what looked to be small glow worms, all of them emanating the same blue glow as Marcus had been, guiding their path into the darkness below.

The steps continued for some time, occasionally levelling out onto landings that led into various side chambers along the way, though these were dark and damp and didn't appear to contain much at all. Continuing down to the base of the stairs, they eventually reached a chamber that contained two tunnels heading off in opposite directions, as well as a central path leading forward.

Once the party had made it onto the landing, Higant closed his eyes, and his golden glow returned. Marcus, seemingly reacting to the return of Higant's power, instantly ignited with his own ethereal blue.

"We take the central path," Higant proclaimed to the rest of the group.

He didn't hesitate—he just advanced, with Marcus right behind him.

Along the walls of the rough-hewn passage were ornate trails of a gold mineral that seemed to both reflect Higant's glow and react to Marcus's energy, coming alive with gold flecked with blue, humming with energy and lighting their way through.

After walking for some time, the space between the ceiling and the floor began to narrow, and just as they were beginning to think they'd have to start crawling, the tunnel opened up into one of the largest natural caverns they'd ever seen.

Almost perfectly spherical, the walls were smooth, with similarly round boulders scattered around the outside of the inner circle. In the middle of the chamber was a circular metal plate, adorned with patterns and words of a language long forgotten. Ancient as the place must have been, the plate was pristine, as if it had never been touched.

"The Chamber of Life," said Higant, almost to himself.

Even stranger than its configuration and immaculate interior was the way the chamber made them *feel*. They felt lofty. Open. Aware. Alive.

Vandrune had managed to keep himself quiet thus far, but was dying to explore the depths of the knowledge that Higant apparently now had unfettered access to.

"What is this place, my boy? What was it built for, and why are we here?"

"It would take lifetimes to explain," Higant said with a sad smile. "At its most basic, it is a place where life was found, and then lost—where past became present and future alike, and where time, space, and the creatures that inhabit them all found harmony."

Frederick gave a wry smile. "If that's the simple explanation, I'm loath to imagine the longer version."

Without responding, Higant started to walk towards the centre of the chamber.

Crimson looked on from behind one of the boulders in awe. She knew exactly what this chamber was for—or at least some of what it was capable of. The texts that the truants had uncovered in the Citadels, apparently created by the same ancient civilisation, had given her a far greater use for the Cascade than wanton destruction.

In one fell swoop, she would elevate the truants to the world's dominant power, destroy the mages who had persecuted them ... and rewrite history.

With one hand, she retrieved the Blade of Ki from her back, then drew the wicked curved sciver from the scabbard on her waist. Speaking soft words into the sciver's blade, it started to glow a dull green.

While the rest of the party had begun to investigate the metal plate, Pip had started to explore the chamber's outer walls, and had inadvertently stumbled across the boulder Crimson was hiding behind.

Eyeing each other with surprise, Crimson was the first to react. She leapt forward and wrapped her inner elbow around his neck, her eyes flaring a bright, angry orange.

In response, both Higant's and Marcus's energy flared, and the whole room turned to face her. Kyruarth was already busy gathering power, preparing to fire it in her direction.

"Ah, ah!" she shouted. "I wouldn't recommend it."

She held the Blade of Ki to Pip's throat, her sciver pointed towards Kyruarth. Not wanting to aggravate the situation, Pip stood as still as a statue.

Crimson spoke very softly to Pip, and he relayed her message.

"Have the boy remove the Bands, and don't tempt me to ignite the power of the blade," Pip said slowly. "It'll kill you before you have the chance."

Vandrune made eye contact with Higant and nodded.

The light around Higant dimmed. Kyruarth made a show of releasing the energy he'd generated, but secretly kept enough of it at the ready to strike if necessary.

Marcus, however, glowed even more fiercely.

Higant reached up and touched the bands on his upper arms, causing them to release and slip down over his elbows. The moment they left his wrists, his irises reverted to their usual colour, and he looked like his old self again. He let the bands fall to the floor and then kicked them towards Crimson, leaving them about halfway between them.

"Let Pip go, Crimson," said Marcus. "You've hurt enough people for a lifetime. I won't let you hurt anyone else!"

Crimson burst into laughter.

"Hurt people? Do you think I asked for this life? All I've done has been in service of righting the wrongs committed against me and my people. You mages hunted us, forced us to live in shadow and slaughtered us like cattle, just because we were different!"

"It was never a matter of difference," said Kyruarth. "We were never meant to draw power from the earth. I don't condone what the mages of old did to your people, but the planet's resources are not infinite, and the wounds you leave do not heal. By stubbornly clinging to your ways, you doom yourselves, and threaten to doom us all."

"Shut up!" Crimson yelled. "Did your mages even try to explain that to my parents before cutting them down where they stood? I don't think so!"

Her eyes smouldering, she felt a surge of resonance, then smiled.

"It doesn't matter. The time for talk is over."

Kyruarth, who'd been holding his power in his right hand, felt a tug on his arm, startling him into releasing it. There was another tug on his left leg, then one on his other arm, and in moments, all four of his limbs were bound and held taut, dragging him into the centre of the metal plate and holding him aloft as if he were suspended by invisible cables.

"Vandrune," he said, "we may have a problem."

CHAPTER THIRTY-NINE

THE CASCADE

"It's a little more dire than that," Crimson said smugly. "You, Kyruarth, are the core of the Cascade. The seal has been broken, and the connection is complete. There's no stopping the Cascade now!"

For the first time ever, as Kyruarth struggled against his bonds, the others saw concern creeping onto his brow.

"You have to stop this, Crimson!" Marcus shouted, taking a step towards her. "There has to be a better way!"

"You come any closer, and Pip here gives us all a lesson on the on the Blade of Ki's power," she laughed, bringing its edge closer to Pip's neck. Then, she turned the blade in her other hand to take aim at Higant. "Or would you prefer your friend gave us an education on scivers?"

Marcus stopped and stared at her, his eyes pleading.

"I don't understand. I saved Fanton's life back on the road. You were in tears. After I healed him, for a moment, I ... I thought you might abandon this madness."

As she listened to Marcus, Crimson's eyes shifted from fiery orange to a ruby red.

Was that really what had happened? She couldn't remember. Her tone softened almost imperceptibly.

"You couldn't have healed someone that far gone. It was impossible for even the most practised healer, let alone someone of your age."

"And yet he lives, does he not? I am the Guardian Dracco, Crimson. I possess power drawn from the spirit realm, and the ancient power of dragons," said Marcus. "However close to death someone might be, so long as they yet live, I can save them. I have that power now."

Tears streaked down Crimson's face. She remembered now— Fanton's broken body lying in her arms as she desperately tried to heal him, to no avail. She remembered how Marcus had started to glow blue as he did now, and had done what she could not.

"You saved him. He was not long for this world, and you brought him back to me," she said, letting her arms fall to her side. "I am ... grateful."

Pip, seeing his opportunity, quickly stepped outside the range of her arms, picking up the Bands of Awe from the ground as he returned to the rest of the group. However agile the old man had been, she could easily have stopped him if she'd wanted to.

Having finished contacting the Citadels, Kabi and Fanton had arrived, keeping out of sight in the shadows. Both had heard the story as told by Crimson, and Fanton was astounded that Marcus had saved him. Why would his enemy do such a thing?

Crimson, lost in her own thoughts, stood with her arms limp at her side, head down. Marcus moved slowly towards her, reaching out a glowing blue hand to touch her cheek. She lifted her head.

"You showed me tenderness once," he said. "It seemed only fair that I return the favour. Despite all you've done, I see now that you were as much a victim of circumstance as any of us are in this world. I hold no hatred for you in my heart. We are not your enemy. We did not give you the pain you feel ... but we can help you to heal, and to move past it."

Crimson's eyes began to shift into a light blue, mirroring Marcus's own. She moved closer to him as if drawn to him, like a soul adrift on the ocean being thrown a lifeline.

Just as she was reaching out to him, Fanton yelled, "Crimson, what are you doing?!"

She shook her head as if waking up from a dream, and her eyes instantly went red hot. She punched Marcus in the gut, then sprinted for the boulder that Fanton and Kabi had been hiding behind.

Just as she dove for the boulder, Kyruarth ignited with white-hot light. His scream echoed around the room, and a shockwave burst forth from him. Vandrune managed to throw up his hands and protect himself and Higant with a shield, and Einfall had dragged Frederick behind one of the circular boulders with William and Katarg just in time, but Pip was thrown hard against the outer wall, his body going limp and sliding to the floor along with the Bands of Awe. Marcus, who was still standing firm in his power, had been winded by Crimson's blow, but otherwise remained unmoved.

The light bursting forth from Kyruarth had grown so bright that the most any of them could see was the shadows cast around the room, and it was only growing in intensity. The room began to vibrate with a resonance powered by hundreds of truants, so thick and loud that it rendered everyone not protected by magic unconscious.

"The Bands, Higant!" Vandrune shouted, wincing with the effort.

Higant looked over to where Pip had fallen and staggered towards him.

At about the same time, Crimson sheathed her sciver and emerged from behind the boulder, beginning to draw vast amounts of power from the earth. Her whole body shimmering with a furious red energy, she began a slow advance towards Kyruarth with the Blade of Ki held at the ready, struggling against the force of the Cascade.

Sensing the danger, Marcus and Vandrune attempted to move towards Kyruarth and come to his defence, the three of them approaching from different sides of the chamber. The light surrounding Kyruarth was making it difficult for any of them to gain any ground, including Crimson. It felt like they were wading waist-deep through mud, and moving only made them sink further into an impossible situation.

Kyruarth let out another loud, painful yell as yet another invisible cable attached itself to his inner thigh.

Crimson had to reach him before they did. It was true there was no stopping the Cascade now, but even with the seal broken, unless she struck Kyruarth with the Blade, it would fail to transcend the barrier of time.

Neleuwan might be destroyed in the process, but the mages would live, the truants would be wiped out, and she would never see her parents again.

As the three of them struggled hard to reach Kyruarth, a golden glow ignited at the far edge of the chamber, catching every conscious eye in the room. Standing in front of Pip, Higant had managed to clasp the Bands of Awe back onto his arms, his eyes alight with the golden glow once more.

Breezing right past Marcus, Vandrune, and Crimson, he walked directly to the centre of the room, completely unaffected by the Cascade.

Unlike the rest of the chamber, the centre was like the eye of the storm—silent, save for the sound of Kyruarth's screams. Higant raised a hand and pressed it against Kyruarth's chest, easing his suffering, if only for a moment. Time itself seemed to slow around then.

"How are you doing, Kyruarth?" he asked, pupils rimmed with gold.

In any other situation, the prophet might have laughed.

"I've been better," he said, biting back the pain.

Higant looked at him with sad eyes. "How do we stop this?"

"Crimson was … right. It's not possible to stop a cascade … once it's been ignited."

"There has to be a way," said Higant. "If there wasn't, the last Cascade would've been the end of us all."

"You have … the knowledge. Last time, the chain was broken … before the ignition. You know … the truth. Neleuwan and I are doomed … but you can still save the others … and protect what's left."

"No. I won't accept that," he said, tears welling in his eyes. "Neleuwan is our home, and you kept Marcus safe. This can't be the end."

Kyruarth screamed again, another invisible cable tethering to his leg.

"I'm open … to suggestion," Kyruarth gasped, trying his hardest to remain conscious. "Is there nothing—in the knowledge?"

"I have looked, Kyruarth. All the knowledge of the ancients at my disposal, and I still can't come up with an answer."

The entirety of the spherical stone chamber, perfectly shaped to concentrate the resonance in the centre of the metal plate, began to shake violently.

They were running out of time.

Higant looked over the mage's suspended form, seeing his arms and legs straining under the pressure being applied in four different directions.

Kyruarth needed some way to counter the binding.

He needed power, and the knowledge to use it.

Ignoring the alarm bells in his mind, Higant touched the band on his right wrist to the band on his upper left arm. The left Band of Awe came free, and he began to falter.

"What are you doing?" Kyruarth exclaimed. "The pressure is too great! You'll be tossed—like a stone!"

Clenching his teeth, Higant began to affix the loose band to Kyruarth's arm.

"If it saves Neleuwan ... what choice do I have? Tell Marcus ... I'm sorry"

Kyruarth wanted to protest—tell the boy that the Bands may have no effect on him, and that it wasn't worth gambling all of their lives on it—but there was no time. Cursing, he closed his eyes and began to chant, attempting to divide his concentration between holding the tension on his limbs so he wasn't ripped apart and protecting the foolish boy at the moment of transition.

Higant took a deep breath, closed his eyes, and detached the remaining Band from his arm. With the last of his fading power, he kept himself steady as he attached the first clasp to Kyruarth's wrist, then slid home the final clasp.

The moment it was done, Higant's body was lifted and sent flying through the air, hurtling outward towards the walls of the chamber at frightening speed.

Kyruarth, who moments before had been in unimaginable pain, felt instant calm and power course through his body the moment both Bands were in place. His body remained locked in the centre of the room, but he was able to counter the tension perfectly, eliminating the pain and returning his presence of mind. Calling the power from within himself, he sent it towards Higant ... and it caught him so close to the wall that his breath fogged up the rock, then gently lowered him to the floor. The rapid change in inertia was still a severe shock to his system, but he would survive.

The vibration in the chamber was reaching a point of complete harmonic vibration. Crimson didn't know what had happened with Higant, but Kyruarth remained tethered, and it was now or never to drive the Blade home. She drove a palm down into the earth, directly siphoning an amount of power that was dangerously close to her limit, turning the ground around her to ash. Her eyes raged a molten red, the thick blanket of energy surrounding her bubbling like lava.

As Higant had before her, she walked effortlessly to the centre of the room, continuing to draw power with every step. She disappeared into the white light, and streaks of red started appearing through the light until slowly but surely it coalesced, turning the whole room from bright white to blood red.

The onlookers could only assume the worst.

Inside the core of the Cascade, Crimson approached the suspended Kyruarth with a grin. Eyes closed and head hung low, there was nothing he could do. He was hers now.

He would suffer for taking her parents away from her ... and with the seal broken—with this much power gathered in one place—his death at the hands of the Blade of Ki would send ripples throughout the timeline.

She would ride them back to a time before her parents had died, and then use all that she'd learned to unravel this wretched world, remaking it in the truants' image.

Brandishing the Blade of Ki, she lunged at Kyruarth, bringing all of her strength and rage to bear.

Kyruarth's eyes flew open, and golden light poured out from them, just as they had from Higant. The wave of power that hit her sent her reeling, skidding backwards and out of the Cascade's core. A moment later, the blinding red light was extinguished, and all of the vibration vanished from the room.

Despite being thrown, Crimson had landed on her feet, and was quickly assessing the situation. Vandrune, Marcus, and Higant had also emerged from the boulders they'd taken shelter behind. In the centre of the room, they saw Kyruarth alive and well, his body aglow with gold, the Bands of Awe affixed to his arms.

None of them had ever witnessed power on this scale before. Even Higant's previous power paled in comparison. This was power in control, with the benefit of long years of experience.

"The Cascade," said Crimson, her face stained with despair. "You ... you stopped it. How? *What did you do?!*"

"Simple," said Kyruarth. "I sent all the pain and power being channelled into me back along the invisible tethers. They were released, and the circuit was broken."

"No. No!" she screamed.

There was no way her Ladies had survived the backlash of such power.

This would be the end of them all.

Crimson seemed about to lose her mind ... until a sudden clarity came over her.

"It doesn't matter. There's enough power in you now that the Blade should have the same effect."

With a manic grin, Crimson regained her molten aura in an instant and bounded towards Kyruarth at speed. She swung the Blade down at him in a vicious arc, but Kyruarth parried it away with an invisible weapon, then dodged to the side. In the same motion, the Blade swung upwards at an angle, heading straight for him. Kyruarth deflected again, but Crimson moved like a leopard—swift, powerful, and tactical. Every time he parried, she was ready with another strike, but at every turn he was there, deflecting and avoiding.

Crimson was howling viciously, trying again and again to gain ground in the battle, but to no avail. Likewise, Kyruarth was hard-pressed enough defending against her savage strikes, leaving no room for any thought of retaliation. They were perfectly locked in combat. To those witnessing the struggle, it seemed genuinely possible that the stalemate could go on forever.

All of a sudden, Marcus's power ignited—but this time was different. He was radiating more power than ever before, and his expression was difficult to gauge. It seemed as if he was acting purely on instinct.

Higant turned and saw his friend moving towards the fight.

"Marcus, what are you doing?"

But Marcus didn't hear him. He continued walking slowly, deliberately towards the stalemate. As he reached the edge of the metal plate upon which Crimson and Kyruarth were locked in the heat of battle, he kneeled down to the ground and placed his hand upon it.

The earth below them trembled, and a flare of blue energy ignited between the combatants and lingered there, forcing them to step backwards. For the shortest instant, they both disengaged, and Kyruarth looked over to see where the power had come from. Seeing Marcus, he gave him an unusual smile.

Blind to all else but the image of her sinking the Blade into Kyruarth's heart, Crimson didn't even register Marcus or his actions, seeing only an opening to lunge for her opponent.

At the last moment, Kyruarth lifted an arm to deflect the strike, and the Blade of Ki collided with the Bands of Awe.

In an implosion of power, the collision of the Bands and the Blade drew in the blue energy Marcus had created moments before, then burst outward from the point of impact faster than the eye could register. It raced up the curved walls of the chamber and reflected back onto the metal seal in the middle of the room, upon which Kyruarth and Crimson still stood.

The concussive force was so powerful that several of the boulders surrounding the centre of the room shifted back a few feet, some of them even rolling slightly.

All in all, the light and heat from the connection lasted for only a couple of breaths ... and then the whole chamber went black.

Higant opened his eyes slowly. The chamber that had been so alive with light and heat and energy was now quiet and dark, and it took his eyes a moment to adjust. The first light he registered was that of the tunnel leading out of the chamber, where the gold mineral along the walls had lit their path. The walls of the chamber themselves also gave off a faint glow, as if charged by the vast amount of power that had just been released.

Soon, he was able to make out more of the centre of the chamber where Kyruarth had been standing.

Instead of Kyruarth or Crimson, there he found Vandrune, his teacher.

Testing his strength and rising to his feet, he slowly walked towards the centre of the chamber.

"Vandrune?" he called out. "What happened? Where did they go?"

In his hands, Vandrune held one of the Bands of Awe. The other was nowhere to be found.

"This was all that remained in the circle," said Vandrune. "It's nothing short of a miracle that it survived. As for Kyruarth and the truant Crimson ... caught up in such an explosion of power, it's difficult to imagine they fared as well."

As the words were leaving his mouth, Marcus emerged from behind one of the boulders.

"Are you saying they're ... dead? Crimson and Kyruarth are dead?"

"It would be foolish to assume otherwise."

The boys felt great sorrow at the loss of someone they'd respected deeply. In his own way, Marcus mourned for Crimson, too. Misguided as she'd been, her life had not been easy, and he'd hoped for a better ending to her story.

One by one, the other inhabitants of the chamber began to awaken, and Vandrune relayed the events they had missed. The Einfall was next to recover after the boys, and she immediately roused Frederick, who in turn woke William and Katarg. It seemed that at some point, while the others were getting their bearings, Fanton and Kabi had skulked away, vanishing without a trace. Where they would go, or what they would do without their mistress, was anyone's guess.

Pip was the last to wake, and took the news especially hard.

"No ... it can't be," he said, weeping for the loss of his friend. "There were still so many stories left to share."

"The sacrifices he made for the kingdom ... for his friends ... will never be forgotten," said Frederick. "I will see to it that his memory is honoured."

"What do we do now, Vandrune?" said Higant. "Has the threat of the truants passed? What of the return of dragons?"

"I wish I had answers for you, Higant ... but with this, all that has been prophesised has come to pass. Whatever comes next, we shall simply have to wait and see," said the old prophet.

"Pip?" said Marcus, approaching him where he sat. "What will you do?"

"I ... I may have lost Kyruarth, but hearing from Ally has been such a blessing, and all of you have given me hope that our daughter will return to me," he said. "If it's alright, I'd like to stay for a while. Something tells me this isn't quite over. I want to see it through to the end."

"You may stay as long as you like," Frederick assured him. "Come. I will arrange quarters for you in the guest wing."

After Vandrune borrowed his ear in private for a moment, Frederick nodded once, then turned to head back up the long passageway with Einfall, William, Katarg, and Pip in tow.

With that, Vandrune and the squires were all that remained in the Chamber of Life. The mage crouched down before them, bringing himself closer to their height.

"I want to thank you both. With the loss of our friend, this may not feel like much of a victory ... but it's important to acknowledge what we've managed to achieve, and how much of that we owe to the two of you," he said. "It's one thing to find power within yourself, but quite another to use it as bravely and as selflessly as you have. Without your interventions, the truants may well have succeeded in their Cascade. At best, we'd have lost the capital ... and at worst, there's no telling what they might've accomplished. All of that is to say nothing of how tenaciously you fought for one another, and managed to return safe and sound."

Still, the boys looked dejected. There were still so many things they didn't understand.

"Rest assured, there'll be time for answers later," said Vandrune. "For now, I think you've more than earned a rest."

He ushered Marcus and Higant out through the passage and up the long, glowing stairwell. As they emerged from the opening, Marcus's downcast eyes caught sight of something on the statue.

"What's that?" he said, kneeling down towards it.

The rune within the recess where the Blade of Ki had resided seemed to have taken on a different form. Where once it had been nothing more than a symbol, it now took the shape of a medallion. Marcus pried it free from the stone, and it was warm to the touch.

"Something tells me it belongs to you as the Guardian Dracco. Keep it close," said Vandrune.

The three stepped over the lip of the fountain and the mechanism clicked again, causing the two halves of the statue to rejoin and the fountain to return to its original position.

"As for you, Higant, I can think of no better home for the remaining Band of Awe than with you. I hope it proves to be enough."

"As do I, Vandrune," he said, his expression sombre.

It pained the old prophet that there was little he could do to lift the boys' spirits. The road ahead would be no easier than this ordeal had been, and there were no words he could say to change that.

"Make no mistake, there is much work to be done—not only to understand the power that each of you possesses, but also how to control it," he said eventually. "In that, I can help. But for now … rest."

Exhausted down to their core, they began to walk towards the castle interior, when suddenly, Vandrune stopped.

Perhaps there was something he could do after all.

"Oh, and one more thing," he said with a smile. "I'll have a surprise for you next week. Look forward to it."

DEPARTURE

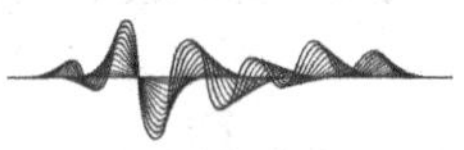

The morning sun beamed into the room, casting a warm glow upon Higant's face. Now squires to the king, he and Marcus had been given their own rooms in the royal wing. Even a week after the confrontation in the Chamber of Life, it still felt good to see the sun rise after so much destruction and loss—and to sleep in a bed after so many nights on the road.

Since the event of the chamber, Frederick had held a public celebration in honour of the departed Kyruarth ... and though few, if any, had known of whom they celebrated, the king had vowed to change that. Humble and reserved as the prophet had been in life, Frederick felt he should at least be recognised for his deeds in death. At his suggestion, in order to occupy his mind, Pip had set about putting his friend's stories to paper.

Impressed by the Einfall's skill, when not guarding the king, William and Katarg trained under her, seeking to push themselves to greater heights and edge closer to their newfound purpose. In private, the Einfall—or in this case, Seren—was often seen at Frederick's side.

Marcus and Higant had been taken under Vandrune's wing, and both of them now spent much of their time under his tutelage. They learned about a great many things, studying prophecy and ancient history, and learning to control their new-found powers. Though much had changed, King Frederick had insisted that the boys continue to perform their duties as squires, feeling it would help to keep them grounded.

Apparently, today was the day of Vandrune's surprise. Neither of the boys had any idea what to expect. Their mood had improved much over the past week as they'd settled into safety and routine, and they'd begun to anticipate it eagerly. All they knew was that they'd been given leave from their duties for the entire day, and at some stage, Vandrune would call upon them. They couldn't picture anything that could surprise them after all they'd experienced, but that only added to their excitement.

There was a banging on Higant's door.

"Are you ready?" Marcus shouted from the other side.

"Just putting my boots on," said Higant, hopping towards the door on one leg.

Rather than wait around all day, they'd planned to take the horses out for a ride. With Kyruarth gone, Vandrune had felt it only fitting that Marcus would inherit Blossom, Thunder's companion, while he took on Numinous. Higant had it on good authority that the stallions approved of their new riders.

Swinging the door open, he saw Marcus standing there and beamed.

Never again would he take seeing his friend for granted.

Kicking his remaining boot the rest of the way on, he rushed out the door with Marcus and headed for the kitchens. They'd been hoping to get a good meal before heading into the field ... but they barely made it down the hall before William intercepted them. It seemed he'd been waiting for them.

"Good morning, young squires," he said, his expression stoic. "The king requests your presence in the reception hall."

"But ... we were supposed to have the day off," said Marcus.

William shrugged. "Sorry, boys. King's orders."

Dejected, they followed him through the castle and towards the throne room.

"Do you think it has to do with the dragons?" said Higant.

"I hope not," said Marcus. "I'd hoped to just be a squire for a little longer."

Arriving out front of the large double door, William knocked three times and waited.

The door opened slightly to reveal Syng, the squire Marcus had come across outside of Vandrune's chambers after finding the baron dead. Another of the king's squires, the three had become better acquainted over the last week, and were fast becoming friends.

Marcus and Higant cocked their heads to the side. What was he doing here?

"Ah, you're here. Well, come in, then!"

The young man threw open the door, and a crowd of people cheered.

"Happy birthday!"

Everywhere the boys looked, they saw faces they recognised—from Pip, to Vandrune, to Jerry, to the former squires of Baron Vandeguild. Every one of the people they'd ever met and loved was here in the reception hall, which had been retrofitted as a party room. Long tables spanned the centre of the room, topped with mountains of delicious food, cakes, and sweets.

As the cheering died down, King Frederick rose from his throne upon the dais, the Einfall at his side.

"Squires Marcus and Higant," he spoke, smiling gently. "It occurred to our esteemed Master Vandrune that young men ought have a day to celebrate their birth. Seeing as the two of you were without one, we took the liberty of assigning one to each of you, and felt it only fitting that you should share it. I hope you don't mind."

Having no idea who their parents were, much less the day they'd been born, neither Marcus nor Higant had ever celebrated a birthday before. Even their ages they'd had to estimate, simply considering themselves another summer older at the turn of the seasons.

Sharing a look with tears in their eyes, they found Vandrune standing at the front of the crowd, and rushed into his arms.

The Chamber was dark and cold. Every fibre of his body ached, even through the numbness and tingling. Slowly, he opened his eyes, seeing the soft, gentle light emanating from the Chamber's walls and the iridescent blue glow of the mineral veins in the passageway.

Hadn't they been gold earlier?

Feeling started to return to his arms and legs, which only made the pain more pronounced. The metal plate beneath his back was cold and hard. Feeling a stinging sensation on his right arm, he reached up to rub it, and what he felt there—or rather, didn't feel—made his head snap to his side. The Band was missing from his right arm. In looking down, however, he saw that the Band on his left arm remained.

He hadn't recalled taking it off. Where had it gone?

Then, he remembered the collision of the Band and the Blade. Perhaps it had been destroyed by the impact.

No, that wasn't right. He'd blocked with his left arm, he was sure of it. Why was the Band that was struck the one that remained?

He slowly rolled over onto his side and pushed himself up, looking around the chamber for any sign of Marcus, Higant, Vandrune, or even Crimson. It would be a miracle if anyone present in the chamber had survived a conflux of that much power. The surge he'd felt from the Band and Blade alone was immense, even before taking in the power that Marcus had ignited. The boy's power had been drawn into Kyruarth's body and combined with the power Higant had transferred to him via the Bands, but it wasn't until Crimson's blade had hit them the power had coalesced.

He looked around, but could not see a single soul.

Rising unsteadily to his feet, he stretched out his limbs, trying to get feeling back in his extremities. Had they really all perished? Without leaving a single trace?

Suddenly, he felt eyes on him. He froze at the unfamiliar presence, slowly turning to look towards the entrance. A figure was moving towards him calmly and deliberately.

In the blue light, he could see that it was a woman. As she drew closer, he saw a striking young lady wearing a simple dress, with a square-cut neckline and short sleeves that cinched at the upper arm. Her waist was accentuated by a thin gold belt, pulling the dress in to show her hips.

Stopping just feet away from him, her eyes were a brilliant sky blue.

"Welcome to the future's past, Kyruarth," she said.

"I am Lilliarth, Higant's mother."

ACKNOWLEDGEMENTS

A dream is not a dream without a group of people who believe in you. My beautiful wife who has listened to my thoughts and ramblings about this book over the last many months and has always supported me no matter my projects. My son who has enquired, offered and suggested ideas for the book including himself, of which he achieved, has been a wonderful ally in the development of characters. To my parents who always supported me over the years and showed me that the human spirit is something to be cherished. My brother and sister and their families who have been there for me and my family when times were tough, their energy is located as part of the story within.

My extended family who has always been there no matter what, you are all an inspiration for the book, for my stories and for the love you have all shared with me and I with you.

To my editor who has helped to shape my written word into a piece of art and kept me on the path to the final destination.

To my writing Guru who helped me with beginning this journey almost a year ago and helped to show me that I can do it with hard work and determination and a lot of patience. Lastly my designer, who worked hard with my vision to deliver a wonderful visual experience.

About the Author

David lives in Brisbane, Queensland, with his wife and son. Outside of his creative pursuits, David is a nurse and has worked in the field for over twenty years, most recently supporting large digital health projects. He believes that life should be interesting, challenging, and fun, and that there's always opportunity in stories that drives imagination.

David is an electric vehicle enthusiast, and is especially fond of Teslas, of which he owns a Model 3. He has a love for acting and has always loved the ability to portray a character. The joy to write a story of my own was something I never thought possible until now.... I hope you enjoy.

www.ingramcontent.com/pod-product-compliance
Lightning Source LLC
Chambersburg PA
CBHW010344220726

48290CB00016B/2619